The Local Truth: White Harbor Book 1

Carlos E. Rivera

Originally published in Australia by Slashic Horror Press in 2023.

ISBN-13: 978-0-6457638-2-9
Cover design by Greg Chapman
Interior design by David-Jack Fletcher and Lee Cross James
Edited by David-Jack Fletcher

*To Jimmy: my constant support and inspiration to
push forward.
Thank you for your patience in the face of all my crazi-
ness…*

*…and to my parents: Please know this story doesn't
symbolize our relationship now,
but our relationship at a different, darker time,
thankfully gone.*

I love you all.

"The Child who is not embraced by the village
will burn it down to feel its warmth."
African Proverb

"Small town, big hell."
Costa Rican Proverb

Prologue

1991
Blight Harbor

Everyone in town had a story about the house at the foot of the hill. The wooden house. The Vanek House, as it was known, although no one with the last name Vanek had lived in the town of White Harbor for over a hundred years. It stood on the corner of Graham Street and Hill Road, where the latter began its winding climb toward the dense, wooded mountains.

The house was two stories high and unpainted, rotten wood peeling from neglect. Every window had been boarded up, giving it the monolithic appearance of a tombstone surrounded by knee-high fescue grass. Vermin could be seen breeding in the grass on the warmer nights, and random hisses, squeals, and chirps kept human presence away with thoughts of what else might be creeping there.

It was built on pilings, from back when Etenia Creek used to overflow during the rainy months, of which there were plenty every year. The creek—now nothing but a pitiful, stony gutter a child could hop over without a second thought—served as the western edge of the property. From there, the covered windows on the upper floor resembled lidded eyes, which, if ever opened, would gaze down upon the rest of White Harbor in silent, eldritch judgment.

On the first floor was a set of double doors held shut with a rusty chain and a large padlock. The narrow porch and wooden steps rising from the front lawn were slanted and broken; large splinters of brown, black, and green—covered in white splotches of mold—stuck upward, like teeth in a jagged under-bite.

It was the type of house that lent itself to stories. Gossip. Rumors. Tall tales? Perhaps some. Others, not so much. For anything, even the wildest idea the mind could imagine happening within the house's walls, there was someone in White Harbor to attest to it being an undeniable fact. From poltergeists and mass suicides to evil cults and concealing the gates of Hell in one of its rooms, there was no story too outrageous for the Vanek House to have been the site, the witness, or sometimes, even the perpetrator.

Some events were genuine, recorded facts. Those were

the rarities, such as the grisly deaths of a family who rented the house, although the landlord had never wanted to rent it before. The family—the Albrights—seemed personable enough and had intended to remodel the Vanek House into a bed-and-breakfast. No remodeling ever occurred, though. They did no work on the property at all, which struck the locals as bizarre.

According to police reports, one night in the summer of 1968, Jonathan Albright stabbed and killed his wife, Penny, his seven-year-old daughter, Sadie, and his one-year-old son, Nelson. He stabbed each of them forty-four times.

The police had found Jonathan Albright dead, sitting at his dining room table, with the knife driven through the upper-left quarter of his body, straight into his heart. The strangest finding by the medical examiner was that, before committing suicide, Mr. Albright had carefully cut and eaten pieces of his wife and children. The examiner recovered forty-four distinct pieces from his stomach, swallowed whole without chewing. The tip of his own middle finger had also been cut and swallowed whole. To this day, there's no explanation to what significance the number forty-four had for Jonathan Albright, or why the distal phalange of his middle finger was also severed and eaten, but it ultimately didn't matter—there were clear victims and a clear culprit.

Case closed.

Events like the 1968 murder-suicide were facts,

but they were not the only truth as far as the denizens of White Harbor were concerned. There were also the known "facts". The accepted "facts". The *local truth*. Events without evidence, but which the townsfolk knew—just *knew*—were true.

Such was the case of Gerardo Valencia, a twelve-year-old boy who went missing for six days during the winter of 1989, when a rare blizzard struck the town. The trail led the police to the Vanek House, where they found Gerardo's corpse. A police officer took a Polaroid of the boy's frozen face and, exhibiting both a lack of sense and poor taste, showed it to some of his drinking buddies. Soon, the whole town knew Gerardo Valencia hadn't died of starvation, dehydration, or even hypothermia, which would've been the likeliest culprit. In mere days, everyone knew the boy died screaming with his eyes frozen open, bulging like white marbles, staring in stark terror at whatever caused his heart to stop, his mouth twisted in a scream so inhuman it had dislocated his jaw.

The autopsy report confirmed the boy died of sudden heart failure, and three of the boy's fingernails were detached as he clawed at the floor in desperation, as if attempting to escape from something that was dragging him by his legs. Apart from that, the boy's body was intact, with no signs of violence or sexual assault.

There were no signs of another person being in the building, no footprints in the dust besides his own, and no signs of the murder scene being wiped down—the house was covered in dust and cobwebs, save for the drag marks leading to where the body had been found.

There was never an official explanation for what Gerardo went through within the walls of the house. The police made no arrests, but the people of White Harbor knew—or at least had a fair notion—of what had happened. The town consensus was that whatever nameless evil lived in the Vanek House had sent the blizzard over the town, which made the poor teenager wander off on the way home from school to seek refuge in the abandoned building. Then, the evil forces dwelling within tortured and frightened the boy to death, while the howling wind muffled his screams.

As for *who* let the boy inside the building, that was also a known truth, even if law enforcement found no evidence of it.

This tacit understanding of events, known only to those who were "from town", developed a local name. It was like a collective mindscape, an ever-growing compendium of folktales, gossip, rumors, nightmares, fears, superstitions, and accepted "facts" the locals referred to as *Blight Harbor*. No one ever lived too long in White Harbor before experiencing Blight Harbor. It was the way one knew they were officially "from town".

Blight Harbor is in that corner in anyone's house they can never turn their back to because of a strange feeling something in the emptiness is watching.

Blight Harbor is in the muffled sound of a man beating his wife, while their next-door neighbor turns up their TV's volume.

Blight Harbor is in the happy "Hello!" from a neighbor's mentally-challenged son, whom one always found so charming and full of joy, until the day they saw him standing in his backyard, masturbating.

Blight Harbor is in the handshake of that elementary school teacher everyone's friendly and social with, but everyone also knows, before moving to town, had been accused of fondling a young boy and, maybe—just maybe—got off on a technicality. After all, his wife didn't leave him, did she?

"That's in Blight Harbor," locals would say, sometimes flippantly, other times fearfully, when a topic would be best ended because it belonged in that dark chest of misery where everything they wished to keep hidden or forgotten got tossed.

People who were not "from town" often made the mistake of thinking Blight Harbor didn't exist, that it was simply a local name for something found in every town. While all the aforementioned things could happen anywhere else, in White Harbor, they had substance. They were an entity—the town's living, bleeding heart. Something ethereal, but tangible, like a light drizzle. Blight Harbor was like the small particles of engine exhaust carried by the supposedly clean mountain air that filled the lungs of every single one of the town's four-thousand residents, both keeping them alive and slowly promoting the growth of cancer cells.

No place in the town's history had ever been the physical embodiment of Blight Harbor quite like the Vanek House.

There was a tall concrete wall to the south of the Vanek property, erected by the owners of the house next door, a well-to-do—or so they'd like the rest of the town to think—married couple, Elijah and Maria Knox. The latter was a real estate agent, and knew the importance of, "Location! Location! Location!" but had been cursed with inheriting her mother's home, which was literally the worst *location* for residential real estate in all of White Harbor.

This was torture for Maria Knox. She was more than aware the sight of the Vanek House could lower their property value the way rot on a tomato spreads to all other tomatoes in the box. So, up the wall had gone, with another wall next to it to block the view of the *other* spoiled tomato nearby—a residence immediately up the hill from the Vanek House. That other tomato, unfortunately, had a worm in it. A worm named Ben Curling.

Ben Curling's home was an ugly, one-story wooden

box with a gray shingle roof, and almost as old and moldy as the Vanek House. In fact, they had both been a single estate until the mysterious Vaneks had segregated it into two plots of land. Two plots which, to the Knoxes' chagrin, placed their pretty little Cape Cod-style home in a veritable checkmate of ugliness, as Curling's creepy forest of a backyard was twice as long as the square where the Vanek House stood, stretching across the entire eastern edge of the Knoxes' property.

Unlike the Vanek House, however, Curling's had gone through the rare fix here and there to make it at least inhabitable, but no care had been given to these repairs to make them blend in with the original building, neither in material nor color. The result had been a patchwork of boards, planks, covers, and panels that made the whole place look like a bunker built by a scavenger. This was only what was visible of the property, as more than half was camouflaged in bushes, trees, and vines, the latter of which crawled up the walls and over fences, reaching toward the shingles in the roof like dark tentacles rising from the depths, wasting away and drying up as they climbed, starving for the touch of sunlight, but being burned by it instead.

Maria Knox knew, even as the existence of the Vanek and Curling houses gradually deteriorated her land value like a pernicious blight, it was the man himself—and the infamy attached to him—that actively ate away at it. If the police had busted Maria with a cocaine lab in her house's garage, it couldn't have done the damage to their property that Ben Curling's name alone did. They had repeatedly tried to sell the estate and move, but no one would touch it. Even people from outside, who knew nothing of the Vanek House or Ben Curling, needed only to gaze at the unpleasant-looking old man sitting on his porch with his two large, black Mastiffs, and they would give their residence a wide berth. There might as well have been a sign at the town entrance that read:

THANK YOU FOR VISITING WHITE HARBOR!
PS: The Knox house is radioactive.

"One day, I made up my mind and went to talk to that man," Maria Knox once said to her younger sister, Wilma, over afternoon tea. It was a custom she felt was oh so European and bourgeois, despite serving the tea in a cheap set she had bought at Greene's, a five-dollars-and-under store downtown. "I walked up to his front lawn. I didn't want to get too close. You know, he has those big black dogs with him at all times. Mastiffs, I think they're called. Mean creatures. Nothing like my little Dottie."

She caressed a tiny Pomeranian sitting on her lap, its tongue sticking out sideways as if its snout were too small to contain the stupid-looking thing. "I only wanted to ask him to please trim the bushes and the trees and to cut those creepy vines. They ugly up the neighborhood, and I can see them all day from the kitchen. They crawl over our fence, and if you rip them out, they leave root marks on the paint. Also, he owns that other building, you know?"—lowering to a whisper as she raised her teacup—"The Vanek House?"

Straightening up, confident nobody but Wilma had heard her, she continued, "Well, he never mows that lawn, either. I can imagine what types of vermin are crawling all over that grass. It's unsanitary! Do you know what I found in my trash the other day? Not one, but three, THREE raccoons! Those things carry diseases, Wilma! Diseases!"

She stared into Wilma's eyes, desperate to sense someone empathized with her ordeal. Wilma simply bit her lower lip uncomfortably and responded by nodding.

"I have three children here, for Christ's sake! Caesar is already a teenager! Don't get me wrong, I know he's a good boy and all, but he's so handsome. What if some floozy from school decides those shrubs beyond the wall are a good make-out spot and *lures* him there? A snake could bite him!"

Wilma's eyes inadvertently glanced sideways at a framed picture on a corner table. Her sister's three children grinned back at her: Paula, a cute two year old, Randall, a skinny nine year old, and Caesar, a twelve year old with bright-red pimples on his greasy face, incipient facial hair, crooked teeth, gigantic gums, and some undeniable signs of teenage obesity.

"Randall!" Maria said, startling Wilma back from her distraction. "That boy keeps going in there to catch bugs for his collection. He's a curious boy, and so smart, a scientist through and through. I think he'll be a biologist like his father. No! A *doctor* in biology. That's why no matter how many times I tell him not to go there, he's always sneaking and crawling around that place like a homeless person! Crawling, Wilma! Crawling on rat droppings and God-knows-what-else!"

Wilma had the impression she *should* say something, but Maria was already in the middle of her tirade, and she would not suffer interruptions.

"And my widdle Pauwy-wawie…" She took in a deep breath, as if summoning the strength to bring forth a memory so traumatic it made her doubt the existence of a loving God. "My baby. My beautiful, beautiful baby! The other day, I saw her eating something off the floor. And I know what you're going to say, Wilma, so stop it right there!"

Wilma's eyes flitted left and right, her lips scrunched in confusion, then looked into the deep brown of her tea. She wasn't going to say anything.

"I know it's normal for babies to just grab whatever they find on the floor and put it in their mouths, but one thing is a shoe, or a toy. It's an entirely different thing when…" She choked a sob. "Oh, my Lord. I tried to get it out of her mouth. I stuck my fingers in there and pulled out…a… You won't believe what it was! Guess what it was, Wilma!"

Wilma opened and closed her mouth like a fish, un-blinking, not sure what to say.

"Guess!"

Wilma opened her mouth to speak.

"A cockroach!" Maria shouted before a word could leave Wilma's lips. "My baby girl was eating a dead cock-roach off the floor!"

Maria wrinkled her nose, raising her upper lip so her two square, white front teeth showed. She closed her eyes, furrowed her brow, shaking one of her hands quickly in front of her face, and shook her head in disgust.

Dottie, the stupid-looking Pomeranian, with the stupid-looking tongue, looked up at her mommy, who was currently looking stupid.

Maria picked up her cheap teacup, brought it to her lips, blew softly on the scalding-hot tea, took the smallest sip, swallowed it, and blew out a bit of hot air, trying to regain her composure.

She shook her head.

Her eyes went perfectly round, and her eyebrows curved upward, trying to convey the greatest horror imag-inable, and so she resumed. "We might end up with the bu-bonic plague here in White Harbor, and Ground Zero will be *that house*! That...monstrosity! Would it hurt *that man* to take a bit of care of it? It's his property, and it's harming ours!"

She took a moment to compose herself and have another sip of hot tea.

"So, as I was saying before, I went to that place. His place. My intention was to be a good neighbor, to offer an olive branch, so to speak. I asked him. I begged him, 'Pleeeeeeease, Mr. Curling. Oh, pleeeeeeease, trim your bushes. Pleeeeeeease, cut those vines. Pleeeeeeease, take care of that lawn', and do you know what that godless troglodyte said?"

Her eyes were now bulging spheres of insanity, almost threatening to pop out of a face to be found in encyclopedias next to the word "indignation" from that day forth. She leaned in, stared right into Wilma's eyes, and whispered, "Nothing." She paused for emphasis, letting the horror sink in, and repeated, "Nothing. He wouldn't even talk to me. He only glared at me with those enormous eyes in that... That...black...face of his."

Wilma stifled a gasp, clutching at the fabric of her skirt.

Maria caught herself. Cleared her throat. "Not that him being Black makes him bad, of course. I'm not one of those racists. I'm glad people like him can own a property that big. Honestly, look at it! It's three times the size of ours!

But I'm not lying to you, Wilma. The moment he glared at me, both his dogs, at once, raised their heads like black sphinxes, with the horns and all."

Unbeknownst to her, Wilma had just repressed an almost inhuman urge to interrupt her and explain that yes, she was, in fact, being racist, and no, sphinxes do not, in fact, have horns. It never ceased to shock her how Maria felt so comfortable spouting her archaic, despicable perspectives. It reinforced the notion that the house hadn't been the only thing her older sister had inherited from their mother.

"Those are devil dogs, Wilma, if I've ever seen a devil dog. They began growling at me. Like he had told them to. Like he had used his mind to tell them to growl at me and scare me away."

She caressed Dottie with hard, frantic strokes of her hand, perhaps a bit too hard, and the Pomeranian let out a single helpless whine.

"I turned and ran. I swear, I never want to see those eyes again, Wilma. That man's eyes are not human. I've had nightmares about those eyes. Nightmares! How is that man allowed to be free? We all know what happened to that Colombian boy two years ago during that blizzard. Who do you think let him into the house? Who has the only key to that padlock? Who locked that poor boy in there with whatever lives there? He did! Old Man Curling did! Drove the boy's mother crazy with grief!"

She inhaled and exhaled slowly. "Anyway, that's in Blight Harbor. Let's leave it there."

Maria had only been expressing one of many opinions White Harbor's residents had about Old Man Curling, but, like her, only dared speak in the privacy of their homes or in small social gatherings.

There was a preternatural aura about the man he didn't seem to be in any hurry to dispel. Ben Curling was an enigma. He invited rumors by the very act of existing. He was a man whose age no one seemed to agree upon. Some people in their fifties swore he had been just as old when they were children as he was now, while others remembered a young boy named Ben Curling living in the house around the same time. If true, this boy would have most likely been home-schooled, since none of the adults remembered attending school with him.

Another controversial theory claimed his asocial demeanor pointed to a lack of education or even mental retardation, but many neighbors had often seen him reading on his porch, philosophy, non-fiction, history, and many other types of literature, which, to others, spoke of a cunning and educated man.

The Curlings, of which he was the only known descendant, hadn't been famous for socializing for as long as anyone could remember, which had only fueled the flames of speculation. Mystery had always enveloped the family. More accurately, perhaps, everyone might have held a piece of the puzzle, but there hadn't been enough pieces in one place, at one time, to put the entire picture together.

Curling spent his time sitting in the rocking chair on his front porch. All day, every day. Like a sitting statue in a park, surrounded by the thick vegetation that enveloped his property.

He sat. He watched. He never spoke.

Sometimes, there would be a book in his hands, sometimes a plate of food, or a drink, none of which anyone had seen him stand up to get. The books the neighbors saw him reading were another topic of discussion. Neighbors claimed to have seen him reading everything from Bram Stoker's *Dracula* to *Of Love and Shadows* to *The Satanic Bible* to the *Necronomicon* itself—human skin binding, metal clasps and all. Then, there was Tiberius Baker, who said he'd once seen him reading *The Hobbit*, and Old Man Curling had apparently been holding it upside down, which meant he was only pretending to read because the man was illiterate.

All the while, as people talked, Ben Curling went on with his routine.

He sat. He watched. He never spoke.

However, even that wasn't always true.

"He buys his food at the market," Mia Elliot once told Libby Grant as if she were really saying, "I saw Goody Proctor with the Devil." She licked her lips and spoke into the phone, savoring the gossip like a delicious chocolate truffle. "You wouldn't believe it, huh? He does sometimes leave that house to get stuff. He comes in really early, as soon as they open, so there are fewer people there. I've seen him studying a tomato before putting it in his bag, like very close to his eyes, sort of transfixed, like he was looking at a human heart, and I know what you're thinking, how the hell does someone look at a human heart? Well, I don't know, I am not a psychopath, but that's the feeling I got from the way he was staring at it, and I'm telling you, Libby, that man was hungry, like he thought the tomato would taste like human flesh and blood if he bit into it. Well, as long as he's eating a tomato and not an actual human heart, I can rest easy, but who the hell knows, right? He gives me the creeps, that man."

"He doesn't just go to the market," Libby Grant responded. "Bennie saw him at the hardware store, too." She now emitted a trembling exhalation that turned into a thin moan. "To think my poor husband shares a name with that ghoul; blame it on my thoughtless father-in-law, like everything that's wrong with Bennie. Anyway, he says the time Old Man Curling came in, he just picked up what he was going to buy off the aisles, plopped it right in front of Bennie on the counter! Didn't even say hello, he just sort of grumbled, 'How much?' then stood there, waiting for Bennie to ring him up. He paid with cash and left. He bought a drill bit and some nails. Oh, oh, and these what-do-you-call-em, wire strippers, wire stripper pliers. Can you imagine what that man is doing with those things?"

People talked, as people do. Stories of Ben Curling making a special guest appearance in town were as rare as Bigfoot sightings, and for many, they held just as much truth to them. Despite this, everyone in White Harbor was familiar with the sight of Ben Curling sitting on his porch with his two black Mastiffs at his feet.

He sat.

He watched.

He never spoke.

Chapter One
The Town that Made You
2022

*T*ime to come home.

The thought alone made Peter Lange want to make a squealing U-turn and never look back. His blue Chevy Malibu rolled up the scenic road that broke from the I-5 toward White Harbor. There wasn't a quick way to get into town, but the drive itself was one of its little charms. The northern route offered some beautiful vistas, which were often the subject of pictures for those who ventured off the interstate. White Harbor was a minor detour on the way to more popular destinations; a swim, a hike, and a selfie before moving on to more interesting places.

Peter, however, was not heading back to his childhood home for something as frivolous as sightseeing. This wasn't a pleasure trip, but a self-imposed, almost religious pilgrimage—a burden which could almost be considered penance. This visit carried an additional weight with it: unfinished business. In his mind, he rehearsed a conversation he'd put off too many times.

Way too many, he thought, as he took slow, long breaths.

The road into town wound through a thick forest and across small rivers and brooks as it skirted the northern Crescent Mountains—a sickle-shaped mountain range that started in the northwest and curved to the southeast, gradually decreasing in height. The mountains surrounded the expanse of land that was White Harbor, looking from the sky like a thumb and index finger, trying to grab a pinch of the Pacific Ocean.

The vehicle rolled up the northwestern flank of the mountains, where the road rose steadily. To Peter's right, a vertical cliff plummeted toward the ocean. Enormous waves crashed against tall, jagged rocks spiking from the water. People called this area Skarsgard's Teeth, and the road that ascended near them was carved into the stone of the mountain. It was like a tunnel missing its outer wall, held up by sculpted rock pillars rising from the edge of the cliff at irregular distances from each other. The entire structure was made to look like it was part of the mountain. This, and a similar road at the eastern end of the mountain range, were the only ways in and out of town. The mountains completely blocked the area from the world before it was colonized.

"It will be nice to see you again," the female voice coming from the car speakers said, pulling Peter back from his thoughts. "It's been, what? A year?"

"A year, a month, and six days," Peter said, as the shadows from the impressive pillars streaked across his face, one after the other, like frames on a roll of film. He glanced at the screen on his dashboard to see the name of the caller; seeing Nadine's name there gave him a sense of reassurance; the familiarity anchored him to a normal world he didn't feel he was a part of anymore. "Wish it were under different circumstances."

He gazed out the window, over the edge, at the waves crashing on the rocks below. Salty water and foam sprayed high into the air, as if trying to grab the car and pull it into the ocean. Peter squinted through the sunlight as he approached the end of the tunnel road.

Nadine sighed. "I'm so sorry, Peter. Sorry I couldn't be at the funeral. With taking care of Angie and all, it was just impossible to make the trip."

"Don't worry," he forced a humorless chuckle. "You checked up on me every day, so you were there more than anyone. Besides, I'm happy you didn't get to witness me turning into a cliché."

"What the hell are you talking about?"

"What was it the *New York Times* said about my latest book? I have it almost memorized by heart. They said, 'The prose is overwrought, unnecessarily wordy, and Lange seems content with simply scaring readers, rather than seeking deeper, more culturally relevant subjects.' Then they said, and this is the part I truly loved, 'Instead of writing about his Latino heritage, which would have been more appealing to a world moving toward more culturally diverse tastes, Peter Lange is only interested in creepy tales, not even avoiding the pitfall of having a male writer protagonist who has a refrigerator wife.'"

Nadine let out another sigh. "Seriously? Are you trying to be funny right now?"

"Well, Miss Schaefer," he said, knowing she hated when he called her that, "I am, in fact, a writer, and my wife is, in fact, dead."

"I don't like you when you get like this. I know it's a coping thing you do, using a bit of dark humor to deal with unpleasant things, but I really think it's inappropriate in these circumstances."

"Well, tough shit. I'm the one who's grieving. I get to choose how."

"I can also choose to hang up since you're being an asshole."

Peter stared out at the waves crashing into Skarsgard's Teeth. For a moment, he lost his orientation and veered toward the edge. Not enough to put him in danger of driving off the cliff, but enough to give him a start.

"I am being an asshole," he said. "I'm sorry. It's been…stressful."

"Is that why William isn't coming with you?"

"It's a part of it. Left him at Jenny's parents' before driving here. I think they'll appreciate having him around. It's like having a part of her there with them, and they'll pamper him into normalcy, or as much normalcy as he can have now, I guess. I've been keeping it together for weeks for him. I need to *not* keep it together for a while, and he does *not* need to see me like that."

"There's also the *other* unpleasant thing you came to do."

"Don't start."

"Why are you going to that place?"

"I have to."

"No, you don't. You do more than enough paying for her care. You don't need to see her."

"Nadine, she's my mother. I haven't seen her in over a year. She's sick. I can't just abandon her like that."

"Yes, you can! In fact, it would be the healthy decision to make. Did you forget the awful things she said last time you came? What she said about Jenny?"

(*That bitch will burn, the Lord will take her! the bitch will burn! You mark my—*)

"About your son?"

(*That little spawn of yours will be nothing but gristle stuck between the teeth of the Lord and He will pick at him with his tongue, but he will never—*)

"That's not her fault," he said, becoming agitated. "It's the Alzheimer's. She doesn't know what she's saying anymore."

"You know that's not true. She didn't have Alzheimer's when she saw us kissing in your backyard when we were kids. She didn't have Alzheimer's when she came at me with those scissors."

(*Whore! Get away from him! You will not corrupt him with your sin! You will not sully him! I swear I'll drag these scissors across your face and men will cringe away from your whore fac—*)

"You know she can't control herself, Nadine. She just gets a little crazy sometimes. We—"

"What, *Norman*? We all go a little mad sometimes?"

With a sudden turn of the wheel, Peter swerved right and pulled over. He found himself at the spot where the road would've made a tight left turn and disappeared down the side of the mountain as it sloped toward town. There was a broad flat rock formation jutting from the edge, following the direction the road would've taken had it continued onward instead of curving left.

He sat in silence for a moment, breathing in and out, each breath deep, loud, and angry.

"Don't call me that." His voice was a hiss now.

He had always hated that nickname. Barry Giffen gave it to him on the day he'd first talked to everyone at The Pines, back when they were all kids. Despite hating it, given how things turned out, he put up with it.

"Norman" had been an obvious reference to Norman Bates, from Alfred Hitchcock's *Psycho*, but Peter, who could not watch movies and didn't own a television, remained oblivious to it. After months of grinning naively when called Norman, his curiosity got the best of him, and he asked Bobby Novak to show him the movie.

Bobby pulled the movie from his vast collection of VHS tapes from back in the day. Two walls with many shelves filled end-to-end with lovingly curated VHS boxes arranged by genre, franchise, and date. Peter could still remember sitting on the plush carpet in Bobby's room as the other boy slid the tape into the VCR, swallowing his nerves as the movie began. Even in black and white, the film was exhilarating to his eyes, which had never seen a proper movie—not up close—that wasn't educational material played during class.

He spotted the similarities with Norman Bates at once, and he understood the nickname. At first, at least. Even if he felt embarrassed by it, he could understand why his relationship with his mother might draw a comparison, so he kept his good humor about it. This lasted until exactly one hour, forty-one minutes, and twenty-five seconds into the movie. Peter witnessed Norman Bates, dressed in his mother's clothes and a cheap wig, wielding a knife, and grinning insanely under a swinging light bulb.

Peter watched, mouth ajar, until that last scene, when an even bigger insult was added. The ending implied Norman had all but disappeared, buried under the all-consuming "Mother" persona. At that point, he stood from the floor in Bobby's bedroom and left without saying a word, humiliated. Not in the same way he'd been humiliated by his own mother countless times, but worse, because now he felt humiliated by his friends. They had been calling him something *that* awful for a long time, and he'd just grinned like an idiot.

Perhaps—he'd realized, with the years and the therapy—what had always bothered him wasn't something as harmless as a wig and a dress. Not even the implications about his mental health. The real reason he'd been so offended, so deeply insulted by that cruel nickname, was the very true existential dread that his mother would one day overwhelm him and diminish him to the point of nonexistence. That he would be nothing but a tiny squall in front of the force of nature that was Martha Lange. In the end, wasn't that the reason Nadine was now calling him that?

She was afraid he would collapse under the weight of his mother.

"I'm… I'm sorry, Peter," Nadine said.

"I know who she is," he said. "I know *what* she is. I know every horrible thing she's ever said." He stopped talking, gazing far ahead at the sky and the ocean.

The place where he'd stopped was known as Blue Overlook, and it was a mandatory stop for any tourist driving into town due to its breathtaking view. A single large tour bus was departing the area as he'd arrived, leaving a trail of white dust, which now dissipated in the wind. He pulled into the large gravel parking zone to one side of the overlook.

"I know she's always been…like that, but it's different now. She's alone, and scared, and confused, and you're telling me to just abandon her?"

"I just think sometimes we make excuses for people, and there are certain things that are inexcusable." Nadine swallowed hard, and her next sentence sounded somewhat choked. "My parents loved each other. I can attest to that. It wasn't an act they put on for the neighbors. They loved each other."

"I know. I remember."

"All it took was once. He hit her once. He lost control and hit her *once*. It wasn't even a proper punch, it was this weak backhand slap in the living room, but he knew. The moment the slap hit—I saw his face during the commotion—he knew he'd changed something, and he couldn't take it back. My mom told him to move out, and he did.

Didn't even argue. He knew he couldn't take it back, because when you love someone, you will argue and yell and shout and even stop talking to each other for a while. But the act of hitting someone, even in the heat of the moment, carries a fundamental loss of respect toward the other person.

"Down the line, they talked and remained civil. When dad got sick, she was there for him the whole time, until he died, but they never tried to get back together." She paused, hearing only silence on the other end. "Peter?"

"I'm listening," he said, not taking his eyes off the perfect blue sky, unblemished by clouds.

"You might rationalize it and say 'well, but your mom was there when he died, so why can't I?', right?"

Peter didn't answer.

"It was one slap," she said. "It cost him a good marriage, and never getting back together. Then, I think about… about the way they *found* you! God, Peter, we've missed you so much since they took you away from her, but what she did to you, I—" She sniffled, and Peter heard the sound of her wiping at a snotty, tear-stained nose. "The way they found you, Peter. It's nowhere close to what my dad did! That woman doesn't deserve to have you next to her, holding her hand as she dies. She deserves nothing but to die alone, and scared, and confused. Then Hell, immediately after."

Peter glanced again at the dashboard screen; he saw the call time increase, making the sudden silence more awkward as each second passed. He sighed. There had been something in that last sentence, something sprinkled along with the grief, like a bitter spice. It was hatred. Hatred toward Martha Lange and everything she stood for. However, he knew her words came from a place of love for him.

His late wife, Jenny, had been the love of his life, but Nadine was his best friend, and she'd also been his first girlfriend—his first kiss, his first heartbreak. Just like her parents, they would never be together, and they both knew it. He hadn't slapped her to deserve this fate, but his mother had made sure she realized just how bad an idea being with him would have been as long as he lived under her roof.

Nevertheless, their love had only grown, their friendship had only strengthened, and they'd only gotten closer despite the years and the physical distance. Nadine always had his back, and this moment was no different.

"I'm not doing this for her," he said after a few moments. "I'm doing this for William."

"She fucking hates William!"

"I know,"

(—*gristle stuck between the teeth of the Lord*—)

he spoke in a calming voice, trying to get Nadine's emotions to subside. "Nadine, his mother died a month ago. He understands what that means, but he misses her so badly. What would I be teaching him if I left my own mother to die alone?"

He was certain this would make Nadine back down, but her reply cracked like a whip. "You'd be teaching him there are some relationships so toxic, even blood ties don't justify keeping them around."

"Point taken." His tone was almost businesslike. "Your disagreement has been noted. I'm still going to do it. Are you gonna fight me for it?"

Nadine took several seconds to answer. "No," she said. "However, I'll trade you."

"Oh no. What?"

Nadine's voice shifted to the friendly tone from just moments before the cloud of his mother came over the conversation. "The guys want to take you out for drinks tonight."

"No, no, no, Nadine," Peter protested. "Not tonight. I'll be—"

"Stressed out from seeing Mother and tired from the long drive. Right. Get over it. I was going to tell them just that, but since you want me to be a good girl and stop getting on your case about seeing that woman, you don't get a choice anymore. So, 8 p.m. Cunningham's. Be hungry, because there will be chicken wings. Be thirsty, because there will be beer."

"Are you serious? Nadine, c'mon. Jenny just—"

"Wanted you to be happy." She completed his sentence. "You'll be here for four days. You can cry and grieve all you want. We'll even grieve along with you later, but we want you to have at least one good night with your friends. Your wife died a month ago. You deserve to get drunk before you get back to being a responsible father."

"Fine," he said. "Just one condition. Just the Vigilantes, alright? No significant others unless the significant other is actually part of the Vigilantes."

"How come?"

"You know. I'll be tired and on edge, and well, Barry's wife… I don't want to deal with all that."

"Why, I do not know what you might be referring to, good sir," Nadine said in a conspirator's voice. "Perhaps the thing you're talking about lives in Blight Harbor, and we should leave it there."

"Funny. See you tonight."

"Talk to you later."

The moment the call ended, Peter stepped out of the car and slowly strode to the edge of Blue Overlook. Each dragging step raised a cloud of dried dirt off the ground, and it soon covered his shoes. A safety railing delimited the edge just a few inches over waist height. Straight ahead, there was nothing but blue ocean and sky. The 10 a.m. sun shone with intensity. Peter scanned his surroundings, making sure no one was coming. Once satisfied he was completely alone, he climbed over the railing and stood on the other side. He took in a deep breath, eyes closed. When he opened them, he turned his head to the left.

In the distance, he could see the wide circle of blue ocean that made up the bay, followed by the land that surrounded it, which seemed to fold upward into the Crescent Mountains—a natural boundary, circling the area almost completely. The skirts of the mountains were covered in trees, bushes, and grass, which carpeted the land, broken only by the occasional rock formation sticking out from among the trees. During most winters, the mountaintops were the only places in White Harbor that became covered in snow, and these four rock formations became highlighted in white, piercing through the winter-darkened canopy of the trees. This had earned them the name of The Horns. This time of year, however, the mountains were lusciously green, and The Horns were streaked and grained in black, gray, brown, and white.

It was the town Peter was gazing at, however. The years passed, but the town always looked the same. One building got replaced by another occasionally, but the reality was the town itself changed little. Sure, the store signs changed. What was a clothing store became a laundromat, what was a restaurant became a pet shop, but most of the town remained frozen in time. A fresh coat of plaster and paint on the same old buildings, the same old families, the same old secrets. Painted over, but always there, like layers under the surface.

New faces, living the same lives.

The phrase "he got out" had been applied to him from the moment they'd removed him from his mother's home, and he'd gone to live with his aunt. Like he'd finished a prison sentence or gotten paroled. It was a phrase often used to refer to anyone who managed to move out of town. "Managed", because it was considered an accomplishment, moving up in life, like removing a boot off a car's tire and flooring it like a bat out of Hell.

He got out, but he always came back.

He feared one of those times he came back, he wouldn't be able to get out anymore.

In one of those buildings in the distance, Mother waited. Did she even know she was waiting? Was she conscious enough to know she was waiting for him to visit? Could the news of Jenny's death have reached her? Did she already know how

(*Look away, son! Look away!*)

she'd died? Was she waiting with a smug smile on her face, expecting him to come and confirm what she already knew?

What was he thinking? Coming to visit her after Jenny's death was beyond torture. Even if his mother wasn't lucid enough to understand who he was, he would wonder the whole time, *Does she know?*

Once more, he closed his eyes and let the sun warm his face. Its brightness shone through his eyelids, and they seemed to glow red and orange when viewed from behind. He took in another deep breath of fresh mountain air, mixed with a hint of saltiness from the sea. He opened his eyes and gazed straight down at the waves crashing on the rock wall. His jaw and his hands trembled, and, for a second, he almost reached back and grabbed the railing, but he knew he couldn't do that.

(*Whoever grabs the railing is a big clucking chicken!*)

He slowly reached down, unzipped his pants, and took a piss over the edge of the cliff. The stream curved left in the wind and broke into drizzle before making it to the water.

Chapter Two

The Embodiment of Evil

1991

"There's this fish on the East Coast," Elijah Knox once said, while sitting at the counter at Chuck Cunningham's bar.

His friends, Neal Parham, and Jerry Lucas paid close attention.

Knox had downed four beers already and was holding the almost-empty fourth bottle by the neck, spinning it, making the bit of liquid at the bottom dance in circles.

"The Northern Stargazer, this fish is called. Harmless sounding name. This thing buries itself in the sand almost completely. Everything but its face, and let me tell ya, what a face. Ugly little fucker. You're looking at a patch of sand, then you do a double take when you see these vile, round walleyes staring up at you, and this mouth, like a down-turned sickle moon filled with pointy teeth. It stays there waiting, unmoving, just staring, until some tiny fish, whose luck just ran out, happens by. Suddenly, it rises from the sand and gobbles it up in a single bite. Poor little fish doesn't know what hit it. At first, it's swimming happily, waving its little fins." He fanned his hands like a fish's fins. "Then, BAM! Complete darkness."

Chuck Cunningham, not even waiting for Knox to order his fifth beer, put it on the bar in front of him. Knox put down the bottle he'd been holding, grabbed the new one by the neck, and took a long swig to give himself a brief, suspenseful pause before he got to the point.

"That man in that house. Old Man Curling." He imbued his voice with disgust, as if Parham and Lucas needed reminding no night of drinking with Elijah Knox was done without the obligatory Old Man Curling tirade. "He sits in that goddamn rocking chair all day, in that mess of trees and vines he calls a home. He reminds me of that fish. A fuckin' Northern Stargazer. Bulging eyes, down-turned mouth, and all." He took another swig of beer and pointed the mouth of the bottle at Parham and Lucas. "Mark my words, gentlemen. One day, some unlucky kid is gonna pass too close to that house, and BAM!" He slammed his hand on the counter, startling both.

"Hey!" Chuck Cunningham turned to him with a warning expression.

"Sorry!" Elijah turned to his friends and lowered his voice to an ominous whisper. "He's gonna gobble that poor kid up. You'll see. That man is a predator."

"Well, I don't know about him being a predator," Jerry Lucas, the local veterinarian, only two beers in, and still composed and eloquent, said. "He certainly doesn't strike me as friendly; I would add unpleasant and downright misanthropic. Predator, however, might be too harsh a word. Those dogs of his, though…"

Elijah's and Neal's eyes opened wide in surprise.

"I know, in normal circumstances, I will never blame a dog for being aggressive. I will usually blame the owner, and it's no different in this case. Mr. Curling, and I'll call him that because of professional courtesy, came in one day with his two dogs. One of them presented symptoms of food poisoning. Vomit, anorexia, lethargy, lack of coordination, you know, the usual stuff when a dog eats something it shouldn't have."

Both of his friends nodded. Elijah, he knew, had had to medicate his wife's unpleasant little Pomeranian on many an occasion, when it ate too much.

"Dog's sick," Jerry said, doing his best Ben Curling grumble impression. "The dog didn't have a leash on,

I should mention. It might have been sick, but it certainly didn't look it. It appeared perfectly capable of lunging at someone if provoked. That dog just stared at me. The other one did likewise. I know this will sound crazy, but it felt like those two dogs *hated* my guts. I mean, most dogs hate coming to the vet. Every vet knows that. They're scared, apprehensive, they whine, they tremble, they urinate, they refuse to move. I'm trained to deal with all that, even angry dogs, for sure, but these things, they *hated* me..."

He stared vacantly for a moment, swiveling his head slowly from one side to the other, replaying the memory to see if he might have interpreted it wrong, perhaps missed some key detail that would explain the dread that clutched his mind now that he remembered the incident.

"I asked Mr. Curling to put a leash on the dogs, and he scowled at me as if I had just insulted his mother. Then, in the most casual tone, he said, 'They won't bite anyone if I don't tell 'em to. They know I'll kill 'em if they do.' I was at a loss for words."

"Maybe you were, but I think that's more words than the entire town has *ever* heard Old Man Curling speak," Neal Parham said, red drunken cheeks and a silly grin on his face. "Seriously, by his standards, that's downright chatty."

"Maybe. He spoke with such confidence, like a man who knew he could say and do anything without the need to apologize. Like we owed him the license to never be questioned. Who knows? Maybe we *do* owe him that, after all the gossip and grief this town has given him."

"Nothing he hasn't brought upon himself," Elijah said.

"Well, I know something you don't, Eli," Jerry said, casting a shrewd glance at his friend. "When you're Black, people look at you differently. Here, I'm the town's veterinarian, but when I go to another town, I'm just another Black man, getting those looks like they're wondering what store I stole the fancy clothes from."

"That's bullshit. It has nothing to do with him being Black! You know better!"

"I know it doesn't help." Jerry gave his friend another meaningful glance with a raised eyebrow.

"Alright, alright, keep going," Elijah answered, waving a dismissive hand.

"I don't know why, I just felt too scared to push on the leash issue." He took another sip of beer. "For God's sake, it's my clinic, it's protocol, and I was still too terrified to follow it. I just told him to bring the dogs into the examining room. I turned to walk inside, took a few steps, and heard Maida from behind the reception desk utter this sudden"— He emitted a loud gasp—"and I turned around to see both dogs were *stalking* me."

He did his best to imitate the posture of the canines, gesturing with his hands when his face or body couldn't.

"Head down, body tense, ears up, tail up. I heard a growl and froze. In my mind, I saw the dog lunge at me, straight for my throat, but just before it did, Mr. Curling came up and kicked him! He kicked his own dog on its haunches! In front of a veterinarian!" He drew in a deep breath. "And I didn't move. I didn't reprimand him. I couldn't. The dog just moved aside. Didn't even cry out when it was kicked. Mr. Curling glared up at me, with even more scorn in his eyes, if that was even possible, and he brought out leashes and collars from his jacket pocket and put them on the dogs."

Jerry took a generous chug of beer and swallowed audibly.

"Now, I know what I just said. I will never blame a dog for being aggressive, and I mean it. Mastiffs are usually nice family pets, and they're very gentle animals, but a Mastiff that's not used to seeing other people, and not taught how to behave around strangers, can be quite aggressive."

"So, which one is it, then?" Elijah said, once again pointing at him with his beer. "You said, in normal circumstances, you would never blame the dog. What did you mean by 'normal circumstances'?"

Jerry nodded. "Again, I know what I said. I still wouldn't blame the dog. Not really. I've seen some angry dogs in my life. Dogs trained to be aggressive, even trained to kill. I've seen abused dogs, terrified dogs, whose instinct is to bite if you so much as move. Not once have I been afraid of a dog. But that stare the dog gave me after getting kicked…" He bared his teeth in a fearful grin and took in air through them, as he moved his head slowly in denial. "*That* scared me. It really did. It was a blaming stare. Like it was saying, 'I won't forget that.' But it wasn't just that."

"Oh, really?"

"Well…" Jerry said, in a high pitch, and followed the word with a tightening of the lips that expressed this was the part of the story he wasn't so keen on telling.

He removed his glasses, rubbed his eyes tiredly, and put the glasses back on.

"A few days later, maybe like a week at most, during breakfast, Pauline told me she'd gotten up to make herself a cup of tea in the middle of the night. She has insomnia sometimes, the tea calms her nerves. Passionflower tea. You know how she suffers from anxiety, but the pills, uh, the pills make her feel weird so, for a few months a year, despite the doctor's recommendations, she stops taking them, to 'cleanse,' she says"—he marked the word with air quotations—"and well, passionflower tea, it, uh, contains this substance called chrysin, which is a flavonoid that helps calm anxiety, and—"

"Will you get on with the damn story, Jerome Wolfgang Lucas?" demanded Elijah, banging again on the counter; this time only eliciting an annoyed sigh from Chuck.

"Fine! Okay!" Jerry—who loathed the middle name Wolfgang—said. "While she was waiting for the water to boil, Pauline peered out the window and thought she saw two dogs, black as night, sitting on the front lawn, panting, and just staring at our house. Fixed on it. She said she hadn't told me because she thought she'd dreamed it. After all, they weren't acting like normal dogs. 'They didn't look right,' she said. She wasn't sure if it was just a reflection of the moonlight or some other source of light, but she was convinced their eyes were bright blue, like luminescent blue. This just made her dismiss it all as a dream even more, and it got all mixed up with the memory of her making tea that night. Only, I don't think she dreamed it.

"I didn't tell her what I was thinking because I didn't want to scare her. Anxiety, you know? I said nothing because the morning after she had *supposedly* seen the dogs, I woke up and went out to get the newspaper, then the smell hit me like a punch. It was feces. Definitely feces, but they smelled sick."

"Like when you've been constipated for three full days, and Taco Bell makes it all come out at once?" Neal Parham said, earning a disgusted expression from his friends. "Whaaat?" He shrugged, not quite grasping what he'd said that might deserve such a look.

"Thank you, Neal," Jerry said, "for the lovely mental image. As I was saying, the smell hit me, so I turned to find the source and there they were: two massive piles of dog excrement on our lawn. It appeared they'd been there all night.

They weren't fresh. I examine dog feces for a living, so I knew that much. They were several hours old, and yet they smelled as if half-digested chunks of meat were stuck to them and had been rotting for days."

"Now, who's the one providing the gross mental images?" Neal said.

Jerry eyed him with annoyance. "Thinking rationally, well, dogs have a great sense of smell, so they could've located my house but, I'm telling you, the more I think about it the less sense it makes. It just doesn't! I live on the opposite end of town from Mr. Curling. The dogs have never been at my house. I doubt the man even knows where I live to have pointed the dogs in my direction, and this is just something dogs *do not* do. They don't track a person's house out of an entire town to take a *SHIT*—"

Elijah and Neal flinched, he assumed, on account of how uncommon it was for him to use foul language.

"—on someone's front lawn out of spite; and still…"

He guzzled beer from the bottle thirstily, as if seeking comfort, as if he needed the liquid to push down a bite of bread stuck in his throat; needed it as much as Pauline, his loving wife, sometimes *needed* passionflower tea to go to sleep.

"Still, it unnerved me. Every time I went out for my evening jogs, I kept stopping and looking back because I sensed—I just *sensed*—a pair of vicious black dogs, as if they were real muscle and fur, with blue glowing eyes, stalking me, with their heads down, bodies tense, ears up, tails up, and drooling for a bite of my flesh. I imagine when they finally catch me, and all the while, as they rip me apart down to the bone, I scream and picture that man's hateful stare when I told him to put the leashes on the dogs, but his angry face turns into a grin, and I see him grinning. And in my screams, I regret—God as my witness—I regret the moment I mentioned those god-damned leashes because now Pauline's a widow because I couldn't keep quiet about the damn leashes, and that man's still grinning, grinning because *he* commanded his dogs to kill me. He commanded them to track down the asshole vet who put a leash on his babies and eat him whole; well, almost whole. They'd leave some recognizable parts—some of my face or my left ring finger with the engraved ring still on it—then drag the carcass back to my front lawn and shit me out for my wife to find all that's left of me."

Jerry went quiet. He stuck the bottle in his mouth and didn't stop drinking until his bottle was empty. He raised a hand and signaled for Chuck to bring him another.

"That's in Blight Harbor, man," Elijah said, patting his friend on the back. "Leave it there."

The three men took a silent drink almost at the same time.

Neal Parham shook his head. Looking dissatisfied.

"No," he said. "You know why I can't just leave it in Blight Harbor like you guys?"

To his friends, he appeared to have sobered up all of a sudden.

He pulled a Polaroid out of his pocket and slammed it on the bar.

"This is why."

The very same Polaroid he'd taken two years earlier, showing the twisted, terrified face of Gerardo Valencia.

Elijah and Jerry gasped as they saw the image.

Even Chuck Cunningham stopped what he was doing and looked down at it. A trancelike sense of dreadful ceremony wafted in the air, like Neal had asked for a minute of silence for a child two years dead and in the ground. Nothing but skeletal remains by now. A dry memory.

"How would you feel if that happened to your kids?" He gazed into the eyes of his friends, moving from one to the other as he spoke. "Your three kids, Eli. Maria would lose her mind, wouldn't she? She'd be in a straitjacket locked in Lighthouse Rock for the rest of her days. What if it was your boy, Jerry? Pauline would dive off a cliff. You, Chuck, can you picture Jess like this? She's a strong kid, but this face isn't because of weakness. This is some unholy shit, right there."

Looking uncomfortable, Chuck waved a hand in

front of Neal's face. "Neal. There's no need for this. I think you've had en—"

"I know I'm probably gonna have a pretty horrifying death sooner rather than later." Neal stated this matter-of-factly, no joking intonations or cynicism in his voice.

Jerry tried to intervene. "Neal, please—"

"'The Curse of the Parhams', am I right? You've all heard of it."

"That's a myth, Neal. Your family isn't—"

"The hell it isn't," Neal gave a single throaty chuckle. "My dad bled to death in his truck. He got drunk, crashed into a tree, the bottle broke, and he cut his femoral artery on impact. My grandma got torn apart by coyotes, while her children watched." He once more shot glances all around with a sarcastic smile. "Who knows what the hell's in store for me. I've made my peace with that. But just thinking this"—he tapped on the Polaroid—"could happen to my boy, Freddie, or my baby girl, Laurie, how can I just leave the whole damn thing in Blight Harbor?"

His friends stopped trying to interrupt. Their gazes moved flittingly among each other to see if he might actually learn to read the room and shut up.

No luck.

"Dorothy Parham, my ancestor, she worked at the Vanek House almost a hundred years ago. Guess who she worked with? Rickward Curling. Ben Curling's ancestor!

Three families living in that place at one time. The Vaneks all died, the Parhams are cursed, and the Curlings inherited the property. Now, you look at this"—he tapped on the picture again—"and tell me Curling had nothing to do with it. Tell me we should leave it in Blight Harbor, and take the chance of our kids ending up like that.

No one answered.

Just sat, taking disheartened sips from their beers.

If anyone were to listen to those stories—only a handful of the many exchanged among the inhabitants of White Harbor—they would assume they didn't talk about the Vanek House, but Old Man Curling. This would be incorrect, nothing but a superficial assumption. People telling these stories were adults, and adults—by the benefit or misfortune of having lived longer—inherently saw other people as the source of evil, not inanimate objects.

It's true adults can embrace superstitions, religious beliefs, abstractions, and magical thinking: "The Devil made me do it", "It felt like I had stepped out of my body", "These shoes bring me bad luck at Blackjack."

Yet, the adult mind needs to find someone to blame, an embodiment of evil—a living vessel for these superstitions, beliefs, and abstractions to act through. The adults that talked about Ben Curling weren't aware talking about him was nearly the same as talking about the Vanek House.

Children, however, understood this distinction. Hard logic was not a burden to them, and they could see the sources of evil adults often overlooked. They could see the man, and the evil *behind* the man, like an invisible puppeteer. Because of this, the children's stories talked about Old Man Curling, but in relation to the Vanek House, almost as if he were the house's appendage. The moving arm on an action figure, not the mechanism which moved it. They recognized whatever was wrong with Old Man Curling was inseverable from the Vanek House.

"I guess Freddie really screwed the pooch, huh?" said Bobby Novak, a short, blond boy of eleven, somewhat chubby, with keen, blue eyes, sitting on a rock and wearing a black *Terminator 2: Judgment Day* t-shirt so new the print on it was still thick and glossy.

Bobby wanted everyone at school to know he'd been the first kid in his class to watch the movie, even if he technically wasn't old enough to have done so. Getting into the movie theater to watch an R-Rated movie being only eleven, he thought, made you quite cool. "Well, here's what I know…"

His classmates were standing or sitting around in one of those tribal gatherings that used to form after school, back in the days before humanity collectively decided that smartphone screens were more interesting than other human beings. Children and preteens of all ages, social cliques, and ethnicities paid close attention to Bobby's story—or as much attention as one could expect after a long day of school.

The topics of the day were the Vanek House and Old Man Curling, as an unexpected glimpse into the death of Gerardo Valencia, a boy whom many of them had known, had just seen the light of day, two years after his death.

Earlier that morning, Freddie "the Hyena" Parham had been sent to the principal's office and was later seen leaving with his dad, Neal Parham, who picked him up in his police cruiser. They all knew Freddie hadn't been arrested by his own dad, of course. Officer Parham had simply been on patrol at that time, but given how big Freddie's screw-up had been, it was certainly a fitting image.

Bobby, who had been the first to know of the day's events since he was Freddie Parham's closest friend, witnessed most of it, and told the story in the gathering at The Pines, to the best of his knowledge.

Freddie happened upon the fateful picture while searching

his dad's desk for a box cutter, and he knew right away what the glossy square with the white borders at the bottom of the drawer was. He'd heard his dad go on drunken tirades about how the whole town was going to Hell if a young boy could just die so horribly, without the possibility of catching the culprit. Gerardo hadn't been the first child to die under strange circumstances in White Harbor, but he had been the most recent, and certainly the first Freddie's dad had seen in person since becoming a police officer.

Following that uncontrollable impulse that often overtakes young boys to do mischief, Freddie put the picture in his backpack and brought it to school, and he meant to show everyone and their uncle the horrible frozen face of Gerardo Valencia.

The Polaroid wasn't quite clear—the surroundings were dark, and the flash had overexposed the subject—but what half the school got to witness that day was still unforgettable. Gerardo Valencia's face with his cold bulging eyes, like a fish in a freezer, and his twisted, eternally screaming mouth. One of his hands was visible as well, in one corner of the photograph. Though blurry, they could all see it was curled into a claw, and one fingernail was missing, replaced by the reddish-brown of frozen flesh and blood.

Freddie Parham became a hero that day. He knew his destiny was to draw a horror graphic novel like the ones in the pages of *Taboo* or *Twisted Tales* when he grew up. He could draw amazing horror creatures. Many times, he'd shown his work to Bobby, and assured him his future involved making it big by scaring people. The Polaroid was just a little practice, Freddie said, and laughed in the high-pitched "Hee-hee-hee!" that had given him his nickname.

That morning Freddie had been in his full glory. He broke social norms, he made people gasp, he made people scream, he avoided being caught by any of the teachers, he stuck it to the man, and he pushed the boundaries to sate the world's morbid curiosity. He also made one mistake: he completely failed to consider someone might tell.

It had been too tempting. Sylvia Nguyen. Conceited bitch. Teacher's pet. Her eyes with big, round glasses, nearly glued to her notebook, carefully re-writing the previous class's notes in clean, girly calligraphy.

Bobby had warned him not to. Other girls at school might scream, or curse him out, or slap him for showing them the picture, but Sylvia was not like other girls. Sylvia didn't conform to the "don't be a snitch" rules that governed other children. However, by the time Bobby finished his warning, he knew it was too late. He knew the look in Freddie's eyes. It had gotten him in trouble so many times before, and now it was directed at the narrow space between Sylvia's face and her notebook like a crack in a prison wall through which an inmate could see the sunset.

Giving in to his base instincts, Freddie pulled the

picture out of his backpack, took it by a corner between his thumb and index finger, and shoved it in that narrow space right in front of Sylvia Nguyen's eyes.

Even Bobby, who wasn't one for mischief, had to admit the scream that followed was glorious.

Sylvia Nguyen had pipes that could wake the dead. She immediately turned around, eyes wide in terror, and pointed her finger straight at Freddie, who was already laughing, but his laugh was short-lived, as Sylvia shouted without a hint of holding back, "HE'S GOT A PICTURE OF A DEAD BOY! HE'S GOT A PICTURE OF A DEAD BOY!"

"Well, you know the rest," Bobby said. "Miss Brighton took him to the principal's office and his dad took him home in his police cruiser." He thought, *That drunk jerk is going to beat him within an inch of his life, and right in the places where the clothes cover the bruises.*

There was a quiet in the crowd of children around Bobby, as if paying respect to a fallen comrade. It was clear some of the other kids knew of Freddie's predicament. Neal Parham's alcoholism was a well-known fact, and that he beat his son wasn't known to all, but even if they didn't know, they all agreed Freddie "the Hyena" was in deep shit.

This was the sort of conversation that was common in The Pines, as the students at Garland Elementary called the gathering of pine trees behind one of the school buildings. The Pines were a safe place for all who came. Bullying, fighting, and all kinds of discrimination were forbidden. Outside—in the world—you could have wealthy parents, or be good at sports, or be the most popular kid in school, but here, in The Pines, your opinion was worth the same as that of any poor, awkward, unpopular basement-dweller.

Ancient Greeks would've been proud of the mature little *Agora* that had sprouted near the school, created by the children themselves. Of course, even the ancient Greeks fell short of the equality that existed in this hallowed place, as they used to exclude women, foreigners, and even male Greeks from other cities. At The Pines, everyone's opinion was welcome.

One only needed to briefly glimpse the place to understand why children had gravitated toward it for generations. It had the cover of trees—in this case, pines, which never lost more than a third of their needles between the summer and fall, and never in the winter—it had plenty of rocks to sit on, it was close enough to the school buildings to get there quickly after the bell rang, but it was far enough and in a downward slope so the eyes and ears of school staff were blind and deaf to what happened there. It was an unspoken understanding among the children this was what made this one spot so special. The area was unviolated by adult presence, hidden from the eyes of authority. It had naturally evolved into a microcosm of civilized balance, a tiny utopia—an unusual, self-regulating, neutral zone.

"Who saw the picture?" Bobby asked, trying to break the silence and move the conversation to more interesting topics before everyone got bored and called it a day.

A smattering of hands rose slowly. Then more. Then more. Over fifty percent of those present, in fact.

"What do you think happened to Gerardo in that house?" asked Jess Cunningham, Chuck Cunningham's daughter, a red-haired girl with freckles, full cheeks, and a fluffy perm. "That face is gonna give me nightmares. Do you think Old Man Curling did it?"

"Nah, that wasn't Old Man Curling," said Leroy Howe from one side of the circle.

"It was the house," said Royce Howe, his twin brother, from the other side of the circle, as if continuing his sentence.

They never sat close to each other, so it always sounded like they were speaking in stereo. Royce had just removed his Walkman headphones, and the rest could hear the lyrics to "Mama said knock you out" still coming from them, which raised the question of how he'd heard his brother speak with the headphones on. It was the little parlor trick of the Brothers Howe, and they seemed to be aware of the disorienting effect it had on others.

"Old Man Curling works for the house," Royce said.

"But it's the house that does the killin'," Leroy continued.

"I think you might have a point there," Bobby said. "But he probably gets something out of that. My dad told me one day Old Man Curling has been watching over the house since the beginning. He's supposedly two hundred years old. If you ask me, I think it's the house that keeps him alive. That's why he stays close. I think the house turned him into, like, a vampire, or something, and the way it works is he feeds on people's blood, right? Then, he pukes some of the blood inside the house, and the house feeds on it in exchange for eternal life. It's a symbiotic relationship."

The other kids around him—some sixth graders like Bobby himself, like Jess and the twins, others a few years younger—exchanged glances and murmured about the genuine possibility an honest-to-God vampire might live in town. Their minds, like those of most preadolescents, were still balancing atop the fence between the fantasies that populated the imaginations of children and those new, entirely different fantasies, which would soon replace them in adolescence.

"Wait, though," interjected Callum "Droopy" Baker, a fifth grader whose drooping eyelids, perpetual dark circles under his eyes, and sagging cheeks made him appear like he was both sleepy and melting at the same time. "Doesn't Old Man Curling spend the entire day sitting on his rocking chair, out on his porch? If he was a vampire, he'd burst into flames when the sunlight hit him."

"Well, yeah, I guess," Bobby said, puffing his cheeks, realizing Droopy Baker might just have a point. "His porch faces north, though, so no direct sunlight hits the porch."

"What about the sides of the porch?" asked Droopy. "They're open to the east and west."

"Uh…well, there's a house uphill to the east, so it covers it in the morning, and there's the Vanek House to the west, and that covers it in the afternoon. There you go. No sunlight."

"Not buying it." Callum shot back.

"W-well…" stammered Bobby, still clinging to his story, "…I said he's *like* a vampire or something. Maybe he's a different type of vampire. Maybe he's immune to the sun. How about that, huh? And don't forget what my dad said. Old Man Curling *is* at least two hundred years old! That is a fact!"

Callum regarded Bobby with those sagging eyes of his. "I think your dad's full of shit." His robotic monotone left unclear if he was making fun of Bobby, or if he actually believed Bobby's father was, indeed, a man whose insides had become engorged with excrement.

"Will you both please stop?" interjected Nadine Schaefer, an auburn-haired girl the same age as Bobby, with a V-shaped face and high cheekbones, taking pine needles in her fingers and breaking them into one-inch zigzagging chunks. "I think we all agree the house is evil. Old Man

Curling is a tool of the house, but almost no one knows what made the house like that. My grandma knows, though. She told me there used to be a witch cult that gathered there."

Nadine glanced around the group and became aware they were observing her with expectation. She was the tallest of the sixth graders and the tallest girl at school. She was proficient at basketball, an avid runner, and one hell of a baseball player. This gave her the title, so coveted in the pre-2000s era, of "one of the boys". She had the added benefit of being one of the pretty girls at school, which meant the boys worshipped her, the girls wanted to be her, but she was down-to-earth enough no one thought she was arrogant about it.

"The one story that always stuck with me was about what they did when someone in the cult died. Grandma said during funerals—which always happened at night—the whole cult would gather in the Vanek House and light candles, so those windows up there glowed like"—her eyes widened—"flaming eyes, and the shadows inside made it seem like the eyes were *moving*. She said there used to be this noise coming from the house, like chanting, and screaming, and moaning. She said it sounded sad, but also *angry*, like they were angry at God."

Murmuring and nodding from some of the other children, as though they knew what that sounded like, knew it from experience, even.

"Like they were asking for repayment for the person who died. Then, after the funeral, they walked—*the entire congregation*—and they carried the coffin toward Clive Memorial, which doesn't sound that strange but, before they started marching, they'd set the coffin down in front of the house and surrounded it, and they continued chanting, and screaming, and moaning while they brought the corpse out, but now the dead guy could stand on his own."

She surveyed the crowd to find rapt gazes from every direction.

"My grandma said they made him walk to the cemetery, following him slowly, weeping and clamoring toward the heavens. Once they got to Clive Memorial, the dead guy climbed back into the box, all by himself, then they closed it and began pouring dirt over him. During all this, they just kept chanting and screaming, and chanting and screaming, non-stop."

"It's called a coven."

Nadine turned her head toward the voice. It was Droopy Baker, one of a handful of kids thoroughly unimpressed by Nadine's popularity. "Huh?"

"It's not a *cult* of witches, it's a *coven* of witches," he said.

"Witches can form cults, too."

"No, they form covens. People form cults."

"Witches are people." Nadine was confused.

"Well…sure. But they're, like, people who worship the Devil."

"Oh!" Nadine's lips formed a nearly perfect O, and she nodded slowly. "I see. They worship the Devil. You mean, like…a cult?"

"Don't make me get a dictionary!"

There was no humor in his thinly veiled threat.

"That's all bullshit," said Barry Giffen, the bulkiest of the children, in a loud voice. "You're all talking bullshit. A family used to live there when my momma was younger, just the dad, the mom, and two children. The dad killed them with a butcher knife and ate them."

Barry was built like a linebacker for a college football team, despite being no older than the rest of his classmates. He was one of a smattering of well-known bullies, but here at The Pines, he was one more of the bunch, regardless of whether the others liked him, and many of them certainly had reasons to hate his guts. Most, even those he didn't bully, wondered why he always came here and joined the conversation. He didn't seem to like any of them in the slightest, and yet, he was there, every day after class, like clockwork.

"There was no cult," he said. "No witches, no walking dead, no vampires. The house just possesses you to do evil things. My momma said when they found the dad, he had already eaten the kids and his stomach was all swollen and purple, and you could even see the shape of some of their body parts pushing against his belly from the inside. It was like they'd reanimated there, and they were being digested alive. He was already chowing down on the mom's leg when the police arrested him. He took a bite out of one cop when they tried to restrain him"— he paused for dramatic effect, and to let the whispers of "ewww" and "grossss" quieten—"but he tore his throat right off. My momma saw the ambulance carry the mom's body out, leg stickin' out from under the blanket, all chewed up and bleeding."

Someone coughed in an "Ahem, ahem" manner.

Barry swiveled his head with annoyance to see Droopy Baker, with his fist covering his mouth the way a TV detective would do, right before beginning an extended monologue about his findings to point an accusatory finger at a person in the room, declaring them the murderer.

"Ambulances don't pick up corpses in murder cases," he said flatly. "The coroners do. Also, they don't use blankets, they use body bags to put the—"

"Shut the fuck up, or I'll punch your nose through your skull!" Barry said, raising a fist.

"Fair enough." Droopy held his tongue, going forward.

"You know, I heard the cannibal story, too," croaked Wilfrid Ingram, his blue eyes looking huge behind his thick glasses. He was wiping potato crisp crumbs off his lips. "But I heard it was Old Man Curling who ate his family, and that's why he has none left. They say the reason he guards the house is that's where he butchers the people he eats, because each person he kills in the house feeds the demon that lives there."

"No, man, there's some voodoo going on in that house," countered Royce Howe. "This is some Marie Laveau, Haiti to New Orleans, zombie Bokor necromancy shit."

"Curling is a descendant of Marie Laveau," continued Leroy Howe with a nod. "He's not two hundred years old. He's about a hundred and something. His mother sent him from New Orleans to White Harbor to spread voodoo across the country."

"But then," Royce continued, "when he tried to turn someone into a zombie, he made the mistake of doing it *in* the house because he didn't know there was a weird power there. So, the house turned the spell on him, and now, Curling is a zombie that serves the house!"

Leroy shrugged, and chewed a nail, like this was old news. "And he takes people there to feed their souls to the house. That's what happened to that Valencia boy. Just ask our grandma. She's seen Old Man Curling up close."

"She says he smells like a dead man."

"Well, that sounds close to what my gramma told me," Daley Hines said. "She said those two black dogs he has are the Devil's dogs, and he gave them to Old Man Curling to guard the house. She said there used to be three, one for each of the heads of Cerberus, and they were born out of the house's floorboards, but the third one, the biggest one, was too hard to control. So, Old Man Curling killed it, and let the house swallow it back up, trapping its spirit in there, and he must feed it with souls, so it's not released again."

The conversation quickly turned into a quick-fire session of theories, bouncing from one side of the circle to the other, with increasing speed, like a game of hot potato.

"Old Man Curling killed a woman in the house a hundred years ago, and her angry spirit haunts the house."

"There's a black orb floating in the air on the second floor, and it's a portal to hell that is slowly expanding."

"Each room in the house has the skeleton of a crucified baby, and each baby is one of Old Man Curling's children that he sacrificed to the house."

"Old Man Curling has the key to the door that will unleash the apocalypse."

"There's nothing supernatural in the house. Old Man Curling is just a kiddie-diddler, and he does it in the old house."

"You're all wrong," said an unfamiliar voice from outside the circle.

Everyone turned their heads to see a short, thin, black-haired boy, roughly eleven years old, standing with his back toward the slope that led to the school buildings. The boy was pale as freshly fallen snow and slightly freckled, which seemed to hide what little of his Hispanic heritage there was—the genes from his mother, whom he took after, had all but erased it. He was gripping the straps of his plain, brown leather backpack with both hands as if an invisible line were tethering it to a tree branch, keeping his rickety body from collapsing to the floor.

"Least I think you are."

"Oh, yeah?" Barry said, staring the boy down with a twisted lip and a challenging scowl. "Who asked you, Lange?"

"I..." Peter Lange stammered. "I...just... I just thought since you were... Since you were all here...talking, I could—"

"Could what?" Barry stepped forward, causing Peter to take a step back and almost trip over an outcropping root.

"Uh, nothing." With a clumsy jerk and a spin of his arms, Peter regained his footing and, with haste, turned on his heels to walk away. "I'll just... I'll just leave."

"Yeah, you better. Wouldn't want your crazy mom to come after us."

"No!" Peter spun, the mortification written all over his face. "M-Mother would never—"

"Oh, Mother would never!" Barry imitated the frightened boy. "Whatever you say, Norman!" He laughed.

"I d-don't know who Norman is."

"Go ask Mother!" Barry's tone was scathing.

Peter froze in place, his lips shaking, failing to form a word. Any word.

Barry, seeing the effect he was having on the puny kid and relishing in it, couldn't resist, and took one more step toward him, a wicked grin on his face. He loomed over Peter.

"Leave him alone, Barry!" Bobby Novak called out, pushing him back and standing between the two boys. "The Pines are a safe place! You can't do that here!"

Barry rolled his eyes, remembering the penalty for fighting in The Pines, a penalty that had been passed down from generation to generation, and even bullies did not dare to challenge. He sighed, turned around, and went back to his spot in the circle, leaning against a tree.

Bobby turned around to face Peter. "There," he said, patting the boy on the shoulder, and noticing how he flinched away, which made him grimace with sympathy. "Come on, sit with me. Nice of you to join us at last!"

Peter regarded him nervously and gave a brief, scant glimpse of a smile.

There was an intrigued silence that took over the group as Peter Lange crossed the circle to sit next to Bobby on the rock. They all knew Peter from class, but none of them truly *knew* him. Few of them had actually spoken to him, only in group assignments he wasn't allowed to do on his own, and even then, he only spoke when absolutely necessary. There was only one thing everyone knew about Peter Lange besides the fact he was a quiet boy, and it was something everyone, even their parents, appeared to agree with; a *local truth*: Martha Lange, his mother, was as crazy as a sprayed cockroach.

Nadine Schaefer remembered a time she and her mom had been shopping for clothes. They were coming out of Betsy's Fine Clothing, one bag in hand for each, and just as the sunlight hit their eyes, the sound of shouting and weeping assailed them from their right. At first, she was confused, as the sound didn't seem to go with such a beautiful summer day, with such a magnificent blue sky, and the exhilarating joy of shopping with her mom. She even thought she might have imagined it. However, both Nadine and her mom turned their heads to catch the sight of Martha Lange coming in their direction, dragging her son by the arm down the sidewalk. Fingernails dug into his skin, and she shouted a litany of religious nonsense as the boy wept and pleaded and apologized for whatever sin the crazy woman had been condemning him to Hell for.

The woman's hair was undyed, a mixture of auburn and gray, long and unkempt, hanging in strands down to her small breasts. It was hair that wanted to be wavy but had been forced into almost-straight submission by hours of furious brushing. The woman was wearing a long sleeve buttoned blouse, red with tiny white dots. She wore a blue skirt that hung to her ankles. She had no make-up on, no rings, no bracelets, no necklace, and though Nadine couldn't see past her long hair, she was sure she wasn't wearing any earrings. But the image that got forever recorded in Nadine's memory, like a photograph, was the blood. Tiny drops of blood, not big enough to be streaming down the boy's arm, but undeniably there, where the fingernails ruptured the skin, fingernails bordered with a tiny red line as the blood got caught under them.

Nadine's mom's face had lost all color, and an expression she hadn't been able to understand fully passed over her eyes. Her mom sighed as Peter and the insane woman walked by, and she muttered, "That poor boy."

She had said nothing else, but Colleen Schaefer was visibly uncomfortable for the rest of the day, as if something was gnawing at her mind, as if she witnessed something suck out all the joy from the world. She didn't ask her to try on the new dress they'd bought that day like she normally did. She didn't cook dinner. Her dad made some pasta instead, while her mom stayed in her room saying she had a headache.

Nadine had always seen her mom as a strong woman but, that day, she had seen her as powerless for the first time.

"You all know Peter," Bobby said. "He's my neighbor. He's cool."

There was a smattering of hellos and plenty of awkward glances exchanged among those present.

"Hey," Peter croaked.

"So, Peter, you were saying?" Bobby asked, with an encouraging tone of voice. "About the Vanek House and Old Man Curling?"

"Uh, yeah," Peter hesitated. "Moth…" He stopped and cleared his throat. He threw a flitting glance at Barry as if the large boy would rise and suddenly punch him into the ground, like he was playing Whack-A-Mole. "My mom… she told me the actual story behind the house. She told me why I should always stay away from it."

"Oh, well, that's a real fuckin' trustworthy source, right there," Barry said.

"Barry!" Bobby shot a warning stare at the much larger boy.

Barry sighed, crossed his arms over his chest, and averted his gaze from him.

"She never lies," Peter said, his voice low and serious as he stared intently at Barry.

When Barry glanced back, he saw Peter Lange was

completely serious. That mousy little shit that had come in, so shy and unsure. The boy he'd pushed against walls, and tripped up, and made fun of, and shoved into a locker more than once, was one hundred percent sure of this one thing.

"Mother never lies! Never!"

"That's alright, Peter," Bobby said, placing a hand on his shoulder in a placating manner, ever the paladin. "Tell us."

"My mom once told me Ben Curling inherited the house from his parents. It's been in his family a long time."

He made a pause. Many eyes, filled with anticipation, were pointed directly at him.

"That's all?" Barry said, like his momma had served him salad for dinner, and in a challenging tone added, "Where's the scary shit?"

"I'm getting to that," Peter said.

Chapter Three

Memories of Age

2022

She glanced at her hands. Bony, spotty things covered in what looked like tracing paper that had been crumpled and stretched. Its translucent quality revealed the veins underneath, like blueish roots contrasting with white tendons that were working, pulling, and releasing under the skin, as the calloused tips of her thin fingers passed over the beads.

The movement of her fingers was delicate, meticulous, rounding out each bead, as if remembering a wooden texture that was no longer there from repeated use. As she went from one to the other following their black string, each bead's surface felt identically smooth, yet there was memory in that smoothness, memory of so many prayers and litanies, spoken while aged, hard, yellowed calluses polished the wooden surface, day after day.

Each finger moved in succession, rising and falling, accompanied by the soft mumbling of wizened lips. The words, spoken in a language not of this age, not of the modern world, droned on with hypnotic progression, as her head nodded up and down with a constant cadence.

"*Doikaat gozun-Uolmin yggshe*," the voice, emerging from deep within the woman's chest, said. She breathed in deep, exhaled, and continued. "*Uolkaat Uolmin-koda sen.*"

Another breath, another exhalation.

Her eyes were closed, her brow was furrowed. Her eyeballs moved erratically from one side to the other, underneath her eyelids. Something was not quite right. Perhaps she should open them and see, but that would mean interrupting her midday prayer, and she could not. She *would not*.

"*Ivmyzno trievekaat Uolmin-yevin sen.*"

Something she recognized now.

The birds had gone silent.

People were not as observant as she was, so they rarely noticed. In White Harbor, every day around noon, all birds went quiet, coinciding with her midday prayer. Only the Faithful noticed. Only they knew why the birds went quiet, as if fearing a lurking predator. They were too busy, those other people. Their attention invested in short, meaningless lives that had no other end but darkness and the horror of nothingness, for if there was something to call "horror", wouldn't it be that? Not the childish lake of fire of the Christians, nor the repetitive cycle of the Hinduists, nor the walls and boiling water of Islam. No, the actual Hell was nothingness. Body and soul erased. The reason people sprung awake in terror during dreams of falling was that nothingness followed, and there was no more unimaginable horror.

"Quelmyzno trievekaat conilvi-fredthun sen."

She wondered where Peter was. Most likely chasing after his father, seeking reassurance and love, as if those things could come from any other but God. Peter was only six, but she could see the boy was weak and full of worldly curiosity, which would make him lose focus, and one day make him stray from the path.

Next bead. She had to focus.

"Edoakaat gozun-Uolmin yggshe."

Next bead. Her mind kept getting distracted today.

"Edoan eikaat Uolmin-koda sen."

Next bead. She was criticizing the boy for his lack of focus, and here she was, getting distracted at the most important moment of the day.

Focus! she commanded herself.

"Ykop takaat conilvi-fredthun sen."

Next bead. She had to clear her mind!

"Uolkaat Uolmin-yevin sen."

Then there was Hector. Her husband. Ignorant, if there was one word to describe him. Useless, if there were two. Still clinging to that infantile religion full of fantasies and greed she found so laughable. The majority weren't always the wise, and Hector's religion might have the numbers, but not the wisdom. A religion of gold and money and pretense. Her God was a God of stone and dirt and water and light, who asked for naught but that which you have from birth.

Next bead.

"Uolmin megdikaat Uolmin-koda sen."

Sure, he had acquiesced a little. Perhaps to make *her* also acquiesce to his sin and get off his back. He agreed to join the Circle, but he asked for time. Time! How dare he? Man must not ask for time from God, but willingly give their own, because time is God's. Sure, he joined the gatherings. Sure, he made the offerings. But did he have the courage to commit? Would he do what God asked of him when the time came? No. She was certain he wouldn't.

Next bead.

"Edegikaat conilvi-fredthun sen."

Of course he wouldn't. It was always up to her. He only followed because he was cowardly—a third word to describe him! She smiled as this occurred to her. He followed because he was a foreigner with no other family. An ignorant, useless, cowardly foreigner, raised with the culture and beliefs of peasants. What did she ever see in him? Why had she debased herself to be with him?

Next bead.

"Otpoi ujigokaat Uolmin-yevin sen."

Hector was making her have to work harder when she needed to be stern to ensure Peter didn't stray from the path. That boy loved the world. She could see it in his eyes, but she already had a plan. She had beaten the world out of him, and to an extent, had held his curiosity at bay, but it had never been enough. Curiosity always crept back in, like a chronic disease. She already knew how to draw the inquisitiveness out of him. The solution was in her own home, all along, and she knew the right moment to test it.

Next bead.

"Tjenaf egoikaat gozun-Uolmin yggshe."

Peter aside, what had been happening with the strange daydreams she had been having? The one from that morning had been particularly confusing. Terrifying, even, and she wasn't a woman who scared easily.

She left her home, intending to go to the store to buy some flour, eggs, and butter. She would've sent Peter if he hadn't been at school.

School. She grunted in annoyance.

She had briefly considered homeschooling him—no need to expose him to the world, when his love for the world was already hard enough to contain—but Hector, ignorant, useless, cowardly Hector, had insisted. He had promised he would take it upon himself to work on the boy's nightly teachings of the *Uolminar* if she agreed to let him go to a normal school. She had said no, but Hector had his ways of making her agree. Ignorant? Perhaps. Useless? Perhaps. Cowardly? Perhaps. Persuasive and manipulative, though? Those were two adjectives of which she wouldn't spare him. They fit the man like a glove, and so she—her lips now stretched indignantly into a thin line—acquiesced.

That morning, people on the street stared at her as she walked to the store. *Let them stare*, she thought. She was a woman of power, so she would always draw envious gazes. The strange events began as she turned the corner and walked into the grocery store. The small grocery store owned by Darryl Stockman.

She stopped cold.

Her breath caught halfway down her throat, and her eyes went wide with shock. There, on Stockman's counter, was a man in a strange light-blue gown. Even through the blood and pus-soaked bandages, she could see the man was covered in wounds and burns, and when he turned his eyes in her direction, one eyeball was pure red, with the pupil as black as the

(*Nothingness*)

darkest cave. The man's teeth were exposed. He had no lips, as if his lower face had been scraped off. There were gaps between those teeth, and his horrid grin was brown and black over the scant remains of enamel white. He was missing the lower half of his left arm and both legs were gone.

The bandages covered most of his body, but she could see dark fluids soaking them, seeping through them. Moist cloth had been applied to most of his burned skin, and brown, red, and black could be seen in glimpses of parts not covered, with lines of pink marbled throughout. A coat of a strange slimy substance also covered the visible burns and wounds.

The man moaned something unintelligible through the ruins of his exposed teeth. His eyes were wide with confusion. He was saying something, but she couldn't understand what.

"Ooueeryyyuuuuuh."

She could not speak. When she turned her head to glance out the store window, the bright sunlight made her squint. It was a beautiful morning, and she could hear cars and people. Everything out there appeared normal, but in here there was a burned man on Darryl Stockman's counter.

Why?

"Ooooueeeeeeryyyyyuuuuuuuh!" the man repeated, sounding more alarmed.

Who are you? she realized with increasing agitation. Her chest rose and fell as her breathing deepened. *He's trying to say, "Who are you?"*

She opened her mouth to speak, but at that point, a young man suddenly came into the store. A strangely familiar young man, a young Asian boy—possibly a homosexual, judging by his soft demeanor and fine features. His breath was labored as he spoke her name in a soft, almost infantilizing tone.

"Martha!" he said, sounding relieved.

How dare this effeminate boy speak to me with such familiarity?

"I mean, Mrs. Lange!" He grinned with perfectly white teeth. "You gave me quite the scare. I've been looking all over for you!"

She believed she remembered him now. The boy that came to mow her backyard. The son of that Chinese family who lived downtown and owned a restaurant. *King's*, she thought, *it was on King Street, near the market. That's the name of the place.* A garish abomination of red and gold and mirrors all over the walls. The restaurant was on the first floor, and the rather large family lived in an enormous apartment on the second floor. *Why is he here? Why is he talking to me?*

Instead of answering the impertinent boy's question, she turned to the man—the burned, dismembered man on the counter—and pointed straight at him. Instead of appearing horrified, she made sure to exude poise and concern. Like a person of her prominence would.

"That man needs help," she said, not sure there was anything the boy could do about it. "Why would someone put him on the counter like that?"

The Chinese boy turned to stare at the burned man, puzzled. His gaze returned to her, then went back to the man.

"Well, answer me, boy!" she commanded. "Answer when your elder asks you a question, or do they not teach you that in China?"

The boy tensed, clearly irritated. He grinned again with that stupid white smile, and said, "Remember, Mrs. Lange, I'm Korean, not Chinese."

"I don't care whether you're Chinese, Korean, Japanese, Filipino, or some lidded-eye Vietnamese that snuck into a military boat when we were coming back from Vietnam! I asked you a question! Why is that man on the counter? Why isn't anybody helping him?"

The boy's grin lost some of its shine. It remained quite stupid still—as per her judgment—but more in line with the respect she deserved.

"Mrs. Lange," he paused, pondering, "I..." He stammered, took in the image of the burned man again, then his eyes reacted as if he had remembered something, and turned to face her. "I am actually here to get people out of the store, so when the ambulance gets here, there won't be any people in their way. I saw you come in, so I ran in to let you know."

"Oh," she said. She shot a compassionate glance at the burned man, whose eyes were pointing directly at her, even that one burned red eye, with the black hole for a pupil. "But...I need butter, flour, and eggs. What am I supposed to do? Walk all the way downtown to another grocery store? I have to get lunch started!"

"Tell you what," the Chinese, or Korean—or whatever—boy said. "I'll walk you home, and afterwards, I'll—"

"I don't need you to walk me home!" Her lip curled upward, her face became full of indignation. "I'm perfectly capable of walking on my own!"

"I-I know!" He raised a careful palm toward her. "I just meant, because of all the commotion, with the ambulance and the, uh"—he glanced at the man—"the fire department, it might be unsafe. Please allow me to walk you home. I'd be happy to. I'll go to Harbor Grocers myself and get you your groceries."

"I don't know that store!" She shot back.

He grimaced. "Becker's. I'm sorry, I'll go to Becker's."

"Becker's is more expensive than Stockman's."

"Uh, yes." He raised an index finger as if he had already considered this. "But Becker's doesn't sell eggs by the dozen, Mrs. Lange. They sell fifteen per carton, so you get more bang for your buck."

She paused and considered the boy for a moment. It surprised her he would know something like that. *Well*, she thought, *the Chinese were famous penny-pinchers, and knew many ways to save a dollar, so who said Koreans weren't the same?* In all her years, she hadn't considered going to Becker's for eggs, so she hadn't known about this. She found her opinion of the boy with the stupid grin swayed positively, despite her reservations about him.

"Fine. Have them in my house by nine, or I will never again hire you to mow my lawn."

The boy grinned at her. There was something knowing about that grin she didn't like, once more, moving the dial on her opinion back toward dislike.

"Don't you grin at me with that stupid face. I mean it. A shoddy job you do in my backyard already. Just give me an excuse not to hire you again."

"Nine o'clock, Mrs. Lange. I promise."

"Good." Her mind temporarily disengaged from the fact a burned man was lying on top of Stockman's counter.

"I'll even get the good butter," he added. "I'll get Land O'Lakes."

She opened her mouth to add something.

"Unsalted," he cut in before she could. "It's the one my mom used."

"Your mom bakes?"

"She used to." For only a second, his smile disappeared, but quickly came back. "Best cakes and pies I ever had."

"Well. Your mother is right. That is the best butter if you want quality and a good price. Good for her. She's very smart."

"Yeah, she, uh…she is."

He smiled and approached her and tried to get his arm under hers to walk her home. At first, she recoiled, but he responded with a gesture that told her she would be safe with him. She didn't fully trust him, not just yet, but if it saved her the trip all the way to Becker's she would accept.

As they turned to leave the store, she turned her head toward the man on top of the counter. His burned red eye followed her as she exited the store. The black void of that eye's pupil seemed to expand and pull her in—it wasn't pulling only her, but the entire store. The room around the man's head was fading into something else. Something she couldn't quite make out.

Another place.

She noticed something about him she hadn't seen earlier. A tube hung from the side of his mouth, like the tubes that dentists used to suck out a patient's saliva to prevent it from building up inside their mouth. She realized the man's attempt at talking to her a moment ago had gotten him drooling, and saliva fell in a thin line from the corner of his mouth.

As she walked home, with the Chinese boy holding her by the arm, his grip was gentle but firm, as if he were trying to prevent her from pushing him off or letting go of him. She was confused to find the street was no longer a street, but some kind of hallway, all aquamarine-colored walls, white floors, doors at either side, and a steel handrail splitting the wall in two. The people in that hallway were unfamiliar, miserable, and sick.

A woman in a doctor's coat came toward them and continued walking past, hurriedly, without even regarding them. And the boy at her arm, she now noticed, wore hospital scrubs. Had he been wearing them all along? No. No, he hadn't. He had been wearing shorts and the shirt he used to mow the lawn. When had he changed? Did he look older now?

The lights above were fluorescent, but not the same fluorescent lamps she was used to. The fixtures were strange, and the type of light was white, but steady, not the buzzing fluorescent tubes of the hospitals she knew, and why was she walking down a hospital hallway? This was clearly a hospital. What route home was this boy taking her through? The air was chilly, and the almost liquid echoes of their steps down the hallway made her shiver. She was disoriented. A nauseating dizziness came over her. Suddenly, any thought of letting go of the Chinese boy left her.

No, he's not Chinese, and he's not a young boy. The thought came out of nowhere, from some dark cavern in her mind, where decades of knowledge were still stored like books in an abandoned library, where a lonely scholar tried to salvage the tomes before the mold overtook them. *He's Korean, and he's Peter's age. He's forty-two. He's forty-two, and he's Korean, and his name is Chang. No, that's his last name. The boy's name is Raymond, Raymond Chang. That's why I always thought he was Chinese, because the last name always sounded*

Chinese to me, but he's Korean. His name is Raymond Chang, and he's Korean. Raymond Chang. Raymond Chang. R—

"Raymond," she mumbled in a feeble voice, feeling like, at any moment, she would lose her balance and swoon, right there, on a floor that appeared cold, that *felt* cold, even through her slippers. She didn't want to be alone in that place. The notion of getting lost forever in a labyrinth of sterile and exact-looking hallways terrified her, and her grip on the boy's arm became tighter.

"I'm here, Mrs. Lange," he said in a warm tone.

They walked together like that, in uncomfortable silence, until they got to the door to her house, and once inside, the nightmare abated, because it couldn't have been anything but a nightmare, could it? She hadn't crossed a hospital hallway to get to her house. That was ludicrous thinking. It had been the shock of seeing that burned man, his arm and legs gone, lying on top of the counter at Stockman's—it had affected and disoriented her.

"*You know,*" the forgotten scholar's voice said, but she pushed it aside as nonsense. What did she know? What was there to know? She knew all she needed, and most of her world was in order. In control.

She was home now. She'd have a glass of water, rest for a while, and get working on dinner. Chicken pot pie seemed like just the right thing. There was flour and butter, and a couple of eggs, and if she got started on the crust soon, it would be ready in time. Peter would be back from school soon. He was about to turn twelve in a few months and start middle school. Where had the time gone?

He had grown up so quickly, so shoddily, and she'd had to make up for lost time straightening him up after Hector left. It was just like Hector, he'd made the boy crooked, that man—that ignorant, useless, cowardly man—and she'd had to do all the work herself to get Peter back on the straight and narrow, and there were still bends she'd have to fix, even if she had to break every bone in his body to set it straight, but she was up to the task.

You know.

What nagged at her, however, was how often this had been happening. Small moments when she had been going through her daily routine, and something would be amiss. Something wouldn't fit, something would be out of place. A picture would not be on the wall where it was supposed to be. She wouldn't be able to find her favorite blouse, or her kitchen utensils would be nowhere to be found.

You know.

Out of nowhere, everything would be back, but there would be people in her home, around her neighborhood. People she didn't know. When she gazed out the window, she couldn't make out the Vanek House across the street and down the slope. It would be a garden, but not her garden, which she had so carefully tended and filled with plants and flowers and herbs for her cooking. It was larger, expansive, a garden that couldn't possibly fit within the bounds of her property, and there would be paths—winding, bewildering paths—in that garden, and she'd go outside to investigate, and would often get lost in those gardens, under the canopy of the trees. There had been no trees in her garden, no trees in her backyard. She would feel so lost, so scared. Whenever she looked at her reflection, she was dressed in—

You know.

—clothes that weren't hers. They *looked* like the clothes she'd normally wear, but she hadn't bought them, she hadn't picked them. She hadn't even put them on, and their smell wasn't like the smell of her detergent, they didn't smell like clothes that had dried in the sun. She always hung her clothes to dry in the sun. These clothes smelled like a drier, and not just any drier, a large drier, where bulk amounts of clothes were dried together, and she'd call, "Peter?" and no one would answer.

You know.

"Peter?" she'd call again. "Come here this instant, boy! Your Mother is calling you!"

Nothing. No one would answer. No one would come. Then *he* would be there. The Chinese boy. The boy who mowed her lawn,

(*—not a boy, he's 42, not Chinese, but Korean, and his name is R—*)

84

with that hypocritical, condescending, stupid, white grin. Talking down to her. She would complain, and she would argue, but her fear of being somewhere alien would get the best of her. Her confusion, her disorientation, they would overcome her, and she'd acquiesce.

She would always acquiesce.

The Chinese boy would bring her home.

You know.

Home?

You know.

Was she home?

You know.

Where was she?

A bird chirped from a tree outside. She gasped. She had lost focus. Midday prayer. She had stopped her midday prayer halfway through. How could she have been so irresponsible? She would have to start over.

"Forgive me, my Lord," she whispered with trepidation.

First bead.

"*Doikaat gozun-Uolmin yggshe.*"

Next bead!

"*Uolkaat Uolmin-koda sen.*"

Next bead!

"*Ivmyzno trievekaat Uolmin-yevin sen.*"

The bird went quiet. Next bead!

"*Quelmyzno trievekaat conilvi-fredthun sen.*"

Next bead!

"*Edoakaat gozun-Uolmin yggshe.*"

Next bead!

"*Edoan eikaat Uolmin-koda sen.*"

Next bead!

"*Ykop takaat conilvi-fredthun sen.*"

Next bead!

"*Uolkaat Uolmin-yevin sen.*"

Next bead!

"*Uolmin megdikaat Uolmin-koda sen.*"

Next bead!

"*Edegikaat conilvi-fredthun sen.*"

Next bead!

"*Otpoi ujigokaat Uolmin-yevin sen.*"

Next bead!

"*Tjenaf egoikaat gozun-Uolmin yggshe.*"

"Mom?" another voice said, coming from the ether.

You know! said the voice of the forgotten scholar, louder each time.

She would not let herself be distracted! Next bead!

"*Yevinmyzno trievekaat conilvi-fredthun sen!*"

You know!

Next bead!

"*Ferpevakaat Uolmin-koda sen!*"

You know!

Next bead!

"*Eeva torkaat nivoc syl!*"

"Mom," the voice said, sounding much closer. Was that a hand on her shoulder?

You know!

She needed to shut it out! Last bead!

"*Tjenaf egoikaat gozun-Uolmin yggshe!*"

"Mom!" the voice said. The hand shook her shoulder slightly.

Her own left hand flew up to slap the intruder hard across the cheek. Her hands were small, bony, spotted, and wrinkled, but they were hard, and their knuckles jutted out like tiny sharp rocks in the soft sand of a beach. The back of her hand struck the intruder's skin. There was a whip-like crack, followed by a pained grunt.

She didn't need to turn her head to know who the trespasser was, but she turned anyway, and scowled with piercing blue eyes that were as fierce now as they'd been in her youth. Her gaze regarded her visitor with anger—but also with a heightened sense of pride and dignity that would shrink the largest of men—and so this puny boy would easily be crushed under the weight of that stare.

"You will not belittle my title by reducing it to those three casual letters, boy." She hissed, and her words were like an evil wind blowing through the spaces between her teeth. "You will respect me and all I stand for."

His breath caught in shock and his shoulders sank, even as his hand still rubbed his cheek.

"You will respect my title, my place, and my very granting of your existence. You will address me as *Mother*!"

Peter gawked at her with shock. It was plainly visible in his terrified face. Ignorant, useless, and cowardly, as always, just like his father. But it was what she expected of him. She expected respect. She expected fear and reverence.

To the left of where Peter stood was the Chinese boy with his hospital scrubs, staring at her in almost as much shock as her son. The boy probably didn't just mow lawns. He was probably a hospital janitor, out on lunch at this hour. Who had let him into her home? It didn't matter. Let him watch. Let him watch how a true mother brings her disrespectful son into submission. Let him watch her son be disciplined.

"Say it!" She commanded.

Peter stammered for a brief second. "Y-yes," he said. "Mother."

The birds in the tree outside resumed their singing as if they'd been holding their voice in for far too long.

Chapter Four
No Details

Harborites weren't too preoccupied with the idea of death. It was a concept they were accustomed to more than most people. The people of White Harbor mourned their dead just as much as anyone else, but when it came to the passing of someone *outside* their immediate circle, their reaction was less: "Oh, that's so terrible, I feel so bad!" and more: "Oh, I guess it was their time." Death was frequent in White Harbor, but locals didn't pay as much attention to it as they probably should.

It was only those who managed to "get out" that began noticing those around them didn't die as frequently as before. Even though they noticed this, few—which was to say, almost none—had the ingrained curiosity to investigate deeper. They accepted it as a fact of life. The shock of other people's passing was kept away in the reinforced steel safe they called Blight Harbor. The curious thing, however, was this safe was portable, and they carried it with them even outside the bounds of the Crescent Mountains, and once feelings were locked in the darkness of that vault, there wasn't a need to retrieve them ever again.

Peter was a notorious example of a person who "got out," and he'd gone through this phenomenon. After child protective services had taken him away from his mother at sixteen, he hadn't experienced the death of anyone close until Jenny's passing.

There was a part of him that had found this sudden deceleration in obituaries rather odd, but he hadn't dwelled on it much. It hadn't felt unnatural to him. Living outside White Harbor, he'd read, seen, and heard news of people dying—accidents, illness, crime, war—but no one close to him until the untimely death of his wife.

Whenever he found out someone he actually knew had died, it was always someone from White Harbor. Every single time. Nadine's parents, for example.

Even as a writer, someone who was expected to dissect events to their tiniest causes and largest consequences, the idea never clicked in his brain. He didn't feel the need to study or understand it. It was just how life was. He was quick to dismiss that line of internal questioning, as if a voice in his mind was telling him, "Never mind that. It's not important."

Peter was back in White Harbor now, however.

This wasn't a large city, like the ones he'd known, but a small town, and small towns had a way of never forgetting, even when they *pretended* to forget. They had a way of submerging you in a flood of memories. Those who lived in White Harbor and those who got out had all built dams to hold back this flood. The difference was those who lived in town were still immersed in Blight Harbor, which gave them all they needed to reinforce the dam and hold those unpleasant memories at bay.

People like Peter, who had gone far away, still had their dam, but they had let it deteriorate. They let cracks and leaks form. Meanwhile, the volume of memories and fears and secrets never stopped accumulating, like concentrated liquid trauma. Metric tons of pressure that had nowhere else to go. In the end, all that held them back was an unsound, eroded structure waiting for a flash flood to make it crumble.

That flash flood for Peter might just be the appointment he had that day at noon.

He had almost two hours to kill before visiting his mother at Clarendon Hospital's elderly care wing. He resolved to take a drive around town and see if he could spot what had changed since his last visit. It was a good time waster, and he figured he could stop for some groceries—he'd be too exhausted to go shopping after talking to his mother.

He drove his car down from Blue Overlook, the hills to his left, and the ocean to his right, and he did his best to clear his mind, trying to prepare for his appointment with Mother. Calm was difficult to come by, though, when the source of his diagnosed anxiety and depression was waiting for him, even if she didn't know he was coming to visit.

Peter noticed Greene's had closed. He supposed the five-dollars-and-under business model was not well suited for today's economy in small towns with fewer customers. Most likely, Natalie Greene—Mrs. Green's daughter, who'd taken over after her mother's passing—had decided to sell lower-quality items or attempted to raise the prices. Neither of these things helped a business keep customers, and in such a small town, losing just a couple of shoppers took its toll. He wondered what Natalie Greene was doing now that she didn't have the store. He'd ask Nadine for the town update later.

What time is it? The dashboard clock read 10:20 a.m.

Only ten minutes had passed since he'd left Blue Overlook.

Someone had decorated Jerry Lucas's vet clinic with some huge cat and dog decals. It looked nice. Or would've looked nice if they at least fixed a crack that grew diagonally across the wall and through the new decals, making a poor German Shepherd appear like it was being decapitated. Old Lucas was still in good health the last time he'd come to town, and the clinic was still open for business. Still had his name on it, too.

That's good, Peter thought.

Jerry Lucas was a good man. Too bad about his wife's passing, though. Suicide.

10:22 a.m. Really?

The streets were almost empty. The kids were at school, and the adults were at work. It wasn't lunchtime yet, so it made sense. Most people he saw, he didn't know, and he had this weird notion they should know who he was, not so much because he was a well-known writer, but because he'd grown up in town. Whenever he caught someone's eye as he drove with the window rolled down, he would give them a goofy smile, like saying, "Hello…it's me…Peter."

He passed Cunningham's Bar, which was closed at this hour. Jess had taken over for her dad a few years ago, but Old Chuck still came some nights and shook hands, spoke with the regulars, and worked the bar. He worked slower than before, but always friendly, unless someone got a bit too drunk or rowdy—which wasn't unheard of in towns like this one—but he just needed to give Jess a quick nod, and she'd kick any drunk's ass out with ease. If said drunk happened to be too big for her to physically manage, there was always Peggy, her shotgun, which she kept hidden behind the bar. She, fortunately, hadn't had to point Peggy at someone in a long time.

According to Nadine, Mrs. Cunningham was alive, but she stayed home most of the time. She was legally blind now and had osteoporosis. As if that weren't enough, she had almost no cartilage left in her knees, so she couldn't walk. Nadine went to visit her often, since she enjoyed being read to. She said Mrs. Cunningham was still pleasant to talk to and was in a good mood a majority of the time.

Jess's younger brother, Peter remembered woefully, was a different story. What had happened to him had been both sad and unexpected. He went away to college and didn't come back alive. He died of alcohol poisoning during a frat party. The whole town thought Old Chuck would up and sell the bar, wanting nothing more to do with alcohol, but to everyone's surprise, he simply passed the business to Jess, who made it thrive and expanded it into Cunningham's diner.

The last time Peter had been in town, he spent some time talking to Old Chuck Cunningham, and he could plainly see, even six years later, his son Jonah's death still hurt. He blamed his son's demise on being far from home and nothing else.

"My boy had never drunk before that," Old Chuck told him. "I've owned the bar for decades, and I've always kept my taste for liquor on a leash, with varying degrees of success, mind you. Jonah, though, he was terrified of the bottle. I made sure of that. I'd always show him the worst drunks, whenever I could, and asked him, 'Do you want to end up like that man over there? The one in the gutter, with his friends laughing at him? The one the girls stay away from because he stinks of booze? No? Then never touch liquor. We sell the poison because they want it, but we don't touch it.'"

Old Chuck forced an emotionless laugh before continuing. "Showed him Neal Parham once—God rest his soul—fulfilling his family curse. Drunk and unconscious, he was. Poor Neal was on top of a pile of garbage bags in the back. Still had his shirt on, but that was all he had. Some no-good teenagers had taken his shoes, his pants, and his underwear. Wang to the wind, he was. And the only reason they'd left the shirt on him was he'd thrown up all over it. Nice shirt, that one. Such a shame."

Old Chuck paused a bit, cast a longing glance to his right, as if he could see through the wall in the direction of the frat house his Jonah had died in, and Peter imagined he could see all plausible scenarios in the world that could have led to him ending up with a lethal alcohol level in his organism. All plausible scenarios, except the one in which Jonah had taken a bottle and put his lips to it. Old Chuck only shook his head, sniffed, and wiped the beginnings of a tear with the back of his index finger.

"No, my Jonah didn't drink. Not willingly. They did that to him."

He never specified who "they" were, but Peter could

guess with ease. Hazing wasn't truly something that had disappeared from frat houses. Not entirely. Old Chuck still managed to crack a smile, and a joke, and a laugh, but some of the light had faded from his eyes.

10:28 a.m.

Peter harrumphed.

This isn't working, he thought to himself. *Shopping it is, then!*

He parked his blue Malibu parallel to the sidewalk in front of Harbor Grocers, and from the moment he got out of the car, he noticed something different about the store. The sign above the doors was new, the same as the logo, but it wasn't that. He couldn't put his finger on it. Just as he was about to figure it out, a pedestrian passed in front of him and their eyes met for less than a second, and once more

(Hello…it's me…Peter)

he nodded and smiled like a dork. The passing woman seemed a bit confused, nodded back, and continued walking. Realizing he'd done this outside his car, face to face with another person, he slapped his own forehead and blurted out, "Dork!" under his breath, which just earned him an even more puzzled look from the woman. "Oh! No!" he said. "Not you! Me… I'm the…dork. Sorry."

She turned her gaze away from him and continued walking.

Peter approached the glass double doors of Harbor

Grocers, which opened with a rolling, swishing sound, and he was quickly enveloped in that distinctive aroma exclusive to grocery stores. It was the smell of disinfectant, fresh vegetables, meats, bread, pastries, cleaning products, cardboard boxes, and other groceries, all blended into something that should've smelled unpleasant, but was actually welcoming.

Homelike.

Once he entered, what he'd noticed from outside became apparent. The space was larger than he remembered. When he was a child, this supermarket used to be called Becker's. Ten years earlier, they had changed its name to Harbor Grocers, when Sam Becker Junior took over the administration from his father. However, even last year, when Peter was in town, the place had been the same store he'd known since childhood, only slightly remodeled.

The Beckers, it seemed, had since expanded.

"Well, look who came to visit!" said an older man in his late seventies, sitting behind the cash register. "Famous, superstar writer Peter Lange, quite the celebrity!"

Peter chuckled with embarrassment. "Well, 'famous', 'celebrity', and 'superstar' seem like a stretch, Mr. Becker," Peter said, shaking the man's hand with a sincere grin. "Also, they're redundant."

"That so?" Samuel Becker Senior said, grinning back. "Tell me. Have you been on TV? Talk shows? All that hubbub?"

"Uh, well, yes." Peter's palpable discomfort at talking about anything with the word "fame" and all of its synonyms sprung up visibly, like a rash. "Couple of times."

"Then, you're a famous superstar celebrity writer as far as us simple Harborites are concerned. And we're very proud of you, so it bears the redundancy. We even thought of throwing a welcome party for you, but Judy thought it'd be too much. You ask me, I think it would be worth it. Welcoming the town's favorite son after an entire year."

Peter grinned with as much sincerity as his embarrassment would allow, and his face warmed, blushing as he usually did when someone gave him anything approaching a compliment. He didn't miss the fact Sam Becker was keenly aware he hadn't been in town for nearly a year.

Small towns had a way of never forgetting.

Becker Sr. remained a staple at the store, and Sam Jr. took care of the management and finances. The last time Peter talked to Sam Jr., he'd told him—when he suggested it was time for his dad to retire—the old man became indignant and said, "You'll have to drag me out from behind that cash register with my feet pointing up, inside a body bag! Don't make me regret giving you the keys to the store!"

"I like what you've done with the place." Peter nodded toward the far end, where they'd knocked a wall down to join the store to the next building. "Oh, I see it now. You expanded into Rockwell's."

"Bah!" the old man said in that dismissive manner only old people could declare something as unimportant, unnecessary, or unwelcome. "That's Junior's doing. I agreed to the name change 'coz he said it would sound more like 'the town flagship store'. Town flagship store, my wrinkled, sore, pimpled, white ass. It doesn't need to be a flagship anything. It's a grocery store, that's it! Junior went and created an internet page!"

He scoffed.

"We're not Amazon, up there in Seattle, with their technology stuff, and their web ordering, or whatever you call it, we're a small…town…store!" He poked the counter with his index finger with each of the last three words. "People come. People say hi. People exchange the usual courtesies. People buy. People leave. Maybe, sometimes, they stop and gossip, and that's the appeal. It's personalized! Who's going to buy stuff off the internet in a town this small, huh? Everything is a few blocks away from everything, and we're only 4325 people, last I counted. Well, twenty-six, now that the Feltons had that baby boy two months ago, God bless 'em. And only He knows how long we've been around that number, and it ain't increasing anytime soon, let me tell ya.

"An internet page, can you imagine? Nah." He shook his head. "Let Amazon have those. Don't need 'em. By the time they take over the damn world, like one of those science fiction empires, I'll be long gone, and Junior can turn this into like a drone factory for all I care. They have those drones now, you know? Amazon. The day I see one of those approaching my backyard, I'll consider it as invading private airspace and shoot it out of the sky. What's that bald, sinister-looking Amazon sonuvabitch owner guy gonna do, huh? Send an old man to jail for a drone that costs what he'd call pocket change?"

Peter let out a hearty laugh.

"Oh, you think I'm joking, right?"

"I don't think I've ever seen an Amazon drone outside publicity videos, Mr. Becker. I think they have them tied up in permits or something."

"No! They *got* the permits, now! Finally, got the permits. Soon they'll be spying on all of us, those things. I'm glad I won't be here for that. Oh, but, Junior, he calls it 'Advancement' with a capital A, like it's a good thing to have robots flying in our neighborhoods. I've read and watched a lot of science fiction in my time, son. I grew up in the heyday of science fiction. I've seen what comes from letting robots run around all over the place."

Peter laughed again.

"Oh, my gosh." An elderly woman with a big grin came from the aisle closest to the cash register. "Got him started on Amazon, didn't you?" She regarded the old man with humor, but also a bit of annoyance. "Stop talking Peter's ear off, you dusty relic of a man. He's probably busy!"

"How are you, Mrs. Becker?" Peter said, returning the grin.

Judy Becker's face turned serious the moment she locked eyes with Peter, causing his expression to do the same. Her expression wasn't an unpleasant one. It showed empathy and concern. She lowered her head slightly and a shrewd gaze greeted him from over the translucent pink of her glasses' rims. "How are you, Peter?" she asked, and Peter sensed that wasn't the question she was truly asking. She was asking: "How are you dealing with your wife's death, Peter?"

"I'm…"—he considered for a few seconds—"I'm doing okay."

"Oh, bullshit! Of course you're not!" she exclaimed with a dismissive wave of a hand.

Peter was so shocked by the way she'd blurted her words, he just stood there with his mouth half-open.

"How could you be? Grief is a bitch. I mean, this one"—pointing to Sam Sr.—"annoys me like an itch at the center of my perineum, but he's *my* itch, and I've grown accustomed to him."

"Appreciate it," Sam Sr. said.

"Oh, shut up, you!" Mrs. Becker gave him an irritated glance. "If something took him away from me, I don't know what I'd do. I'd be crushed!"

Peter's mouth went shut like a glove compartment.

"Judy!" Mr. Becker said. "Watch that mouth!"

Little by little, Mrs. Becker's expression changed with realization, which became horror, and finally, full-blown embarrassment. She turned her head toward Peter, her fingers softly tapping her upper lip, as if she were playing a tiny, invisible harmonica, her mouth working nervously. "Oh, my boy, I'm so sorry. I didn't mean to use that word."

"That's fine." Peter forced a smile. "I know you didn't mean it in a bad way."

(*"Look away, son! Look away!"*)

"No, sweetheart. It's not fine. It was insensitive of me. Let me make it up to you. Oh, I know what I can give you. I'll be right back."

Peter shook his head. "Mrs. Becker," he said, now feeling mortified again, extending a hand toward her, "that's unnecessary."

"Just be quiet and let me make it up to you." She turned around and headed toward a door behind the cash register. Peter knew this led to the Beckers' garage, since the store was next to their home. "First, this stupid old man nearly talks you into a stupor. Now, here I go, opening my big mouth and saying something so abhorrent. Be right back. You go about your business. Don't let me delay you."

The short white-haired lady disappeared behind the door, which swung back and forth, until it stopped.

"You see that?" Becker Sr. said. "That's called sixty years of marriage. She fucks up, but somehow finds a way to include *me* in the fuck-up, like she's saying, 'Yeah, but he fucked up, too!'"

Peter chuckled. His eyes darted toward the knocked-down wall. "What happened to the Rockwells? They'd had that shoe store forever. I thought Pam was going to take it from her parents once they retired. You know, since Stanley got out of town after getting married."

Becker Sr. seemed uneasy, which only heightened Peter's interest.

"What happened?"

Becker Sr. considered for a moment. Realizing he wouldn't escape from providing some kind of explanation, he sighed. "Oh, alright. I'll tell you, but only because you're from town. This is no business of any outsider. No details, though! Just the general stuff, because Judy will just about bite my head off if she finds out I told you this after what you're dealing with."

"Sure. I won't say a thing."

"I mean it, Peter! Do not insist! No details!"

"No details," Peter repeated. The fact the older man was so emphatic about this made him want details even more.

"Well, after the cancer took Collin Rockwell, Stacy Rockwell took over her husband's store for a while, to give Pam time to learn the management end of the business. That way, she could take the shoe store, and Stacy could retire. That was the original plan, anyway."

An unsettling sensation overcame Peter, like he knew he would hate the rest of this story. He licked his lips, nodded, placed his hands on his hips, and continued to listen.

"And whaddaya know? The cancer came back around for poor Stacy, same as with her husband. Except with Collin it was the lungs, with Stacy it was the colon. Too young the both of them, to be honest, but I'm biased, I think, me having gone to high school with Stacy and all." He shrugged.

"Plenty of people go younger than they should in this town," Peter said, nodding.

"That they do." Becker Sr. gave him a sharp gaze with a raised eyebrow. "Shouldn't be surprising, to be honest. I guess it was just their time. Only a handful of people make it past eighty in this town. Judy and I, we're in the lucky few even approaching that age." He knocked on the counter. "Knock on wood. Don't wanna jinx it."

"When did Mrs. Rockwell pass? Couldn't be more than a year. When I was here last, she was doing fine."

"Let's see, it's July now," Becker Sr. said, his eyes rolling upward as he tried to remember. "I'd say August, September, last year? It was just devastating for poor Pam. She closed the shoe store. The plan was to close for only a month, while she did her grievin', got all the matters of their home and business in order, but then…" His eyes wandered away with some unease. "Then it was Pam's turn to go."

"Whoa, what?" Peter blurted in utter shock. "Pam

Rockwell is dead? How? How does that even happen? She was younger than me!"

"Well…" The old man swallowed hard and moistened his lips. "Remember, I said no details, so I'm holding myself to that. You ain't getting no details from me, Peter, I'm sorry. I know you're probably used to people just doing what you want, with you being a celebrity and all." He waved his palms in the air, side to side, comically, as he said this. "Let's just say tragic accidents don't take age into account. Went out exactly a month after her mother."

"Oh, my god. That's awful!"

"That, it is, son." Becker Sr. ran his hand down his mouth, stretching out the skin of his cheeks, his wrinkles disappearing briefly. "Makes you sort of wish it had ended there." He added in an under-the-breath voice that indicated it hadn't ended there. He averted his gaze, as if fearing he'd said too much.

"What?" Peter asked. "What does that mean?"

Sam Becker Sr.'s blue eyes gazed up at Peter's, and for a moment, the jovial old man appeared his age. Dark bags of skin under his eyes, and his teeth slightly yellowed from a bad smoking habit, one of his incisors a slight shade of gray.

"Stanley?" Peter asked.

Becker nodded with a grim mien.

"Stan Rockwell is also dead." Peter reacted like he was in some kind of cruel, hidden camera show.

"Stan had to drive from Seattle to see about his sister's funeral. Now, just picture how he must've felt, just a month after putting his mother in the ground. He packed up, put his family in his SUV—wife, two boys, two girls."

"No," Peter said, as if that simple word could stretch an arm into the past and put a stop to what had so obviously happened.

"Yes," the old man said, nodding. "Not sure at what point exactly, but a couple miles before reaching Centralia, it appears Stanley nodded off. Rachel and the kids were asleep, too. That's how the truck got 'em."

"Jesus!" Peter said, his face aghast.

"Now, here's the thing. My cousin Dave, who's with the Seattle police, said the weird thing was there were no tire marks. The SUV just made a beeline past the median strip and into oncoming traffic. No attempt at turning away or stepping on the brakes. Dave said this could imply it all happened so fast Stanley and his family didn't wake up at all before the crash. Or..."

The pause Sam Becker Sr. made gave Peter a profound sense of trepidation, like all the blood from his body had simply drained down toward his feet, leaving him cold and empty.

"Or what?" he asked.

"You know, Peter? I think the alternative is too unthinkable for my old mind to truly consider." His blue eyes drove themselves into Peter's. "Too damn unthinkable. And if you ask me, it's better if they didn't see it coming because they were all asleep."

Peter nodded, trying to wash away the unpleasant thought, wishing he could scrub it entirely away, rip it out, burn it, before it grew roots in his mind, and he could never remove it as if it were a relentless weed.

"What happened to 'no details'?" he asked with a mirthless chuckle, trying to make light of the conversation.

"I didn't give you details," the old man said, refusing him the comfort of lightness. "Details, my boy, would give you bad dreams, and something tells me you don't need more of those right now."

Peter nodded and forced a dim smile. "I'll just get my stuff, if that's okay. I'll be back before Mrs. Becker brings whatever she's getting."

"Oh, I know what she's getting." The grin Sam Becker Sr. gave Peter returned some of the pleasantness from before. "You're in for a treat, son!"

"Good!" Peter grinned. "Can't wait!" He turned and grabbed a shopping basket.

"Hey, Peter?"

He turned toward the old man again.

"I'm sorry. I didn't want the conversation to take such a dark turn." He seemed genuinely apologetic. "We really are happy you're in town."

"Thank you, Mr. Becker."

If the old man only knew the darkest moment of Peter's day was now only…

What time is it? He checked his phone. *10:45 a.m.*

…an hour and fifteen minutes away.

As he left Becker's—Harbor Grocers—with his groceries and an enormous slice of strawberry cheesecake that looked like it would taste like high-calorie, homemade sin, Peter waved goodbye to the Beckers.

The cheesecake decided for him. He called Doris—the live-in housekeeper at the house in the mountains he and Jenny had bought a few years back—and told her he'd be making a stop there before continuing with the less pleasant part of his day. He had to drive home and put the cheesecake in the fridge, because he would sooner jump off a cliff than let Judy Becker's immaculate dessert spoil. He would have enough time to drive up to his house on the eastern hills, past the location where the old Vanek House used to stand before the fire of '93, and past where his childhood home still stood. He'd get home—Doris would welcome him with a tight, motherly hug he desperately needed—take a shower, change clothes, and he might even fit in a fifteen-minute nap. All to mentally prepare for the appointment with his mother.

An hour and ten minutes after his conversation with Sam Becker Sr., Peter entered Clarendon Hospital, preparing himself for one of the most unpleasant conversations of his life—and there were plenty to choose from.

Out in the town, beyond his awareness or care, White Harbor's inhabitants continued on with their own lives, oblivious to the fact that, for many of them, these were the last days of their earthly existence, and, for many others, even worse things awaited.

Chapter Five

Bobby Novak
1991

B obby nervously glanced around as he stood on the opposite side of the road from Peter's house. His eyes moved in all directions, scanning for any suspicious movement. If Peter was correct, at noon his mother would be distracted with her midday prayer. Once started, she wouldn't be able to stop for any reason—which sounded strange and ominous when he paired the concept of prayer with the eccentric reputation of Peter's mother. Peter said at that hour he'd be able to sneak out. He had preemptively told her he might need to go to a classmate's house to copy some notes and might go for a walk afterward. The important part was to not let Martha Lange see him leave with another kid, which would make her suspect Peter was lying.

Peter's home was on Hill Road, two houses up the

slope and across the street from the Vanek House, while Bobby lived four houses up from Peter's.

He'd always been curious about the strange, lonely kid he saw from time to time at school, or taking walks around town or, on rare occasions, sitting by himself on a park bench simply marveling at the trees, as if their swaying branches were wondrous things from a fairytale. A few times, he even tried to speak to him, but Peter always seemed apprehensive about exchanging more than a few words, before excusing himself and leaving in a hurry.

Despite that, Bobby thought he had a good eye for people, which convinced him Peter was friendly and nice.

Bobby's gaze took one last 360-degree survey of the surroundings. He didn't know why. After all, the only person he should be worried about was inside Peter's home, probably performing some strange chants or rituals, like the ones he always saw witches perform in Freddie Parham's horror movies. His eyes stopped, however, when he caught sight of Ben Curling, staring straight at him from his porch. It was as if the man knew some mischief was afoot.

You're being paranoid, Bobby thought. *He just stares at anyone in this general area, and you're the only person on the street right now.*

In a hurry, he put two fingers in his mouth and whistled once toward Peter's house. Five seconds later, Peter came out, closed the door, and ran to Bobby.

"Why the backpack?" Bobby said, pointing to the brown leather backpack strapped to Peter's shoulders.

"I'm supposed to be studying," he said. "If Mother sees this in my room, she'll know I'm lying."

"Got it. We have to go get Leroy and Royce. They told their parents they'd be going to my place, and I told my parents I'd be going to theirs."

"Does that actually work? Wouldn't they just be able to figure it out with a phone call?"

Bobby considered this for a moment. "It's gambling. We're gambling."

"What?"

"It's, uh, we're sort of hoping they don't call each other, and if they do, we're already outside, so we can make something up on the fly."

"So…lying?"

Bobby put his hand on Peter's shoulder. "Peter…not everybody's your mom." He nodded toward his bike. "Get on the bike. We still have several stops to make."

2022

The courtyard of the Lighthouse Rock Mental Health Facility was empty, save for one person: Bobby Novak. He sat alone, like he did every day, letting his mind relax with the sighing whisper of the wind, having lunch under the shade of a big leaf maple.

The mental health hospital where Bobby worked had been built on a small island one mile off the coast of White Harbor, after the lighthouse that had once stood there was hit by a gigantic tidal wave. The wave hit the lighthouse at just the right structural spot and the perfect angle to knock down the entire top third.

The event had puzzled engineers of the time, who'd had no choice but to blame it on a badly reinforced structure. Once the evaluation committee saw the high cost of reconstruction, the low large-vessel traffic in the area, and the distance from land, they decided not to rebuild the beacon. Rather, they'd find a better use for the land. They decided the best use for Lighthouse Rock was to build a psychiatric hospital, to treat mental patients, both local and from the surrounding counties, as a way of properly splitting the bill and making the most of the location with the least strain on their budgets. To make this notion more appealing, they also built a separate wing to house and treat those who were—at the time—dubbed "the criminally insane".

The bottom two-thirds of the lighthouse had been repaired and integrated into the new building, and the spot where the top of the lighthouse had crashed had been turned into a monument, now the centerpiece of the courtyard where Bobby sat eating a roast beef sandwich and drinking a Coke. They had even put a plaque on the monument that read:

WE REMAIN A BEACON OF WELLNESS FOR THOSE WHOSE MINDS ARE LOST IN THE DARKNESS.

Bobby had always considered this contradictory. How could a lighthouse beacon that had crumbled to the ground from shoddy construction, and could no longer serve its purpose, be a symbol of recovery?

He appreciated the sentiment, though. In fact, he believed every person with a psychiatric condition could be rehabilitated, or at least be given enough stability to lead a dignified life. He hoped to rehabilitate someone dear to him, the person who had inspired him to become a psychiatrist. Though his childhood friend, Freddie Parham, was still a patient of this facility after almost thirty years—or, more accurately, a killer found not guilty for reason of insanity— Bobby still held hope for him. He believed with all his heart that Freddie could come back from wherever his mind had gone after the things he had seen and the things he had done.

Day after day, Freddie spent his time in the rec room, or in his own room, drawing and painting, using charcoal and assorted paints Bobby himself brought for him. He wasn't a violent patient—except for that one incident with a security guard—despite the things they'd accused him of doing, and they did not consider him a suicide risk.

Bobby would speak to him often, and Freddie would sound like the person he'd always known, only older and with more maturity, even if it was a stunted maturity—an unfortunate side effect of being locked up for most of his life. But out of nowhere, in the middle of casual conversation, a strange phrase, or a bizarre concept would sneak into Freddie's speech. He talked about things he called "The Exiles", or he rambled on about "the true town behind the town", or he recited and repeated random facts about the number forty-four. The latter, in particular, always evoked a certain unsettling memory in Bobby, which he couldn't put a name to. He meant to investigate further, but kept either forgetting or postponing.

These moments in the conversation felt to him like chatting with a respected relative, only for them to blurt out a casual remark about Holocaust denial. It brought a disturbing air into the room, a chilling, oppressive dread made more intense by the joyful grin on Freddie's face when he talked about it. This topic that terrified Bobby made Freddie positively giddy.

Finally, there was that phrase he repeated incessantly, but refused to write, no matter how many times Bobby asked him to. Listening to it over the years, and on recordings, he had approximated it to something that sounded like, "*Jennaf eggo-ika-at gozun uolmin eegsheh*." While Freddie stubbornly refused to write it, insisting it was the language of God and he wasn't worthy of writing it, he provided Bobby with its meaning.

Once, after a lengthy conversation, the phrase had simply exploded out of Freddie's lips, almost convulsively, like it had taken over him, and he'd simply had to say it. It reminded Bobby of a preacher speaking in tongues. This was followed by Freddie's hyena laugh and a prideful grin. Bobby took this opportunity to ask him what the phrase meant, like he had so many times before. Except, this time, Freddie said, "Alright, Bobby, only because you're the best friend I'll ever have." He remembered the clarity, the sobriety in his friend's eyes—it was a moment of lucidity, so absolute, his face almost glowed with zealous emotion.

"God will feed," Freddie said and stared at him with bright, impassionate eyes.

"What do you mean? Like, is God going to feed his followers, or…?"

Freddie only responded with an impish little chortle and said no more on the subject.

God will feed.

Bobby took another bite from his sandwich. A shudder ran down his back.

It was a phrase so simple, but the fervor behind it,

the fanaticism he had seen in Freddie's eyes, had turned those three words into the image of an enormous creature, dark but maddeningly beautiful, and terrifying beyond comprehension, rising from the line of the ocean with an open mouth that disappeared at both ends of the horizon, swallowing the sea, the earth, and the sky, and every creature in them.

As Bobby tried to push the image out of his mind, a noise caught his attention, and he swiveled his eyes up at the sky. He noticed a flock of seagulls gliding just beyond where the canopy of the maple ended. He realized something unusual had happened. Something he had simply ignored. But now, in the courtyard's quiet—with the ridiculous plaque in front of him, insisting on the ridiculous mission statement—it slowly snuck up on him: a minute earlier, all the seagulls that surrounded the island had gone quiet.

They were noisy creatures, so it should have been hard to miss. He probably wouldn't have noticed if it weren't because they'd briefly restarted their squawking, only to stop again, all at once. He was just coming off his memories of Freddie's ominous words when the cacophony resumed.

Had this happened before? He had that strange feeling in his gut that told him it had. He wasn't certain when. He was sure this time it was absolutely true, though. At the time of the silence, there were seagulls flying overhead, and some near the rocks at the edge of the isle, but they were quiet.

This has happened before. I know this has happened before.

He made a mental note to pay attention and ask around the hospital if anyone had noticed this as well, and he would remain vigilant the next day to see if he noticed a similar behavior.

The thought came with no small load of existential dread, though: had so many years of exposure to mental patients driven him a little insane?

He took another bite of his sandwich. A pair of seagulls stared at him, perhaps expecting him to throw them a piece, or waiting for him to leave to peck at his fallen crumbs.

Bobby stared back.

God will feed.

Chapter Six
Royce Howe
1991

Bobby sat on his bike's top tube, trying to make it seem like he wasn't struggling to pedal from such an uncomfortable position. Peter, in contrast, looked quite content while sitting behind Bobby, gripping his shoulders.

Royce caught up on his bike to the right of Bobby, and Leroy appeared on a skateboard to the left.

"So, Bobster," Leroy said with an impish grin. "You seem to be moving kinda fast in your relationship with Norman."

"This is technically your first date," Royce continued, "and you're already between his legs."

"Oh, ha, ha," said Bobby, with a voice completely devoid of humor.

"And you, Norman," Leroy said. "Mother's gonna be disappointed that her boy just spread his legs so easy."

Royce moved his hand up and down in a stabbing motion. "Shwee! Shwee! Shwee! Shwee!"

Peter responded with a naive grin. "I don't get it."

Royce and Leroy shared a look of surprise.

"He's so pure!" Royce said.

"No wonder you're so taken with him, Bobby!" Leroy said.

"Alright!" Bobby said, huffing with each push of the pedal. "You guys are up! Who's next?"

Leroy kicked once on his skateboard and said, "Well, when we synced up for your stupid plan, our bottom picks were the Hyena, second to last, followed by Barry."

"Then, your buddy the Hyena said he'd get there on his own 'coz he didn't want us showing up at his place right now."

Leroy raised a hand, performing a drinking motion. "Probably, he doesn't want us to see his dad racking up points for the ol' Parham curse."

"Yeah, so the Hyena took himself out of the equation."

"And because we're just that lucky, we got Barry."

"And I think I speak for the both of us when I say, what the fuck, Norman?"

Peter lowered his gaze. "I have my reasons."

"Are you sure he's cool?" Leroy said and kicked the pavement again.

120

Peter nodded.

"I trust you, man." Bobby flashed him a reassuring smile.

"Easy for you to say." Royce turned his head toward Peter and lost a bit of control of the handlebars, causing the bicycle to wobble slightly. "Whoa!" He regained his balance. "Easy for you to say, 'coz you're not risking Barry-mother-fucking-Giffen's mom calling our house to ask if he's there! I mean, Droopy, we could've made it work, but Barry? Man, adults talk, you know? They look stupid but aren't."

"Wait," Peter said. "So, Bobby's going to your place, you guys are going to Bobby's, and Barry is going to your place?"

"Yeah!" Royce spoke with an exasperated expression. "Can you believe that shit? 'Coz our parents totally won't!"

"Barry's mom won't call your parents," Bobby said, annoyed by the conversation, then he canted his head to the right, as if considering. "It's Cal I'm worried about."

"Why?" Peter said. "Where's Callum supposed to be staying?"

Bobby swallowed hard. "Cal is telling his parents he's staying at Barry's place."

"Oh, fuck," Royce said.

"Well," Leroy said. "We can only hope Droopy's broke-ass parents haven't paid their phone bill and can't actually call Barry's mom."

2022

Royce was home rinsing the dishes and putting them in the dishwasher. His wife, Lillian, was at work, and just like she did every weekday—since she worked nearby—she would drive home, have lunch with Royce, and drive back to the municipal building, leaving him to pick up the table and clean up.

Royce worked from home, creating content for his streaming channel, doing music reviews of assorted genres. He was quite the prolific creator, and it paid enough to help him pursue his actual dream, which was not just reviewing music, but creating and playing his own creations. He recorded, mastered, and sold his music for other content creators to use, or to be played at events. He was even invited to attend big venues, often in larger cities, where he would DJ for the crowd.

His name, both online and in the club scene was DJ RALA, short for "Right Arm, Left Arm", and pronounced "Raylah"—which was interpreted by many as the casual pronunciation of "railer", from the colloquialism "railing", which was commonly understood as "fucking". He had literally only meant it as an acronym for "Right Arm, Left

Arm", but if fans wanted to think it meant something more cred-worthy, he wasn't planning to correct them.

They might, however, be disappointed if they found out this man—whose name evoked such images of debauchery and sexual prowess—was, in reality, a forty-one-year-old man, with the world's most precious daughter, in a devoutly monogamous marriage with a Municipal Finance Director.

This was the reason he kept his personal life completely separate from his DJ life. He liked to think people might imagine DJ RALA was, at this moment, lying by his pool, under the summer sun, with a "girlfriend-for-pay friend" doing a long line of cocaine off his presumably large, exposed member. However, Royce Howe—streaming entrepreneur, father, husband, and average penis-haver—was currently rinsing the dishes and peering at the tree outside his kitchen window.

I could hang a nice swing from that large branch for my baby girl. Though, as he considered the tree itself, he realized something odd.

Tracy, his four-year-old, had taken him by the hand just four days ago, and made him follow her to the backyard, pointing excitedly at the tree. "Look, Daddy, the birdies! The birdies!" she'd said with glee, because she'd seen a bird's nest up there from her bedroom window. He lifted his daughter in his arms so she could marvel at the tiny chirping birdies closer.

He had zero knowledge of ornithology, but he promised Tracy he would find out the name of that type of bird for her. He'd planned to do that later today, since he actually had the time for bird sleuthing. He knew he'd mostly be doing it for his own curiosity, because Tracy honestly didn't care. All she cared about was that they were the most beautiful birds in the world until the day she saw another bird and automatically declared it the most beautiful bird in the world. She had already named them Mommy Birdie, Daddy Birdie, Kenny Baby, Bebe Baby, and Tasha Baby, and those names worked just fine for her.

From the moment he'd found out about the Birdie family, he'd been quite attentive of the goings-on at the Birdie home in the tree, if only to make sure no cat or other animal harmed them, and none of the babies fell off the nest and have Tracy find it injured on the ground. He would also leave water and some food nearby for Mr. and Mrs. Birdie to pick up easily.

Because of this level of attention, he'd gotten used to the baby birds' constant peeps and the parents' constant calls and random chirping, but he now realized, just a moment ago, the peeps and chirps had stopped, started, and then stopped again. It wouldn't have been so strange in normal circumstances, except it happened all at once. There was no random peep from a bird that went quiet after the others, like a kid in a choir that missed his cue to stop singing.

They all literally stopped at the same time, started again at the same time, and stopped again at the same time. Now, here they were again, happily peeping and chirping, and he wasn't certain, but he was convinced they'd also resumed at the same time.

He had this strange prickling sensation on the back of his neck. A foreboding tingle, like standing with your back to a window during a cold, breezy day. He felt this had happened before, but how could he possibly know that? It was such an insignificant phenomenon that he couldn't imagine a reason he would remember it happening before. Yet he was almost certain.

What's up with that? he thought, as he clumsily placed a rinsed dish on the rack. He might investigate that too, while attempting to determine what species the Birdies were, and whether they had a tendency to go quiet out of the blue for no reason.

Chapter Seven
Barry Giffen
1991

There was a knock at the front door.

They were here.

The irritated exhalation that issued from Barry's chest made him feel like he was deflating, but once the volume of air in his lungs had reached zero, he felt like he needed to continue further down—was negative deflation possible?

Barry was already dressed and ready to go out, but as he sat on his bed staring at the door, he wondered if this was such a good idea after all.

He glanced around his room as if he could find an excuse lying around. Having to clean his room might have been a good one, but one disadvantage of being so obsessive about order meant his damned room was spotless. Not even a sock out of place. Sitting on his perfectly made bed made him uncomfortable, since he had to be sure not to forget to smooth the wrinkles once he stood up.

Should've sat on the chair, he thought.

He regarded the many posters of musicians and bands he liked, covering the entirety of one of his walls: The Who, Depeche Mode, Kate Bush, Blondie, Judas Priest, The Kinks, Queen, Led Zeppelin, The Smiths, R.E.M., David Bowie, Ramones, and many others, forming a collage of artists that only clicked together in his head.

There was another wall covered with posters of soccer teams and soccer players. Maradona, Asprilla, Lineker, Valderrama, Schillacci, Klinsman, Baggio, Romario, Cannigia, Higuita, and other names no one in the entire town would even care to know about, much less know how to pronounce. While in the U.S. of A. football was king, Barry didn't care much for it. He was in the school's soccer team and was eagerly awaiting the 1994 FIFA World Cup. He cheered like crazy in '88 when the United States was selected as the host country. His dad was alive back then and cheered along with him, promising he'd save money to take him to at least one game. He guessed he'd have to go for both of them now that he was gone. He just needed to save enough for a ticket. When the time came, he would figure out the bus fare and where to sleep. He'd sleep on the street if he had to.

Another knock at the front door.

Go away, go away, go away!

"Barry!" His momma's voice, yelling from the bedroom. "Are you planning on opening the damn door? I have a headache!"

Fuck. No choice now.

"I'm going, Momma!"

"Goddamn it! What do I have to do to get some sleep in this house?"

It's almost 1:00 pm. Maybe if you hadn't spent the night out drinking with Mr. Parham…

He stood up and smoothed the wrinkles on the cover and headed out.

He opened the door to see one of the Howe twins standing outside, his hand raised, ready to knock again.

Barry greeted him with a snarl, bulging eyes, and clenched teeth. "Knock again and they'll need the jaws of life to pull your brother's head out of your ass!"

"Hey, Norman?" Royce shot a scared look at Lange.

"Hi Barry," Peter Lange said with a shy wave, standing next to Bobby Novak. Barry couldn't help thinking he'd let the little twerp con him into joining their stupid group.

"Did you tell your mom you'll be staying at Royce and Leroy's?" asked Bobby.

Barry stared at him as though he were the dumbest person in the universe and shut the door with a bang.

"I don't need to tell her shit. Let's go!"

He removed the lock and chain off his bike, mounted it, and started pedaling.

2022

Barry had gotten off the phone with Nadine, who'd called to confirm the plans for the night and hurried to call his wife, Maryann, to let her know. He knew she wouldn't like it, but he hadn't asked for anything in a long time. Maybe he would get lucky, and her mother wouldn't be nearby when she picked up. Maryann was much more manageable when her mother wasn't there to fan the flames. And oh, how she loved fanning them. She was basically a fart on a lighter, the unpleasant old cow.

As the cell phone rang, he leaned back in his chair and tapped his thick fingers on his desk. He noticed the small, translucent, standing plate that read, *Barry Giffen: Import & Export Logistics Manager,* wasn't aligned with the edge of the desk, so, with one thick index finger, he pushed softly at a corner until it was aligned. He also aligned the keyboard… and the screen…and the stapler…and the notepad, and the pen, and the entire wheeled cabinet under the desk.

He wasn't anxious.

He wasn't nervous.

He could have this conversation without it becoming "a thing".

He jumped, and his heart skipped a beat when Mary-ann's voice came up on the phone.

"Hello," she said, in the cheery tone she had when she still didn't know who was calling.

"Oh, uh, hi," Barry stammered. "Hey, hon, how are you?"

"Oh, hi hon," she answered back, and her tone went down just an octave, enough for the change to be noticeable. Sure, she called him "hon", but there was this unpleasantness to the way her voice changed once she recognized him. She didn't sound glad to talk to him. It sounded more like: "Oh, it's you."

As if the change of tone hadn't been enough to dishearten him, he heard a whiny voice in the background say, "Who is it?" and he tightened his jaw in frustration. Therese, his mother-in-law.

"It's just Barry," Maryann said, speaking away from the phone, then came back. "What's up?"

"Listen, hon, I was, uh, talking to Nadine—"

"Schaefer?" she asked with some distaste. The question itself seemed to be asked to show antipathy, since she was the only Nadine they knew.

"Yes, Nadine Schaefer." He nodded, even though his wife couldn't see him.

"What did she want?"

"Well, Peter's back in town." He made it a point to

grin widely. People on the other end could hear you when you were smiling. "She was planning a get-together tonight at Cunningham's."

"I can't make it tonight. I might take Mom out for dinner."

There was an awkward pause that stretched until the Heat Death of the Universe.

"Oh, I didn't know you were going out tonight."

"I might. Just wanted to keep my options open."

"Well…" He noticed how his fingers were now tapping the desk furiously, and he had to will himself to stop doing this. "Look hon, since, in your case, the plans are options, and my plans are more concrete, maybe I should be able to go out with my friends?"

"Are you smart-assing me?" The phrase came out like the crack of a whip.

"Wha—"

"So, what you're saying is my plans are irrelevant, only because I'm still putting them together. Is that right?"

He could hear she had him on speaker now, as her voice attained an echo it didn't have before. He could also hear her mother whispering things to her in the background. He could picture the horrible, bespectacled, bad-purple-dye-jobbed cow standing right next to her, with that evil smile she got on her face whenever Maryann chewed him up, a disgusting facial expression which somehow showed indignation and arousal at the same time. The old monster got her rocks off whenever she heard her daughter stamp him out.

Tapping. Tapping. Tapping. Fingers tapping.

Stop it!

He spoke again. "No, that's not what I—"

"Also," interrupted Maryann, "I know your friends, too. We all went to the same school *and* high school together. Since my plans are so *optional*, how come you're going out for drinks, but I can't come with you? Isn't it an *option* to take your wife with you?"

"Well, it's just supposed to be the old gang," he said nervously, feeling himself diminishing. "I'm sure Peter will come over for lunch or dinner one of these days. I could even ask him to sign a book for you. You like his books, right?"

"I don't give a crap about Peter Lange's signature."

He could hear his mother-in-law whisper something that sounded like, "You tell him," in the background.

"His last book sucked. You know what I do care about? If you go out with 'the gang', or that ridiculous name you used to call yourselves as kids, the 'Vigilantes', who's going to take care of Daniel and Gabe? Who will make Gabe's formula and get his bottle ready? Who will heat Daniel's food? Who will put them to bed? Who will do their laundry? You have a three-year-old and a one-year-old. Who will take care of their needs while you're out drinking with the Vigilantes?"

"I, uh…" Small. He was becoming small. Diminishing. Vanishing. Disappearing. Nothing. He was nothing. His voice was becoming a soft whine. "I thought…"

"You thought what?" she asked, already knowing the answer, but wanting him to say it.

"I thought maybe you and your mom could take care of them for just tonight?"

An audible gasp came from the background. *The cow, the horrible old cow!*

"Oh, you thought that, did you?" Maryann actually scoffed loudly at the very notion, at the gall, at the audacity she obviously sensed in his request. "You know what? Go. You go. You go, do that. Have fun. Enjoy yourself while neglecting your family and ignoring your children. How responsible of you."

"M-Maryann. Hon, that's not fair. Every day, I come in at 6, feed the boys, play with them before putting them to bed, and do all the other stuff. I'm only asking for one—"

"Go! Just go! I'll take care of the boys. Don't worry. I'm glad I have Mom here to support me, since you clearly aren't interested in doing your part for this family. I think I should evaluate if I want you to still be a part of this family at all."

Tapping. Tapping. Tapping. Small. So small. Meaningless. Nothing. Just nothing.

He had to contain himself for a moment and reflect

on what he would say next, but it was hard hearing that woman in the background whispering things to his wife. He sighed softly, away from the phone as to not incur in Maryann's wrath any further.

"Thank you, hon," he said meekly.

"Don't thank me."

He heard the old woman—the old cow—whisper something to his wife.

"Thank God your kids are too young to realize how irresponsible and neglectful their father is being right now."

She hung up, and he peered at his fingers. They weren't tapping on the desk anymore, but his fingernails were digging into the wood. The nameplate had moved a bit with all the tapping, so he raised his hand from the desk, put out a trembling finger, and re-aligned it.

His attention was called now to the sound of two crows outside the window, those two crows had been cawing like mad when he'd been speaking to Nadine just minutes ago, to the point of being insufferable and distracting, and during the call they'd gone quiet.

After the call with Nadine ended, they resumed their raspy kraas and caws, but now that the memory came back to him, he hadn't heard them once during the call with Maryann. Maybe he'd been too distracted by his wife treating him like a subservient slave and the mental image of his mother-in-law whispering, "Whip him harder!" to her, but he was not convinced that was it.

The crows were now cawing again.

Barry rolled his office chair toward the window and shut it hard enough for the crows to be scared away by the sound. There were two pictures carefully taped to the window, and upon closing it, they'd aligned perfectly with his eyes. Daniel and Gabe, his reason for existing, his reason for hanging on, his reason for putting up with those two. He rolled back toward his desk, his broad back now hunched over. He ran his hands down his face and over his beard with a deep sigh of frustration and impotence.

Chapter Eight

Callum Baker
1991

"Gotta hand it to Droopy's family," Royce said, regarding Callum Baker's home. "They sure know how to make a trailer *not* look like a trailer."

"That's mean," Bobby said, giving him a side-eye. "Also, it's not a trailer, it's a mobile home."

The group had stopped in front of the pretty blue-and-white home where Callum lived with his parents and his younger brother and sister. The mobile home was spotless, with hanging plants adorning its makeshift porch, a small flower garden at the front—a family of gnomes and all.

"Don't get us wrong, man," Leroy said. "It's definitely the prettiest mobile home in the park. Doesn't look poor at all! I mean, check out that other one over there. If that shit ain't haunted, I don't know what it is."

"Just because a family lives in Lumenwood, it doesn't mean they're poor."

"True, true," Leroy said. "Except, Droopy *is* poor. He works part-time at Rockwell's, putting shoes back in boxes and cleaning up, otherwise he wouldn't be able to afford school supplies at all. He can't even afford clothes. The other day our mom gave him a bag of our old clothes because his parents couldn't buy—"

"Bro!" Royce said, jumping in. "Shut up!"

Leroy noticed everyone had gone quiet as death, and he turned toward the front door to see Callum already standing there, giving him the most humorless death stare he'd seen in his entire life.

He was wearing a red shirt with faded white and gray geometric shapes in the chest area, and a red and black flannel on top.

Leroy pointed at the shirt and turned to Bobby. "See? That one was mine."

Callum's eyes flitted to each of the members of the group, and said, "You brought bikes?"

"Yeah, why?" Royce gave him a confused expression.

"Well, you and Leroy have been my gracious benefactors, so, since I'm living in poverty and squalor, you'd know I don't own a bike. I can't follow you unless you drag me behind like an outlaw in a Western."

"Oh, crap." Bobby, being the one that originally showed up on a bicycle, stared at him with a guilty expression. "I'm so sorry, Cal. It was my fault."

After an awkward silence, Leroy said: "I brought a skateboard."

"Well, how considerate of you." Callum pantomimed examining the skateboard. "Does it come with a passenger seat?"

"Uh…" Peter raised his hand.

"We're not in class, Norman." Royce rolled his eyes. "You don't have to raise your hand."

Peter put his hand down with an embarrassed smile. "I was just going to say, why doesn't he ride on one of the other bikes, like me?"

"I'd take him on mine, but my top tube is too diagonal." Royce pointed at his bike. "I'd ride us into a gutter or something."

"Jesus, you're all a useless!" Barry said, rolling his bike toward Callum.

Royce turned toward Peter with a wide glare of concern. "You know he's gonna kill us, right? He's gonna kill us, and it will be your fault. I just want to put that out there, so you think of that as he's crushing our skulls."

Peter shook his head in response. "He won't."

"Here." Barry kicked a three-inch metal bar attached to the rear wheel's hub. There was one on either side. "I got footholds. You can ride with me. Stand there and grab on to my shoulders."

"Thanks," Callum said with hesitation.

"Hey, Cal!"

They all turned to see Callum's mom, a pudgy-faced woman with such a perfect motherly smile it was impossible for most of the boys not to smile back.

"Oh, hey, Mom." Callum was about to step onto a foothold.

"Hope you kids have fun. Be careful, alright?" She wiped her hands on an apron that had seen plenty of use. "Hi Leroy, hi Royce, hi Bobby."

They all greeted her with the type of big, polite, nervous smiles that children often reserved for their friends' parents.

She noticed Peter, and at first didn't seem to recognize him. "Peter Lange, right?"

"Yes, ma'am. Nice to meet you."

"Nice to meet you, too. Such a pleasant surprise to see you hanging out with the other boys." She nodded her head toward Barry. "Is this the boy whose house you're all going to? Barry, right?"

The other boys exchanged glances, realizing she didn't know Barry, and she had no idea what to expect.

Leroy pictured Barry suddenly going berserk and tearing the sweet lady to shreds like an angry bear.

What they saw next was far more terrifying.

Barry flashed a bright smile at Callum's mom, and with the nicest, politest voice they had ever heard come out of the large boy, he said, "Yes, Mrs. Baker. Nice to meet you! Don't worry, we'll take good care of Cal! We have dinner early at my house, and my mom's making some fried chicken and mashed potatoes for dinner, so when we bring him back, he'll already be full."

She smiled back and nodded with satisfaction. "That's great! So nice to meet you, too, Barry. I won't keep you, boys. Alright, you have fun!"

She walked in the house, while they stood there gawping at Barry, who kept smiling as the door closed. He looked like he'd been possessed by an alien body snatcher.

"It can act human," Leroy whispered to his brother.

"If it breeds, we're doomed," Royce whispered back.

The door finally closed.

"What are you waiting for?" Barry turned to Callum, no longer smiling. "Get on."

Callum climbed on the footholds.

"Hold on to me, because if you fall and crack your skull on the pavement, I'll just keep pedaling."

"Good," Royce said to his brother. "It can't imitate humans for extended periods."

They all mounted their bikes and began pedaling away. As Barry's bike rolled forward, Callum lost his balance and almost fell back, then grabbed on to Barry's neck and pulled himself forward, ending up with his arms clumsily wrapped around his neck.

"Stop hugging me, or I'll push you off the bike."

Callum steadied his footing, stood straight, and placed both hands on his shoulders. "Sorry!"

2022

The library of Ann Summers High School was not as frequented as it used to be when Callum Baker was in school. Who needed library books—most of them dog-eared and covered with drawings of penises and tits on the pages, from years and years of being lent to inconsiderate students—when computers and cell phones existed?

He did not oppose cell phones, computers, and technology. He wasn't that kind of adult, and he couldn't blame the kids. He knew they now seemed to have an innate ability to communicate with technology that people of his generation barely had the luck to get in on during high school so as to not be completely incompetent. They could not, however, match the ease today's kids had to locate any kind of information they required in mere seconds. It was equal times admirable and alarming.

Access to knowledge was now nearly omnipresent, but the information wasn't curated most of the time, or it was *overly* curated most of the other, leaving only a small percentage of actual, verifiable, peer-reviewed knowledge that still needed to strive for relevance against people who simply refused to believe anything that came from official sources.

Still, given the choice, he would vote in favor of the Internet and not against it. He had to admit, deep down, it was improving the world more than it was worsening it. What people mostly saw on the news or popping up on feeds was mainly the depressing, horrible stuff, while the good worked mostly in silence. Just the idea scientists across the globe could share their knowledge with each other, instead of working in silos, meant people who could enact change for the better had a shot at figuring out how to move forward despite those who would wish to stop them.

All those things considered, though, Callum loved the smell of books, of paper, of bindings. He loved the feeling of a page sliding over another, almost sensually, to reveal the next two pages' worth of knowledge. He loved the sound of a hard cover on a large book opening, the weight of it, or better yet, the almost inaudible crinkling of leather-bound books, which were now so rare. They seemed to creak like treasure chests holding untold discoveries.

Sitting behind the library's front desk, rimless glasses on, in front of two rows of bookshelves, set parallel from each other in neat, organized rows—more than most comparable schools got now, thanks to him pulling on some personal strings—he was finishing his notes on one of few available historical accounts about the first colonizing party that made it past the Crescent Mountains, and the infamous blizzard that had nearly killed them all.

He had been working on something, something he'd been studying for a while now, poring over books, and maps, and documents—and yes, websites. Something he wasn't ready to share with the rest of the world, something he was slowly uncovering and piecing together thanks to his constant reading about the town of White Harbor—its origins, and certain phenomena which made it a unique, isolated, little bubble of strangeness.

If he hadn't spent most of his time in a mostly empty library—and yes, again, had access to Google—he wouldn't have gotten as far as he had in as short a time.

The door to the library opening interrupted his thoughts, followed by someone's steps approaching. If it was a kid, he'd just wait for them to approach if they had a question. He had just read a full copy of Gerardo Valencia's autopsy report he'd procured from a well-connected friend, and he was now moving on to an article about the history of the Parham family. Specifically, the Parham curse. It had been such an undeniably compelling tale with so much "evidence" to support it—all circumstantial, all based on folk tales, gossip, and assumptions—it was quite a hard myth to debunk.

But debunk it, I will, he thought with a sense of pride.

He was so immersed in his research it startled him when a female voice said, "Hey."

He glanced up to be greeted over the desk by a woman's lips, which felt soft and familiar. Instinctively, he kissed back. When he finally saw who he was kissing, he saw it was Sylvia. He got startled for a moment, until he regained his wits and remembered she was his girlfriend—she was also, he reminded himself with trepidation, the high school principal.

"Wow, it's becoming so easy to catch you off guard when you get into those books," the stunningly beautiful Sylvia Nguyen said. "Or maybe, after six months of dating, I'm just getting better at sneaking up on you."

Callum turned his head left to throw a quick glance at the library's double glass doors, which led straight to a hall that would be filled with students once the bell rang. "Should we be doing this right now? I mean…the students…"

"Jesus, Cal," Sylvia said. "You can be a killjoy sometimes."

"Syl, you're my boss." He adjusted his glasses, which had slid down his nose. "It's not ethical. People can't know we're going out."

She rolled her eyes and the corner of her mouth stretched sideways in a tired smirk. "Who cares if anyone knows, Cal? Stop being weird. Nobody cares."

"Are you sure? Mrs. Shue keeps giving me the worst evil eye every time she sees me. I think she suspects."

"That's because she hasn't liked you since we were in high school," Sylvia said as plainly as her voice would allow.

"Oh," he said robotically.

"And because she knows."

"Oh."

"What I'm saying is, it doesn't matter, Cal!" Her brown eyes glanced at him. She pushed the glasses up on his nose before he could do it himself again. "I don't pay your salary, and everything I do with budgeting is reviewed by the superintendent. So, relax. There's no conflict of interest!"

He gestured at the shelves full of books, many of which he'd requested. "Well, technically—"

"No." She put a finger to his mouth. "No, no, no. No more 'technically'. Well…maybe one more. Nadine asked me to come to Cunningham's tonight, and you are obviously invited, too. *Technically*…I said yes on your behalf."

"What? But, Syl, they don't know!"

"Nadine already knows. I told her after our second date. You know I'm not good at not telling."

"I can't go tonight." He gestured toward the books and papers in front of him. "I'm busy. The project. The publication. This is important!"

"Look." She approached him and cupped his cheeks

in her palms lovingly. "I love that big brain of yours. I love how thorough you are. It's the sexiest thing about you, but we have never gone out with our friends as a couple. Lange will be here only for four days, so this is our one chance. We're going. Are we clear?"

Callum sighed and let his shoulders fall, defeated. In his expression, his cheeks sagged, and the bags under his eyes—which had disappeared as he'd grown into adulthood—reappeared and became more pronounced, making him temporarily resemble the awkward, weird kid he'd been throughout his school years. He nodded with a marked lack of enthusiasm.

"You're cute when you make that face." Silvia kissed him on the cheek and started walking toward the doors. She got them halfway open but seemed to remember another thing she'd come to tell him about. "Oh, that's right. Did you notice the thing with the birds?"

"What thing with the birds?"

"They went quiet suddenly. You didn't notice? The mountains are right there." She gestured toward the large windows and a fence only a couple of feet from them, beyond which trees of all kinds abounded.

"There's no actual external ventilation here, Sylvia, not sure if you've noticed. There's air conditioning. We can see outside but not hear anything. What do you mean the birds went quiet?"

"*Technically*," she said, highlighting the word again, "they didn't *just* go quiet. They sort of got quiet, came back, got quiet again, and now they're back…again."

Callum seemed more confused about this event raising any kind of notice than the event itself. "Don't they do that, like, all the time?"

Sylvia did something Callum found adorable: an exaggerated upward turn of the eyes with a finger going up to her mouth, as if in thought.

"Well, yes. Except, this time, it was weird enough that people started talking about it. I got it from Tom, who was out with the kids from his biology class, collecting leaf samples. Then, Kelly, that new gym teacher, she said the trees around the baseball field went quiet."

"That doesn't mean anything. It's hearsay, nothing scientific, just a coincidence."

"You must think very little of my scientific method, sweetie," she said with a sarcastic smile. "I got curious. I wanted to test it. So, I called Victoria at Garland Elementary. You know how The Pines are like right there, and trees surround the entire school? Garland is five blocks from here. Therefore, what would be the odds it would also have happened there, and out of everyone there, Victoria noticed it?"

"She did."

"Of course she did!" Sylvia raised her hands in triumph. "Not just that, they were also talking about it there, so several people there had noticed it. So, we have the same event: birds sing, birds go quiet, birds sing again, birds go quiet again, birds sing again, reported in two places that are five blocks apart, at the same hour, and confirmed by people in both places. What do you think it means?"

Callum's eyes went round with curiosity and excitement. "I have to test this."

"I can help you."

"I love you."

His cheeks turned an intense red hue, realizing he'd said this for the first time and it had just come out so easily.

"And you should." Sylvia blew a kiss in his direction and walked away.

Chapter Nine

The Grieving Mother: "Roberta"
1989

As he came in from the freezing cold and closed the door behind him, Peter had never in his life been so glad to be home. He expected to be quickly enveloped in his house's warmth but was surprised to find, while inside it had been warmer than the post-blizzard weather he'd walked in from, the house was still colder than he'd expected. Was the heater on the fritz? He took a quick survey of his home.

He was taken aback by how dark the house was for a winter afternoon. Peter soon realized the electricity was off. Out of nowhere came a soft popping sound, like a tiny bird-shot pellet falling on a polished tile surface, and he noticed the fireplace was on, and the wood was crackling and popping as it burned. Mother was sitting on a high-back chair close to it, with a book resting on her lap and both hands resting on its front cover.

She looked like a painting one would hang on the wall in a living room. A living room where another middle-aged woman would sit by the fireplace, looking like a painting one would hang on the wall in another living room, where yet another middle-aged woman would sit by the fireplace, looking like a painting one would hang on the wall in yet another living room, and another one, and another one, and another one.

It's no use, Mr. James, it's middle-aged women all the way down, Peter thought, feeling quite clever but having a challenging time remembering which was the actual quote he was paraphrasing. *Turtles,* he remembered. *It's turtles all the way down. Where did I read that? It's going to drive me crazy.*

"Don't just stand there, boy," Mother said in a sleepy voice, her eyes fixed on the fireplace, immersed in her own thoughts. "Come and kiss your mother."

Peter hung his leather backpack on a hook by the door and hurried by her side. She slightly raised her cheek, and he gave her a kiss.

"You're late," she said.

"I'm—" he stammered. "I'm sorry, Mother."

"That's fine." She spoke in a pleasant manner, which was not typical for her. "Where were you?"

"I stayed a little longer inside the school. I thought I'd wait out the snow until it got better to walk home."

"Smart boy." She stayed transfixed by the fire, not even turning her head to look at him. The flow of the flame cast a dancing reflection of light on the surface of her eyes. "Just don't let it get too late when you do that. Don't let it get dark."

"Yes, Mother." He surveyed the house to make certain that the electricity was indeed off. "Was the power cut?"

"Well, of course it was," she said regretfully. She finally managed a fatigued smile in his direction. "Your old Mother has been distracted these last few days. I forgot. I made the payment this morning, but, with the snow and all, we probably won't have power through the night. I'm surprised they made you go to school today."

He nodded. "I heard the other kids saying that."

She let out a single chuckle from within her chest and smiled. "You heard the other kids, huh?" She glanced at him again. "They weren't saying it to you, I'd imagine. You 'heard them' talking to each other."

"They don't talk to me, Mother, and I don't talk to them," he said hurriedly. "You know that."

"I know. I'm sorry it has to be that way, but you don't need them, Peter. You don't." She gestured toward a small, upholstered banquette to her right, in front of the fireplace. "Sit."

Peter sat down, his arms straight and his hands clinging to the edge of the seat, mystified at the strange mood that had taken over Mother.

2022

"Sit!" Mother said from her chair by the hospital window, in the tone one would use to address a disobedient dog, soon to be scolded.

Peter still had his hand pressed against his cheek from where she'd backhanded him not five seconds ago.

"I said, sit," she repeated. The lucidity in her eyes had been one he hadn't seen in a long time, and it had only appeared in that stare after commanding him to call her "Mother", as "mom" was too informal a word for someone of her stature.

"Uh, Pete," Raymond said from the door, sounding a bit shocked by his mother's sudden physical aggression. "Will you be okay?"

"Yes," Peter said, sitting down on a chair next to the bed. His cheek still felt hot, and he rubbed his hand on it. He kept his eyes on his mother, as if she were going to stab him in the gut if he so much as took his gaze away from her. "I'll be fine, Ray. Cunningham's tonight?"

Ray said, "Yeah," and Peter felt his friend's reluctance to leave him alone with his mother, even though he couldn't see his face. "See you tonight."

"If the crazy lady doesn't kill you," he imagined his friend thinking immediately after, as Ray's footsteps disappeared into the hallway.

"So…" Mother's eyes became barely slits as she gave him a knowing smile, studying him intently. He remembered the way her eyes narrowed when she knew he was hiding something and wouldn't admit it.

"Did you break that plate?"

"No, Mother," he would answer, as shards of dishware lay on the floor.

"Did you tidy up your room?"

"Yes, Mother," he would answer, with clothes and toys hurriedly thrown in the closet.

"Were you playing with yourself in the bathroom?"

"No, Mother," he would answer, his skin clammy as he closed the bathroom door behind him, blushing.

She would always know.

She always knew when he'd been bad. Even before she asked, she knew. He would always admit to lying, and he would always pay the price. Nothing, however, could have prepared him for the question that today accompanied those narrowed eyes.

"How did she die?" she asked.

For a moment, Peter's eyes widened in shock as he stared at her. She knew! Mother knew! She knew about—

"My sister was always so meddling," she said, her hands clasped together on her lap, that dreadful rosary wrapped around one of them. "Taking my son away from me was a sin that could not be forgiven. I knew she'd pay for that. God promised me she would. I just didn't expect her to die so soon. What are you now? Eighteen?"

It took Peter way too long for the shock to move out of the way of the brain synapses needed for him to grasp his mother was talking about his aunt Constance, who was well and alive at her home.

"Mother," Peter said. "Aunt Constance isn't dead."

Slowly, almost in sections, his mother's face began to quiver, crumble, and twist into a malevolent glower. She looked cheated and betrayed. If flames had come out of her ears and nostrils and the corners of her lips, he wouldn't have found it at all surprising.

She stood up from her chair, quickly, with an agility Peter would never have believed her capable of, and turned her back on him, indignant. She gazed out the window and her hands were together under her belly. He could see her shoulders rise and fall as she breathed angrily.

"I will deal with her," she said. "I understand now. That's what the Lord wants. He wants me to handle my family matters. He's already done too much for me. Some burdens must fall on my own shoulders, and I must be strong to carry them, not just bear witness."

"Mother, stop. Just, please st—"

"Who died, then?" she asked softly, almost casually, as if asking who was at the door. "Do not lie to me, boy, because I will know it. I know your eyes when you've been crying. You are a weak and sad boy, not a real man, so I know you have been crying a lot, and I know someone dear has passed away." She stared at him over her shoulder. "Out with it. Tell your mother who…" her speech trailed off. She stood there with the window to her face, silent, waves of realization radiating out of her.

Peter heard a "ch" come from her lips, but he didn't hear the actual word until, out of nowhere, she repeated it.

"The bitch," she said. "The bitch died. Didn't she?"

She turned her head and gazed at him. Her eyes were filled with a revolting sort of joy. Those were the eyes of a person overcome with gladness, of a person who has seen God fulfill a promise and seen their faith rewarded.

1989

Mother continued to gaze dreamily into the flames of the fireplace. Peter observed her forlorn expression, something rare for her. She sighed, which made him even more concerned.

"Are you okay, Mother?"

"I was doing some food deliveries this morning, before the snow hit. Passed by the Valencia place." She gave him a knowing glance. "You know. That boy?"

Peter nodded. "I heard he was going to start middle school next fall."

"That he was," she said with sadness. "Not anymore. This shouldn't have happened. Not like this," she sighed again. "I went to deliver lunch to his mother. She was not well, and she wouldn't accept my help."

Earlier that day, at the end of her food deliveries to various businesses and houses in White Harbor, Martha reached a small house on the north side of Burkle Park. It was a sunny and bright day, despite the snow that accumulated on the ground and at the edge of sidewalks here and there. She rapped on the white door of the bright yellow home, which gave off an old-world, cheerful charm.

The vivid yellow of the house was almost reminiscent of a fairytale, with its mullioned windows edged in white, and a garden that, had it been spring, would have been bursting with colorful, joyful flowers. Roberta Valencia was a kindergarten teacher, and her colorful home and big yard reflected that love of children, but life had only blessed her with the one. Gerardo, who was now dead.

While Martha had to put up with sideways glances from so many of the residents of White Harbor, Roberta was welcoming and pleasant. She had been Peter's kindergarten teacher and, where other mothers and teachers regarded her with fear and scorn—*Envy*, she thought—Roberta always had a smile on her face, and often shared a cup of coffee with her.

Roberta had legally taken her husband's name, which was not a custom in Colombia, where they'd come from, or in any part of Latin America. When Martha inquired about it, she joked, "I only did it because, otherwise, it would keep confusing the gringos."

Martha could understand this. People had been confused when she'd legally changed Peter's last name from Rojas—Hector's last name—to Lange, after Hector disappeared. She wanted nothing of the man to remain in Peter's identity.

Roberta, coincidentally, practiced that ridiculous religion Martha's ex-husband used to practice, and this, Martha knew, would mean they would face the dark, cold nothingness of the void, in the end. Despite this, she had found herself liking and respecting the woman. She was the closest outside the Circle she could call a friend.

The door opened, and there stood Francisco Valencia. At first, he reacted to the winter cold outside his front door by blowing into his hands. The moment he saw Martha, there was surprise in his eyes, and a bit of a twitch in his mouth, as if he had stopped an involuntary reaction of some sort. He smiled widely and said, "Mrs. Lange, how can I help you?"

"How are you, Francisco?" she said, with perfect Spanish pronunciation of his name. "I thought I'd come by and leave some food. I made some macaroni and cheese and some salad for you and dear Roberta."

Anybody who would've witnessed Martha smiling at that moment would have been astonished to see her do so with such earnestness. She reached into a large, unadorned tote bag she carried slung over her shoulder and brought out two large Tupperware containers.

Francisco regarded the containers in Martha's hand and said, "Oh, Mrs. Lange, you didn't have to do this."

"I did," she said immediately. "I can only imagine what you must be going through, and I know you probably can barely think of eating, much less preparing food. You know I pride myself very much in my cooking, and this is very simple, but it's comfort food for me. I thought maybe a little home cooking would make Roberta feel a little better. After all, what are friends for?"

Francisco seemed uncertain what to say, judging

by his expression. Finally, he took the two containers in his hands and said, "Thank you, Mrs. Lange. I'll make sure she gets this."

"Can I see her?" she said hurriedly.

He hesitated. "She just took some pills, and she's in bed. I think she wants to sleep the afternoon off. Maybe some other time?"

"Please." Martha's tone was pleading, and Francisco regarded her now with not just puzzlement, but a little alarm. "I need to talk to her. I promise I will be quick."

He squinted, looking slightly perplexed. "Okay, Mrs. Lange, that's fine." Hesitating, he moved aside and held the door open for her.

What awaited inside the house was the polar opposite of what Martha had seen outside. Even at this hour in the morning, the house was dark and dreary. The beautiful windows from inside were curtained and barely let any light in. The house had an unclean smell to it, of garbage bags that needed taking out, and dishes that needed washing. There was an open box with leftover pizza crust on the coffee table in front of the TV, and a dirty sock lying alone on the carpet beneath it—a young boy's sock. The surface of the dinner table was glass. It hadn't been wiped in many days, and crumbs and stains now fed tiny ants.

To the right, there was a closed door with small, rect-angular, adhesive markings where a poster with some South

American soccer player had been before. This had been young Gerardo's bedroom. She could see a single piece of tape still clinging sadly to the door, with a torn corner of glossy paper, from when the poster had been ripped away by a grieving mother or a grieving father in a moment of despair.

Photographs were laid face-down on the shelves and mantles, and lighter-colored rectangles on the walls revealed where other pictures had been removed. Photos of Gerardo, she knew.

As she followed Francisco through a threshold into a small hallway, they passed a bathroom that smelled as if it hadn't been cleaned all week. She brought her hand up to her mouth and remembered how impeccably neat Roberta's house used to be kept. The floral scent of her furniture polish still lingered in her memory from those days when she'd pick up Peter from kindergarten, and Roberta had been kind enough to allow him to play with Gerardo while she had the time to come pick him up after her afternoon deliveries.

As they reached the spot where the hallway turned left to find the bedroom, she swiveled her eyes to the right, where a large garbage bag sat on the floor, full of boy's clothes. The bag was still open, like a hungry mouth, waiting for more memories of the dead boy to be fed to it. The long sleeve of a red sweater hung out of the bag like a fuzzy tongue.

"*Mi vida,*" said Francisco, walking into the master bedroom, his voice drawing Martha's attention toward the door to the left. "*Martha Lange viene a verte.*"

Martha spoke Spanish after years married to a Costa Rican immigrant. How could she not, especially when considering Hector Rojas was the kind of boisterous buffoon that talked even through his elbows? It was something she had found charming about the man…back in the day.

"*A qué viene esa mujer?*" Roberta's voice sounded spent, tired, and empty. She had asked, "Why's that woman here?" The wording of that phrase, though short, had not come with the friendliest of connotations. She did not feel discouraged, though. She knew what grief could do to a person.

"I just wanted to see you, Roberta," she said from behind Francisco.

He hurried into the room, almost as if Martha had been pushing past him. Glancing at her over his shoulder, he seemed to indicate she was being rude, yet she didn't care about his opinion. She was here to show her sympathies to someone she cared about and respected, and this man—as men often did—was standing in her way. Without even waiting for Roberta to respond, she walked inside and sat at the edge of the bed, near Roberta's feet.

She found herself gazing into a face that was so pale and hollow; it felt like gazing into the face of death itself. Roberta's appearance was that of a gray mask, with dark circles underlining reddened eyes. Her nose was also reddish, and the outer layer of its skin was peeled from so many tissues wiping at it. Wetness surrounded the nostrils. Her hair was matted, crow's feet had been drawn from the corners of her eyes, mouth down-turned and toad-like. Here sat a woman who knew impossible pain.

"How can I help you, Mrs. Lange?" said Roberta, staring at her in confusion.

"You?" Martha gave her a kind smile. "I need nothing from you, my dear Roberta. How could I ask for anything when you've just suffered an insurmountable loss?"

Roberta grimaced, as if those words, instead of comforting her, stung.

"And call me Martha. I'm no stranger and Peter is no longer in kindergarten, so no formalities, please. I am so deeply sorry about what happened to your son."

"Thank you," Roberta said with a nod. Her voice was almost inaudible and wet, its sound like the last two drops of rainwater that fall off the edge of a leaf into a puddle.

"No need. I avoid places that are teeming with people, and young Gerardo's funeral was…let's just say, there were so many people who loved him. I wanted to do something a little more personal for a friend like you."

"A fr…" Roberta raised her eyes to her, then to her husband. Martha didn't notice him responding with a shrug. Roberta brought the tissue up to her nose and wiped again. It must have been quite painful to wipe such a sore nose.

"She, uh," Francisco said. His voice grated on her, but she bore it out of respect.

Why is he still here? Yes, I have come to pay my condolences to both, but I especially came to see Roberta, and I do not appreciate his interruption...or his presence.

"She brought some food."

Roberta smiled politely, but uneasily, at her.

"It's still warm," Martha said, trying to shift the focus again to herself and the purpose of her visit. "It's almost lunchtime. Let me serve you a plate!"

Without waiting for a response, Martha sprang from the bed, walked to Francisco, swiped the containers off his hands, and headed toward the kitchen as if it were her own home.

She put the plastic container aside while she expertly took a tray from the kitchen counter, opened the cabinets to find a plate and a cup, pulled out a spatula from a drawer, and a fork she placed on the tray. She got the lid open and up floated the wonderful smell of the four cheeses she used on her macaroni and cheese: Gruyère, cheddar, Brie, and a nice powdering of Parmesan on top—with just a pinch of perfectly crisped and crushed bacon mixed in with the latter.

Instead of just shoving the spoon in and plopping the mac and cheese on the plate, she took the spatula and cut a line across the container, slid the spatula underneath, and pulled the whole chunk out. Strands of cheese and creamy gooey deliciousness poured out of the edges of the spatula, but before they fell off, she had already placed the perfect square on the plate. She opened the second container and served the salad, a simple green salad with lettuce and arugula, and found some balsamic vinegar and croutons in Roberta's kitchen to sprinkle on top of it. Finally, she opened the refrigerator and found a pitcher of iced tea. Roberta had the habit of putting lime juice in her iced tea, but nobody was perfect. She poured the tea in the glass, put the pitcher back in the refrigerator, closed the refrigerator with a swift kick of the back of the shoe, grabbed the tray, and hurried back to the bedroom.

Two pairs of confused eyes greeted her in the bedroom, staring at her in astonishment. They were not expecting this level of kindness and service from a woman of such stature as her, she told herself, but quickly reminded herself the Lord asked for humble hearts and one could take pride in one's work, but not feel superior for a job well done, as a job well done is done for the Lord.

"Here." She carefully set the tray in front of the sitting, grieving woman. "Eat. I promise you'll love it!"

Roberta glanced at her husband, as if expecting some kind of action from him. Give her approval, perhaps or, most likely, an interjection that would stop her from having to eat.

"Uh, Mrs. Lange," Francisco said. She did not correct him or ask him to call her Martha. "We're so thankful, but Roberta isn't feeling much like eating this past week."

"I think Roberta can speak for herself, Francisco." Martha's tone was sharp and icy.

"I'll eat," Roberta said hastily, her grin strained as she glanced at her husband and then at Martha. "I haven't eaten a thing in two days, and this looks just perfect. Thank you so much."

Roberta grabbed a forkful of mac and cheese, stuck the fork through a few leaves of lettuce, and shoved the whole thing in her mouth. She grinned forcibly at Martha as she chewed.

"It's good, right?"

Roberta nodded, still chewing the mouthful.

"Can you taste the Brie?"

"Dahwut?" Roberta said, her mouth still full.

"The Brie? The cheese I put in the recipe. It gives it that extra creaminess."

"Mmm-hmm," Roberta exclaimed, nodding enthusiastically.

For a moment, she ate in silence, Martha watching over her every bite. Roberta took a drink of iced tea, turned to her, and spoke. "I'm sorry, Martha. I don't mean this to sound rude. You know you're always welcome to visit, but…" She paused, as if carefully choosing each word, "…why are you here?"

Martha was a little taken aback, but simply brushed

it aside in her mind. "I wanted to see how you were doing. I was worried and wanted to check up on you, bring you some food, and see if you needed anything else."

"You didn't have to."

"I did." Martha grabbed her hand in support. "I could never abandon a friend at a time like this."

"A friend?" Roberta said. "Martha, we've barely spoken in years, since your son left kindergarten, other than a polite hello, when we've run into each other."

"Well, I always smiled and said hello back," Martha said, becoming increasingly confused. "Didn't you notice that, you silly woman?"

"I thought you were just being civil. Same as I was."

Martha stared at her for a few moments, inspecting Roberta's face for some sign of insanity or a clue to her being facetious. She finally snorted and smiled. "Oh, stop being silly. Sometimes friends don't talk for a long time, but they are there when it most matters, such as I am, right here, right now. Just like old times, when I used to come pick up Peter, and you would make coffee, and we would sit down and talk like sisters from different mothers."

Roberta's expression went dead serious. "Martha," she said, the earnestness in her voice underlined by her pale, drawn, mourning face. "You were a visitor at my home. I was being courteous. Other than me answering questions about Peter, you did most of the talking."

There had been an edge to Roberta's words, sharp as a hidden blade, which Martha hadn't had the interpersonal skills to sense. Roberta was quickly transitioning from confused to polite to having exhausted her social ability and wanting the intruder to leave.

"Alright," Martha said, still keeping her manners above all else. "I can admit I haven't been the most present friend, but—"

"We're *not* friends." Roberta's death mask of a face was now expressionless, a stiff mannequin face.

A silence stretched forever in that room. The air had turned into thick molasses, and the three of them were suffocating in it.

"I can see you're very affected by what happened to your son. You're not yourself."

"You know nothing about me. You know nothing about my son."

"I know how you must be feeling," Martha said back to her, with pain in her voice. "I understand."

"How?" The word came out like a shard of ice. Roberta put the tray aside and sat up straighter. "How can you possibly know that? Did you raise Gerardo? Did you give birth to Gerardo? Did you carry Gerardo for nine months in your belly?"

"No, but I—"

"Nine months I carried him!"

"*Mi vida*," said Francisco, seeing his wife beginning to lose it.

Martha, sitting on the bed, felt suddenly baffled and terrified, watching Roberta go from one to eleven in seconds. Perhaps, if Martha had been a different person, she would've stayed quiet, excused herself, and left, but she was who she was.

"Roberta, I have a son, I know what it's—"

"Nine months!" The words exploded out of her. All the pent-up grief burst out like the contents of a pressure cooker. "Nine months that felt like a lifetime. When you carry something that long in you, it *becomes* you! Then, we have to either push them out and tear ourselves open, or they cut us open. Then, we wait, for the longest seconds in the fucking universe, just hoping, just praying the next thing we hear is our baby crying, just so we know we're lying there in our own filth and blood, but we did our job right! We stuck the landing! We got them here safely! Time to spend years, and years, worrying about every single threat that could come their way. Is it a flu that's going to take them from us? Is it a car that's gonna run them over because we didn't see it coming? Or is it sudden infant death syndrome?"

"Roberta, my dear friend, there's no need to—"

"Shut up!" She stared at Martha, her face now full of tears, lips trembling with anger and disgust.

"I got so good at taking care of my Gerardo, it made

me a better kindergarten teacher, because I knew their parents were as afraid as I was, so I wanted to make it easier on them, and why? Because you think once they make it past the kindergarten bump, they can take better care of themselves. You think you can relax, but no. There's this thing in your head, '*But what if? But what if? But what if?* Kidnappers, rapists, bullies, drugs, another motherfucking flu!"

"There's no need for that kind of—"

"I said, shut up! You can never relax! You never get to relax! You fear, and you fear, and you fear! You love and you fear! And most parents spend their whole life loving and fearing, and their fears never come true, but mine did, and I would give anything in the universe to continue fearing!"

Roberta scowled at Martha, upper lip trembling and covered with tears and snot that were now flowing freely without the intervention of a tissue.

"I know that fear, Roberta. I know how you feel. I am a mother, too."

"Oh, you know how I feel, do you?" Something pulled at the right corner of Roberta's lip, forming a tremulous, deranged, sarcastic grin. "Last time I checked, Peter is still alive, and you are still destroying his childhood. Something in that house killed my son. Your son is alive, and yet you've always treated him worse than you treat an animal—"

"That's not true, I only discipline him like God—"

"Fuck God!"

"Roberta, *mi vida, por favor!*" Francisco said, in utter shock at his wife's blasphemy, and did the sign of the cross.

"I meant *her* God," she said, pointing her reddened nose at Martha. "Neither our God nor yours saved my son, but mine didn't tell me to treat mine like a slave, like a mongrel. Gerardo was loved." For a moment, her face cracked, as if the anger was gone and weeping would start, but soon, it twisted again into a visage of indignation. "Oh, I remember the belt marks on Peter's arms and legs. I do. I remember how some weren't just red, but purple and black. And yet you still have your son, and I had to see my Gerardo's face, the way it had twisted, the way it appeared. Even dead, he was screaming. Did you see the picture that imbecile, Neal Parham, showed his friends at Cunningham's? No wonder his family's cursed. You have to be soulless to do something like that." Her eyes fixed on Martha with a look of fiery contempt. "I had to see that face in person at the morgue. You treat your son like garbage, and you still have him, but I loved mine and was raising him right. He was going to be a good man, but I had to see my dead son's face *like that* on a cold slab. My only son."

"It doesn't have to be like that!" Martha said, out of nowhere, once more missing her cue to stop and bow out.

"What?" Roberta squinted at her, as if Martha had just become blurry in her eyes.

Martha, knowing this would be her only chance to

say her piece, spoke. "It doesn't have to be that way!" The words came out hurriedly and continued before Roberta had a chance to interject. "Gerardo's death was a tragedy, one that was not meant to happen, but maybe, maybe if you pray to God—"

"What?"

"—maybe, if you renounce your ridiculous religion, those fantasies and fables, and pray to the *true* God—"

"What?"

"Mrs. Lange, please, you're upsetting her."

"—the Lord is real, he's tangible, he's true! He can do wonderful things! Nothing is out of His reach!"

"Get out!" Roberta snarled, a guttural, almost inhuman sound.

Martha's face took on the impassioned countenance of madness only true, unbridled belief could bring to a human face. "I was going to come to you earlier." She brought out a thick, leather-bound book from her tote bag, and held it before her, and caressed it with her palm. "Bring you the word of God, before all of this happened, before that man, Ben Curling, let your son into that house, and—"

"Mrs. Lange, please, leave!"

"—all of this tragedy unfolded."

"I said, get out, you crazy woman!" Roberta hissed. "I will not let you use my son's death to come preach that bullshit in my house!"

"It was my fault!" Martha beat her own chest with a fist, now weeping passionately. "My fault for not having come earlier. My fault for not bringing my friend into the Circle soon enough."

"GET OUT!" Roberta shouted, throwing the tray with her food at Martha, the contents of the plate hitting her blouse, leaving a smear of sticky macaroni and cheese.

Martha took a step back, but she did not stop her proselytizing, interrupted only with a grunt the moment the plate hit her. "Just cast aside that false God of yours, embrace the real God, and he might bless you with another son, one that may replace the one you lost!"

"What did you just say?" Roberta now growled, throwing her covers aside. "Do you think I want to *replace* Gerardo?"

"I didn't mean it that way."

"He was my son!" She slid off the bed.

"*Mi vida*, please, calm down!"

"How dare you?" She stood up. Rage coming out as spit, accompanied by a string of insults in Spanish: "*Puta! Bazofia! Gonorrea! Morronga! Malparida! Pichurria! Lengua viperina!*", which roughly—and not in that order—translated to: "Two-faced, insignificant, badly bred, hypocritical, revolting, insufferable cunt!"

"Roberta, *por favor!*" pleaded Francisco.

While Martha understood Spanish, half of these insults were Colombian, and she was not familiar with them, but she understood enough of them for the message to hit home at full strength. Still, she continued. "There's no need to insult me. I'm trying to help."

"My Gerardo was irreplaceable! He was my life! How dare you suggest I would want another son just to replace him? He was a person. A human being." She reared back. "Unlike YOU!"

She pounced on Martha, a feral beast out of control. Both women fell to the floor. Roberta straddled her and began choking her.

Martha was in shock for a few seconds. She tried to push Roberta off but found her to be stronger.

Francisco ran toward his wife, but as he tried to put his arms around her, she turned and bit down on his arm, having completely lost control. Francisco screamed and stood up, clutching his bleeding arm. He took two steps back and tripped on the food tray that was lying on the floor and fell on his ass. The back of his head hit the solid wood footboard of the bed. He rolled in pain on the floor, groaning and clutching his head.

"I'm going to do Peter a favor," Roberta said, her hands clamped around Martha's throat. "I'm going to do that poor, sweet, kind boy a favor, and I'm going to remove you from his life before you do to him what that house did to my Gerardo."

Martha's panicked blue eyes met hers from a face reddened with strain.

Roberta's mind was in a wrathful haze. Her vision had shrunken to a small circle in which all she saw was the face of the woman she was trying to kill. Indeed, she was trying to kill her. She had tormented her own son for a long time and had now insulted the memory of her beloved Gerardo.

She could remember the bruises on Peter's skin, the scrapes on his knees, the sad and broken face of a child who had put up with abuse for too long, despite his young age. For a long time, she'd considered going to the authorities about it, but her husband and other people in town kept advising her not to.

No more. She would be a passive coward no more.

In her mind loomed the face of Gerardo, her baby, his tiny crying face as they handed him to her, swaddled in blankets, and she remembered falling in love with him immediately. She saw him as he grew, as he changed, as he became his own person. She saw him smiling; she saw him playing. Birthdays, Christmases, vacations, moments of joy that for twelve years they had shared as a family. How could this monster believe anything could replace the person her son had become? She saw Gerardo in high school, saw him graduating valedictorian, saw him in college, and, later, married with children of his own. Finally, she saw his face on the morgue's cold metal slab. The bulging eyes, the twisted mouth, the broken capillaries all over his pallid skin, the clawed hands—the image that had killed those future memories that would never come to pass.

She could still hear that voice, the voice of reason, trying to make her realize she was about to kill another human being, and there was no turning back from this. But that voice was far away, lost at sea, muffled, lost in the haze and the loud roar that had filled her head from the anger, the indignation, and the unfairness of it all. This woman, this ghoul, still had a son. Roberta no longer did. It was an affront to every belief she'd ever held dear.

It was at that point she realized something had changed. Martha's appearance had shifted from red and terrified to composed and serene. Her blue eyes stared coldly back at her. Why wasn't she scared? Why wasn't she feeling the lack of oxygen the pressure of her hands was bringing upon her?

Her strength left her as a chill went up her spine, and she let go of the strange woman, and she sat there, straddling her, speechless, mesmerized.

"I thought you were my friend," Martha said in a calm but accusatory voice.

The words filled Roberta with unspeakable dread.

"Get off me," Martha said. A flat, emotionless command.

The impulse to get away from the woman as quickly as she could made her spring up to a standing position and take two steps back. Her eyes shot a glimpse to her left. Martha's right hand was still clinging to the leather-bound book. The book had a strange symbol engraved on its cover: a long, jagged, vertical line with two horizontal lines across it, both slightly angled upward from left to right. From the lower tip of the upper line started a half-circle, like a sickle going downward, until it crossed the vertical line.

Her breathing became deep, and she was suddenly aware of everything around her. Gone was the tunnel vision from the raging haze, and now she could see Martha stand, and she could hear her husband groaning in pain behind her.

"I was wrong about you," Martha said, not taking her terrible gaze away from hers, the book now hugged against her bosom. "Your family wouldn't have been welcomed into the Circle. I thought you were worthy of the Lord's gift. I was so sure, but I can see now you and your husband are lesser people. Lesser people who spawned an even lesser son."

Roberta tried to rage at this but found she couldn't.

She couldn't move.

Spit came out of her angry, snarling lips, but she couldn't move.

"I offered you a gift from the Lord. A new son. A new life. Yet, you dare throw that offer back at me, the same way you threw the food I brought you." Martha regarded the spilled food, the plate, the fork, and the glass, then turned to Roberta. "You say you don't want another son?"

Tears were now spilling down Roberta's cheeks. She was terrified.

She. Couldn't. Move.

"Well, I came here today to grant you a gift, and I'll do just that. I'll give you what you want." She stared into Roberta's eyes. "Pick up the fork."

"N—" Before she could finish the one syllable, her body bent down against her will and grabbed the fork like a child would hold their first eating utensil—full fist around the handle with the tines pointing down. She stood back up and held the fork in front of her, as if to get Martha's approval. "I'm sorry," Roberta whimpered. "I'm sorry. Please."

Without saying a word, Martha fixed her gaze on her abdomen, and with no hesitation, Roberta lifted her shirt with her left hand and plunged the fork a few inches under her belly button.

She did this once.

Again.

Again.

She was horrified to see the bright red blood running down her pajama bottoms. She didn't scream. She couldn't scream. Martha wasn't letting her scream, but she was feeling every single sting of pain as she cut her lower abdomen open with a tool not made for cutting. The fourth stab buried the fork all the way in, almost to the handle. Her face was red, her eyes were bloodshot with tears, and no matter how hard she tried, she could not scream.

Roberta wiggled the utensil left and right, left and right, opening up and widening the wound, forcefully cutting through skin, fat, muscle, and ligaments. She wanted to faint, but she couldn't faint, either. She was not allowed to. She was not allowed to move. She was not allowed to scream. She was not allowed to faint.

When the cut was several inches long, Roberta reached into the wound, first with two, then three, then four of her fingers, and finally, her entire hand. She could feel the air from her lungs empty in a scream, but what came out was a weak exhalation.

Air without a voice.

Francisco eventually recovered from the pain and removed his hands from his head, noticing they were covered in blood. Although, the fact he was conscious indicated the injury wasn't too serious, perhaps a minor concussion. He shook away the dizziness and confusion long enough to see his wife from behind, standing in a puddle of blood. There was a fork in her right hand—*Is that blood on the tines?*—and her left hand was doing something in the general area of her abdomen.

Before he could make sense of this, he watched in paralyzing horror as his wife pulled out *something* from her abdomen, something he couldn't identify as anything else but a torn portion of flesh. She tossed it to the floor with a revolting splat before reaching *inside* her abdomen again, only to pull out another bloody, bulbous mass of tissue that had something like fleshy tubes, with ends that appeared she'd ripped them off whatever they'd been attached to.

His wife stood there, silently, with this pink, purplish lump in her trembling hand, dripping blood into the expanding puddle. Right before he could scream her name, the shape of a woman—Martha, with her big bag hanging from her shoulder—walked past his field of vision heading toward the bedroom door and saying: "Call 911 if you don't want her to bleed out."

The moment Martha disappeared, Roberta's body crumpled to the floor, and she screamed raucous screams. She convulsed in pain and became more and more covered in red as she rolled in the blood on the floor.

He regarded her and, only for a second, a hysterical, unwitting giggle escaped his throat, and he put both hands over his mouth to stifle it. The scene before his eyes was so disgusting, so incongruously wrong—his wife rolling on the floor, screaming and kicking her legs at the red puddle, like a child having a tantrum. The thought assailed him again, and the laughter escaped him, now uncontrollably.

Whether caused by shock, by cumulative tragedy, by temporary insanity, or a run-of-the-mill concussion, he started laughing, and he couldn't stop. His laughter sounded painful. It sounded like screams. Like it was rending his insides. His eyes showed terror most pure, but his drooling mouth laughed, and his laughter joined the screams of his wife.

He thought he had seen the most horrifying thing the day he saw his son's twisted, dead, screaming face, but the image of his wife rolling and kicking on the bloody floor after ripping out her own uterus would fill his nightmares until the day he died.

If this was going to be his life going forward, why not laugh?

Peter ran his fingers over the banquette's upholstery, licked his lips, and said, "Are Gerardo's parents going to be alright?"

"No," his mother said. "How could they?"

She turned her head to him. "They lost something that cannot be replaced."

His mother's mind was working, her eyes shifting. Something had happened to Mother that had shaken her. He didn't remember a time when he'd seen her like this. She'd always been unflappable, solid, monolithic, but this day she appeared frail and tired, and even to his inexperienced eyes, Mother had become something she'd never been—she was doubtful. As if to confirm this, her next words were shaky, almost teary.

"I think God can do anything." It sounded like a personal affirmation. She caressed the leather-bound book on her lap.

I think? Peter wondered if he'd heard her correctly.

"I don't believe, however," she added, "that all His marvels are things the human heart would want, even if they come from Him." She wiped at her nose with the back of an index finger, almost as if in a daydream. "There are things even I wouldn't want." Her eyes went again to the flames, and tears welled in them.

"Mother?" he asked, now truly worried. Those words, if his mother had taught him anything, were blasphemous and wrong. Was this some trap? A trick? A test?

"There are things I'd never want God to replace, even if he offered." She gave him another look, her expression pleading. "Promise me something, Peter."

"Yes, Mother. Anything."

"Promise me you will never set foot in the Vanek House. Promise me you will stop going there."

"I never go there, Mot—"

"Don't lie to me," she cut him off quickly. "I have never lied to you, so don't lie to me. I know you go there. I know you sit at the edge of Etenia Creek and stare at that house. I have seen you meander around it, sneaking through the grass, trying to take a peek through the blocked windows. I once saw you running out of the front lawn when Ben Curling's dogs began barking at you. Tell me the truth now."

Peter didn't hesitate to reply. Mother rarely gave chances to retract one's statements, so he wouldn't waste this one, especially when it was so obvious she knew. "Fine, Mother. Yes, I've been to the Vanek place. I'm sorry I lied. I didn't want to worry you. It just calls to me, you know? I wander around it and I make up stories in my head. Ghost stories. Scary stories. They keep me entertained. Mrs. Burton says I have a very active imagination. She says I should express it more, because she thinks I'm very creative, but I tell her I can't, because God doesn't like that. So, I just keep the stories in my head."

He was expecting her to slap him. Once for lying to her, and twice for imagining fictional stories, which were lies, too. Instead, she said, "Good boy. You did good, standing up to that teacher. She doesn't know what's good for you." She squinted straight at him. "Is that all?"

He nodded. "Yes, Mother. That's all there is."

She sighed, as if in relief, or—in his paranoid mind—forcing herself to believe him. "Good. Promise me you will never approach that place again. Go around it. Don't linger close to it, and above all things, *never* enter that house. Is that clear? Never."

"Yes, Mother. It's a promise." He hesitated. "May I ask a question?"

"You may," she said, and leaned back in her chair. The shadows from the fireplace played with the contours of her cheeks, brow, nose, and lips.

"Why are you worried about me going there?"

She sighed again. "Because today I saw what would become of me if I lost you. That dead boy's mother had been an inch from losing her mind. To the point, all it took was the slightest push for her to go completely over the edge of insanity. I saw myself in that woman. Peter, I cannot lose you."

"Why, Mother?"

"Why?" Her expression showed the very question was offensive. "Because I love you, you stupid boy. You are my life. I love you, and I will never let anything harm you. Ever."

Peter sat in silence, his fingers playing around on the cushioned surface of the banquette's upholstery. Never, not once, had his mother said those words to him. Tears welled up in his eyes, but he did not actually cry. He allowed himself to feel moved by these unfamiliar words his mother was telling him, and tears were something he'd always associated with pain and punishment, so he allowed himself to feel joy.

His mother loved him.

Chapter Ten

Angela Schaefer

BEFORE

The story of how Angela Elyse Schaefer (Undergraduate) and Robert Preston Novak (Psychiatry Professor) became an item would've made a reader of cheap romance squeal with delight. They began their relationship as acquaintances, but over time, it grew into a friends-with-benefits arrangement, which later deepened into something more.

Angela had been a precocious teenager. She'd lived fast, fully, and unapologetically. She'd dated on occasion, but her casual encounters had been far more numerous. She was the kind of girl boys circled—like sharks—unaware the petite teenager with the sweet, infectious smile was a megalodon.

Bobby had been an anomaly, though. A glitch in her usual standards. He was ten years older than her, clean cut, blond—she'd never liked blonds—not fat but thick-bodied, and he was an absolute dork. Yet there was something so disarmingly adorable about him. He somehow ninjaed his way into becoming her first proper boyfriend, the sneaky bastard. The fact they were officially in a relationship had crept up on her, and before she knew it, they'd spent nine years together; nine absolutely wonderful years.

It had been a slow process. They had peripherally been in each other's lives forever, considering Bobby and Nadine had been close friends since middle school, but Angela had been just a toddler at the time. He was a constant presence in her home during her childhood and her teenage years, but had little to no interaction. Why would they? She was basically a child back then.

That changed when she attended college at Willamette. She was an undergraduate and intended to attend law school, and he had a job teaching at the university. He spent four days a week on campus and drove back to White Harbor during the weekends.

All Angela had needed to know he was interested was the dumb expression on his face when she approached him in the cafeteria.

With a playful lilt to her voice, she said, "Hi, Bobby! Long time, no see!"

He was speechless, shocked for a few seconds, gawking at her. It was as if he was seeing her for the first time.

Angela knew the look well.

He finally spat out a clumsy, "Oh…hi!"

Like a fish on a hook, she thought with a salacious grin. She just needed to let him think it was swimming away with the worm before firmly reeling him in.

Her intentions, though, soon hit an unexpected wall.

If she'd taken the time to know Bobby during the years he frequented her home, she wouldn't have confused the geeky shirts, the heavy metal, and the video games, with the cliché of a basement nerd that would jump into bed with any girl with low enough standards to have him.

Her miscalculation was that she didn't count on Bobby being a gentleman. Even if he was obviously attracted to her, he maintained clear boundaries. Angie wouldn't turn eighteen until four months after that first conversation, which meant Bobby would not lay a hand on her. No matter how much she tried, or how much she figuratively threw herself at him, Bobby was swift at dodging, and this only made her want him more.

Finally, the day came.

When the candles were blown out on her birthday brownies—a result of her friends forgetting to buy a cake—and the party had ended, a slightly drunk Angie phoned Bobby and, without beating around the bush, said, "You're taking me to dinner tomorrow."

"Oh, am I?"

"Yes."

"Why is that?"

"Because you didn't come to my birthday party. I invited you."

"I didn't think it would be appropriate. Your sister is one of my best friends. I'm much older than you, and I'm sure some of your friends are in my classes, so I'd stick out like a sore thumb." He paused. The silence was awkward on his end only—Angie loved listening to his arrhythmic breathing. He continued: "I sent you a gift and a card, though. Did you like them?"

"You sent me a tank top. An old, black tank top. A used, old, black tank top...in a frame."

"You don't know what it is?" He sounded surprised. "I thought you might."

"Well. It's framed, so I'm guessing it's a collecti…"

She stopped talking.

"What?" he asked.

"Oh, my God… You're kidding me, right?"

"No. That's one of the tank tops worn by Linda Hamilton in *Terminator 2*. It was one of my favorite movies as a kid, and you've always loved sci-fi and horror, so I thought you might appreciate it. Remember when I told you, a few months back, you looked like a young Sarah Connor? You laughed and said you didn't, but totally blushed. *That* told me you were familiar with the movie, so I took a shot."

"I don't know what to say." She left a too-long-for-comfort silence. "Except…this is so…*creepy*, and you're a *fucking perv* because I was underage a few months ago, and we didn't have a relationship close enough for you to be giving me expensive movie collectibles like this, you *freak*."

"I'm sorry. So, you're saying you don't like it?"

She left another long silence.

"I love it," she said, "and you're taking me out to dinner tomorrow, regardless, alright? You didn't come to my party. I feel personally insulted."

"Sounds fine. I'll come by at seven. *Hasta la vista, baby!*"

Another awkward silence followed. Felt by both of them this time.

"Ew…gross," she said. "You need to work on that creepy approach, man," she laughed. "Make that eight. Nobody goes out at seven. God, you're old."

That first night was more fun than it had any right to be. Bobby was as dorky and awkward as she was sure he'd be on a date, but he was so delightful. They laughed, and discussed bad movies, and went for a walk after dinner, and simply talked for hours, almost making up for the years they hadn't even acknowledged each other.

There was, however, one thing that stood out among everything they did that night, and it was that after four months of wanting to fuck Bobby into unconsciousness, she had not wasted her opportunity.

And, oh dear God, Bobby's dick.

One day, while sitting at the bar at Cunningham's, Jess—being as blunt as usual—casually told her people were talking about the sounds that came from Bobby's house whenever Angie visited him. The pounding, the moaning, the screaming, the growling.

"People think the damn place is haunted, or someone's getting killed in there," Jess said. "So, one night, I pass by the place and, what do I hear if it's not my dear friend Angie crying out like a possessed woman, and my old buddy Bobby growling like a rabid beast? Seriously, girl? *That* good?"

At first, Angie grew warm in the face. She nodded yes, to her best friend's wide-mouthed astonishment, but Jess grinned mischievously and said, "Oh, you better give me details, you dirty slut, or I swear you're not welcome in my bar anymore!"

Angie remembered laughing hard, taking a sip of her drink, and going into every minute detail of Bobby Novak and his extraordinary dick, a flawless one-size-fits-all wonder of phallic engineering.

It wasn't just big, she told Jess. The shape of it, the girth of it, the weight of it, the *proportions*. If there was a Fibonacci Ratio, but for dicks, it would be based on Bobby Novak's dick; it would be called the Novak proportion, the Golden Dick proportion. It was perfect in every way; the

190

way it rubbed against her, the way it fit inside her, the way it felt in her hand.

After giving it some thought, she realized the notion was juvenile and ridiculous, but if she was honest with herself, it had been her motivation to stay for the first three months. Bobby's dick was a thing of beauty. She couldn't give it up. It was addictive. Sure, Bobby was sweet and smart and fun, but she'd found him kind of excessively geeky, even for a young woman who considered *herself* excessively geeky. He was kind of long-winded, and sometimes even a little tedious, but—Jesus-on-a-flying-saucer—she *loved* Bobby's dick.

There were all the *other* things he did to her as well, of course.

Bobby, unlike most men, knew it wasn't all about putting it in and pumping away like a piston. No. Bobby knew the external areas, the middle areas, all the right spots. The circular rubbing, the flicking at the right angle, the alternating between the tip of the tongue and the whole tongue. He even had a technique she dubbed "the @ sign" that made her cling to the mattress as if it were about to take off flying into space with her on it.

Bobby was a master of his craft. He was like those artists that can paint vistas on a grain of rice, or build an entire galleon inside a bottle, or make a few brush strokes on a canvas that seem abstract at first, but evolve into the perfect orchid, a drop of moisture on a petal and all. Bobby was an artist, a connoisseur.

This had only made her want to keep up with him because she had a reputation to defend—she would not lie down and let him take all the credit. No way. She would show him she could give as much as she could get, and she showed him a couple of techniques of her own he'd not been expecting and which made him holler with unbridled pleasure.

As she got drunker, with Jess encouraging her, she went into this business pitch of taking a cast mold of Bobby's dick and selling "The Bobby" (registered trademark). They would become millionaires in a year and retire to Italy or somewhere else in Europe, but she tore down her own proposal for two reasons: One, even if she could replicate the shape, she didn't think she could replicate the "feel", how it was both rock hard, but sort of cushy, for comfort. Two, she was selfish and didn't want to share.

As she got even drunker, she stopped talking about Bobby's Burj Khalifa of a dick, and began talking about how no man had ever been so attentive, how he treated her like there had never been a more important woman in history, how he worshipped the tips of her fingers with soft kisses, and how, when she got a cold or the flu, he was always there to take care of her, not minding if he caught the flu as well, just to make sure she wasn't sick alone.

She talked about how Bobby was communicative and always involved her in decisions that impacted them both, how he valued her intelligence, and above all, although she was studying to become a lawyer, he'd always encouraged her artistic side. She had sometimes dabbled in oil painting, and the results, she admitted, were an affront to the concept of art itself—or at best, mediocre—but he'd shown her how therapeutic this was for her.

She showed Jess a picture Bobby had taken of her one morning when he'd woken up and noticed her painting by the window, the sunlight shining down on her as she sat in the square of light that formed on the floor. She was wearing nothing but the shirt Bobby had worn the previous night. He'd quietly taken his phone in his hand and snapped the picture without her noticing. She had been painting him while he slept, completely nude, but tastefully covered with the sheets.

It was while showing Jess that picture that it came out: the phrase she hadn't yet told Bobby, but which she wasn't able to contain anymore.

"I love him."

While remembering that moment, alone in her bed, a tear left a thin wet streak across Angela's face, not making it to the pillow because it had pooled in her ear.

"I love him," she had repeated, to Jess's astonishment.

She loved Bobby Novak.

Bobby Novak, who had been her ex-boyfriend now for five years.

Bobby Novak, who hadn't come to see her for weeks after she'd returned to White Harbor, bedridden, ugly, corpse-like, puking and shitting herself as she waited for death.

She loved Bobby Novak, and Bobby Novak hadn't come to see her one last time.

Had those nine years meant nothing? she wondered during those endless days and nights in which she waited in her lonely bedroom for him to visit.

Four mint-green walls delimited her sad little kingdom. Her bed, a dubious throne, where she didn't sit but lay, as dust and cobwebs accumulated underneath. The sky above her kingdom was made of square, white ceiling tiles, whose only hint of color was given by cobwebs near the joints and the cornices, which had turned gray, giving her the feeling that every white cloud had a gray lining.

Her closest servant was a bedside table on casters, which often held food or medicine, neither of which seemed appealing to her. Her royal carriage was a wheelchair, which sat forgotten in a corner from the moment she figured out it was faster to stumble or crawl toward the bathroom than asking to be sat on the wheelchair and taken there.

She was queen and ruler of everything her eyes beheld, which wasn't much to speak of. Her gaze would travel to her right, over the zigzagging pattern of her carpet's gray and brown fields, toward her kingdom's northern bounds. There, two tall, white closet doors guarded a haunted forest of memories of dresses, and suits, and shoes she could no longer wear.

If she followed the pattern across the fields to her left, her land came to a stop at the bathroom door, her southern limit. Beyond that passage lay bogs of nausea, putrid smells, humiliation, and pain. Many a time she'd been forced to kneel there, emptying the contents of her stomach as tribute to the ruler of that accursed land, who did not recognize her authority.

A single window behind her headboard prevented her from ever seeing the sunlight from her throne, only a reflection of it on the wall that blocked her view of the world to the West. It also cast a rectangular glare on the TV screen on that wall—her only source of entertainment—where jesters and mummers waited on equal-sized rectangle boxes for her to point her scepter at one of them to make them dance. Here, in the lonely moments of the day, her thoughts sometimes turned darker than she'd like them to, and she wandered into them as if they were a thick forest sunlight couldn't penetrate. It was the only thing she could do aside from watching whatever generic streaming content was available, which became less appealing with each passing day.

She spent her time cycling through streaming apps, all of which looked the same to her by now. Nadine was paying for her to have as many options as she could to keep her entertained, only for her to lie here and use her remote as a shovel to dig through tons of garbage, sometimes finding a rare little gem hidden underneath the pile, and those were getting rarer every day. All she saw at this point were rectangles with titles, shouting, "Look! Look! Content! Content! Consume! CONSUME!" It gave her an odd feeling of gladness she would no longer be here by the time the whole industry collapsed in on itself and the world went back to shadow puppet theater in caves and got the entire cycle started again.

There were no mirrors in her bedroom—she'd had them all removed. One had been on her vanity table, which she sold. The other had been a full-length mirror, in front of which she used to get dressed, mixing and matching clothes and accessories to go out for drinks, or a hot date, or a courtroom appointment. Mirrors were a thing of the past for her. They were relics of a time when those things mattered. When they were options. What was the need for mirrors now? She'd never put on make-up, or a fine dress, or a suit again.

She was the youngest female lawyer of her graduating class to make partner at her firm. She would also soon be the youngest female lawyer of her graduating class to die of gastric cancer. Next time she wore make-up, it would be someone else putting it on her, as well as dressing her, after stuffing cotton balls in her mouth to make her cheeks seem full, gluing her eyes, sewing her mouth shut, fixing her hair.

She'd feel embarrassed if some ghostly version of herself remained in the world, which could witness her dolled-up corpse being put on display like Sleeping Beauty in front of her friends and family. She pictured a ride, like at Disneyland, in which they'd pass by on carts as sad music played and animatronic people and forest critters wept for the dead lawyer princess.

She hated thinking Bobby might see her like that. Just imagining it made her wish for a closed casket.

Well, what if he decides not to attend our funeral? the insecure part of her inner self said.

Of course he'll go, the reasonable part of her inner self replied. *He has to.*

Not necessarily, Insecure Angie said. *Don't you remember right before our last date? He only showed up as a last-minute decision.*

Well, yeah! answered Reasonable Angie. *That's proof right there. We thought he wouldn't show up, and he did.*

Angela remembered how she had mentally braced herself for Bobby not to show up for their farewell date five years earlier. She'd decided to move to Portland when offered a job at McCullough, Larson, and Sharpe, one of the most renowned firms in the state. Bobby took the news she'd be leaving as well as expected: the man had been a wreck.

They agreed to go out on one last date, "The Angie

and Bobby Greatest Hits Final Tour: Once More, With Feeling!" But Bobby was such an emotional mess, she could have put money on him not showing up, on getting that one final text: *I'm sorry, I can't.*

He did show up, Reasonable Angie insisted.

They went out that night, agreeing not to see it as a breakup, but a postponement, until he finally worked everything out to leave White Harbor and move to Portland with her. After all, it wasn't that far, only about sixty-five miles. In the meantime, he could drive there whenever he wanted.

We knew the truth, though. Insecure Angie would not let it go so easily. *We knew, even as we discussed it—dorky good-guy Bobby Novak would never leave White Harbor. He's too used to it. It's his home, it's part of him. If life is a role-playing game, Bobby's a Non-Playable Character, the generic townsperson, and if by some unearthly miracle he ever moves out, he will never be happy someplace else, and we've always wanted him to be happy, haven't we?*

It had been obvious to the two of them. Sure, he could drive to Portland and see her there. Sure, she'd come visit White Harbor once or twice a year, but it wouldn't be sustainable. Neither of them was built for long-distance relationships. Eventually, it would start feeling like two strangers traveling a long distance for a booty call. Two people imposing their presence for a few days on the other's personal space and routine.

A routine they would no longer be a part of.

Angela decided for the two of them. It would be their last date. No argument about it. One last night together. Bobby was older, but he was more sensitive, so she would try not to break the illusion the long-distance thing might work out. After that night, though, she planned to find excuses, or be too busy, or have no room in her calendar, until he finally gave up and moved on. Something, however, told her making those excuses would be unnecessary. Something told her Bobby also knew this was the end. It was a silent understanding between them.

Another decision she made was, if it was going to be their last night together, there would be no morose, heartbroken lovemaking, with pauses for tears. No goddamn way.

Instead, she fucked his brains out.

She rode Bobby's remarkable dick with fierce, maniacal intensity, until he'd cried out loud enough to wake the neighbors. Four times they'd gone at it that night, and she was sure, even now, Bobby could still feel her on top of him, her legs clinging to his hips like a clamp and grinding on his white, freckled skin until it turned red with friction.

They said their goodbyes the next morning. They kissed. Neither of them wept, not in front of the other, at least, and that was a mercy.

She said goodbye to White Harbor, and five years had passed in the blink of an eye. How fleeting was the past when you felt the end of your life so near. They had talked on the phone a few times and gone for coffee twice—once when she'd been in town for the holidays, and once after her mother's funeral. After that, she decided she didn't want to come to White Harbor anymore.

The cancer had other plans, though. It forced her to move back from Portland, puking at least five times a day, forty pounds skinnier, and with a death sentence confirmed by her usual doctor, as well as by the second and third opinions she'd sought.

Bobby hadn't even called. For weeks, she remained in bed, her body racked with vomiting, crying with whatever moisture she could spare for tears.

We should call him, Reasonable Angie said. *It's better to know.*

We have to respect his decision, Insecure Angie said. *Even if it hurts. It's better this way. He shouldn't see the horror we've become. We should let him keep the memory of the woman we used to be.*

How will that help?

It won't.

With a weak, trembling digit, Angela wiped away the tear on the left side of her face. She felt both parts of her mind grow further apart, to the point it didn't feel like two parts of herself but two completely separate people talking to each other.

200

I think Nadine knows why he won't visit, but she doesn't want to tell me.

Why would she do that?

Maybe he found someone else. Maybe that's what my sister doesn't want to tell me. He found someone else, and his new girlfriend isn't comfortable with him coming to see his ex-girlfriend, the one with the sex-positive reputation. The slut. The whore. The practice hole for every boy in town.

Stop this. You're only hurting yourself.

There were more tears now. More tears than one finger could wipe away, and she let them roll down both sides of her face in rivulets, pooling in her ears and spilling over, soaking her hair.

It's my fault. It's my fault for leaving. I could've been a small-town lawyer, and a damned good one, but I was too ambitious. I chose my career, success, money. I left him alone for years, and another woman won his heart.

She gasped as another thought flashed in her brain. Insecure Angie had grabbed hold of her pain and now ran with it.

What if it's a man? I hadn't even considered that!

Oh, c'mon, how could you be so stupid? interjected Reasonable Angie. *If Bobby was gay, we would know. We have enough evidence to the contrary.*

You're right. It's settled then. He met a woman; she won his heart, and it's all my fault.

Maybe. It almost felt like Reasonable Angie had admitted defeat and joined Insecure Angie in her despondence. *Maybe you're right. Maybe it's* our *fault.*

The dark thoughts kept boiling and swelling inside her. How could he have not come? How could he have abandoned her so completely? What could she have possibly done to him to not even deserve a call when she was dying?

She felt so hurt, so humiliated, so furious, so worthless, and with this darkness in her mind, she weakened and fell into a restless sleep.

NOW

"CONSUME!" shouted the rectangles on the TV screen.

She didn't feel like consuming that day. She felt like thinking. Especially because something strange had caught her attention. There were trees in the backyard and beyond the house's fence. Many trees with many birds that sang all day. They made the quiet moments just a tad less quiet, and prevented them from becoming completely devoid of sound, which was a concept that made her uneasy.

Silence.

Her life had always been anything but silent and static, so even in these moments, having the birds outside sing-ing helped her feel like there was life out there. By listening to it, she was connected to it, and therefore, still alive. But the birds had gone quiet all at once, which wouldn't have been anything of notice if they hadn't suddenly started chirp-ing again, only to once more fall into tomblike, disquieting silence.

If Nadine hadn't been late with her lunch today, she might have missed this, but she'd been on the phone for a while with Peter, and that had delayed lunch. She'd been alone at precisely this moment to notice the phenomenon. The birds had gone quiet, and her connection to the world outside slipped away with every soundless second, pushing her mind toward the dark thoughts.

Nope. Not doing this anymore. That's over.

She wasn't letting the dark thoughts take hold any-more. She had promised, and for almost six months, she'd kept that promise—most of the time.

One night, over six months earlier, she'd been es-pecially weak from not being able to keep any food down, and the intravenous nutrients weren't making her feel better. Feeling spent, she closed her eyes and dozed off, only to wake up to a strange keening sound and a frightful pressure on her right hand, which felt as if it was about to crush its frail bones.

Her eyes opened to a blurred world. Her hand was

stuck. She pulled, but it wouldn't move. Before her eyes, outlined against the dim light coming through the open door from the hall outside, was a terrifying, dark shape. It was a small, stumpy creature, shorter but bulkier than a child, and what appeared to be its head barely rose over the edge of her bed. The head approached her fingers. She felt breath coming from a mouth. Steaming breath coming from what she pictured to be jaws, primed and ready to bite her hand, which she now realized was wet and covered in a slimy substance.

Is that drool? Blood?

She was too groggy to tell, and too weak to scream or break free from the monster's grip, which was strong despite its small size.

Her chest heaved with panicked breaths. She inhaled as deeply as she could. Wanted to scream, despite a sore throat and strained vocal cords from the day's constant vomiting. That didn't matter. She *had* to scream; she had to call for help.

She opened her mouth.

She felt…*lips?*…on her, and whatever scream had been inside her, rushing to come out, vanished.

The lips delicately kissed the tips of her fingers, with tenderness and care. It was almost as if her hand were made of mist that had mysteriously taken shape, and any sudden movement would make it dissipate. Yet the grip was firm, desperate, as if a drowning person were clinging to her hand as she pulled them out of the water.

Her vision cleared a little more. Her eyes adjusted to the shadows and the dim light from the hall. The shape was not a short creature, but a kneeling person—a kneeling man—who was sobbing as he softly kissed the tips of her fingers. With enormous effort, she used the last of the deep breath she had meant to form into a scream, and barely mustered the strength to whisper, "Bobby?"

At the sound of her voice, the figure started convulsing into uncontrollable sobs and wet mumbling that sounded like the words, "I'm sorry," over and over.

Minutes later, after composing himself, Bobby turned on the light and sat beside her on the bed. Even after all that time, she'd left that side of the bed vacant, and she'd never even paused to consider why.

As it turned out, just like she'd been apprehensive of him seeing her turned into literally half the woman she'd been before she left town, he'd been afraid of her seeing him so incapable, and so useless, and so impotent to help her.

"It was something I couldn't fix with chicken noodle soup, a couple of blankets, and streaming movies for a few days," Bobby said.

"Well," she said weakly, "chicken noodle soup, blankets, and streaming movies are pretty much the sum of my entire existence at this point. So, you've been missing out on aaaall this." She weakly raised a hand and moved it in front of her, gesturing toward her mint-green room. Her lonely little kingdom. She turned her shaking head toward him, and a weak smile touched her lips.

"I'm so sorry. I should've been here. I should've actually been *there*."

"Where? In Portland? Why? We would've ended up back here, anyway."

"You wouldn't have had to go through it alone, the diagnosis, the sickness, the move."

"Maybe, but at least you were lucky to miss today's puking session. I felt like the girl from *The Exorcist*, just spewing pea soup all over the bathroom. Don't go in there. It's traumatizing, it might break you. I'm fairly sure my head spun from the vomit pressure. Looked like a garden sprinkler on high."

She smiled again.

Bobby chuckled, and to her surprise, leaned in and kissed her. There was so much love in that kiss she felt capable of standing from the bed, and walking, and skipping, and twirling, and dancing.

Gazing at her with a smile, he said, "You're beautiful."

"I didn't brush my teeth after the last time I puked."

"I know." He gave her a grossed-out smile, and the both of them burst out laughing, until Angie placed her hand over her stomach and groaned in pain, though still struggling to contain her chuckles.

She tilted her head to one side, rested it on his arm, and said, "Stay."

And he stayed.

While Nadine would not allow Bobby to move Angie into his own house, and accepted no argument in favor of it, she gave Bobby a key to the house so he could come and go as he pleased.

Every morning, he would kiss Angie before leaving to take the ferry and go to work at the psychiatric hospital on Lighthouse Rock. Nadine had gotten permission to move all her classes to the afternoon, so she would watch her in the mornings, make her lunch, and then a nurse would watch over her in the afternoon. Bobby would come in the evening and bring her dinner—usually some kind of liquid stock with something soft for her stomach—and feed her.

They'd sit down and talk. And talk and talk and talk. Then watch one of the sci-fi, horror, or fantasy movies they loved, and fall asleep together. He was there to hand her pain pills, and he was there to carry her to the bathroom when she got sick, or to bring her a bedpan when the vomit came too quickly for her to stand up. Despite everything, he smiled, and he kissed her, and he loved her, even if she saw herself as the ugliest creature on Earth.

Against all odds, the three months the doctor had

given her stretched into four, into five, into six. She didn't know how much Bobby's presence had helped—people said those who feel loved and happy are prone to feeling healthier, and she was inclined to believe them.

She had no delusions about recovering, though. She was still going to die. She knew this, but now, she would enjoy her last days instead of watching the hours grimly count down to the inevitable.

Bobby or Nadine occasionally sat her in a wheelchair and rolled her out to the backyard, where she could feel the sun, and she could once again paint her mediocre paintings, and she could feel alive, at least. Yes, she still felt her body withering away, but not as quickly and not as painfully.

They had even begun making love again. It was different. Less frenetic, gentler, but just as wonderful as she remembered. What had been moans and hollers had turned into whispers, exclamations of pleasure, and deep breathing that accompanied long gazes into each other's eyes.

"I have a request," she said one night to Bobby. They had been sitting on the bed watching *The Return of the King*. The lights in the room were off, and the screen's glow flickered on their faces. Bobby gave her an inquisitive glance. "When it's clear that it's time. You know…my time?"

He nodded gravely at her.

"I want to watch these with you one last time."

"These what? These movies? *The Lord of the Rings*?"

A small smile tugged at the corners of her lips as she nodded. She could feel how her movements had become less clumsy. She had put on a few pounds, and the color had returned to her cheeks since Bobby had been there with her.

"The Extended Editions!" She pointed a warning finger at him. "God help you if you put on the theatrical ones!"

"I wouldn't do that." He sounded genuinely wounded at the suggestion. "I'm not a monster."

"Good," she said with a nod. "I've always liked that conversation between Gandalf and Pippin when it seems the battle is lost," she sighed with dreamy eyes. "About how death is just another path we all must take. I like the imagery, you know? This gray curtain of rain rolling back, and then you see it…"

She peered up at him with anticipation.

Bobby chuckled, and in his face, there was so much love it made her feel her heart would explode.

"What? Gandalf?" said Bobby, doing his best Billy Boyd as Pippin impression. "See what?"

"White shores," she said in a dreamy tone, reverting to her normal voice, "and fields of green stretching as far as the eye can see, sun rising over all."

"Well, that ain't too shabby." Bobby's voice broke.

Angela turned to look at him with a raised eyebrow. "That ain't too shabby?" she said in an amused tone. "You sound like bootleg subtitles."

"Why? You were paraphrasing too!" Bobby giggled softly. "Did I ruin the moment?"

Angela regarded him in silence.

"No." She slid down the bed to lay her head on his chest, her voice breaking, too. "You're here."

The singing of birds reached her ears again, pulling her out of her memories. Tears of gladness welled up in her eyes. She was connected to the world again. She was part of the living, and the dark thoughts hadn't gotten a hold of her.

Sure, the shows on streaming were getting boring, but watching them with Bobby hadn't. Watching a bad movie with Bobby and hearing his commentary on it and criticizing the bad special effects and the poorly written characters felt like watching a documentary about a bad movie, which was actually pretty interesting.

The last few months had erased the word "never" from her mind and "maybe" became a concept again.

Maybe taking the mirrors out of the room had been too much. How did she know she still looked bad? After all, the only times she saw her reflection lately were in the bathroom mirror after throwing up, and nobody looks good after puking their guts out. Her countenance might have improved a bit, and she might be robbing herself of watching that improvement.

Maybe one day Bobby would like to see her with make-up on, and not so pale. It might not even be about Bobby and *for* Bobby. She might just want to put on make-up, admire herself in the mirror, and feel like a pretty girl again; and sure, he made her feel like one even without make-up, but *she* wanted to *feel* beautiful, even when he wasn't around.

Maybe one day she could put on a pretty dress—it was summer, after all—and maybe Bobby and Nadine would take her out in her wheelchair. The queen in her royal carriage, out in the town, maybe get some ice cream. She could actually have ice cream as long as it had no lactose. Maybe she could dress up like her mom when they used to go out as a family, and she could put on make-up, and the three of them could go out for ice cream.

Yes. She would do that. She would propose that to them. If they said no, she'd guilt them into it until they said yes.

She heard steps coming up the stairs. Nadine was bringing her lunch. Time to start operation "guilt my loved ones into taking me on a day out".

Chapter Eleven

Nadine Schaefer
1991

A denim skirt with black leggings underneath. That part, at least she had already decided on. She didn't know what places they might crawl into, and she didn't want to give the guys an accidental peek of the goods.

The green or the yellow? Nadine put the blouses in front of her in the mirror, switching back and forth. *Green? Or yellow?* She let both of them dangle at her sides, holding them by the hangers. *Why do I even care?*

"Fuck it. Green it is."

She tossed the yellow blouse on the bed and put on the green one. *Too pretty.*

She had to dress in a way to make it clear she wasn't trying to be attractive. She wanted her look to be more understated, not flashy or attention-seeking. If anyone said, "Hey, let's go climb rocks, have a fistfight, then roll around in pig manure," she wanted to make sure no one would reply, "Oh, but Nadine can't, because check her out, all dressed up."

Why. Do I. Care?

She dug around in her closet, and among the many hanging clothes, noticed a green and blue flannel shirt. "Ugh, no. Half of them will wear some kind of flannel." She kept browsing through jackets and shirts and sweaters and cardigans, but her eyes kept darting back to the damn flannel.

*Half of them will wear…*she sighed, defeated. *Fuck. Fine. That makes sense.*

She threw on the flannel and rolled up the sleeves, and she hated the fact that it felt so damn right for the day's mission.

She tied her hair back in a ponytail, grabbed a pair of black Doc Martens, put them on, and headed for the door.

Let's go.

Her dad was in the living room, playing with her two-year-old sister. She ran up to them, gave a kiss to little Angela, pinched her on the cheek and said, "Whyyyyy? Why do you have to be so damn cute?"

"It's genetics," her dad said in a loud, bragging voice. "She gets it from her dad."

Nadine kissed her dad on the cheek. "You wish. Love you, Dad!"

"Where are you going in such a rush?"

"You know Peter Lange?"

"Yeah?" His reaction to the name was one of concern.

"He's meeting some other kids from school at Burkle Park this afternoon. He called me yesterday, asked me if I wanted to hang out. Thought it'd be cool."

"Okay." He spoke while still appearing to be worried. "You sure that'll be safe? That Lange woman is kinda nuts."

"Dad." She gave him a grave stare, but still smiling pleasantly. "When have I not been able to take care of myself?"

She gave him no time to answer and ran out the door.

2022

Nadine wasn't her usual jovial self as she brought the tray of soup up the stairs. She couldn't process the fact Peter was visiting the person who'd most hurt him in his life. That he was doing this willingly, over some imposed sense of familial duty, was baffling to her. The idea wasn't going down well.

Speaking of going down well, while on the one hand she was glad Angie was enjoying a fulfilling relationship—even one that seemed confined to the walls of this house—it annoyed her she couldn't complain about the constant "night noises" that came from her room.

She wasn't a prude, she reassured herself. She'd had a healthy—if somewhat infrequent—sex life, and she was glad Angie could get as much as she could during the worst moment of her life.

Do they have to be so damn loud, though? That's like forcing the hungry to watch you eat. Or, well, hear you.

She shook off the mental image that had sprung up in her brain: her little sister, happily bouncing up and down on a mechanical bull with Bobby's face, waving a pink cowgirl hat in the air and shouting, "Yeehaw!"

What made it even more irritating was both of them seemed to think they were being super quiet. She could hear Bobby whispering to her sister, "Honey, shh! Be quieter, your sister's in the next room," and her sister's giggly, girl-in-the-throes-of-ecstasy voice, whispering back, "Right! Sorry! Keep going!"

She sighed as she reached the top of the stairs.

This was part of her daily ritual. She compelled herself to not turn her head right, not turn toward the closed door to her mother's bedroom—the one that used to belong to both her parents. The room was vacant since her mother's death, four years back. A heart attack.

Following the funeral, Nadine and Angela went into the room, tidied it up, and did their best to replicate how their mom had arranged her belongings. They made one alteration, though. They took out the picture they knew she kept in her underwear drawer, a picture of her and their dad's wedding, both so youthful and happy. A picture she believed they didn't know she kept there.

"Only once." It was the lesson she taught them after her divorce, in tears. "You can love him with all your heart. You can feel like your soul will break from missing him so much." She grasped the hands of her daughters with her own. "If he hits you once and stays under your roof, he will do it again. Only once, and that's the end of it. You can forgive, but never forget."

Knowing her mother, she would've felt mortified to know her daughters were aware she'd kept that picture. Worse still, that some nights she held it in her hands and sobbed quietly in her bed. She didn't want her essential lesson to her daughters to be spoiled by her still loving their father and never loving another man again. She would've felt the picture undermined the message, and so it needed to remain hidden, but the walls were thin, the girls were curious, and dried tears left salty stains.

They had taken the picture and put it on the nightstand next to her side of the bed. Nadine's mother had forgiven her father for his grievous mistake, but she'd never forgotten. Nadine was forty-two now. She was no naive child, and she knew her parents hadn't just remained friends. They probably continued seeing each other and spending time together as two people who were madly in love, but never again under the same roof. She could even picture the exact words Colleen Schaefer must have said to Andrew Schaefer. "If you don't want a man doing to those two girls what you did to me, it will have to be this way." Nadine could also picture her father nodding in agreement.

From the day they put that picture on the nightstand, neither had dared enter the room. Maybe someday, Nadine would gather the courage to go into that empty room, inhabited by the ghosts of two people she loved and missed, move her parents' things into storage, save for maybe a couple of keepsakes—the picture, for sure—and make that room her own. Even if she didn't feel she could inhabit the room where her mother had lived, loved, suffered, convalesced, and died in, as her own bedroom, potentially she could turn it into her office, a somewhat neutral space of work she could slowly make her own, until she became comfortable with it.

What's Angie's room gonna be? a voice from her thoughts said cynically. *A gym? An S&M dungeon? Much use you'll get for either of those two things.*

"Stop it," she whispered to herself. "That's awful."

She might just end up selling the house and moving to Portland. Her sister owned the Portland apartment, and it was vacant.

Sure! No ghosts at your dead sister's old apartment at all, silly!

"Shut up!" she said again to herself.

As she let her gaze move down, she remembered the tray and the soup and turned left toward Angie's room. She walked down the hall and reached the first door to her right. She held the tray on the flat palm of her left hand, and with her right, she turned the knob. "Alright, Angie, I made your favorite! Chicken noodle—"

Her mouth clamped shut so fast it sounded like her teeth were snapping together, and suddenly, her mind was blank as to why she was there. It was like when she went into the kitchen and forgot what she came to do, so she stood there, a stupid expression on her face, while her mind displayed nothing but a loading screen.

She forgot where she was. She forgot *who* she was. Nothing she was seeing made sense, and she was enveloped in a thick miasma of numbness.

Before her, on the bed, was her sister. Lying motionless, one hand lying on her stomach, and the other hanging limply off the edge of the bed. Her head turned away, one eye just partially open, her mouth slack-jawed.

"Ang—" she started, but her mouth went shut again, so abruptly her teeth made a loud *clack!* Her mouth worked for a second or two, her eyes searching her sister for any reaction to her presence. In a dumb tone of voice, she said the first thing that came to her head. "Angie, are you dead?" she said, and of course, it sounded stupid, but it was all she could think of.

Angie didn't move.

Gingerly, almost as if she'd walked in on her sister in the middle of a peaceful nap, Nadine placed the tray on the bedside table. Not even a drop of soup spilled over the edge of the bowl. The tray didn't even make a sound. Her hands ran down the fabric of her pants, smoothing it out. There was a strange calm in her mind, a gel-like thickness to the air, and she felt cushioned by it.

She scanned her sister's body for movement. None was apparent. She focused on her stomach and noticed it wasn't rising and falling. Her sister wasn't breathing.

A switch flipped.

Nadine snapped into action. "Angie! ANGIEEEEE!". She grabbed her sister in her arms and raised her torso to a sitting position. The head hung first backward as she went up and dropped forward heavily when the torso went upright. "Angie! Angie! Nonononononononononono! Please! Please!"

She gave her sister soft slaps on the cheek to which she didn't even react. Tears rose, welled behind her eyelids and were close to spilling over, but before they could, Nadine's body moved without even thinking. Her palm reared back, and she struck her sister's cheek. The slap cracked loudly and echoed in the barely furnished room.

"OOOOOOOWWWWWWW!" Angela exclaimed, bringing her hand to her cheek. "You psycho!"

"Fuck!" Nadine said, suddenly letting go of her sister,

standing up, turning, and taking an angry step away from her. "You cunt!"

She turned back around, mouth agape in anger, astonishment, and horror—mostly anger—which only continued to rise, as she saw, despite rubbing her cheek with her hand, her sister was grinning.

"Oh, you do *not*!" she said, pointing a finger at Angela, who now started chuckling. They were low staccato chuckles coming from deep in her chest, and her grin was now wide, showing her teeth. "You do *not* do this to me, Angela Elyse Schaefer!"

"I thought you wouldn't fall for it." Angela was openly laughing now.

"How could you do that?" Nadine gestured dramatically with an open hand. "I thought I had lost you! I thought you were dead! How could you do that to me?"

"I'm a lawyer." Angela shrugged, as if that answered the question.

Nadine's fingertips went to her temples and her lips pursed together for a full two seconds before blurting out, "WHAT?!"

"I'm a lawyer," Angela repeated, and snickered. "I have no conscience. Well, I sort of do, but can turn it off sometimes. That's really helpful, you know? Also, I'm pretty good at staring down people on the stand, so I can hold my eyes open for a long amount of time. There are also the acting lessons I took with that theater group in Portla—"

"Shut up!" Nadine said. "Just shut up!"

She stood there, just gaping in disbelief at her sister. Her baffled expression only accomplished making Angela burst into uncontrollable laughter, her body shaking as her hands clasped her stomach.

"Why would you do something that horrible?"

"Theatrics can help you negotiate agreements."

Nadine stared at her sister as if she'd spontaneously sprung into a monologue in Mandarin with a perfect accent and intonation.

"Sometimes it helps to show the opposing party what they can end up losing if they don't agree to the terms. It's great for plea bargains."

"What…" Nadine started in a subdued voice, "could you possibly want to negotiate that would justify this?"

"I want to go out with Bobby," she said matter-of-factly, with an emphatic nod. "I want to get dressed up, I want to put on make-up, I want to feel fucking hot with my handsome boyfriend pushing me in my wheelchair all the way to Seaside Park, where he'll buy me an ice cream. I want to feel the sunlight on my face. I want to sit and watch the ocean for a while. I want to feel the grass on my skin. I want to see people playing in the park. I want to pet someone's dog. I want to ride the Ferris wheel, the little swan boats, the merry-go-round, and the roller-coaster."

Nadine's complete lack of amusement at what she'd just heard seemed to pulsate from her with each heartbeat. "Let me see if I understand this. You traumatized me," she enunciated each word carefully, "by making me think my only sister was dead"—she licked her lips, closed her eyes, took a deep breath, glared again at her sister—"because you wanted to go to the park and have ice cream and go on the rides."

"Yes," Angela answered with a nod, assuming a perfectly straight sitting position on the bed. She coughed softly once and rubbed her stomach softly, as if to assuage some slight discomfort. "Should you not grant my request, I will die, and you will continue on, knowing you did *not* grant your sister her last wish. I will also haunt you from beyond the grave."

"You are a thirty-two-year-old woman. You're a professional. Not even a thirteen-year-old would pull this stunt."

"I fail to see your point. Are you not negotiating, then? Should I die now?"

"No!"

"Okay, so from your quick response, I infer you will agree to my terms. Am I correct?"

"Yes!" Nadine said in a burst of resigned anger. "Fine," she huffed in annoyance. "We can go to the park tomorrow, alright?"

"Yay!" Angela said, raising her hands in a V with joy,

but quickly letting them fall halfway down in exhaustion.

That she could lift her arms like that, even briefly, when just a few months ago her sister couldn't have even fed herself, was all Nadine needed to drain away any remnants of her anger.

"Roller-coaster is out of the question, though!"

Angela brought her hands down to her thighs and placed one on top of the other formally. "I am willing to make that compromise."

Nadine rolled the little bedside table with the lunch tray close to the bed. "Brought you your food. I'm guessing you feel strong enough to eat on your own?"

Her sister nodded back at her as she grabbed her spoon and put it in the bowl.

Nadine gave her a quick, unenthusiastic smile. "I'll come back for the plate soon. I want to lie down for a bit."

"Nadine? I heard you talking to your boyfriend a moment ago."

"Peter's not my boyfriend."

"Oh, I see," Angie said, and again assumed her formal sitting position. Coughed softly once more and contained a slight grimace. "Could you please, Ms. Schaefer, answer yes or no to whether the following statement is accurate? Are you, Ms. Schaefer, confirming you will not be pursuing a romantic relationship with a best-selling author, who was recently widowed, and you are prepared to die a spinster?"

"I am not a spinster, and Peter and I are only friends."

"Ms. Schaefer, could you please state, for the record, when was the last time you had a penis in you?"

"Angela!"

"Three months? Six months? A year?"

"It has not been a year!"

"Ms. Schaefer, did the last penis you have in you belong to a Clifford Reed, a fisherman, whose idea of dirty talk was telling you the best thing about his work was the smell, because it reminded him of your private parts?"

"You're disgusting! Oh, my God! He never—"

"Or have you forgotten his penis was ever in you, Ms. Schaefer, because it was, and I quote a previous statement, 'So tiny, I didn't even realize it when he put it in'? Did you or did you not make that statement, Ms. Schaefer?"

"I told you that in confidence! You're being so immature! Stop this, right n—!"

"Please, answer the question, Ms. Schaefer."

"You know what? I don't have to play along. I'm done with this conversation. I'm leaving."

As Nadine walked out and was about to close the door, the last words that reached her ears were: "Your Honor, I ask that this witness be found in contempt!"

Already outside the room, Nadine sighed. Through the door, she could still hear Angela's laughter devolve into wheezes and grunts, which did nothing to make her sound any less joyful. She felt so annoyed, but also so happy Angie now had enough energy in her to mess with her like she always used to. Angie had always insisted she give the relationship with Peter a second try. She was just a little girl when she and Peter were an item, but she eventually told her the entire story about them dating, about their first kiss, and about the insane woman who had come at her with scissors.

Angie had known Peter mostly as Nadine's friend, but she'd always been perceptive. She always knew the feelings were still there. Nadine visited him a few times at his aunt's place, but by the time she decided to ask him out, Peter had already met Jenny Morton. Most importantly, he was happy with her, and Jenny was exceptional, and worldly, and witty, and just a wonderful human being, who became almost as good a friend to Nadine as Peter himself. She would've never moved a finger to get between two people she loved so much, respected so much, and who were so clearly made for one another, and eventually the feelings stopped—or at least, stopped being acknowledged. She was happy with her simple, small-town life as a schoolteacher, Peter was happy being married to Jenny, and she was happy with the friendship they shared.

She pondered, however, now that Jenny was gone, what happened to those old feelings? She owed Peter respect for his grief. She owed Jenny respect for their friendship. She wasn't even sure it would be appropriate, wanted, or even healthy for her to bring those old feelings back to the surface.

There was no way, after such a long time, to redefine that relationship.

Peter was her friend. Nothing more.

Chapter Twelve

The Dreaming Mother: "Jenny"

"Tell me," his mother insisted, as if the news were imperative to her very existence. "I want to know how she died."

Peter was overcome with disgust and anger at the deranged joy he witnessed in his mother's eyes. She wasn't fully lucid. She didn't know what year it was, or how old he was, or how long she'd spent wishing death on his wife. But she was lucid enough to savor the joy of hearing of her passing.

"That's not why I'm here, Mother," he said with his head down. "I'm not going to—"

"You will tell me! You will obey me and tell me how that filthy woman died!"

He stared daggers at her. Had Nadine been right? Had this been a terrible mistake? Was there no hope for his mother? He had come here to find common ground, to find vestiges of a relationship that could still be salvaged, but how could anyone find common ground with a person who rejoiced in the death of a loved one? He'd come all this way with a purpose, and sometimes compromises needed to be made to get the other person to listen.

It reminded him of when he'd refused to remove a sexual assault scene from *Survive the Fallen*, the last part of his trilogy. His argument had been it was a pivotal scene in the book, and it was the only way to truly cement how irredeemable the character of Creed Collins was. His publisher argued the scene was too graphic. It was needless, it felt gratuitous, it appeared exploitative, and they wouldn't publish the book unless the scene was removed.

He fought the decision for a long time. He insisted the scene was needed, and they were not seeing the big picture. The character of Creed Collins had been seen as an antihero in the story up to that point, and he'd become one of his most popular characters—one the readers connected with. He needed to ensure there were no lingering doubts about the character's irredeemable qualities by the final third of *Survive the Fallen*. He gave in to the publisher, but still kept a tamer version of the scene. He'd found having Darlene, the protagonist, tell the events from her perspective, allowed her the chance to keep her agency in sharing only the details she felt comfortable sharing, as well as making Creed

Collins's demise more impactful. He pleads for her help, and she only throws a knife at his feet and escapes, leaving him to fend for himself against a horde of thousands of undead creatures, where he's ultimately devoured.

"Well, what are you waiting for?" Mother pushed, putting an end to his meditations.

"Our house burned down," Peter said hurriedly. "She died in the fire. That's all you get. No details."

"She burned," his Mother said with an obscene grin stretching her upper lip. "The bitch burned, just as I predic—"

"Mother, stop!" He wanted to punch that grin off her face. That self-satisfied, revolting grin. He knew despite the maze her mind had become, she could still picture many scenarios of how Jenny had died, but none would be as horrible as the truth.

It began as a spark.

The way a piece of broken glass, if hit by sunlight at the right angle, can start a forest fire. Sometimes it's the smallest things that grow into unexpected outcomes. Only, this time, it was a literal spark. Not the one that started the fire that took Jenny's life, but the one before it.

The first fire.

Their first house.

Of all the alarming places it could've started, it had been in William's room.

The fire department had later determined the source of the fire had been a malfunctioning night light in his room. The defect caused it to overheat, and a spark set fire to the drywall.

Nobody was injured, and apart from a severely blackened wall and ceiling in William's bedroom, there was no big tragedy to mourn—or so Peter thought. That broken night light left almost invisible embers in Jenny's mind, simply waiting to be stoked.

Jenny had convinced herself the malfunction was due to the house's wiring, even though she paid two separate electricians to verify the wiring and panels were in perfect condition.

In the end, Jenny said she'd feel more comfortable if they moved somewhere else. Even before she and Peter tied the knot, the house had been hers, so it was her call to make. Thinking this would help Jenny sleep more soundly, Peter didn't oppose the idea. They came across a lovely house in Hillsboro, a quiet city, with hospitable people and a lot of nature to ignite his creativity when he sat down to write. They bought the new house fully furnished, so moving in was a breeze. They didn't unpack everything right away, they were in no hurry. All the things they couldn't immediately find a place for could sit in bags in the basement for now. They wanted this to be the most hassle-free move they could do.

While life in Hillsboro was everything he'd hoped for, Peter could see the fire still haunted Jenny's mind.

When Jenny was seven years old, there was a fire in her home, and it had been a traumatizing event for her. At one point, while exiting the house, her skirt caught on fire, leaving a visible scar on her left thigh.

When Jenny told Peter this story, it hadn't seemed like the fire still haunted her. She'd gone to therapy as a kid and worked on her fears. For as long as they'd been married, there was never a sign of this still troubling her. She had no issue lighting and using a gas stove and was quite experienced at being the grill master at barbecues, never feeling anxious around fire. All she seemed to have left was the scar on her thigh, which, now that she was an adult, was a tiny blemish he would've mistaken for a birthmark if she hadn't told him the story.

Now, however, it seemed like the notion of William burning to death in a house fire was a constant concern to her.

Those tiny embers of fear remained in her mind, and they would come out in subtle ways, like her asking him if he smelled smoke, or turning the stove off and on several times, until she was sure it was, indeed, off. After tucking William in, she always made it a point to double-check all his appliances before she departed. There were also the nightmares, during which, according to her telling, she was trying to save William from burning alive.

One evening, as if blown upon by an evil wind coming from a dark cave, one of those small, hot coals started to burn brighter and hotter.

The night in question, Peter was in the middle of a peculiar dream, in which he was involved in a conversation with a fascinatingly charming carnivorous plant that asked him if he would consider allowing it to eat his kidney, as he only needed one to live.

Peter, sitting down to an entertaining game of chess with the well-spoken botanical wonder, in the greenhouse of his Victorian manor, was politely explaining that giving even one of his kidneys would mean reducing his lifespan and health, and so he couldn't comply with the plant's wishes.

The plant, adjusting its top hat using an elongated green leaf, proposed a compromise. If they got legally married, it would actually own half of his kidney, which was perhaps a more suitable deal than his whole kidney.

Peter pondered about the mechanics of such a marriage, with the plant from time to time asking for half an organ to sustain itself; however, as the plant seemed quite courteous, despite its anthropophagic tendencies, he promised to study the legality of such a proposal.

It was then that the King, who observed the game of chess from a throne three-hundred feet high, through a golden spyglass, thought it opportune to pronounce sentence on whether a sentient vegetable could make a suitable spouse for a grown man, when——

"Let go of the torch!"

Peter jolted awake as the bed shook abruptly.

"Let go of the torch *now*, William!"

It was Jenny.

Confused, and barely making sense of his surroundings, he finally made out the shape of Jenny walking toward the window. She had apparently jumped off the bed, causing the mattress to shake. Her blanket was lying on his side of the bed.

"Do what your mommy tells you! Please!" She begged, gazing out the window, into the darkness.

"Jen, what's going on?" he said with concern, only to be entirely ignored.

"No! Look at your hands! Look at your hands! They're burning! Let go of the torch! Your arm is burning! It's burning!"

Peter hurried around the bed and stood in front of his wife to see her eyes were open, but she wasn't seeing him. He placed his hand on her shoulder, but she didn't react to his touch. She shook her head in desperation and sobbed. "No, no, no. His arm is burning. His skin. His skin is burning! Please! Please! I can't reach him! Somebody, do something! My baby is burning!"

"Sweetheart?" He breathed, trying not to startle her, realizing what was happening.

"No! My baby is burning!" She brought her hands up to her face, as if to cover tears, but they stopped in the air, a full inch away from her eyes, the palms turned toward her.

"Jen," Peter said. "Jenny? Baby?" He once more put his hand on her shoulder, and this time, he began caressing it. He found it unnerving how she seemed to cry into her tense, clawed hands while they just hung in the air—her eyes open, no tears, but she was crying, inconsolable. It filled his imagination with a picture of her, in her dream, wearing a clay mask an inch thick. A face with no face, only two holes for the eyes and a hole for the mouth. She was clawing at the mask in despair, which explained why, in the waking world, they were an inch away from her face.

She blinked. She gasped. Her eyes found him, confused. "What's the... What is the... What's the... What's going on?"

Peter ran a hand softly across her cheek and said, "You were sleepwalking, Jen."

"I was?"

Peter nodded. "Yes, but there's nothing to worry about, alright? I'm here, and you're here, and we're fine, alright?"

She gave a nod, still showing confusion.

He wrapped his arms around her to let her know she was safe and loved.

For the rest of the night, Jenny slept soundly. Peter didn't. She had nearly given him a heart attack with the way she'd jumped off the bed. He left a lamp on and studied her every move, her every breath, her every turn, the way her eyes rolled and swiveled in her sleep. Watching for signs she would once again stand up, not knowing what it would mean if she did.

When Jenny came down the stairs the following morning, the aroma of freshly brewed coffee, toasted bread, and cinnamon filled the air.

"Oh, my God, what is that smell?" she said with a smile, as she entered the kitchen, almost floating in clouds of fragrance, and reached the table. "French toast?" She sat down, marveling at the smell of the moist delicacy on the plate in front of her, and her eyes rolled up in decadent pleasure. She turned to Peter. "Oh, you're a monster. You know I shouldn't. I'm still trying to lose the Spring Break pounds!"

"You've earned it," Peter said, pouring coffee into a large mug in front of her that read: "The Doctor is OUT until the Coffee goes IN."

William's cheeks were round and puffed up as he struggled to chew the massive bite of perfect, sweet, eggy toast. "Eeg haf swiced bananas and mable syrrip," he said with difficulty.

"Well," Peter said in a pleasant tone. "*We've* earned it. We're all tired from the move, and we just need to relax."

William swallowed. "Mom! Eat! C'mon!" He laughed. Little pieces of toast were stuck to his teeth as he smiled.

"You little traitor," she said, squinting at him. "You know what? When I get addicted to these, and I'm all fat and happy, I'll start paying more attention to my plate than you. I'll stop cooking and I'll just eat. Then what will you do, young man?"

She raised her eyebrows at him.

He laughed and shrugged. "Dad will make me toast," he said, pointing a fork at his dad.

"Oh, so you're in cahoots, then?" she said, squinting at Peter. "That's called mutiny."

Peter raised his hands in a "don't look at me" gesture.

"Well," she said, taking the small bowl with banana slices, tossing them onto her French toast, and smothering them in maple syrup, "if I'm going to be a fat mom, I'll be the happiest, fattest mom in the universe." She took a big bite of French toast and moaned with joy. "Mmmmmm!"

"Yeeeeeeah!" William cheered, raising his fork,

laughing out loud.

Jenny grinned at her son. "So, how are you liking the new house, young man?"

"I like it. My room is huge!"

"You know something?" she asked him in a conspiratorial tone. "My room is huge, too. Don't tell your dad because I'm moving my stuff into it tomorrow."

She turned toward Peter, laughing. William laughed with her, too. Peter was laughing with them, but she noticed how his expression cracked slightly when her eyes met his.

"Are you okay, baby?" she asked.

"Yes!" Peter said. "Nothing that can't wait."

That night, Jenny came home from work to find Peter sitting at his desk. For now, Peter's office was simply a desk, a laptop, and the chair he sat on, hunched over and looking as if he were trying to crawl into the screen. Soon, he'd have this place full of shelves with books, and papers hanging from walls, and sticky notes, and handwritten charts, detailing the moment a character entered the story to the moment that character exited it, and everything in between. It would transform into one of those rooms in police shows, covered in photos, and copies, and cutouts, and post-its connected by pins and red string.

She walked up behind him, put her arms around him over his shoulders, and rested her chin on his head.

"How's the book going?" She kissed him on top of the head. "Did you kill that guy I don't like?"

"Well, if the lady of the house wants my favorite character dead, I guess I have no choice." He pretended to type quickly. "And the ground caved in under his feet and he fell a long, long way down, into a dark pit…"

"And?"

"Aaaaand… Oh, okay… And he shat himself after hitting the bottom. Everyone else lived happily ever after, and they did not shit themselves. The end."

"Good," Jenny said reassuringly, and kissed his head again. "Now it's a bestseller."

"That's not what you came to ask, is it?"

Jenny put on a show of being offended, her mouth dropping open in shock and her eyes wide. "It totally was. That guy was an ass. He deserved to fall down a mine shaft—"

"Pit."

"—pit, and to shit himself! It wasn't letting me sleep at night that he might make it alive and un-shat to the end of the book."

"Jen," Peter said, his eyes rolled upward, even though he couldn't see her with her chin on his head.

"Ugh." Jenny rolled her eyes. "I just gave you the cue to get into the damn topic. Why can't you just take it?"

"So, you remember?" Peter closed his laptop and turned his chair around to face her. "Any comments?"

"Is that really your first question?"

"No. But you scared me half to death, and I'm worried as hell, because you've never done that before. I'm kind of just putting the most general question out there and we can take it from there."

"I'm sorry."

"Baby, no," he said. "You don't need to apologize. You didn't even know it was happening. C'mere."

He took her by the hand and pulled her close to him.

She sat on his lap, and he kissed her gently.

"I'm worried, too," she said, resting her forehead against his. "It's probably just a side effect of the move and the fire and all."

"Should we seek help?"

"No, sweetie. No. It was only once."

"It has been building up for a while. Ever since the fire, you've been having nightmares and night terrors."

"Okay," she said, and took his head in her hands. "I agree. What's happening to me is not a normal reaction—"

"Don't say that either."

"Listen to me. It isn't. Nightmares, night terrors, then slowly recovering—that's the normal progression. Nightmares, night terrors, then sleepwalking—that's escalation."

Peter nodded in agreement.

"If I may ask for a minor concession," she said, now placing her hands on his shoulders.

"Really? You just had me kill my favorite character, and you still want to ask for more stuff? Who do you think you are, missy?"

She slapped him on the top of the head playfully. "Shut up, stupid."

"The abuse I have to suffer in this marriage is astonishing." He noticed she was just staring at him. "Okay, stupid shutting up now."

"One point doesn't make a line, right?"

"Right."

"I propose we put the therapy on hold. Not because I don't think I need it. I probably do. I just want to give myself time to settle into the new house, see if this helps me get back to normal. There's the possibility the sleepwalking might have been a one-time thing."

"Jenny—"

"Peter. It only happened once. Just once."

"I don't think it's that simple."

"If it happens again, I will set the appointment for the very next day. I promise."

Peter gave it some thought and reluctantly nodded his head. "Fine."

She kissed him again. "You know me. You know I take our mental health seriously. I won't toy with it. I just want to try the 'tea and relaxation' route before going down the therapy and pills route."

A week passed with no sleepwalking incidents.

A second week passed and, apart from a few nightmares, no sleepwalking.

On Tuesday of the third week, Peter woke to find himself alone in bed.

He patted Jenny's side, but all he got was the softly cushioned sound of his palm against the mattress.

Bathroom?

The bathroom door was open, the lights were off.

"Jen, are you in the bathroom?"

He threw off the covers, rushed to the bathroom, and flipped on the light switch. He was dazzled by the reflections of the white LED lamps against the tiles and the steel fixtures. Once his eyes adjusted, he was met with an empty bathroom. Jenny wasn't there.

He stepped back into the bedroom and noticed the door to the hall was open. He was surprised he hadn't noticed this before, but he'd made a beeline toward the bathroom and hadn't paid attention to it.

His pulse quickened slightly.

There's no need to be worried. He tried to be reasonable and not jump to conclusions. *She probably just went downstairs for a cup of tea.*

His mind launched a rebuttal. *What if she attempted to go downstairs while asleep, slipped, and then tumbled down the stairs, and ended up with a broken neck?*

He pictured it as if he were standing on the landing, staring at the bottom of the stairs: Jenny's body sprawled on the floor, her head facing right, her chin touching her right shoulder, and her left eye staring up at him, dead, but open and accusatory.

(*No, officer, I did not push my wife down the stairs,* the voice in his head said. *You see, she sleepwalked, which is something she'd never done before we moved here, and she tripped and broke her neck. Yes, I do know my rights. Why do you ask?*)

Peter hurried to put on a pair of slippers and rushed out into the hallway, heading straight toward the stairs, but trying simultaneously to hold back the panic that was seizing him. He was about to pass William's bedroom when he noticed the line of light that shone from the space under the door, and he stopped. There was usually light there, but it was blueish-white from William's night light—after the incident, they'd purchased the best one in the market and plugged it into a special socket that cut the power at any sign of overheating—the glow he was seeing was warm and yellowish, like the one from William's bedside lamp, which had no reason for being turned on at this hour.

Careful not to let irrational fear get the best of him, he cautiously approached the door and turned the knob little by little, pushing the door in slowly. A vertical line of yellowish light grew as it opened inward.

The image that assaulted his eyes froze him in place in bafflement: Jenny was crouched next to William's bed, her back turned to him. In front of her, there was something round, like a ball covered in some kind of thick fabric, bobbing up and down. Where the blanket continued down toward the foot of the bed, something shook violently.

It took him a moment to process what he was seeing until he noticed the same Sesame Street pattern on the blanket was covering the bobbing round thing.

It was William's head.

His mother had thrown the thick blanket over his head and had tightened it around his neck. The boy thrashed as he choked.

"Jenny, no!" Peter ran toward his wife, and he grabbed the blanket with one hand firmly, shoving his other arm between William and Jenny, and without even thinking, he pushed her with all his strength.

Jenny flew backward and hit the closet door, just as Peter removed the blanket from over William's head. The boy breathed in deeply and let out a desperate wail, coughing, his face red. Peter had never been happier to hear his son cry since the day he'd been pushed out of his mom. Peter checked him over, raised his head to see if his neck was injured, and the boy just had a red mark that went all around it. He pulled William to his chest and kissed his forehead.

"It's okay, buddy. Everything's okay."

Peter swiveled his head toward Jenny. He was worried he might have hurt her, but felt a deep rumble in his chest as he tried to suppress the primal anger rising in him. He knew she hadn't done it on purpose. She was sitting on the floor, legs pulled in against her chest, one arm wrapped around the knees. Her hand was covering her mouth and her green eyes were wide open.

She shook her head in horror and shame.

"It was a wet blanket," she murmured, making no sense.

"What?" Peter held his weeping son tight.

"It was a…like a wet blanket, like to run through fire, I…" She brought both her hands to her face and her voice quivered. "Oh, my God! What did I do? What did I do?"

Peter stared at her, using every ounce of willpower he could muster to force himself down from his defensive posture. Memories of the damage his mother had done to him flooded his mind like lava rising through a volcano, and he repeated over and over in his mind the same phrase, reminding himself: *Jenny is not my mother, Jenny is not my mother, Jenny is not my mother.*

He put out his right hand and curled his fingers in a beckoning motion. Jenny leaned forward, took his hand, and crawled hurriedly toward him. She put her arms around them both, burying her head in Peter's chest and apologizing to their son.

Jenny slept in the guest room that night, and William slept with his dad. The next morning, after William left for school, Jenny approached Peter in the living room. He was lying back on a reclining chair, his face unshaved, hair matted, left forearm covering his eyes.

"The entire house was on fire," she said, regret pouring out of each word.

Peter moved little, but an almost imperceptible turn of his head toward her showed he was listening.

"I remember running through the flames, up the stairs to William's room. I closed the door to keep the smoke out. Out of nowhere, I found this wet blanket. You know how some people say a thick wet blanket can help you run out of a fire if it's a short distance? I don't even know if that's true, but in the dream, it was. I didn't even question why there was a soaked blanket there. I just put it around him, and I thought if I tightened it around his neck, the smoke couldn't get to his face." She let out a hysterical chuckle.

"Now, I realize that makes no sense, but in the *dream*, it made sense, you know?"

"I know," Peter said in an exhausted breath. His arm still covering his eyes.

"I just got off the phone with Dr. Cook. She scheduled me for first thing tomorrow morning." She paused and swallowed loudly. "Do you think he'll ever forgive me?"

Peter remembered the way William had eyed Jenny that morning, as if she'd been some monster from a nightmare, awkwardly smiling at him from across the table. "We'll talk to him tonight about what happened. He's a smart boy. He'll understand. I'm sure."

"Will *you*?" she asked.

No! The thought rushed through his mind like a bullet train. *No, I won't forgive you. You hurt my son. You hurt our son. You know about my mother. You know! You know what this looks like to me—JennysnotmymotherJennysnotmymotherJennysnotmymother—Stop this, now!*

"Yes," he said.

"You know I'm not her." She eyed him in that familiar way that told him she knew exactly what he was thinking.

This got his attention. He put his hand down on the armrest and glanced in her direction, bags under his eyes.

"I know the things she did to you made last night's situation very triggering, but I think you know this is not the same."

246

Peter nodded. Of course, it wasn't. How could he be so unfair? So judgmental? Jenny had never and would never hurt her boy, for any reason.

He got to his feet and approached his wife. He gazed into her captivating green eyes and lovingly caressed her auburn hair, which had taken on a slightly reddish hue since her recent salon visit. "I love you," he said. "I love how you just know what I'm thinking before I say it. I love how you can bring it to the surface, so it doesn't just fester inside my brain."

"What about you?" She put both palms on his chest. "Do you know me?"

"Of course I do." He peered adoringly into those eyes that had mesmerized him from the moment they met. "I don't think you would ever do anything to hurt William. Not on purpose. You're a remarkable mom."

She kissed him, and they stood in the living room in each other's embrace for a while.

"Although." He noticed her body stiffen as the word left his lips. "You do know my standards for motherhood are just about the lowest. Subterranean. Like, as deep down as the Mariana Trench."

She slapped him hard on the chest. "You idiot."

"Ow... I deserved that, but it was totally worth it."

"Look at you, making jokes about your mother. Some would call that progress."

"Some would call that trivializing trauma."

"I like my way of putting it better." She smiled at him. "Do you know what I would really love to do right now?" Her voice was laced with a playful tone as she bit her lower lip.

Peter glanced over his shoulder. "We haven't done it in the kitchen yet. There's that huge metal table that looks just perfect for—"

"I would love to sleep."

Peter exhaled in relief. "Oh, thank God, I'm so sleepy I wouldn't even be able to get it up with a Liebherr crane."

They kissed again and headed up the stairs to have a long, pleasant nap.

It would be the last one they would have together.

Peter awoke to *Ordinary World* by Duran Duran, the sound distant yet beautiful, reverberating through the night, coming from downstairs. One of Jenny's favorite songs. His eyes darted toward his cell. It was 3:02 a.m. The first thing that truly alarmed him was the smell of smoke. His hand went to Jenny's side of the bed to find it empty.

He hurried from the room, the sound of his slippers slapping on the ceramic tile of the hallway. A glow came from the first floor of the house and up the well of the stairs, a terrible orange with dark black shapes made of smoke that moved toward the ceiling.

How did it get this bad before I woke up?

"William!" he yelled.

If there was a fire, the first thing he needed to do was get his son out of the house. He was about to head to William's room when his voice rose suddenly from downstairs, calling out in terror.

"Daaaaad!"

Peter ran.

As he reached the stairs' landing, he could smell the acrid smoke of the flames as they licked the ceiling of the first floor.

"Oh, my God!"

He kept running down without pausing to consider his own safety. He slipped on the second to last step and hurtled forward, bumping and sliding across the floor. He groaned in pain and opened his eyes and was greeted by the sight of flames and smoke, forming a swirling painting; spirals of yellow, orange, and black played across the ceiling.

"Daaaaad!" William screamed. "Daaaaad!"

He stood, already setting his legs in motion. The song was so loud he could hear it even over the roar of the flames. It was coming from the kitchen, which was where most of the smoke was coming from.

"William!" he shouted, and crossed the threshold

from the hall into an inferno. A sea of roiling smoke flooded the kitchen's ceiling. The only reason it hadn't yet reached the floor was the stove had a hood with a duct that went all the way to the roof; the smoke was being sucked up into it. Jenny was standing in front of the stove, motionless, barefoot, in the oversized blue shirt she'd been wearing as a sleeping gown, and she had William clutched by his wrist with her right hand, and no matter how hard the boy struggled to break free, her grasp was too tight, and wouldn't let go.

The song, coming from a wireless speaker on the kitchen counter, minutes away from being melted by the fire, was coming to the point in which singer Simon Le Bon mourned—when compared to the news of war and need across the world—their own tragedy was insignificant.

William was coughing.

Jenny wasn't, despite all the smoke rushing past her head toward the duct.

"Mom, you're hurting me!" William shouted. "Let me go! Let me go! Mom!"

Coughing, Peter ran to his wife. He stood in front of her and grabbed her by the shoulders. "Jenny, c'mon, wake up!" he shouted. "We have to get out of here!"

There was no reaction from her. She didn't even blink. Her eyes were red and irritated. He tried shaking her by the shoulders, but he might as well have been shaking a store mannequin.

He crouched and tried to loosen Jenny's grip on his son, but her fingernails dug deeper into the boy's skin, keeping him in place. An image flashed through his head—his mother clutching his arm when she was upset, back when he was a little boy. The more he struggled, the deeper her nails dug.

William screamed. "No, no, Dad, that hurts! Stop!"

Peter realized he'd have to carry both of them out if he was to have any hope of saving his family.

"Alright, buddy," he said to William. "I'm going to have to lift your mom, alright? She's probably not going to let you go. She's stuck in a bad dream," he coughed. "Do you understand what I mean? It's what we discussed at dinner today. Say you understand."

"I understand," William said, wiping his teary eyes.

"Good," he coughed some more. "I need you to be brave for me, alright?"

"I will, Dad."

Coughing, Peter stood up and was about to put his arms around Jenny's waist to lift her over his shoulder, but by then it was too late to notice she had been holding something in her left hand the whole time. He couldn't react quickly enough. He saw her lift the wooden meat tenderizer and swing it sideways, striking him in the temple, rendering him unconscious as he dropped near the cabinets beneath the sink.

Before his consciousness faded entirely, Peter's head filled with the soaring, mournful sound of the guitar riff from *Ordinary World*. It distorted, became choppy, then stopped completely as the flames consumed the speaker.

William watched his dad go down and stay down. In his ears, the sound of that song became distorted into slurred moans, and chopped-up screeches that sounded like the calls of monsters in a bad dream, yawning awake and giggling.

He couldn't believe what his mom was doing.

Moments earlier, she'd taken him by the hand to the kitchen, saying she would make something delicious for him as an apology for what she'd done the previous night. He couldn't understand what she meant. After all, he wasn't allowed to eat this late at night—it would cause him nightmares.

She put on some music on the little black speaker. It was that song his mom loved, which she set on repeat. He liked the song, but she normally didn't play music this late. At least, he guessed she didn't, since he was always asleep at this hour, but she probably didn't since she might wake up her dad, and tonight in particular, he was probably tired after what had happened the night before.

She stepped to the stove and rotated a knob. It took

her a little too long to start the lighter, so there was this sudden fireball that went *Phoomph!,* startling him. After that initial scare, it was just the regular fire from the burner. She didn't put a pan or a pot on it, she just let it burn for a while, gazing into the fire. His mom seemed distracted. She wasn't speaking anymore; she wasn't moving. She simply stood there with the firelight shining in her eyes.

"Stay here, sweetheart," she finally said, and went to the laundry—just beyond the kitchen—and came back carrying a mop with a wooden handle. A fluffy, hairy mop that looked like someone had braided a long, white wig. In her other hand, she held some kind of plastic container. It was white, with a red nozzle. He'd seen it before.

His mom put the mop's head on the kitchen burner, the handle laid out over the stovetop and the kitchen counter, the tip touching the wall.

"Mom," he said nervously, "what are you doing?"

Without answering, his mom turned the cap on the plastic container and poured its contents all over the kitchen counter, spraying the walls and the hanging cabinets above. A small wooden pantry also got sprayed by the strange liquid, which had no smell.

It's that liquid Mom and Dad use on the grill… Lighter fluid.

By now, the mop's head was burning with a long yellow flame.

"Mom?"

His mom stood beside him and took him by the wrist. "There. We're safe now."

Chills went up William's spine when he saw his mom smiling at the fire. The flames crawled up the mop handle, and another *Phoomph!* sounded when the lighter fluid on the counter caught fire, followed by the wall, then the cabinet above.

"Mom, you're scaring me! We have to go!"

"There's no need to be scared," she said, smiling. "You see, sweetie, I figured it out. How to keep us all safe."

William tried to move away, but his mother wouldn't let him go.

"We can't let the house burn down while we're sleeping." Her words were robotic, soulless. "So, we have to burn it down while we're awake and watch it burn. That's the only way we'll be safe."

The song faded out. The singer squealing out something that sounded like, "Every world is my world", or "Any world is my world", which was a strange thing to say, in William's mind. The song stopped. A second of silence passed. It started again. The pleasant sound of an acoustic guitar that would end in that foreboding phrase.

"Mom, please," he begged, grabbing her hand. The flames were quickly surrounding them, and the heat was unbearable already. He was sweating profusely, but to his surprise, his mom was completely dry. No sweat at all, as if she were outside on a brisk spring day. "Please, let's get out."

His words went unheeded, and he kept trying to pull his mom along with him or get away, to no avail. This went on for seconds that felt like hours, screaming desperately, as the fire turned the entire kitchen into an oven, and smoke filled the ceiling. It was at this moment his dad appeared.

William felt the same level of hero worship for his dad as he did an emotional bond with his mom. The latter was being shaken to the core because his mother seemed to have no interest in running from certain death, and he desperately wanted to escape, but didn't want to leave her alone. The former had a sudden excited spike when he saw his dad charge into the kitchen, through fire and smoke, ready to be the hero William knew he was.

His excitement was shattered when his mother brought out that wooden hammer out of a large pocket in her sleeping shirt and smashed it against his head.

His dad collapsed in a heap on the floor, and for a moment, he thought his mom had actually killed him. He shrieked in terror and despair. William saw his dad was breathing, yet there was blood all over his forehead, and he kept shouting out to him, but there was no answer.

His mom didn't move an inch from her post in front of the stove. She kept smiling, and now that the music stopped, he realized she was still humming the song under her breath. He couldn't make out words, but little bits of the melody were still discernible. It was an entranced, distant, zombified version of the melody, and it made the hairs on the back of his neck stand and prickle.

A sequence of three or four notes brought to the surface the ending phrases of the song, the "Every world is my world" phrase he found so bizarre, but there was another, sung almost in response, saying—what was it?—"I will try to survive"? "I will learn to survive"?

William watched in escalating dismay how burning pieces of the ceiling now fell to the floor, and he dreaded one of those pieces landing on him or his parents and setting their clothes on fire.

Learn to survive!

He was coughing non-stop now. The heat was so bad his skin was red and sore. He thought frantically, trying to find anything, anything he could use that wasn't on fire. The first thing he saw was the sink, his dad unconscious in front of it. The sink was metal, so it remained intact, but he assumed it had to be very hot. He didn't recognize the material of the cabinet doors, however. They weren't burning, or else his dad would've been on fire, too.

An idea hit him like a light from Heaven.

He saw the top of the tall glasses his parents drank from during dinner. They hadn't washed them yet, so they were sitting inside the sink.

Stretching his body and pulling his mom's arm along with him as much as he could, he approached the edge of the sink and tried to reach for one of the glasses, but he was too short and they were at the very back of the dish pile. His dad was lying at his feet, and without even thinking about it, he climbed on top of him and quickly reached for the glass. His underarm pressed against the metal sink and it was sizzling hot, searing his skin with a blinding hiss. He cried out.

(*Survive!*)

His fingers couldn't reach the faucet's handle, so he grabbed the mouth of the glass with his open hand, and began tapping the handle with the bottom, so it slowly turned.

The heat was dizzying, but this was his one chance—as his dad had always told him—to be brave. Soon, water poured over his hand—warm at first, cold a few seconds after—and the relief of its touch was immediate. He turned the glass in his hand, and he held it now with the mouth facing up, letting it fill with water as much as he could, before—

The glass slipped from his hand and hit the bottom of the sink, smashing into shards.

His heart stopped beating for a few seconds until he remembered there was another glass within reach. One last chance. He quickly reached for the other glass, held it under the faucet, and it filled up as quickly as the gushing water would allow. This time, he only filled it halfway, to avoid it becoming too heavy and having it slip again. He stepped off his dad's back and hurried once more beside his mom. He had been holding his breath, he realized, because he didn't want to cough and drop the second glass.

His mom was grinning widely. Her enthralled grin and her humming, that seemed to come from inside a witch's house in a creepy tale, scared him deeply.

(*Any world is my world. Every world is my world.*)

While she didn't sweat from the heat and she didn't cough from the smoke, her eyes were red and irritated, and tears flowed from them, forming two wet lines on her cheeks that glistened in the light of the flames.

He gathered every ounce of strength he had and hurled the water from the cup, still cold from the faucet, at his mother's face.

Her eyes widened in shock, and she gasped in surprise.

Jenny was jolted awake by the sudden cold that hit her face.

She let out a startled, high-pitched shriek of confusion.

Blurry vision. Blinding light.

Her eyes stung as if she'd poured vinegar on them.

"Where? What?" she blurted, her face soaked.

Then she felt the heat. Sudden. Crawling into her

eyes and nostrils. Her entire skin screaming with a burning sensation like billions of microscopic needles piercing her.

She coughed. Someone nearby was coughing, too.

"William!"

Close. He was close. He was coughing.

She let go of something in her hand, a handle of some kind with a heavy object at the end, and it clattered over the roar of the fire as she began rubbing her eyes. The splash of water had slightly helped moisten them, along with the tears.

Barely, through the blur, she saw her son on his knees coughing, and a little further, by the kitchen sink, was Peter. Unconscious.

She went down on her knees to avoid the concentration of smoke at the top and she put her hand on William's shoulder. "William, what happened?" She felt stupid for even asking this. She knew. The entire house was burning.

I did this! I set the house on fire! I killed us all!

She held her son with one arm and tried to shake Peter with the other, but he didn't move. She could see the blood, now dried on his temple, and her eyes caught sight of the meat tenderizer lying nearby.

"I did this! I did all of this! Oh my God!"

"William! Help me pull your dad away from the cabinets." Her voice was urgent, fearful, but sure. "Grab under his shoulder. Hurry!"

William nodded and grabbed his dad's arm.

Jenny grabbed his other arm and yelled, "PULL!"

They both used all their strength to pull Peter's body toward the middle of the kitchen. They were surrounded by fire, so the center of the kitchen should be the last place to ignite—or, at least, that's what Jenny hoped. She needed to buy time to get William out of the house and return for Peter.

Jenny noticed the falling debris from the ceiling. Their previous house was lost to them. This house was supposed to be a new beginning, and now she could picture their life as a family ending in tragedy because of one neglectful mistake. She had to protect Peter. She had to shelter him from the fiery ceiling tiles, which fell like birds hit by a volcanic blast. Nearby, there was a cutting table made of metal. Moving him under it would take too long. She had to move the table, which was not heavy. It would certainly be hot, though. It had a thin lower deck at the bottom to store utensils and pots. Even if she could lift him onto the lower deck, there was the risk of it cooking her husband like a flattop grill.

She turned to William. "Take off your shirt, sweetie, give it to Mom." Her son did as he was told, and she wrapped his pajama shirt around her hand.

Coughing, her nose tucked under the fabric of her shirt, she ran toward the cutting table and crouched beside it. With the covered hand, she knocked out everything that was on the lower deck. Pots, pans, lids, jars, a full vegetable basket went flying all over the place. Onions with dry skins rolled toward the wall and caught fire. The moisture inside them caused them to bubble and pop.

Down on the metal table's lower surface, she found a small cleaning towel and wrapped it around her other hand. She punched the lower deck upward as hard as she could. Until one of the corners detached, then another and another. She grabbed the metal surface with both wrapped hands and tossed it aside. It landed in a leaning position against the refrigerator doors. Quickly, she stood and placed both covered hands on the edge of the table. Even through the fabric, she could feel how hot it was.

She pushed the table, moving it over Peter until he was almost fully covered, save for the lower third of his legs. She removed his slippers and rolled up his pajama bottoms, so no fabric was exposed. "Please, don't die. Hang on, I'll be right back."

She hoped the hot surface of the table was high enough off the floor as to not slow-broil her husband, but given the circumstances, there was little else she could do.

She tucked William under her oversized shirt and lifted him in her arms as if the boy weighed nothing. "Put your arms around me, sweetie."

William embraced her hard, and she ran out of the kitchen and into a nightmare hellscape of flames and black smoke that formed faces with red eyes and dark, cancerous lumps—beasts with coarse voices that growled deep as they consumed everything around her. As she did her best to find a way out through the flames, she could see chairs, tables, ornaments, all of which had taken on an evil appearance. The blazes had turned them into negative space, black silhouettes in abstract shapes within the glow, with shimmering edges and flickering, angry, bright patterns where empty holes used to be.

The way to the front door was blocked by a raging inferno. The windows were unreachable. It was hopeless. There was no way out, only—

"The basement!"

There was a clear path to the basement door. The large underground space would eventually catch fire, just like the rest of the house, but there was a considerable amount of material and structure separating it from the first floor, so it would give her some much-needed time, as the fire would not burn immediately through the gaps between the beams, or so she hoped. There was also the basement window that led to one side of the house at ground level. She could push William to safety through there.

What about Peter? How are you planning to get him into the basement?

"One crisis at a time," she mumbled angrily to herself.

How did I let things get this bad? Why didn't I go to therapy?

She knew what was behind the nightmares, the terrors, and the sleepwalking. She convinced herself she'd put all of that behind her, and here it was, back with a vengeance, burning down her new home, when all she'd needed to do was to go to fucking therapy.

She felt William cough under her shirt. The acrid smell of smoke was overwhelming.

Jenny ran toward the basement door, pulled it open. No orange glow down there, so it was likely the fire hadn't reached it yet. She flicked the light switch to her right, praying to all heavens and all gods from all pantheons the fire hadn't yet burned through the basement cables. Two lights, one shining over the stairs and a lamp down in the basement, came on.

Thank you!

She ran down and immediately headed toward the basement window, taking notice of the points through which the fire was already filtering through from the first floor. She took a small ladder that was resting against the wall, opened it awkwardly right next to the window, and climbed it, holding William with one arm. She poked her head to see if there was any danger or burning debris outside. It looked safe. "Go on, William, out," she ordered, letting him out from under her shirt.

"Mom, what about…you and…Dad?" William spoke between coughs.

"I'll go get him right now." Her face became even more serious and emphatic. "Go out. Now. Do not stand next to the house. You make it out there, and you run, you *run* all the way to the front of the house, don't stop until you reach the sidewalk across the street. You hear me?"

William nodded.

"Be careful crossing. Look both ways, alright?"

William nodded again.

She pushed him up, and he fit easily through the window. His feet disappeared as he ran toward the front of the house. She needed to get her husband, but there was the matter of bringing him down to the basement and up through the window. She glanced around the space. She had precious little time—the lights were already beginning to fail and she could feel the heat from the spots the fire was finally burning through.

There!

When she returned to the kitchen, the flames were reaching Peter. She watched him, still dizzy, gradually regaining consciousness, but not strong enough to stand on his own. She hurried to him, a dolly cart she'd borrowed from her dad in tow. She had put a large bag of garden soil on top of it, held in place by a truck-bed strap, secured tightly. She took the shirt and the towel she'd placed on Peter's stomach and once more wrapped her hands with them, and pushed the cutting table off him. She grabbed him from behind, arms under his shoulders, and pulled him with all her strength, until he was all the way on top of the dolly. Coincidentally, one-third of his legs hung off it, the same way they'd stuck out under the table.

Not ideal, but it is what it is.

She laid his head on top of the bag of soil and used another strap to tie him to the dolly.

As she was going around to grab the pull lever and get the hell out, a chunk of ceiling fell down next to her, almost crushing Peter. She screamed and was shocked at how quickly the fire was eating away at the second floor. There were pieces of blackened debris on top of him. She swiped them off quickly, grabbed the pull lever, and started rolling him out of the kitchen, kicking pans and pieces of burning cabinets that might stand in her way. Just as they were making it out of the kitchen, an enormous piece of the second floor caved in, and through the smoke and dust, she could make out the shape of a bed. The guest bed where she'd slept the previous night, crashing down from above.

She hurried toward the basement door, and now came the unpredictable part of her plan: she needed to push her husband down the stairs.

She'd found two large bags of clothes, blankets, quilts, and cushions they'd left in the basement until they could have time to fully settle themselves into the new house. She'd arranged the bags at the bottom of the stairs, praying they would cushion Peter's inevitable crash against the basement wall. The bag of soil she was using as a counterweight to prevent the dolly from flipping over as it went down the stairs. Although it wouldn't make the crash less violent, it would stop Peter from breaking his neck.

"Okay," she said, breathing in and out, as if in labor, then bursting into sudden, convulsive coughing. Once she recovered enough, she took one last look at Peter and said, in a tiny voice, "I'm sorry, baby."

She pushed the dolly, and it went bumping and tumbling down the stairs. The loud clatter of metal clashing against wood and concrete assailed Jenny's ears. She ran behind the dolly as if she could do anything besides hope she hadn't just killed her husband.

(*Yes, officer, I did tie my husband to a dolly and push him down the stairs into a burning basement. You see, I was trying to save him. Yes, I am a doctor, and that was the smartest idea I could come up with. What's your point?*)

The dolly crashed against the bags of fabric and sofa cushions, but there was nothing about the crash that seemed dampened in the least. She stopped in dismay when the first sound that assailed her after the crash was Peter screaming in pain.

"Peter!" She hurried to unstrap him from the dolly.

Peter's left ankle was twisted at a terrible angle. "I'm so sorry. It was the only way!"

"What happened?" He groaned with confusion in his eyes.

She helped him to his feet, and just as he put an arm over her shoulder, the electricity went out completely and the light bulbs died.

"Mother*fucker*!" Jenny growled with frustration.

Darkness enveloped them, but as her eyes adjusted, magma-like blobs of fire filled her field of vision, burning through the ceiling, breaking the darkness. The lighting was just enough to see their way, but soon they'd have a ceiling covered in flames, and it was the worst scenario she could think of. Jenny led a limping Peter to the window and told him: "Climb!"

"No, Jenny," he said, shaking his head. "You go first."

"You can't climb without my help. Put any weight on that foot, and you'll scream louder than if I stepped on one of your balls. Go!"

Peter hesitated, then gave her a nod. He climbed the small ladder, pulling himself up by holding the edge of the basement window and Jenny pushing him by his buttocks.

As she helped her husband, the ceiling came into view. Several of the blobs of fire bled into each other, fusing together to form a large, glowing, fiery amoeba, and small flaming pieces of ceiling were falling now into the basement.

"Hurry, baby, please," she said, as Peter crawled out of the window onto the grass. Once out, he turned around and put out a hand for her.

She was about to take his hand when she caught something out of the corner of her eye, and she couldn't help but stop. While the ceiling above her now burned like the sky itself was aflame, what called her attention was something at the deep end of the basement, where the light seemed dimmer.

A silhouette.

Negative space in the reddening background and the clouds of stirring smoke.

The shape of a woman stood there, but not *really* there. A woman who seemed familiar.

(*I've seen you. All these months…in my nightmares*)

A woman who couldn't possibly be in their house. The most terrible dread filled her, and her hands trembled. A sudden urge to call to that woman creeped up her innards. She wanted to see if she responded to the name crawling around in her brain

(*Martha!*)

but she feared calling out, because after everything that had happened the last two nights, she didn't think she could bear hearing the woman answer her call.

"Jenny!"

She was suddenly startled and turned to see Peter's

hand, now glowing in the light coming from the fire above.

"Hurry!" he called.

She rapidly ascended the ladder, held his hand, and climbed onto the window frame. As she got her head out, she looked to the street to glimpse William, looking tiny, standing on the sidewalk across the street. She felt she could hear him calling out to them, but in reality, he was too far to be audible.

Where are all the people?

The house had been burning long enough. The street should've been teeming with onlookers already. Someone should've called the fire department. Why couldn't she hear sirens? She gazed past her husband's head, and she could see a clear sky with no stars, but there was a full moon, and perhaps it was the smoke, but it looked blue—bright electric blue—like a shiny, silver plate in the sky.

"Where are the fire trucks?" she asked weakly, going into a coughing fit.

Peter gazed out toward the street, to see exactly what she'd seen: William and nobody else. "I don't know. Doesn't matter. C'mon. Hurry!"

Out of nowhere, there was a horrible creaking, and the creaking was like the sound of grinding teeth, and nails on chalkboards, and breaking bones, and choking throats.

It was the sound of Hell coming from the house it-self.

Peter—still coughing, still dazed, his ankle still screaming in pain—was trying to pull Jenny through the window. As her upper back was almost through, the burning house made an agonizing groan, and the world was alive with the sound of breaking and splitting. Before he could repeat, "Hurry!", the window frame cracked and the upper part of it broke at an angle, the point digging slightly into Jenny's back.

She cried in surprise and pain.

"No!" he shouted.

"It's pressing into my back," she groaned.

"Can you still move?" He clung to her hand.

"I think so." She grimaced, clenching her teeth together. "But it hurts. It hurts a lot."

"You can do it, baby. C'mon! You can do it!"

Jenny wiggled her way out of the tight space. Peter could see the tip of the broken frame leaving a rust-colored line down her back—what he was certain would've been crimson red in daylight, and this line expanded slowly, soaking her oversized shirt. Jenny stopped, panting, whimpering.

"I can't." She sounded defeated. "This is all my fault."

"Look at me! The woman I love just got her child and husband out of a burning house, all on her own. You don't mean that."

"I do. I really can't. It hurts too much." Her voice became tiny, like a little girl's. She hated how whiny she sounded.

"C'mon. You said the same when you were giving birth to William." Peter flashed his pinky at her. "Remember? You obliterated my finger because of how hard you were grabbing my hand, and I nearly passed out for a damn pinky."

Jenny chuckled with exhaustion, despite the pain, despite the terror, despite the urgency.

"Not you. You kept screaming, 'I can't', mixed with every profanity you knew, while you continued to pulverize my finger, until you pushed *that boy*"—Jenny swiveled her head, glanced at William, and Peter could see her mind working. He was trying his hardest not to show how afraid he was. He had to keep her pushing—"out of your body, and still had the strength to take him in your arms and give him a kiss on the forehead, while I was still recovering from the pain in my damn pinky!"

Their boy was so far from them, all the way across the street. The strongest reason they had to continue living.

"Now, c'mon. You can do this!"

She stared at him fiercely, nodded, clenched her jaw tighter, and once more tried to wiggle out of the basement. There was furious determination in her face, but also the absolutely racking pain of having a sharp piece of wall cut a line down her back like a chef's knife through fresh salmon. She screamed and screamed, and Peter tried to ignore the other sound that accompanied the screams—the cracking and groaning of the house.

"C'mon!" He kept pulling her hand. "C'mon!"

She gave one long pull, screaming her throat raw. She stopped again, but this time, it didn't appear she'd meant to. She pulled but wasn't moving an inch.

"No." Her eyes filled with despair. "I'm stuck. My shirt, it's stuck to a nail or something. The fabric is bunched together, so I can't rip it loose."

Alarmed, Peter crawled closer to the house, and he could feel the heat on the other side of the wall. He was in shock by Jenny's ability to even function with that much heat so close to her body. He grabbed at her shirt to pull her away, but another groan rippled through the house, and the board that made up the window frame collapsed further. There were now two jagged pieces of wood sticking into Jenny's back, as if the house just didn't want to let her go. The blood saturated her shirt even further.

Jenny clawed at his arms as she screamed in pain.

"Jenny, wh—"

The wall in front of Peter, weakened by the fire, exploded outward, and the flames, finding more oxygen to consume, now blazed out of the quickly expanding hole.

Peter rolled out of the way without even thinking

and gawked at the tongues of fire coming from the house. Jenny covered her head from the flames that were dangerously close, singeing her hair. He turned again onto his stomach and crawled toward her, but she put her hand out.

"Stop!" she shouted.

He did.

"Listen!"

Groaning. Creaking. Roaring. Breaking.

She shook her head. "I can hear the first floor breaking above me," she said hopelessly. Coughed. "It's about to come crashing down on me."

"No!" he yelled, ready to crawl toward her again.

"Stop, dammit! Just once in your life, can you fucking do what I tell you?"

He froze.

"Think! What just exploded up there? What's right above me?"

Peter noticed a considerable hole in the wall above Jenny, and despite the flames and the smoke, he could make out the outline of the box standing tall and ominous against the outer wall of the kitchen. He understood now. What had exploded had been the compressor, the cooling gas in the tank behind the refrigerator. It had overheated and exploded. The explosion would've normally gone through the doors, but they were blocked by debris, and the weakened wall had made it easier for the explosion to go out that way.

"Mom!" It was William's voice. "Dad! Hurry!"

The voice was approaching.

No! Stay away! Peter thought.

"The house is falling down!" William shouted.

"William, stay away!" Jenny shouted before Peter could. "Stop him, Peter!"

Without a second of consideration, Peter went up on his knees and dove toward the incoming boy, shielding him from the heat the best he could.

Jenny regarded them both in tears, now barely visible through the flames and smoke. "My two guys," she said, forcing a trembling smile, broken by a fit of coughing. "I'm so sorry. I—"

The black box of the burning refrigerator dropped through the floor, and Jenny's upper body angled upward. Her arms went up, as if she were at a baseball game and she was part of the crowd making a wave. It was the image that went through his mind before he saw her disappear, swallowed by the smoke. The second floor of the house finally gave in to fire and gravity, causing the burning kitchen wall to collapse inwards.

He couldn't even scream, but he could hear his son wailing in his arms as he used his entire body to shield him, and soon they were both enveloped in smoke. He could hear the flames roar and the entire house cave in on itself with the raucous sound of splintering wood and shattering glass and groaning metal, but the worst sound of all came immediately after.

The most blood-chilling screams he'd ever heard assaulted his ears.

He turned his head toward the house, and from the depths of his soul, he cursed the wind for letting him see what was unfolding beyond the black veil of smoke. Those screams, which sounded like they couldn't come from anything human, belonged to his wife.

The refrigerator falling onto her lower body, and the collapse of the house, hadn't buried her and killed her instantly. The refrigerator had instead crushed her lower body and pinned her against the basement wall, and as the entire window frame and wall had broken around her, it had pulled her upper body up, as if held at a sixty-degree angle by a tension wire.

His beloved wife, his dear Jenny, was visible from her torso up in the house's rubble, as if she were standing waist-deep in it. She looked like a figurehead on the prow of an old, wrecked ship. An obscene effigy, and like a proper effigy, she was burning, and she was screaming as the hungry flames that came from the remains of the house consumed her. Her arms flailed, her hair quickly disappeared as if it were itself becoming fire, and her skin burned and dissolved away as black and red spread like an infectious flesh-eating bacterium. He watched in revulsion as bursts of blue flame appeared and burned briefly as the pockets of fat in her body boiled and caught fire.

Like a sudden lightning bolt, William's name flashed in his mind. His son gawked at his burning mother, silent. No screaming. No tears. Just wide eyes, gazing in disbelief at the image that would be etched forever into his memory to never vacate his nightmares. The boy's mouth worked as if trying to say something. The moment a sound left his mouth, Peter immediately shielded him again with his body.

"Look away, son!" he said. "Look away!"

Peter, not heeding his own words, turned his head toward his wife. He couldn't look away and he had no one to shield his eyes. In a horrified fugue, he wondered how long a human being could feel their own body burning before losing consciousness. It had been merely a minute, but it had turned into an eternity, and during that eternity, Jenny screamed and screamed.

Wait, he knew this. He had written something about this before. Burning is the most painful death a human being can experience, but the pain doesn't last long. Once the skin and the nerve endings burn, there is no pain.

Jenny stopped screaming. She stopped moving.

He stared at her, still in a fugue. *Her skin burned completely and her nerve endings, too.* The thought was almost too calm, too detached, a purely scientific statement. *She feels no pain now. That's good. Is she still conscious?*

Jenny wasn't moving. Suddenly, she convulsed. She shuddered. The horror of this was worse. Of seeing her burn, knowing she couldn't feel pain anymore. Of knowing she was *aware* that she was burning, that her body was being consumed by the flames, without being able to feel herself dying.

It was so much worse.

She opened her mouth again, and he prepared for her to scream once more, but nothing came out. She remained like that.

Still.

Soon, flames licked out of her gaping mouth, like swift, bright, reptilian tongues.

She kept burning.

Burning.

Burning.

At last, the sound of fire sirens lilted closer and closer, as well as the sound of people screaming and shouting from the street. Futile sounds.

None of them mattered.

Jenny was burning.

Peter sat quietly. He let the second slap his mother had just given him sting. He didn't rub his cheek with his hand. The moment he'd shouted, "Mother, stop!" the slap had come out of nowhere. Like thunder when the curtains are closed, and you don't see the lightning to expect it. The beads in her hand left a print on his cheek.

Mother stood before him. Fire in her eyes.

"How dare you raise your voice at me? I've never known a more shameful example of a son. I told you what would happen if you married her. Disobedience has a price. I've paid for mine long enough, and it has cost me dearly. Now, you know what it feels like. In a way, it was your fault she died."

Peter's eyes flashed at her, filled to the brim with anger. In other circumstances, he would've hated her, but in his own mind, he had installed subconscious controls that would not let him even think of that word in relation to her. He couldn't hate his own mother. He simply couldn't. It wasn't right. One couldn't hate one's own mother. It was unnatural. No matter what they'd said or what they'd done.

"Take those eyes off me, boy. Lest the crows gouge them out."

Peter's gaze lowered to his feet as he spoke with a deliberate and steady voice. "I don't know if you'll remember what I'm about to say, but I came to say it. I *need* to say it, and you will hear me, Mother."

"Look at him," she sneered with a mocking musicality to her rough voice. "He thinks he's brave. He thinks he's a man. He thinks he has some authority in my house."

"This is not your house." His voice dripped with a boldness just barely laced with cruelty, which was the most he could manage in her presence. "This is a hospital."

Her vile countenance broke, her expression going from solid stone to shapeless dough.

"No. This is my house. You do not lie to your mother. This is my house, and you will respect me!"

"This is the elderly care wing of a hospital." Peter stood up from the chair. "You're in a nursing home." He let the cruelty snake back into his voice. It felt good. "*I put you here.*"

Mother shook her head, walked back toward her chair near the window.

"And if you ever expect to leave this place, you will listen to me, and you will listen to my terms, and maybe you can die with some dignity in a proper bed, in an actual home."

She sat down. "How dare you?" She seethed with anger, the sound of her shallow breathing echoed in the room. "Cursed son. Disobedient son. Aberrant son. Unnatural son!"

"Don't listen to me," he continued without acknowledging her words, "and when I leave town in four days, I will never come back until I'm sure you've died here. Alone, confused, and forgotten."

For a moment, he could see fear, insecurity, humiliation, terror, all cycling through her expression.

However, a second later, Mother straightened herself. The weakness in her face faded, replaced by a look of steely determination that her eyes now held, a reminder of the fierce dignity and pride he was used to seeing.

"Speak," she said.

Chapter Thirteen

Freddie Parham
1991

The day was bright, and sunlight peeked through the leaves in Burkle Park as if the trees were full of fireflies. Spots and splotches of light appeared and disappeared as the wind made the leaves and branches dance and sway, drawing blobs of light and shadow on the cobblestones and on the paper of his drawing block. The shifting light made drawing a little dizzying—almost dreamlike—but it was helpful, given the subject of his drawing, to have this strange oneiric mood.

There was a pervading quiet in the park. People rarely came to this park because it was the smallest in White Harbor, and not as well kept as Seaside Park—the largest one in town—but suited Freddie's tastes just fine. The trees had been permitted to grow more naturally, not constantly trimmed, cut and reshaped. He liked the figures the branches formed, and the way moss and epiphytes—he'd learned that word in biology class—grew on them, when in other parks, they would've been removed, or thought of as ugly.

If he turned his head left, he could see the house of Gerardo Valencia's family, beyond the trees. It was yellow, which made it visible even at the other end of the park. He knew the house was for sale—after Gerardo's death, and after the family had moved out, when the kid's mom went crazy. They would definitely have a very hard time selling it after what happened. One more house in White Harbor haunted by tragedy. He couldn't really understand how the Vanek House was considered *the* haunted house in town—hell, he couldn't understand how the Parhams, his family, were considered *the* cursed family in town—when so many others still had dark tales feeding Blight Harbor. He could almost point at each house as he rode his bike through town, going: *Killed her husband. Killed his wife. Killed their children. Killed their parents. Killed themselves.* Morbid little tales, and sad little ghosts behind bright-colored paint and pretty gardens.

His eyes rolled down toward his sketch. He wasn't super happy about it, but he could improve on it afterwards. The tentacle coming out of its mouth was missing something, but he liked the idea of how its back was bent forward and each arm was fused to each leg by their skin into a single limb. Maybe a hand at the end of the tentacle? No. That would just look ridiculous.

His attention was pulled from the drawing by the

sound of three bikes and a skateboard coming to a halt in front of him.

"About time," Freddie said, and put his drawing block in his bag. "I was about to go by myself."

The other kids dismounted.

"You didn't bring a bike?" Bobby asked.

"It's two blocks that way." He pointed. "It's close. I can walk."

"Your house is pretty far from here, so that doesn't make sense either," Callum said.

"I like to walk, alright?"

Callum stared at him, his gaze lingering, before he finally shook his head, unconvinced.

"Fine, I rode my bike into a rock and the wheel bent, so I walked here. It's exercise."

"That's okay," Peter said. "Let's just walk there. I think Bobby needs a rest."

"That would be awesome." Bobby gave Peter a grateful squeeze on the shoulder as he wiped the sweat from his brow. His shirt was soaked.

Freddie swiveled his head in Barry's direction.

"Well, I'll be damned if I wasn't already." He regarded the big boy, his curious eyes moving up and down his figure without an ounce of the fear other kids awarded him. "You crazy bastards brought Barry the Brickhouse."

"Any objections?" Barry said in a threatening growl.

"None from me." Freddie let out his signature giggle. "If it's true that Blight Harbor lives in the Vanek House, I'd be curious to see what it brings out of someone who's spent their life pretending to be tough."

"Aren't you afraid of what Blight Harbor might do with a freak like you?" Barry said.

Freddie raised his hands, shrugged, and giggled again. "I'm an open book! Nothing to hide!"

"Freddie," Peter said. "C'mon, take it easy. Barry's not a bad guy."

"Yeah, man," Leroy said, his voice dripping with sarcasm. "He's not a bad guy. He only tortured all of us our whole lives, and he's verbally abusive, and might actually strangle us all…but he's found Jesus now! He's not a bad guy!"

"C'mon!" Bobby said. "Quit it! We're all friends here! Well…" He shot a glance at Barry. "Barry's a new friend. That's all. I trust Peter's judgment on this. He has his reasons. Don't you all realize we're about to do something really awesome? We're about to go into the Vanek House! Can we just stop bickering?"

They all exchanged awkward glances.

"I think the reason we're taking shots at each other *is* because we're going into the Vanek House," Royce said. "We're nervous, man! We're letting off steam!"

Bobby smiled and surveyed the surrounding faces.

"But, c'mon, aren't we all excited?"

They all smiled and cheered triumphantly.

This would be a day they would never forget.

2022

At the criminal patient wing of Lighthouse Rock, Freddie Parham sat quietly in his room—listening to the gulls outside go quiet, like they did every day at midday—while the Mother of the Faithful said her prayers. He was not worthy to say the midday prayer because he was cursed. He was stained. He was filthy. But he had been given at least one phrase. The Lord, God, had granted him at least that one phrase, in His infinite mercy, and the phrase came with purpose. The phrase hinted at his redemption.

"*Tjenaf egoikaat gozun-Uolmin yggshe*," he whispered, and he grinned so widely he resembled the filthy animal that had been his nickname for so many years: a hyena. And he was just as filthy, but just as pure in purpose and in focus.

The birds resumed their calls, went quiet, then started once more.

He was waiting.

Waiting.

Waiting.

Like he'd waited all these years, and she'd told him it was time. She'd told him he could redeem himself and redeem his family. God could forgive him and forgive all the Parhams that had come before him. The key was in the one phrase the Lord had granted him.

"*Tjenaf egoikaat gozun-Uolmin yggshe!*" He repeated through grinning teeth, stained red from biting his own lower lip in excitement and pious euphoria.

God will feed.

Yes, He would, and Freddie Parham would set the table.

Chapter Fourteen

William

His grandma, who was sitting at the edge of the bed, kissed him on the forehead and ran a hand through his hair after tucking him in. She regarded him lovingly, still with the warm palm of her hand on his head, and said, "I love you, William."

"Me too, Grandma," the six-year-old boy said, his head poking from under covers with a space print with rocket ships, stars, planets, and moons.

"Thank you, Grandma."

"Your green eyes, though. Your eyes will always remind me of your mom."

"They remind me of my mom, too," he said with love in his small voice. "When I close them, I can see her."

Grandma was about to cry, but she was smiling.

"That's because she's always with you. Here." She gently tapped his head with her index finger. "That's why you can see her when you close your eyes." She placed her palm on the left side of his chest. "She's also here, in your heart, and while she's here, you will never be alone."

She kissed him again and stood up.

"Time to sleep, young man."

"Young man" was what his mom used to call him, and his grandma called him that, too, but he wasn't a man yet. If he'd been a grown man, he would've been able to save his mom, but he hadn't. He had only stood there, watching, and had moved way too late. Even if he'd made it to her side, what could he have done? He knew one day he *would* be a young man, and later a grown man, but what good would that do if he couldn't save his mom? For now, he supposed, he would try to enjoy the way his grandma said it. Everything made him think of his mom before the end, and the memory of how she'd died was almost too painful to bear.

He shivered slightly.

"Please, Grandma, don't forget the night light."

"Of course not." She tapped on a small light plugged in near the door and the entire room was filled with stars and moons and planets in soft white light. "Good night, young man. Sweet dreams."

Grandma left the room and softly closed the door.

He had spoken to his dad that afternoon. Dad arrived safely at the other town where he and his mom had the other house, the house he'd only been to a few times. Dad said he'd gone to see the ocean, and to drive around town, and he'd gone to a grocery store for food, and a nice lady he knew had given him a huge piece of strawberry cheesecake. Dad said he would save him some in the refrigerator and bring it when he came back home.

William told his dad about his day, about the new school, and how everyone was being nice to him. He said he'd gone to the playground with some of his new friends, and they'd played there—on the swings, and on the slide, and there were these big colored pipes that looked like giant worms you could crawl through from one end to the other.

As he remembered the call, he became sleepy.

He also told his dad he wished Mom had seen him at the playground. Dad said she'd seen him from Heaven, and it filled her with joy to see him play with his new friends.

William was sad sometimes, but he avoided telling his dad. Dad was sad all the time now, and he thought he didn't notice, but he did. He always made that face in which he smiled only with his lips, not his eyes. It was a weird face. Dad had told him he needed to be a brave boy at Mom's funeral, and he promised Dad he would always be brave. So, he would not tell him he felt sad or scared sometimes.

William felt the softness of his pillow beneath his head as he drifted off to sleep.

Blinking.

Dad said he was going out with friends that night and he would be okay.

Blinking again.

He was happy his dad was going out with friends, too.

One more blink.

William opened his eyes. He realized he'd fallen asleep for a moment, but was now awake. The night light was off and there was only moonlight coming from the window and—

"Don't scream," said a woman's raspy voice.

He almost did scream, but instead took in a sudden gasp and pulled the covers up to his nose. His eyes caught the shape of an old woman, standing in the corner near the window, where a band of blueish moonlight came in but didn't hit her directly. He could see her shape, and an outline of her face, but no details.

He had seen this woman before. She had been in his dreams before. She never talked. She never moved. She was always off in a corner, or somewhere behind him, or standing still in the shadows. Always looking. Always staring.

This didn't feel like a dream, though.

He was suddenly too scared to even move.

No, I have to be brave! I have to be brave!

His breathing became quick, his heart felt like it

would break out of his chest. The old woman stood in the corner, and he couldn't make out her eyes, but he was certain she was staring at him, and he opened his mouth to scream.

"I said, don't scream," she repeated.

He didn't know if it was because he was still half asleep and tired from playing so much during the day, or if he was fainting with fear, but his eyes blinked closed and open and closed, and, against his will, he once again drifted away into unconsciousness. In his mind, he kept thinking: *It's a bad dream! It's a bad dream! There's no old lady! There's no old lady!*

He opened his eyes again, and there she was, sitting on the edge of the bed, completely naked. The light of the moon was gone from the window, so he could just barely see her, but he knew she was naked, and he could see she had her back to him. He tried to scream again, but his voice didn't come out.

"I told you not to scream." Her voice came out in a sleepy grumble. "You didn't obey, so now you *can't* scream."

(*Every world is my world*)

It's a bad dream! It's a bad dream!

"I wanted to say I'm sorry." The woman in the dark sounded calm, but he realized, even in his panic, that she also sounded sad.

William tried to scream again, but only air came out.

"I didn't want it to come to this," she said.

He attempted to move away, but she had a firm, claw-like grip on his leg, and he could feel her fingernails digging into his skin, even through his pajamas. It hurt terribly, but he couldn't call for help.

"I had no choice." Her voice was a toad-like croak. "It didn't have to be like this, but she took him away."

William tried to push the woman off the bed, but his hands passed right through her. Impossibly, her claw still gripped his leg, and his attempt at pushing her had only made her tighten her grip. It hurt so badly he tried again to scream, but nothing would come out.

"It was the same with your mother," she said, and despite the pain, this made him stop and just stare at the shape before him in horror. "She had to die because she was standing in the way."

With the utmost fear, William realized his eyes were adjusting to the darkness, and now more details were visible of the naked old woman. She was scrawny, all bones and hanging skin, which moved like strings—or strips, or worms, or things that moved around to form her shape—and he started trying to slap the things away, but his hand passed through them as if they were nothing but air that was the color and texture of flesh.

"I only want what's mine." Her voice was a weary mumble now.

He kept slapping at the intangible mass that was

inexplicably holding him in place. The hand that wasn't a hand. The worms in the shape of a hand.

"It's what I deserve," she said.

William gritted his teeth and shook desperately. He could feel the fingernails now deep in his skin, and he could feel them wriggling underneath.

"I just wanted to say I'm sorry." She slowly turned her head toward him. "It's not something personal."

Out of all the terrible things he could think of with his young mind, instinctively, he knew, the most terrible would be to see that face. He didn't know what would happen, but he wanted to avoid seeing that face, now halfway turned in his direction. There was only air as he tried pushing her away. He screamed, but there was no sound.

"It's just what's right, but it won't be personal…"

He wanted to close his eyes now. Why couldn't he close his eyes now? He didn't want to see! He didn't want to see!

There it was, and it was worse than he could imagine. The face was human, just barely. The worm-like things wriggled and moved—slimy, glossy, reflecting light that simply wasn't there—and they moved in and out of each other, and through each other. Forming and unforming shapes that roughly drew a face, a terrible face, and that mouth with no teeth had a long, pointy tongue. The tongue moved by itself, extending, and contracting, like a worm when the point of the fishing hook comes near. It moved independently from the rest, even when the creature wasn't speaking. The most terrifying of all was there were no eyes, only two black holes, like caves in the middle of that shapeless, infinitely moving mass of living tissue.

The next words came out of a mouth that hung open—the jaw unmoving. Her tongue wriggled back and forth, with a life of its own, like a snake. A snake made of fleshy worms.

"It will not be personal either"—The tongue, the horrible tongue, and the nails digging into his leg, wriggling, burrowing under his skin—"when I come for you."

Suddenly, William realized he could scream.

And he screamed.

His eyes—which he thought were already open—flew open, and it was morning, and sunlight came in through the window, but he could still see an outline of the empty black sockets and the wriggling tongue floating in the air.

William jumped in surprise when the door to the room opened, but it was only his grandmother. She surveyed her surroundings with an expression of deep worry. "William, what's wrong, honey?"

The boy flew out of bed, ran toward her, threw his arms around her waist, and cried with loud sobs, more akin to all the screaming he hadn't been able to let out during the bad dream.

Chapter Fifteen

A Handful of Silver

1989

A moment of silence passed after Mother told him she loved him. Peter became pensive, a nagging voice in his head saying there was more to Mother's change of demeanor than she was letting on.

As he stared at the fire, he heard her sigh.

"Out with it, boy. What's on your mind?"

"I'm sorry, Mother. I don't mean to question you…"

She smiled, and while the smile appeared sincere, her eyes appeared tired and old. "You'd like to know why you should stay away from the Vanek House, don't you?"

Peter nodded.

She licked her lips, and her hand caressed the leather binding of the book on her lap.

"Do you know…" She seemed to be piecing together old information from different parts of her memory "…how the curse of the Parhams came to be?"

"No," he said. "There are a lot of stories, but they sound made up."

"They are." There wasn't a hint of doubt in her voice. "Only a few know, and those who know won't tell. That's what the rabble of this town call Blight Harbor—an ignorant name for a serious thing. People in this town know the Parhams are cursed, but that's all they know."

"And are they, Mother?" Peter's eyes filled with wonder and interest, his imagination running miles ahead of him. While his mother didn't allow him to watch television or movies, he sometimes took a book from the library, and he had a secret place where he would hide the books. Somewhere Mother couldn't know about, since the punishment for reading "lies" would be severe. In those books, he read of magical artifacts, potions, mummy curses, vampires, sorcerers, ghosts, and many things that, according to the authors, could curse a person. "Are the Parhams really cursed?"

"Yes," she said plainly. "The curse dates back to when White Harbor was nothing but a growing settlement around the 1880s. The curse of the Parhams started with a boy. He was probably your age. His name was Walter Parham."

1882

Walter Parham, the youngest and shortest of five children born to Isaac and Dorothy Parham, was, by far, the most troublesome of their brood. Walter was often called mischievous and wicked by other parents, as he had the tendency to throw rocks at girls and kick boys with unbridled glee. More than once, his embarrassed parents had spanked or whipped him in front of neighbors as both apology and penance when he'd snuck in to steal bread or fruit from other people's property.

The whipping was particularly savage the day young Walt stole, killed, plucked, roasted, and ate a chicken from one of his neighbors, all by himself. Isaac Parham whipped the boy over a rock. The entire roasted chicken came spewing out of his mouth in a spray of ungodly vomit that landed on the offended neighbor's leather boots. This had only made the whipping that much worse.

The boots were quite expensive.

The apotheosis of Walt Parham's mischief, though, came one afternoon, after school, when the boy thought it a good idea to sneak into the local church, break into the tabernacle, and take the golden cup he'd seen the local priest get from there so many times before. He always saw the adults drink from its contents, but he was never allowed to.

"Not yet," his father kept saying. "Patience comes from God, Walter. Wait, and your time will come."

Wait. How he hated that accursed word. What did his father know about the cruelty of the word "wait"? It was an imposition that made his skin itch with exasperation. His father, a local carpenter, was an adult, and adults could do whatever they wanted, so they couldn't possibly understand the evils of the word "wait".

It was ridiculous, Walt thought. He didn't have to do what adults told him to do, because nobody told *them* what to do. Well, maybe God, he corrected himself, but what did God know about patience when nobody ever told *Him* to wait?

Certainly, there was punishment for disobeying God, and there was punishment for disobeying his parents. A cane, or a belt, and the pain they could inflict; he was familiar with all, but they seemed a small price to pay for the absolute pleasure of doing whatever he wanted, whenever he wanted. Punishment was the price he willingly paid in exchange for entertainment.

The liquid inside the cup was a captivating, dark red that looked delectable. People often licked their lips after sipping from it. Reverend Burgess always said it was the blood of Christ, and it shocked him to realize it was Jesus's blood the adults were drinking. He couldn't even fathom that! It was madness. No matter how many times his father tried to explain the logic behind the ceremony, he always came out of the conversation with a single takeaway: adults were drinking blood, and it apparently had a delightful taste because it was the blood of Christ, who kept just giving it away to people.

No one would've ever accused Walter Parham of carrying the weight of a brilliant mind.

He had tasted human blood before. His own. Once, when he'd crashed face-first into a tree, while running away from his father's whipping cane, and it had tasted like licking one of his mother's copper plates. He'd also had blood sausage, made with pig or chicken blood, and he'd found it delicious. Maybe there was something about this "blood of Christ" that made it taste like blood sausage, but somehow liquid? Christ was known for performing miracles, after all. He'd turned water into wine—the fact that what the adults drank at church was, in fact, wine never occurred to him—so why couldn't he turn blood sausage into something drinkable? Regardless of the specifics, he had to try it, and waiting for his father's permission was not an option.

Walt, not finding the sacramental wine inside the tabernacle, only an empty cup, allowed himself to go around the altar and into the sacristy. He searched around, opening cabinets, and scattering their contents all over the floor until he found his prize. When he found the wine, he retrieved the priest's vestments from the floor, where he had thrown them, and determined he would dress up. He wasted no time in pouring and downing cup after cup of sacramental wine from the pretty golden chalice he'd found—he was now dressed as a priest, so he was entitled to it, he thought confidently.

At first, the wine tasted bitter, like spoiled fruit, but as he continued drinking, it became a shifting, almost living, blend of tastes and smells that swirled into each other—from bitter, to acidic, to sweet, to a thing he could only describe as a "fruity vapor" that caressed his palate, flowed from his throat, and up the back of his nose.

So, this was what Christ's blood tasted like.

Reverend Burgess emerged from his quarters, putting on a coat and hurrying toward the church, where an awful racket was coming from. Such unthinkable noises could only mean evil was afoot, and in God's home, of all places.

It was he who found the appalling scene. He walked into the church to find Walter Parham, drunk and nearly unconscious, on the altar floor. The obscenity of what had transpired was a sight to behold.

In the boy's drunkenness, he'd apparently taken ink he'd found in the sacristy to the wall right under the altar's large crucifix and, with his fingers, in large, bold letters, he had written a single sentence: "Reverend Burgess hides a tiny cock under his tunic." The priest thought, in a speechless trance of utmost horror, the boy had impeccable calligraphy for one so young and so inebriated.

The little heathen had pulled down some red fabric from the altar walls and worn it around his shoulders like a long cape, perhaps pretending to be King George III— post-madness, obviously. The Reverend could see the cape, befouled and stained with ink, tied around the boy's neck, and strewn across the altar floor, garish and dramatic, like those vulgar portraits by those Italian and French painters. Coincidentally, the boy's right hand had its finger pointing laxly, reminiscent of *The Creation of Adam*.

He could also see the trespasser—surely still in his King George III fugue—had pranced around the church, his soles soaked with ink, leaving black footprints all over the floor. Speaking of the boy's shoes, he thought to himself, in a horrified reverie, where *were* his shoes now? The Boy— capital "B", with emphasis on plosion, as he would refer to Walter Parham from this day forth, lest his name carried the curse of his heresy—was barefoot. It didn't take him long to determine he had used the shoes as projectiles to shatter two of the church's windows, one to the left and one to the right.

A rancid puddle on the floor nearby told him the Boy had also put out several candles using his urine, while standing on a chair. Finally, as Reverend Burgess approached any semblance of human comprehension of this, came the fulfillment of the Boy's life's work—his *piè*ce de résistance—the most absolute desecration of God's holy house Reverend Burgess could envision.

The Boy, out of nowhere, simultaneously began to puke and shit himself on the altar floor. Noxious smells and unspeakable substances gushed from both ends of his body. Then, as if signing this masterpiece, the Boy raised a feces-covered hand to grab the pulpit to stand up, slipped on his own vomit, and fell back down, his hand sliding down the side of the pulpit, leaving five thin brown streaks on it.

His final offense complete, the Boy fell asleep.

The Parhams pleaded for forgiveness from Reverend Burgess. They offered penance, they offered money, they offered prayer. They begged the priest not to damn their godless son to Hell—as they knew he probably deserved for his trespass—and yet Burgess seemed unmoved by their pleas.

Isaac Parham, on his knees, his wife kneeling beside him, said with eyes barely holding back tears, "But Jesus said, suffer little children, and forbid them not, to come unto me: for of such is the kingdom of heaven?"

"Matthew 19:14," Burgess said. "Do not quote scripture to me. I know it." He beheld Isaac Parham sternly as he recited in a quick whirlwind of biblical verses. "Proverbs 13:24: He that spareth his rod hateth his son: but he that loveth him chasteneth him often. Proverbs 19:18: Chasten thy son while there is hope and let not thy soul spare for his crying. Proverbs 22:15: Foolishness is bound in the heart of a child, but the rod of correction shall drive it far from him. Proverbs 23:13-14: Withhold not correction from the child: for if thou beatest him with the rod, he shall not die. Thou shalt beat him with the rod and shalt deliver his soul from hell. Proverbs 29:15: The rod and reproof give wisdom: but a child left to himself bringeth his mother to shame."

He turned his fiery eyes toward Dorothy Parham. "I believe you have been brought to shame many times already by your son, have you not? There is no changing that, and that is your punishment to bear. If you listened to the holy scripture, instead of your hearts deafened by parental love, you'd know God would have expected you to plead for me to punish your son, not spare him, not lessen his punishment. He has the foolishness of a child, but foolishness can also be a mask of evil, and he certainly has a tendency for foolishness, does he not? Therefore, if foolishness can hide evil, how big an evil can such monumental foolishness hide?"

Both parents shrunk and looked away in shame.

"Chasten thy son while there is hope!" he repeated angrily, nostrils on his long, prominent nose flaring. "If thou beatest him with the rod, he shall not *die*!" He emphasized the word "die" as if he had wanted it to be the only word in the English language for these two fools. One word that would crush their souls and submit them in obedience to the Lord. After a grave pause, he continued: "It would fall unto me, since I cannot trust you with objectivity, to assess whether there is still hope for the Boy." He spat copiously this time as he pronounced the "B". "Though, ultimately, it would be God's decision." He gave each one a stern and disapproving look, conveying how he found them unfit to be parents. "Bring him to me."

Isaac Parham retrieved his son—who was still pale and ill from drinking too much wine—and stood him in front of Reverend Burgess. He lowered his gaze, as if not wanting to witness what the good reverend would do to his son. His wife, who was now standing next to him, lowered her head as well.

"Look at me, Boy," the Reverend said, with a soft velvety voice, which, instead of sounding soothing, sounded like the smooth coiling of a thick, muscled snake, as its scales slid over the fabric of its victim's clothes.

The Boy tried to lift his gaze, hesitated, and let it fall.

"Look at me, I said!" A single flex. A tightening of the coil.

The Boy's gaze finally met his—blue, bloodshot, and terrified.

"Did you know the punishment for blasphemy in many parishes, even now, is to brand the sinner on the forehead and pierce his tongue with a red-hot poker?"

Dorothy Parham gasped in terror, tears streaming down her face, as blabbering pleas issued forth from her lips. The Reverend glared at her, and she became instantly quiet, as if struck dumb.

"However,"—he returned his gaze to the Boy—"that is reserved for blasphemy, as I said, which is a sin of the mind and the tongue." He touched the Boy's forehead and his lips with his index finger as he said this. "The punishment is, therefore, fitting for the sin. *Your* sin was not of the tongue, Boy, but certainly of the mind…and the hands." The Reverend touched the tips of the Boy's small fingers, with the same rough finger he'd used to touch his forehead and lips. He was reminded of those tiny digits covered in black ink and feces. "Perhapssss…" The Reverend trailed off as if considering.

The Boy clenched his fists as he trembled.

Reverend Burgess had to suppress a twisting corner of his lips, a sign that would denote worldly pleasure in the fear he was causing the Boy. He could see he intensely dreaded the words that would soon come out of his lips, as the wicked must fear the rapture. *This,* he thought, *is fitting.*

Quickly, in one breath, in an almost orgasmic fashion, he said: "Perhaps we might consider branding your forehead and piercing your hands instead of your tongue."

At this, the dam that held the Boy's tears at bay finally broke, and copious streams ran down his face as he blubbered, terrified.

His parents wrung their hands in anguish.

Three for the price of one. Three sinners good and tortured for their sins.

The Boy, an incorrigible delinquent. The parents, cravens, oozing the sin of mercy, for mercy is also a sin when given to one undeserving.

"The pokers will pierce your hands," he said, salivating more than he felt proper, "and, in doing so, they will bring you closer to our Lord, who felt his holy hands pierced as they were nailed to the cross." He locked eyes with the Boy. "Don't you think that's fair?"

No answer. The Boy was sobbing hopelessly. His face was a mess of tears and running snot.

"Answer when an elder asks a question, Boy!"

"Yuh…" the Boy started. "Yuh…yessss…but I don't want th-that!"

"Oh?" The Reverend feigned shock. "You do not want to be like our Lord, Jesus Christ, who was nailed to the cross and died for our sins. You do not want *that*, or something close to that, even as penance for your wrongdoings. Do I hear you correctly, Boy?"

The Boy shook his head, confused and terrified, as if realizing what he had just said might send him to hell, but the opposite answer might accomplish the same. "No!" He blurted, loud enough for his parents to gasp, fearing he had further disrespected the priest by raising his voice. "I mean… not the…"

"The pokers?" the Reverend said, and he allowed himself the tiniest grin. He had earned it. "After the branding and the piercing, I believe a flogging might be in order," the Reverend added this quickly, not allowing time for the Boy to recuperate—another coil of the snake tightening around the little sinner. Now, as if moving to the time of a dreadful requiem, he tightened yet another coil. "We shall follow that with pillorying."

"No, please!" cried Dorothy Parham, who could contain herself no longer, and she sobbed loudly, unable to restrain herself anymore. "For the sake of my family, of my other children! 'Tis like branding *them*, too! He's a heathen, but they are not!"

"Kindly contain your woman, Isaac Parham." The Reverend did not turn to face him, his eyes were still fixed on the Boy, as if Mrs. Parham's sobs were a slight nuisance not to be allowed to disturb him. "Or do you wish to be seen as soft by God, not only toward your evil child, but toward your disobedient wife?"

The Reverend turned a side-eye in the man's direction.

As if someone had taken hold of his hand, with a

stunned expression on his face, Isaac Parham slapped his wife firmly across the cheek. He bit his lip and closed his eyes, the face of a man forced to do something he found objectionable. The shock on her face registered for only a second, but it confirmed to the Reverend this was something Parham rarely did, or never had done. The Parham woman stood quiet and immobile, eyes still spilling tears down her cheeks, but no more sounds came from her mouth.

Good.

"Pillorying!" He returned to the Boy, continuing the portion of the conversation he had been in before being so rudely interrupted. "Do you know what that is?"

The Boy nodded.

"Your neighbors will laugh at you, throw rotten fruit and mud at you. They'll insult and ridicule you, and all you can do is stand there, bent forward, hands and head trapped in place. The public humiliation of your peers as they shame a sinner." The Reverend licked his lips. "Oh, but it doesn't stop there. Oh, no. Then, you will spend as many years as the Lord wills it in hard labor, in prison."

"I'm…" the Boy tried to say.

"What was that?"

"I'm just…a little boy."

"Oh!" He regarded the terrified parents with an openly amused grin, big, white teeth revealed in menacing joy. Now that the topic of ridicule had entered the conversation, he could grin if he so chose. "He is a little boy, he says. He drank more wine than an adult man can drink. He commits heresy in the house of the Lord, and yet, now, facing his punishment, he is a little boy."

He stood tall, ominous, and menacing, looming over the Boy as if he were a stone statue that would topple over and flatten him. He stood there, quiet, for an instant. "You are a little boy, indeed. You are also a heretic. Never forget that. Heretics know not the forgiveness of the Lord, but you *are* a little boy."

He glowered at the Boy's parents.

"Chasten thy son while there is hope. I bear no hope for this one, if I am to be honest, but I am a man, flawed, and prone to the sin of obduracy, and I will try to find forgiveness in my heart for what your son has done, but hope is not for me to give, only for the Lord. So, take this heretic, know in your hearts he is a heretic, and give him the punishment you feel matches the shame you will feel from now on when you enter the house of God. For the Lord forgives, but he does not forget, and neither, I fear, will this church's parishioners. Hope there is hope, and let the Lord decide what to make of this creature of yours."

Walter's parents bowed their heads. Isaac Parham grabbed his sobbing son by the arm. His grip was hard, firm, and he was opening his mouth to, seemingly, say his thanks and hurry out, when the voice of the Reverend stopped him.

"Where could you possibly be going? I am not finished. I have not given you leave. I said he committed heresy: blasphemy of the mind and the hands. Did you not hear me? I must still give a fitting penance for such a sin."

He regarded the Boy again.

"You will come after school each day, and you will kneel on dried kernels of corn, and you will read the word of our Lord, from page one—*slowly*—until the words drive themselves into your skin like those kernels will. You will do this for an hour each day until you've finished. That will be the penance of your mind. The penance of your hands will be that after you finish your hour of reading, I will cane your palms each day, and with sore hands, you will work to mend the damage you did. You will clean, and you will scrub, and you will carry, and you will work for the Lord, until this house of worship is restored to the glory you befouled and continue until I say you are released from the Lord's service. Is that clear?"

The Boy's red face bobbed up and down in fearful agreement, only seconds before his father dragged him out, having received a nod from the Reverend, granting him leave.

Later that day, Walter Parham received the punishment his father decided was equal to his shame. His father made him disrobe before his sisters and brothers, and caned him. He did this as Walter was bent over the rock they'd forced him to hug so many times before, when his punishment was due. The caning did not stop until his back and buttocks bled, and the boy mercifully fainted with pain.

Walter's father, his sisters later told him, beat him for a full minute afterward to make sure he wasn't faking his unconsciousness. As per their telling, his father was weeping as he carried him, limp—with his pants once more soiled and wet—to the barn where he would sleep until he finished the reverend's penance. His mother also wept as she'd dressed his wounds, but it had been she who requested he be taken to the barn, as she would not have him in the house while his sin was still not forgiven.

The whipping cane left deep, bloodied lines that would mark his skin. They would continue to hurt for weeks and would never fully disappear.

Every day, Walter walked from the school to the church, where he would carry firewood, clean the outhouses, sweep the floors, wipe the glass, trim the bushes, and light the candles.

He started the morning after his befoulment of the church, with his body beaten, bruised, and raw. After kneeling on dry kernels that pierced his knees like daggers, and reading the word of a God that was surely laughing at his misfortune, he ensured no trace remained of his excretions anywhere on the altar. He even cleaned between the boards and the texture of the wood. He scrubbed the ink off the wall and the floors, which was especially hard, slow work. The whole time he did this, he cursed Reverend Burgess, feeling the sting of his caned body. Especially his hands, whose broken skin burned the moment soap touched it.

As he worked, every single day, he mumbled angrily to himself that, even now, he believed Reverend Burgess hid a tiny cock under his robes. He hated the sanctimonious man and swore one day he'd have his revenge. He would not forget his anger. His resentment would never die. It would sit in his heart and fester, and grow, and the right moment would come in which he would unleash all of his anger on the reprehensible reverend.

And his tiny cock, he thought.

However, there was one thing his childish mind couldn't have predicted.

Against all odds, he had slowly begun to forgive. His resentment gradually dissipated. He hadn't forgotten what had happened, or how much he hated kneeling on kernels and having his hands caned—he certainly still hated that. He wasn't suppressing the anger, it was being replaced by something resembling acceptance and peace.

He came to understand that what he'd done, and how he'd behaved in the past, had hurt others. He'd hurt people by stealing and damaging their property. He'd hurt the town by defacing the church, something to which the town had a spiritual connection. He'd never once felt that connection until he became the one in charge of keeping it clean.

As the months passed, he realized it wasn't just him that was changing, but others as well, even Reverend Burgess.

On a sunny Thursday afternoon, he arrived at the tiny pantry where he went to kneel and pray, and found the floor not covered with corn kernels. Fearful he might be punished for being spared his daily dose of pain, he went to Reverend Burgess, who didn't react to his presence. The priest shrugged with indifference and said, "If there are no kernels to kneel on, I suppose you'll have to kneel on the wooden floor, won't you?"

His hands weren't caned, he was simply asked to do his chores.

He noticed the townspeople were talking to him again. The other children could now play with him. One Saturday morning, as he entered the church, Mrs. Glendale passed him by and said, "Good day, Walter. God bless you." He was so surprised by this, he could not reply. He merely nodded and smiled, not knowing how to react.

His parents were the last to come around—perhaps because they knew him enough not to expect a genuine change from him—but they eventually allowed him back into the house.

The change happened one night, as he sat in the barn, quietly doing his homework with a candle on a small desk. He was waving away the night bugs he'd become accustomed to by now, as the mosquito net he'd been given only covered the pile of hay he used as a bed. His mother approached the entrance, but he didn't hear her until she was already standing there. He stared at her, surprised. Her eyes were downcast, her hands clasped together in front of her, but she glanced at him and said, "Your father killed some rabbits this afternoon. I've roasted them with some herbs for supper."

He looked at her hands, almost expecting her to make a plate appear out of thin air with a piece of roasted rabbit and some potatoes. After all, he'd had to eat in the barn ever since the church incident. What shocked him, though, was when his mother spoke again.

"Come eat inside. It's cold here."

With no further words, his mother turned and left him there.

He supped with his family on a proper table, with warmth emanating from the hearth. His mother sat quietly in a chair by the fire. She had excused herself from the table earlier, saying her stomach wasn't agreeing with her that evening, but she'd served the food with a smile and quietly watched them eat from her chair, a Bible resting on her lap.

They were once more a family. He shoved forkfuls of rabbit meat, potatoes, and tomatoes into his mouth. It didn't matter he would've eaten the same meal in the barn as he was eating there. Eating it with his family made it taste better.

His father had taken longer to come around. He spoke to him, but often avoided his gaze. Isaac Parham wasn't a distant man by any measure, but he was proud, and Walt knew what he'd done had brought much shame to his family. When his father approached him, just as Walter was getting close to giving up on a reconciliation, he glanced at him with his hands on his hips—as if to stop himself from just hugging his son—and said, "All is forgiven." He nodded at Walt.

Walt nodded back.

That had been the last word spoken on that subject. He left Walt wondering if his father had meant that as a statement, forgiving him for what he did in the church, or as a question of whether Walt forgave him for the way he'd beaten him. He concluded it had perhaps been a little bit of both.

1887

Change continued as the months and the years passed. He found he'd started enjoying his work, though he wasn't sure when this had happened. He just knew it was true. All that extra energy he'd devoted to mischief now seemed to be focused on his daily work. A sense of pride grew in him about the cleanliness of the floors and the restored windows. The bushes he trimmed were now more beautiful than ever, because of how sharp his eye had become at pruning any wayward leaf. He planted flowers that brought color to the church's garden. There had always been flowers there, but these were *his* flowers, in *his* favorite color. He planted lady's leek, aster, fireweed, columbine, ookow, gilia, and penstemon, all in different shades of purple.

His father once told him certain religions used purple in ceremonies of healing, or of repelling evil. He had always just thought purple was pretty but given all he'd done to atone for his own evil, it was symbolic. "Fitting," Reverend Burgess would say in that severe tone of his.

Before Walt Parham knew it, five years had passed. He was fourteen, and unofficially—but locally accepted as— the church's gardener. His past offense now seemed like a distant memory, which made sense when five years made up nearly a third of your life so far. The world had changed quickly, and people had changed their perception of him as well. Once in a while, his sisters, or another kid at school, or even an adult, would throw a jibe his way, reminding him of that time he did the unimaginable to the local church. He never sensed malice in those remarks and felt they were in good humor. People who once cursed him for stealing from them now invited him into their homes to help with any work he could do for them, and even paid him for it.

Reverend Burgess, however, still kept interactions with him to a bare minimum. Maybe in the good reverend's mind, the Boy, as he always called him, would never fully repay his debt.

He found this not to be the case on the day of his fourteenth birthday. As he stored the gardening tools in the church's shed, Walt turned around at the sound of a floorboard creaking behind him and was startled by the reverend, who stood there silently. A shadow fell over Walter since, despite his age, he was still quite short. He feared he had displeased the reverend, and an additional punishment was now coming his way after years of good behavior.

"Take this," the priest said, holding out a fist with the glint of metal between the fingers. Copper and silver. Coins, he realized. Walt put his hand out and his ears were greeted by the cheerful sound of the coins passing from Reverend Burgess's hand to his. "Your debt has been settled. This is payment for your services."

Walt stared at the coins in his hand with shock, as if the priest had handed him the key to the gates of Heaven. He had never held as much money at one time. His mouth worked soundlessly until the words, "Thank you," spurted clumsily from his lips like drool.

"You have done good work. Take that to your family. They will find more use for it than you alone, but save some for yourself. Not too much, though. Do not let the greedy monster that defiled this church make a return. Your family deserves some of those coins for the shame they bore."

Walt stared at the priest with growing concern and took in a breath.

"Notice I speak in the past tense, Boy. I mean it when I say you've paid your debt, your soul is no longer in danger."

Walt smiled, and for the first time in five years, Reverend Burgess smiled back, none of the petrous expression he often wore on his face when he spoke to him.

"One more thing," Reverend Burgess said, making him stop clumsily as he was about to turn around and leave. He was still smiling pleasantly. "You like purple flowers, I've noticed. Is that right?"

"Yes, Reverend. Very much."

"Why?"

"Well…"

He paused and ruminated on the answer. He knew in his mind the reason, but it was a different feat to put it into words for another to understand. He didn't think he had the language for it.

"My father says it represents the…" He searched for a word, but it escaped him. "Royalty. The *royalty*? The *regality* of Christ?"

"Oh?" the priest said. "Do you mean you wish to appear *regal?*" There was some of the mocking voice the priest had used the day Walter had failed God, which made the boy tense up. "I seem to remember the last time you attempted to seem regal with a red cape. It did not turn out so well."

"No!" He stopped and composed himself. "I don't. I'm not. It represents—"

"Penitence, and the repentance of sins," the Reverend cut in. "I know, and it should be meaningful to you, for obvious reasons."

He smiled again at him, and Walter found it both a relief and a source of shock. Reverend Burgess had smiled twice at him, in a single conversation, after five years.

"I will give you another gift." The priest's smile did not fade. "Not coins or anything of value to anyone, but perhaps precious to you."

Walt's eyes opened wide, and his ears perked up. Another gift? What could it possibly be?

"John Ellis. You know good John, right?"

Walt nodded.

"Long-Lived John is a fine hunter, despite his age, and he has explored more than any one person in town has dared within the boundaries of the Crescent Mountains."

"He also sells the best cut of bacon I've ever had."

"Do not interrupt me, Boy." The Reverend's smile left him for a second but returned briskly. "Long-Lived John once told me of a flower he's taken to calling blue moonbud. He says, in his long years, he'd never seen or heard of such a flower, but it grows on the southeastern end of the mountain range, in the forest."

"What does it look like?" Walt's eyes filled with wonder. "Has he told you?"

"Patience, Boy. Yes, he has. He said the bud of these flowers is perfectly round and pale blue, like blueish silver almost, and they have tender blue splotches that resemble the Man in the Moon. When the flower finally opens, the inner side of the petals is bright purple, almost fuchsine, and the center is silvery blue. That center, John says, seems to reflect the light of the moon because the center glows."

Walt's mouth worked as if trying to say something coherent. What Reverend Burgess described seemed to be not from this world, something dreamlike. He could picture it in his mind and wondered if the real thing would be even close to what he now imagined. He had to know. He had to see it. If he could, he had to bring at least one here and plant it. It would be the most beloved flower in the garden he had toiled in for five years.

"Go." The priest gave another smile, moved by his joy. "Go with my blessing, and I hope you find it."

Walt mouthed the words "Thank you" and left, running.

He bought himself a knapsack with two straps and

a flat bottom, two small clay pots, his own spade, so he wouldn't have to take the one from the church's shed—he didn't want to spoil the reverend's good humor by taking things without permission—and a new pair of boots that would allow him to walk in the woods easily.

He purchased all this and was surprised he'd spent only a quarter of the money the priest had given him. The rest of it, he left on the dining table with a quickly jotted note for his parents. In it, he told them this was his first pay from Reverend Burgess and to expect more. He was going into the woods to search for a flower for the church's garden, and he would be back before nightfall. This, he knew, would not sit well with his parents. His father had said he was already a man, but even a man could be too young to go into the woods alone without proper training. It wasn't something he'd never done before, though, and certainly it hadn't been for as godly a reason as getting flowers.

He walked for hours, searching, to the point he thought, perhaps, the Reverend had sent him on a snipe hunt of sorts, a final penance for befouling the house of God, but he didn't truly think so. Reverend Burgess's smile and advice had seemed sincere and with no malice behind it. In fact, he'd even seemed curious about whether "The Boy" could find the flower and bring it to the church. Of course, Long-Lived John Ellis could've perhaps given some additional pointers. All he had to go by was "the southeastern end of the mountain range, in the forest" which was almost as vague as saying, "Over there."

He kept the slowly westering sun in sight through the tops of the trees, in order not to lose his way, and he estimated at some point, during the search, he'd deviated slightly to the north. He reached the point in which the ground quickly sloped upward, which meant he was at the northeastern edge of the Crescent Mountains, so, if John Ellis's directions hadn't been a tall tale—something he was questioning more with every passing minute—all he needed was to skirt the mountain heading south, sticking close to the woods and he could, probably

(*get lost in the woods forever*)

chance into a patch of unearthly flowers of blue, purple, and silver.

The sky was darkening, and he hadn't yet found the fabled blue moonbuds. He knew he should turn back soon. If he arrived late, he would find his mother fretting with worry and his father growing angrier by the minute. The sky was clear. Not a single cloud. The moon would rise soon, and he could use that as a guide to get home, even if it was dark. It was a full moon that night, so the sky wouldn't be completely black, except for maybe an hour. But what about wild animals? A wolf or a cougar? What about a snake hiding in the grass?

"Don't be silly, Walt Parham," he grumbled to himself. "You've already had all the bad luck you're ever going to have."

A rustling in the bushes behind him gave him a start, and he jumped with a cry, only to turn and barely glimpse some kind of furry creature scurrying from one bush and into another. A raccoon, perhaps, or even a rabbit—he couldn't tell. He let out a breath of relief, but the relief was gone only minutes after, when he realized the sky had darkened past the halfway point, and there was no way for him to get home before the night blanketed the entire west.

He continued to walk until the hill to his left—which was green during the day but was now blue gray in the dark—turned into a low rocky wall that increased in height as he advanced. The sound of birds in the trees announcing their goodbye to the sun soon quieted and there was near-perfect silence, broken only by the rustling of his boots on the grass or their crackling in the dirt. He could hear unnerving crunching sounds coming from behind him, like a gigantic mass moving through grass and branch and leaf, stepping on exposed earth and pebbles, but then, everything would go silent.

The noises shifted, sometimes to one side, then to the other, sometimes ahead of him, sometimes far, sometimes close. There were times that made the hairs on the back of his neck stand on end, when this unseen creature sounded too close and right behind him, as if it could breathe on his neck.

There was a whole other world at night. A world of animals and insects with eyes that saw in the dark. Creatures with pincers and stingers that feared the light but owned the shadows. Animals with teeth and claws that leaped and killed quickly, for the night was the realm of the ambush predator, of the skulkers, of the poisoners, and the sudden leapers. A whole foreign land of creatures that hid in the day and came out to kill each other at night—and could kill him as well, since he was now in their territory. Going by the sounds that surrounded him, he could picture some of these creatures as small and timid, but others he imagined as large and capable of tearing a branch off a tree by merely rubbing against it, but this was all his imagination cooking up horrors, because, in reality, he could see nothing.

All he could do was listen.

The sounds didn't seem to exist in isolation from him; they seemed to sound *at* him. The night hordes were putting on a show for their visitor, for the stranger. For a moment, the sounds were everywhere, as day creatures sought shelter, and night creatures awakened. Their voices deafening, intimidating, chilling. The clamor of the beginning of the hunt, followed by the slow fading of all noise as the hunters and the hunted engaged in the eternal dance of "eat or be eaten".

Once more, he walked under the infinite vault of the sky, in numbing, echoing silence.

They had put on their show and now they were observing him, measuring him, weighing their odds against him. "Can we eat this one?" he figured they asked each other. All it would take for his life to end would be for one confident creature, emboldened by a life in the darkness and the strife of the ages, inherited from its ancestors, to answer, "Yes, I can."

Sounds, other than his footsteps, came again.

Slow at first.

Small sounds.

Quiet noise.

The faraway, mournful hoot of a barred owl, then the rustling he'd heard in the bushes, repeated, but somehow always unexpected.

Silence again.

Something like a snort came from his right, and he spun his entire body in that direction, breathing in and out in a panic. He couldn't see anything, but he knew nothing friendly in the forest would snort loud enough at night to be heard, so he quickened his pace. He felt only slightly convinced the snorting creature had not followed.

From far away came the raspy cry of a heron, which meant turning right would lead him toward a small patch of wetlands where the herons lived. He had to keep this in mind, as the last thing he needed was to sink his new boots into the mud of that nearby marshland, where there would certainly be snakes and bugs, and God knew what else.

The heron continued to issue its grating scream, sometimes punctuated by an echoing squawk. To Walt, it sounded like a crying baby being strangled while a small dog barked.

"God, help me," he mumbled, shuddering.

He knew he should turn around and go home, but he couldn't force himself to do it. After coming this far, he couldn't walk away.

Were there bears in these woods? Most likely. He had never actually seen one, but he'd heard there were. They would probably all be sleeping by now, which was reassuring. But what if he bumped into one in this darkness? It would appear to be nothing but a rock until he was too close to it already. One swipe, one swipe from a bear's claw would more than likely be enough to kill h—

CRRRRAAASHHH!!!

A tree fell down.

The crash was deafening in the relative quiet of the forest. The woods came alive again with the protests of startled animals, and the scream of Walt Parham joined them.

He took off running. His scream seemed to shake something loose inside his chest—his heart, perhaps?

The surrounding forest throbbed with noise. Bird and beast cried out. Animalistic threats. The darkness and the forest repelled the invader. Walter ran. He shrieked madly at the denizens of darkness. His cries begged for mercy. Their retorts said none would be granted.

Run! Run! Run!

In Walt's mind, he pictured the bear, tall and black, taller than a house, taller than the church, taller than the mountain itself, pushing the tree down the hill. A smart bear ripping the tree off its roots with a gigantic paw, trying to block his path.

He noticed the silhouette of the tree. It went down with a thud, a crash, several cracks. It rolled down the hill. Naked branches spun like a tangle of bony, desiccated limbs.

Walt screamed. He ran. The shapes of tree branches rushed past on both sides, swaying in the wind, forming a giant spider made of branches. Branches like disinterred bones that crawled behind him and around him, fast despite its frail legs, and its legs were sharp. Right behind the spider, running on four paws, the bear. The smart bear that had failed to cut off his path but did not relent. Black fur, red eyes crying rivulets of blood, and a snake for a tongue. A bear smart enough to know the screaming boy ahead could not win this race. A bear with a man's voice, shouting taunts of victory toward him, because it knew it would catch him. It knew it would eat him.

"Please! Please! Please! Please!" he cried in huffs and puffs as his legs lost strength. He barely noticed the moment he crossed a shallow brook, his new boots splish-splashing and sending water flying everywhere, soaking his trousers and the bottom half of his shirt.

Soon, and thankfully, just as his endurance was giving out,

(*It's going to eat me! It's going to eat me!*)

he realized there was nothing following him at all. He slowed down, breathless, his eyes wild, flitting this way and that all around him. The knapsack with the clay pots and the spade slowed its bouncing rhythm against his back. His arms flailed stupidly as his run became awkward and clumsy. His legs slowed again, and the motion of his body imitated a clown in a pantomime, running from one end of the stage to the other.

At last, he stopped. He panted. He became aware once more of the surrounding sounds, as he bent forward at the waist and supported his upper body on his arms, hands on his knees. The air was so scarce. There was so little of it. How small his lungs were that they wouldn't allow him the amount of air he needed to do something as basic as to continue living.

As the noises of startled animals gradually settled around him, he noticed there were no longer any bugs flying around his face. No mosquitoes, no midges craving his blood. The moon was rising to his left. He couldn't see it all, on account of the mountain, but enough.

He turned his head just slightly as he wheezed and decided there had never been a thing more glorious in the universe than the moon. At this moment, he could not understand why people spoke in terms of the sun, sunset and sunrise. There was a moonrise, too, and it was proof God existed.

That moon was the most beautiful thing he'd seen in his life. It was silvery blue, a hue he'd never seen before. He'd heard of the Blue Moon, but his father had told him this was just a name, not an actual color. It was the most stunning moon he'd ever beheld, but what he saw next made it pale in comparison.

There, close to a clearing in the woods, on a small spot of sloping, grassy ground, there were flowers. John Ellis's blue moonbuds. They were real. He figured they specifically grew in that patch of grass because every night, the rising moon would cast its light upon them, and they would glow just as they were glowing now. Some of the buds, shaped like tiny spheres, shone like blue fireflies covered in dark blue spots. On the open flowers, he could only see a hint of purple, on account of the darkness, which meant, during the day, it must be a lavish bright purple. Just as Reverend Burgess had described—their center glowed silver-blue, like the buds, like the moon that had risen that night.

Walter ran toward the flowers, and he crouched next to them. He put his knapsack down and was overcome by the impulse of quickly getting the clay pots and the spade out—to take as many flowers as he could, as if they would somehow unearth themselves and run away from him. He stopped, though. He wanted to take in their beauty, to marvel at what he was seeing. Of course, he'd read of plants that bloomed at night, even one known as the moonflower, which was beautiful, but it was white instead of purple. He also knew of a variety that was blue, similar in shape to these flowers, so he figured they might be related, but he'd never seen one that actually glowed in the moonlight.

He took in the flower's beauty, and he reached out with his hand to touch a petal. He wanted to know its feel, its texture.

"Silk," he whispered, as he softly rubbed the petal between his thumb and index finger. "It's silky but firm. Soft, but it keeps its shape."

He moved his face closer, and its scent was subtle and floral, but somehow metallic. *Silver,* he thought. He remembered the coins the Reverend had given him. He couldn't accurately explain what silver smelled like, but the flower's fragrance had a light aroma of silver to it. For a moment, all his worries about the darkness of the night, and the fear of creatures, left his mind, and he allowed his senses to be enthralled by this magnificent flower.

Crunch!

A sound. Hearing was the only sense the blue moonbud's beauty couldn't take, and it was now telling him something was—

Crunch!

—approaching from behind. He froze. His eyes searched frantically, trying to spot danger, but they wouldn't have seen the threat since it was behind him.

Crunch!

Too close. It was too close to move. Too close to stand. Too close to run.

Crunch!

His heart beat faster. His breathing shallower.

Crunch!

Too late. Whatever it was, was standing behind him now. He could feel its closeness, like heat emanating from another body.

Slowly, very slowly, he reached for his knapsack, hoping whatever was standing behind him didn't have the intelligence to recognize he was going for the spade inside.

"Stop," a gruff, gravelly voice said from behind him.

He obeyed.

A person. The voice sounded familiar, but he couldn't place it. He parted his lips to speak. "Who—"

A blunt blow struck the back of his head, and he lost consciousness.

Walter first noticed the light. It was a blurry glow, but no longer the glow of the moon. This was yellow and orange and red. This was a fire. A small one. He remembered roasting the chicken he'd stolen years ago from their neighbor. He'd roasted it over a fire like that one. Small and improvised. It had been delicious. Too bad he'd thrown it all up after his father had whipped him for stealing it.

His vision was still blurry. A horrible pain radiated from the back of his head. He tried to touch the painful spot, but he couldn't move his hands. They were bound in front of him and tied in such a way he couldn't separate his fingers, which were clasped together. His legs were bound, too.

There were two voices coming from two shapes. A leaner one, sitting by the fire, and another larger one standing opposite. At first, he couldn't make out what they were saying. His natural impulse was to scream, but the gag over his mouth would've prevented this. Whoever these people were, they were dangerous, and screaming might anger them and make them hurt him. So, holding his terror in, he listened. He put all his concentration into listening in on their conversation.

"...done," the large figure said. He recognized this as the gruff male voice that had spoken behind him before they knocked him out. "I kept my part of the deal. Now you swear to God, you will leave me alone."

Who is he? He knew this person's voice, but from where?

"I swear." This time, it was the other person. Another

man. The one sitting on the opposite side of the fire. This voice, he was sure he knew, but it was hard to focus.

"No," said the big, standing man. "Swear to God. You don't get to trick me on a technicality."

"Fine," said the sitting man, sounding amused.

No, Walter thought. *It can't be!*

"I swear to God," the man said.

Reverend Burgess!

"I swear to God, and all his angels, and archangels." His preaching intonation confirmed beyond any doubt who he was. "May God cast me unto the fiery pits of hell if I ever speak a word to anyone about your life of sin, John Ellis."

John Ellis. Long-Lived John! Why? Why are they doing this?

"You don't get to judge me," John said to Burgess, and his head turned in the boy's direction. He could see the contour of a silvery beard.

"What, this?" The reverend nodded toward Walter, who could still not make out the men's faces clearly, but he knew. He knew. And if he wasn't so afraid at this moment, he would've felt the punch of the heartbreak caused by this cruel realization.

Why?

"I'm punishing a sinner, John. One who wronged God, and me, and still has plenty to pay for."

"I don't give a damn about your excuses," Long-Lived

John said, his gruff voice anxious and full of shame. "I just want to make sure you'll leave us alone."

The priest let out an impatient sigh. "You have nothing to worry about, John." His voice had that slight hint of mockery that Walter had grown accustomed to since that day, five years ago. "Neither you nor that man you keep telling everyone is your widowed nephew. You have nothing to worry about with me. I will keep my mouth shut. You will answer only to God for your…abominable acts."

"So will you, Burgess. You'll be burning in hell right there next to us, but while we're still living, leave us be. I'm done with this. I've done what you asked. Now, I'm going home. I want no further part of this." He glanced back at Walter, and this time he could make out Long-Lived John's expression. The man was enormous. For his advanced age, he was a wall of muscle and silver hair, roughly shaped into a man. His size and build contrasted with the expression of apologetic grief he was now giving him. "He's awake."

John motioned with his head toward him.

Reverend Burgess glanced at him again. When Walter saw the grin on the man's face, he discovered such evil in it, such joy in the enacting of evil, that sharp dread gripped his heart. Screams now issued from his mouth, trying to push through the gag.

The Reverend stared at him as if he'd been waiting for him to awaken.

334

"I'm sorry, Walter," John said, and in his voice was genuine regret. He turned around and walked away. "This makes me sick."

Walter tried to scream, "Please, don't leave!", but the gag turned his scream into a muffled, unintelligible sound. The large man disappeared into the forest. He could see his head hanging in shame even past his broad back.

Long-Lived John disappeared in the shadows of the forest and didn't turn once to glance at him.

Burgess grinned again. A deranged, pleasured grin he'd never seen on the man. He stood up with a grunt, dusted off his trousers, and walked toward him.

Walter wriggled and stirred like a worm, as if the ropes that bound him would break, by some miracle, and he could escape. He screamed through the gag.

Burgess reached toward his hip, and now Walter could see he had a sheath there, from which the man produced a knife. When the glint of steel flashed in his eyes, Walter screamed again, and kicked, and tried to do everything he could to get as far away from the man as possible.

Burgess crouched in front of him. With one hand, the priest grabbed the ropes on his legs to stop him from kicking him. With the other, he raised the knife, showing it to him, ensuring he got a clear view of the entire blade, and sending the message, if he so much as kicked once more, the entire length of the knife would be soon buried in him.

Walter stopped moving. He fixed his terrified, crying eyes on him.

"Now," Burgess said. "I will remove your gag, and you may ask me your most urgent question." He studied Walter's eyes as if to ensure he understood. "You will not scream. Or…" He swiveled his eyes toward the knife and back to him. "Do you understand?"

Burgess's face filled Walter's entire world. The fire behind him cast his face in shadows, but he could still see his eyes, and his teeth, and his long, straight nose with a square bridge, which almost worked to separate his field of vision in two.

"I will need you to nod, Boy. Do we have to revisit the point about answering your elders again, after five years? Nod if you understand."

Walter bobbed his head quickly up and down.

"Excellent." The priest stood up and went around him.

There was a tug on the back of his head, and for one terrified second, his mind told him this was it—Burgess was going to cut his throat right there and watch him bleed out, leaving him for the animals to feast on. Instead, two hard tugs. Burgess removed the gag from his mouth. He appeared again in front of him, the knife in one hand and the wet piece of cloth in the other. A fierce soreness burned at the corners of his lips, and he could taste blood.

Burgess regarded him with curiosity.

"What would you like to ask?"

A million questions came to Walter's mind, but only one seemed relevant. If he was only allowed one question, only this one was essential. "Are you going to kill me?"

Burgess smiled, finding the question amusing.

"Of course I am." His tone was nonchalant.

A sob built up inside Walter. He wanted to bawl like a child, the child he'd been when Burgess had been about to give him his due punishment. Branding, hand piercing, whipping, pillorying, all had seemed like such complex and excessive forms of punishment, but when the answer was simply death, it carried a numbness with it. It felt so simple, so little, and yet so final.

"Why?" Fat tears spilled over his lower eyelids.

"That's such a boring question, Boy. Is that all? Is that really the last thing you want to know before dying? You know why I'm going to kill you. Try again."

Convulsive sobs pushed up from Walter's chest. He closed his eyes and cried, a shaky moan coming from the depths of his soul. "Please, don't do this."

A hand slapped his cheek. It wasn't a hard slap, but firm enough to shock him into stopping. Trembling, he fixed his gaze on his tormentor.

"Don't beg. It accomplishes nothing. I already told you I am going to kill you. Accept that, Boy. You are fourteen. Not an adult by law, but a man for all intents and purposes. Act like one. You are going to die this night. There is no bargaining, no negotiating. Accept it as a truth and make your peace with it."

Walter closed his eyes, and his chest swelled again, preparing for yet another sobbing fit, but another abrupt slap cut it short.

"Stop that. Ask me."

Because of the way he spoke, it seemed to Walter that Burgess already knew what he was going to ask, and he wanted to answer it, but he *required* the question to come from him first. It was part of a process for Burgess, a sequence that needed to be completed.

"You said my debt had been settled." Walt sniffled, sounding so betrayed, so lost. "Why are you going to kill me if my debt is already settled?"

"Good! See? The question is still why, but it's an educated why, a focused why. You always lacked focus, but your work at the church helped you learn it. For a moment, I thought you'd forgotten your learnings. Aren't you glad you learned that before the end?" The reverend smiled and nodded slowly, as if showing he expected Walter to nod back in agreement.

Walter nodded against every impulse in his mind. There was a wild madness in the reverend's eyes that froze him to his core. He appeared excited to be having this con versation. Wherever this creature had been hiding in the man's heart, Walter had never witnessed it. Those eyes filled with hungry insanity.

"Good. You are right, Boy, your debt was settled. Your debt to the church. Your debt to me, and your debt to God, however, was not. You see." Burgess sat on the ground now, his legs crossed. "I am only a man, and I am flawed, and I have urges."

Burgess regarded the knife in his hand almost as a priceless treasure, a piece of his soul. "James 4:2," he continued. "You lust and do not have; so you commit murder. You are envious and cannot obtain; so you fight and quarrel. You do not have because you do not ask."

He shifted his eyes from the knife to Walter.

"And so, I asked. I asked the Lord how to satiate this lust, how to live with it and not damn my soul, and it seems wherever I go, the Lord giveth. I cannot slay any wayward soul, for there is hope of correction in the wayward, but the Lord has put me in the path of those for whom there is no hope. Children that should be culled before they reach adulthood and do serious damage to others. Like you."

Burgess studied his eyes, measuring, evaluating, trying to see if he was following his logic. A twitch in his eye told him further explanation was needed.

"I am not a monster, Boy," he said with a shake of his head, and an innocent chortle. "If I were to slay a child without giving them the opportunity to find salvation, I would have condemned them and condemned myself. The Lord has chosen me to guide these souls to salvation, not condemn them. There have been many before you, and the Lord has given me sight and the opportunity to tend to them. Young boys, like you, who would grow to be a blight on civilization, and with the quick growth of America, I have been fortunate to have been taken by the Lord to many a town that required to be cleansed of one or several of these misguided souls. You will be the first here in White Harbor. An honor if you ask me."

Walter mumbled something, but he couldn't form a sentence in his current state of panic.

"What, Boy? Speak up. I could not hear you."

"You've…" Walter swallowed, and it felt like a stone, rough and heavy, tore at his throat. "You've killed others?"

"Oh, yes," said Burgess with a casual nod. "Didn't you hear me say there have been many? It wasn't always holy work, admittedly. Before finding God, I lusted for what I didn't have. I envied those who didn't have my urges, but I could not be like them, and so I murdered. I hated my sin, but I hated myself more. I thought I was destined for Hell. Yet God found it in his infinite mercy to listen to my prayers and forgive me, and He has used the lust that lives in me to do His work, and so what I do now can no longer be considered murder, because it's God's work."

Walt stared at Burgess in horror, unable to believe what he was hearing. Who was this monster that had replaced the man of God he knew?

"That brings us to you." Burgess cast a glance down at him with a threatening expression. The man—the monster—walked behind him.

"No, no, please," Walter begged. "Please. Reverend Burgess, I have changed! I won't be bad! I won't be—"

The gag caught him by surprise, slipping into his open mouth and quickly wrapping around his head. Burgess tied it in a knot. Walter started screaming, realizing it was time. Even through the gag, his cries echoed through the forest, and he was assaulted by the sounds of animals responding in alarm. The hoot of owls, the caw of herons, the haunting sounds of birds whose names he hadn't yet learned, and now never would.

Burgess came back around and stood in front of him. The flames cast an infernal dance of fire and shadow on the man's face. Hues of red, yellow, orange, and black played with the contours of his brow, nose, and mouth. It made his face appear inhuman. Unspeakably sinister.

"It is time." Burgess bent down to grab the ropes that bound his hands.

Walter struggled and thrashed, but despite his older age, Burgess was surprisingly wiry and much stronger than him. Soon, he was dragging him by a loop of rope near his wrists. All Walter could see were his legs dragging in front of him, leaving two rows in the dirt, the fire moving farther away with each of Burgess's steps. He squealed like a pig that knew where the slaughter was. His cries cut through the shadows of the forest. He couldn't see where Burgess was taking him, since he was on his back as the man dragged him.

Birds cried, beasts growled, the forest was hungry.

The back of his head hit the dirt, and a jolt of pain flared in the wound left by the blow John Ellis had given him. They had come to a stop. He tried to move, to roll away the moment Burgess let the rope go, but before he could move an inch, the priest was upon him. Turning him on his stomach, putting one leg to either side of his body. Burgess's arms slipped under his shoulders, and he felt himself being lifted. Before his eyes was a rock, a rock that reminded him of the one his father used to bend him over to whip and cane him. This was it, he realized. This was where he would die: on a rock, like the one on which punishment had been visited upon him so many times.

"After these years of seeing you work at the church," said Burgess, laying Walt on his stomach over the cold, rough surface, his arms hanging limp over the other side. "I feel like Abraham, when told to sacrifice his son, Isaac. God made Abraham spare his son because it was only a test of faith. You, my Boy, will not have the same fortune as Isaac, because this is God's will. This is my calling. It does not mean I will not grieve for you, Boy. To sacrifice one you love is the hardest mission God may ask of us, and I can say truthfully that I love you in my own way. Have no doubt."

Burgess bent down, grabbed the loop of rope around his wrists, and attached it to a large metal hook that had been tied previously to the rock. Upon seeing this, Walter realized this was always how his life was going to end. They had prepared this place as a kind of execution yard for this special occasion. Burgess had said he'd be his first sacrifice in White Harbor. How many more would die upon this rock after him? How many would bleed over his dried blood?

"I have to hand it to John Ellis. The man is an indisputable sinner, the most reviled by God, but he certainly found the best spot for me to do the Lord's work."

Walter did everything in his power to break free, but power was the one thing he did not have at this moment. This was the place where he would die.

(*Accept that, Boy*)

"Romans 5:3-4," the priest said, now standing behind him. "Not only so, but we also glory in our sufferings, because we know that suffering produces perseverance; perseverance, character; and character, hope."

Walter could almost picture the man smiling a fatherly smile, as if it was supposed to make him feel better. He braced himself. It was time. He would feel the blade drive itself into his back, and he would die. He wondered if he would feel pain. How much would it hurt? How many stabs did it take to kill a person? Would the priest stab him only once and watch him bleed out, or stab him until his heart stopped beating? He tightened his jaw, tightened his clasped fingers together, closed his eyes, and prepared.

He found, in the end, he had accepted it.

Without warning, the priest's hands clasped the sides of Walter's trousers and, in one powerful motion, pulled them to his calves, where the rope didn't allow them to go further down.

Caning? Is he going to cane me before he kills me? Why would he—

A sudden, sharp pain coursed up his spine as he felt something enter him, tearing him open. Walter cried in pain. What had made its way inside his body was not a knife, though, but something he instinctively recognized once the revolting, disgusting warmth of Burgess's body pressed against him.

Compounding this ultimate of outrages, the older man's breath crept up his neck like a hairy caterpillar, making his skin break out in bumps of revulsion, and the slithering sound of the priest's—no, the *monster's*—obscene, nauseating voice, whispered in his ear.

"Now you know, Boy,"—there was a lewd quiver in his voice—"that Reverend Burgess did *not* hide a tiny cock under his tunic."

Walter growled through a wall of clenched teeth and the fabric of his gag as he endured the unspeakable for what felt like all the ages of the Earth. Eventually, his mind disconnected from his body, as if leaving him. It was at this moment he saw, several feet in front of him, barely touched by the light of the fire, a pile of rocks—not a naturally occurring one, but a man-made one. A cairn. All around it were blue moonbuds, glowing in the silver-blue moon, which was at its zenith. He noticed all the surrounding animals had gone quiet, especially the night birds, which were the most constant source of sound he was aware of.

Something happened.

Something he couldn't explain.

The moonbuds seemed to beckon him.

The feeling of disconnection increased. He was receding into his own mind, and what he found there was red and burning and angry. Like a hundred voices roaring in unison, filled with pain and indignation. An anger he'd never known in his life flooded his chest, a hatred with no comparison in a world that teemed with hate and rage and injustice.

He could still sense his body shake with every thrust from the degenerate monster that was defiling him, but he felt no pain, he felt no bodily sensations, because he did not feel his body. He was in the depths of this roiling, crimson, burning cave of fury. A rage that swirled around him like the fiery insides of a furnace consumed every fiber of his being and his soul. He had yielded control of his self to another entity: the rage.

He could see his own hands move without him making them move, and, to his surprise, he saw them break the rope by simply moving his wrists apart, as if the rope were made of paper. Now his hands were free. He heard himself roar in anger, like a beast—a human voice, stretched into an animalistic howl. Joining that voice came all the voices from the animals in the darkness of the woods, as if they had been held at bay by some otherworldly force, but now were unleashed and joined him in his wrath.

The thrusting stopped, followed by a confused exclamation from the old priest, and he sensed—not so much felt—Burgess slide out of him. The force controlling his body spun him around to face Burgess, who looked confused, terrified, and small. A small man. A small creature. Insignificant and puny.

"What is this?" Burgess said. He sounded far away. Burgess took two steps back, tripped on his trousers, and fell on his bare buttocks. "What are you?" He sounded frightened.

Puny.

Tiny.

Frail.

Walter felt himself pull up his trousers and realized he was walking freely. He noticed the lengths of broken rope from his legs lying in the dirt, next to Burgess's knife.

"God, help me!" The priest shouted in desperation, crawling away from him. "Help me, Lord! Hear me! Hear your servant!"

Walter bent to pick up the knife.

"No! Stay away!" Burgess shrieked. "In the name of the Lord, I command thee, stay away, demon!"

Walter didn't realize the moment his body leaped toward the pathetic man, and he plunged the knife in his chest with such force, the man's body bent completely. His legs sprung up in response as he expelled all the air out of his lungs, accompanied by spit and blood spraying Walter's face.

Walter didn't blink.

Burgess's eyes bulged toward him, his mouth releasing streams of blood that ran toward his ears. He tried to move his lips—to say something—but if any words were coming, any prayers, any pleas, any condemnations, Walter couldn't hear them.

I am going to kill you, Walter thought, and pulled out the knife, seeing the reaction on the pathetic priest's face. *Accept that.*

He started plunging the knife into the man's body, over and over and over and over. He watched the priest react to each stab, seeing the blood soak the man's body, feeling the blood fly in fat, warm globs and land on his face and his clothes. Burgess was like a rag doll at the mercy of his strength, and no matter how much he tried to push him off, he wasn't strong enough to even alter the path of the knife. He tried to protect himself and got stabbed through the palm of his right hand, then through his left forearm. Walter stabbed his stomach, his throat, his arms, his naked cock, his hands, his cheeks, his testicles, his chest, his ribs, and continued stabbing, until there were no places left to stab. But he continued, and as he did so, he counted each stab. He learned a human being could be stabbed many, many times before dying.

Thirty-four, thirty-five, thirty-six, thirty-seven, he counted.

Chest, belly button, clavicle, upper arm. Burgess was still alive. Weak, but still alive.

Thirty-eight, thirty-nine, forty, forty-one.

Stomach, shoulder, chest. Weaker, but still alive.

Burgess, whose body was now a mess of wounds and blood, and whose face was red and slick with thick crimson, stared at him. His eyes were round and white and frightened, highlighted in the mess of red that used to be a human face, visible in the light of the small fire. Those eyes, so scared, so confused, so full of fear.

Forty-two.

He stabbed his left eye diagonally, as to have the blade go out of his temple. Burgess's mouth opened to reveal bloody teeth. He shook orgasmically.

Forty-three.

He stabbed his right eye straight through his skull. This time, Burgess's body didn't so much shake as shudder. The last of his life leaving him. There was still a slight movement in his chest.

Forty-four.

He drove the knife into Burgess's heart, which he'd saved for last, and he left the knife there.

Walter stood from between the priest's legs, bathed in blood, and he regarded his work. Burgess no longer moved. Still, he sensed something was missing. One last thing. Without even thinking, his body crouched, reached between the dead man's legs, and in one hard pull, ripped off his penis and tossed it away into the forest, where any night creature could find it and eat it.

Walter felt himself weaken. He felt his mind creep back into his body, the red-roiling anger receding like a dying fire. His movements were his own again. He staggered backward a few steps. He fell to the ground, exhausted, but something stopped him from falling on his back. The rock was right behind him, supporting him.

Before he lost consciousness, he cast a glance toward the moon, which was no longer silver-blue. Just a normal, pale white moon.

Chapter Sixteen

The First Mother: "Dorothy"

They found Walter Parham at dawn.

Several of the townspeople joined his parents and his oldest brother and formed a search party. They asked Dorothy Parham to stay home and wait, but she did not listen to reason. Even when her husband commanded her to, she would not listen. She rode along with her husband, on horseback—a rather unwomanly act, John Ellis thought, but who was he to judge?

The truth was, he could understand her. That instinctive love and drive can make the most restrictive social norm insignificant. He knew this well, especially because of his involvement in this grim situation.

Before dawn, sleepless, realizing his conscience

would not let him live with himself, John had snuck out of bed so as to not wake Christopher, who did not know of the monstrous thing he'd done.

Maybe that demon calling itself a reverend hasn't killed the boy yet, he thought. *Maybe he won't, after all. Maybe, after everything the Parham boy has done for the church, a smidge of a conscience might convince even that ghoul not to hurt him.*

He knew, even as he closed his front door behind him in the utmost silence, those thoughts were folly, but still felt he had to do something. Even if it was too late for the Parham boy, he could lead the people to find Burgess before he washed the blood off his clothes, and he might be brought to justice. John would turn himself in, too, for his involvement, because he could not live a happy life with Christopher—a life that already meant lying to everyone—while also having to hide his abetment in the violation and murder of a child.

He'd gone to the Parhams and found them as sleepless as he was. The father, weighed down with worry and anguish, the mother staring blankly, pale, and cold. He asked if their son, Walter, had returned the previous night, already knowing the answer. He told them he was convinced he'd seen their son heading into the eastern woods that afternoon, when he'd gone hunting, and at one point he'd heard what he thought was the scream of a young boy, but could not find the source, even after searching for two hours. It was a lie, but he had done so much worse than lie that night.

John had offered to help them track the boy, and a party of some twelve people had quickly assembled. For an hour, at least, he pretended to track the boy, knowing exactly where he was, as the light of the sun already shone from the east. When he finally guided the party to the sacrificial spot Burgess had commanded him to prepare, he didn't expect to be struck dumb by the sight.

The gruesome scene before the party's eyes was a graphic depiction of a nightmare: the bloodied body of Reverend Burgess lay by the remains of a small campfire, where some embers still smoked. He was lying face up—if what remained could still be called a face—naked from the waist down, covered in blood and stab wounds. His eyes had been gouged out, and his manhood mutilated. The murder weapon was sticking out of his heart. There were splashes of browned blood lying all over the dirt and the grass. A bloody trail of four steps led to the place where Walter Parham sat with his back against a rock, staring vacantly, covered head to toe in blood that was not his.

The boy's father jumped down from his horse and ran past the priest's corpse, as if it wasn't even there, his full attention on his son's immobile body.

Isaac Parham shook his son by the shoulders, shouting, "What is this, Walter? What happened here? Are you hurt?"

The boy recognized his father, meeting his gaze with

lost, sleepy blue eyes and said, "I don't know."

John had seen that face before, in veterans of the Revolutionary War who'd witnessed death and depravity in overwhelming amounts.

"I don't know," the boy repeated. "I don't know."

John was crouching near the corpse of the priest, as if needing to know beyond any doubt the demon was truly dead.

May you burn in Hell. Save me a spot, for we will meet there.

John glanced at Isaac Parham, who was still asking his son if he was hurt, incapable of seeing the truth. Who could blame him? This entire scene was unbelievable, even to a person who'd seen everything, like Long-Lived John Ellis.

"The boy is not injured."

John saw Dorothy Parham standing on the other side of the priest's corpse. He hadn't heard her approach.

"Isaac Parham!" she called, and her husband eyed her over his shoulder, puzzlement showing in his eyes. "The boy is not injured," she repeated. "If I can see it from here, how can you not see it so close? Are you blind, husband?"

Isaac Parham furrowed his brow, as if his wife had just spoken nonsense, and he turned to examine his son. John could see him run his hands over the boy's body, and during this, all the boy did was repeat, "I don't know," with that lost gaze of his. "I don't know."

The boy's mind was gone, and perhaps that was God showing some mercy.

John waited, knowing the moment Isaac Parham was satisfied his son was uninjured, the next realization would strike him like lightning.

Parham's hand flew up to his mouth, and he sprung up to a standing position, his head shaking in denial.

The boy at his feet kept repeating, "I don't know. I don't know."

"Do you see it now, husband? Do you need proof?"

Isaac Parham just shook his head, his boy still repeating, "I don't know. I don't know."

"Your son killed a man." Her face was stony and cold. "Your son killed our parish's priest."

John could hear murmurs of shock and outrage from all those present ululating all around. *Say something,* John thought. *Say something.*

"He was not happy with simply soiling the house of God," she continued. "He was not happy with shaming us, especially I that bore him and brought him into this world. He was not happy with that. No. He bided his time, feigning innocence, feigning redemption, while he planned to do this. He killed Reverend Burgess, a man of God."

Murmurs. Whispers.

Say something!

"No." Isaac Parham turned a pale face toward his

wife. "It's impossible, woman. Are you mad? He's such a small boy for his age. How could he have—"

"Look at the blood," she said. "Look at the foot-prints. Look at his boots. Look at *him*."

Parham examined his son and shook his head.

"I don't know," mumbled Walter.

"I felt it," she said, beating her chest. "I felt it the day you made me invite that *thing* back into our house. I felt the demon inside him, and I felt sick to my stomach. I held the Bible in my hands to ward off the evil that came off your son, all the while knowing he had not changed. I had to play loving mother for years, as to not anger the demon inside him, or perhaps it would be I laying there, dead and eyeless."

Dorothy Parham seemed to stare her husband down into submission. He could not deny her words, John thought, at least not about who had killed Burgess. It was obvious to all present.

"But he's so small." Isaac Parham's voice came out as an inconsequential plea that fell on deaf ears.

"We are cursed now, thanks to your son," she said. "We are cursed unless we correct this mistake."

Say something, you coward!

"Nathaniel!" she called to her oldest. "Bring rope."

The young man, hearing his mother's command, turned pleading eyes toward his father, but found no author-ity there now. Only his mother was to be obeyed. He went to his horse, took his rope and, hesitantly, brought it to his mother.

"Mother," the young man said in a pleading voice, "Mother, please. Let's take him to jail. Let the court handle this."

"Be quiet," Dorothy Parham said, with an unnerving calmness in her voice. "Do you want to join your brother in hell for speaking in his favor?"

The young man shut his mouth in obedience and brought his hands to his eyes. He tried his best not to weep.

Dorothy Parham turned to the rest of their party, whose murmurs had grown angry, speaking curses toward the boy, condemning the murderer, and even knowing the answer, she asked, "Will any of you object to hanging this murderer? This heretic?"

Exclamations of support came from the crowd. Nobody would stop this.

Say something! John kept thinking. *If there is the slimmest chance of avoiding damnation for what you did, you must say something!*

"Mrs. Parham," John said, his gruff voice shy and diminished. "I think, perhaps, there is redemption in taking your son to jail yourself. In taking him to justice. Because justice is what should matter most. We do not know what transpired here. We do not know what brought about this savagery."

Dorothy Parham regarded him with icy contempt. Her gaze almost flattened him. "Were you ever married, John Ellis?" she asked.

The question took him by surprise. He hesitated. "Yes. My Norma. She passed away twenty-five years ago."

"Did you love her?" There was an intrusiveness in that question that went beyond just whether he'd loved his wife.

"Yes. Very much. A fortunate man I was," he chose every word with the utmost care, "to have met a woman so understanding, so open of mind and heart."

"I'd imagine so." Dorothy Parham's tone was curt, and he saw knowledge in her eyes, the type of knowledge that is only used when it can do the most damage to those who oppose you. "I would imagine, also, that you would've been angry if someone ever put her to shame, or her memory."

John Ellis stared in surprise at the woman before him. "Indeed," he said, and lowered his gaze.

"Do you have any evidence that would suggest this spawn of mine did not murder Reverend Burgess? Any evidence you would bring into the *public eye*,"—she emphasized those last two words—"that there are attenuating circumstances to what he did?"

John studied her eyes, pale blue and with a glacial rage behind them that could freeze the flames of Hell. Her threat was apparent. He did not care about himself, however. After all, he deserved to die for what he'd done to Walter Parham to protect his own secrets, but what about Christopher? What would happen if Dorothy Parham opened her mouth and said the wrong thing? Both he and Christopher could go to jail or be put to death, and this tragedy would've been for nothing. He meant to turn himself in for his offense later, but he couldn't risk Christopher's life.

"Will you rob me of avenging my shame?" Dorothy Parham asked with a firm voice.

John hesitated again. Lowered his gaze. Shook his head. "No," he said.

Without a word, the matter settled, the Parham woman turned from him, walked toward her husband, and presented him with the coils of rope. "Restore the dignity of your family, Isaac Parham."

He watched in petrified horror as the man took the rope from his wife. Isaac Parham stared at her, with a face that had grown old, so old, older than Long-Lived John himself, in a matter of minutes, but the Parham man did not protest.

The crowd cheered and jeered and condemned the boy as they watched Isaac Parham tie the rope into a noose. John stood in silence, witnessing his own damnation unfold before his eyes. Parham's countenance was grim and corpselike, but he did not cry as he lifted the boy in his arms with care, as if his small son had fallen from a tree and twisted his ankle. There was love in the way he carried his boy, and John's heart contorted in his chest when the boy put an arm around his father's neck and rested his head on his shoulder. Isaac Parham's unblinking eyes filled with grief at his son's tenderness. The rope with the noose hung limply in coils around his arm.

The other men from the party ran past John, one of them pushing against his shoulder, as they followed Isaac Parham, who was now walking toward a tree. A tree with a long branch that contrasted against the eastern sky in this clearing in the woods. The branch was shaped like a hand trying to claw the sun out of the sky before it could fully rise over the mountains, stealing the light from the world. John walked, as if in a dream, behind the group of people, who now stopped, surrounding Parham and his condemned boy.

He couldn't see Parham now, just the backs of the other witnesses, blocking his view of what was happening inside the half-circle that had formed around the tree. He was only a couple steps from the backs of two other men, and his heart jumped, startled, when Isaac Parham's hand appeared over their heads, tossing the rope in the air. The rope rose, drew an arc over the thick branch, and dropped back down.

With his big hand, he pushed aside one of the two men before him. He did this slowly, the way he opened the bedroom door a few hours earlier, as to not make a sound and wake Christopher up. He needed to see. He had to witness the exact moment his place in Hell was secured.

Before him was the Parham boy, sitting at the foot of the tree, the noose already around his neck, and his father crouched in front of him. Parham ran his hand tenderly over his son's head. He placed his palm on his cheek and gazed intently into his eyes—his lost eyes—and he held the boy's gaze in his as he whispered words John couldn't hear. He was glad the sound of those words escaped him, as those were the last words between a father and his son.

The last words his own father had said to him, in another long-forgotten town, had been: "Be gone, you perversion of nature. I no longer have a son. If I see you again, I will shoot you dead." He was certain, if Walt Parham could hear the words his father was saying to him right now, he would have heard something far more tender.

Dorothy Parham, at the other end of the half-circle of people, gave both of them an icy glare, hands clasped together. Nathaniel covered his eyes with his hands, racked with sobs that could no longer be contained. Isaac Parham did not cry as he stood up and grabbed the hanging end of the rope, but his face said more than oceans of tears.

The people continued to jeer and call for the death of the murderer, of the demon who had killed the Reverend.

Parham man closed his eyes, clenched his jaw. Gathering his strength to do the worst thing he would ever do.

Do not worry, Isaac Parham. God's judgment will not fall on you. It will fall on me.

"I found the flowers." Walt Parham's voice. Soft. Happy. Innocent.

The boy smiled sleepily at his parents and his brother, all of whom stared at him in horror. The crowd went quiet. Yes, the boy was fourteen, on the way to manhood, but at that moment he looked like a five-year-old, telling his parents of a wonderful thing he'd seen. The innocence in his voice made John certain this was a punishment unto them all, for they would have to carry the memory of that voice with them to their graves.

"They were beautiful," Walter said, and his voice still sounded distant, but somehow filled with wonder and the purest joy. "They glowed in the moonlight."

John studied Isaac Parham's face, now a pale mask of sweat and shock and appalment. His arms raised, holding the rope, shaking, looking like he was in the middle of climbing it. The man's strength was leaving him. He was sure he wouldn't go through with it. How could anyone go through with this monstrosity having heard that voice?

Dorothy Parham's face was also aghast, but otherwise, the determination had not left her eyes. Nathaniel had turned his back on the scene, and John could only see his shoulders shaking as he sobbed.

As if having nothing more to say on the matter,

young Walter let his gaze wander from his family, and it once more got lost in the ether.

The crowd resumed their insults and calls of "Murderer!" and "Hang him!". Hesitantly at first, but they quickly regained their strength and viciousness, like the first patter of raindrops that lead into an evil storm.

John's eyes did not leave the Parham man. He didn't move.

He will not do it. He will not do it. He will not—

Isaac Parham pulled the rope once. Twice. Three times. He let out a primal, guttural howl of pain from his very core. A roar of grief and desolation leaving his parted lips as he clung to the taut rope with closed eyes and bared teeth, summoning the will to do the impossible and hold it as his son died.

The man might as well have raised a stuffed burlap sack in the shape of a boy. Walter Parham did not react, other than a coarse choking sound that escaped his throat once, the moment the noose first tightened around his neck. He hung there limply, eyes bulging out of their sockets, but young Walter did not move. It seemed as if he had retreated from his mind as he died, robbing the hateful crowd of the spectacle they had been calling for.

Little by little, the crowd grew quieter and quieter. The boy, from their perspective, had violently murdered a man of God. They wanted to see him kick and dance and choke, all the fun things that entertained a crowd at an execution—*Or a lynching,* John thought with disgust—but the boy did not give them that. Just a bulging stare and a tongue sticking out.

Just a grim horror that offered no sating to their morbid desires.

The search party was long gone now.

Isaac Parham had not said a word. He had just climbed on his horse and ridden away with that aged, pale, terrible expression on his face. He didn't even offer to take his wife with him on his horse. She rode away with her oldest son, who hadn't spoken either.

The last words of any relevance had been hers.

"Tie the rope to the tree," she'd told her husband without a shred of remorse. "Leave him hanging. He does not deserve a holy burial."

They took the reverend's corpse with them, in a sack tied over a horse's back. Unlike the Parham boy, he would get a holy burial, alright, but no burial was holy enough to spare him from the eternity of torment that awaited him.

After the search party departed, their spirits low and perturbed, he decided only harm would come from confessing. He didn't care about his own well-being—he deserved whatever punishment he got—but an innocent had died that day because of him, and yet another might die if he spoke. For a moment, he saw Christopher up on that tree instead of the hanging boy. Yes, that might very well be his beloved's fate if John were to speak of his involvement in the events of that night. Christopher would fight for him, no doubt, until someone, somewhere in town, questioned the nature of their relationship, and that would be all. The rabble would have an excuse to label him an accomplice.

He imagined Christopher's beautiful face—a man of five and forty already, but youthful and handsome, still far younger than John—up there, hanging by his neck. He pictured his contagious smile being replaced by a loosely hanging jaw and a protruding tongue, purple and horrible, and his dead eyes staring into his soul, blaming him for letting the ugliness of the world creep into their little cocoon of happiness. No. He would bear this guilt in silence until the day he died, and he prayed the day would come soon, because he didn't believe he could bear it for too long.

"Please, God," he whispered toward an indifferent sky. "Let me have the death I'm long overdue, but let no harm come to him, because he is a good man, with a kind heart. Do not make him pay for my sins."

After everyone was gone, he cut the boy down from the tree. He wrapped him in a burlap sack he carried with Bella, his horse, and found rocks to place upon the body until he was completely covered.

It seemed fitting the boy's body would rest in this place. He would not be alone, as indicated by the other cairn that stood just a few feet away from the rock where the boy had died. John had picked this spot for Burgess when the damned priest had blackmailed him, because he'd asked for an isolated place where he could do his work without the risk of anyone showing up. Because of the horror that had transpired here many years before Walter Parham's death, no person in White Harbor approached this place. It was haunted, people said, and John was certain it was more than likely it was, both figuratively and literally. They called this one spot in the woods "Blight Harbor" because of what had transpired here many years ago—or what they told each other had happened.

Truth had turned into myth, but Long-Lived John Ellis had been here when that other tragedy had happened. He'd lived it. He'd survived it. He'd helped put stones on that other cairn, just like he now put them on the Parham boy's.

Yes, this was a haunted place. An evil place.

He cast his gaze some distance away at that other pile of rocks the crowd had been too busy to notice. The cairn he'd helped put in place many years ago, now surrounded by those horrid flowers.

Those unnatural flowers.

While hunting, John Ellis had walked and ridden every inch of land in the Crescent Mountains. Those flowers only existed here. People didn't know the wild like he did. Those few who had dared come to this place out of morbid curiosity and might have seen the flowers, would've done no more than call them pretty, since it was unlikely they would've come at night and seen them glow like the souls of the dead. Those people didn't know the color of those flowers didn't exist in nature. They would call it "purple" or "fuchsine", but they probably hadn't studied them close enough to realize the color was neither. They likely told themselves the silver was simply pale blue in the sunlight, but even creatures and plants that had a natural luminescence did not glow that specific silvery blue. The insects didn't touch them. The animals didn't eat them. Those flowers caused him a dread that chilled his bone marrow and turned his soul pale.

Yes, this was an evil place.

1989

Peter looked at his mother, and her face was grim. She had finished her tale, but he was not clear on its meaning.

"Mother," he said, curiosity emanating from his pores. "I'm sorry. I don't understand. How does this story relate to the Vanek House?"

His mother gave him a sad smile.

"There are events that sour a place," she said. "The world is in a constant struggle between opposite forces. Sometimes, an event is so heinous, so dreadful, it can shift the balance in one spot for hundreds of years. It can turn it into a hole in the world, and that hole can expand and swallow everything around it. That place will remain tainted until the balance returns, or until something else shifts it in the opposite direction. Do you understand what I'm saying?"

"I think so, Mother. Are you saying something like what happened to Walter Parham and Gerardo Valencia can affect that balance?"

She nodded, a proud expression on her face. "Yes."

"Are you saying it could happen to me, too?"

She nodded again. "Yes. I'm also saying I'll do anything for my God, but I could never do what Dorothy Parham did to her son. I am tough on you because I must be, but what happened today at Roberta Valencia's house reminded me of what the loss of a child can do to a mother. I cannot lose you, Peter."

For the first time since he could remember, Peter smiled lovingly at his mother. He felt moved and warm. His eyes moistened with gladness.

"You won't, Mother," he said. "I promise."

"Good boy."

Out of nowhere, the lights in the house came on,

startling them a little. The hum of the heater and other appliances turning on filled the surrounding space.

"Oh," Mother said. "I guess they reconnected it today, after all."

Peter grinned. "Thank God."

She smiled at him again, stood up, and placed the leather-bound book on the chair she had been sitting in. She ran her hands over her skirt, straightened it, and said, "Come with me. I want to show you something."

2022

His mother scowled at him, a mixture of bewilderment, indignation, and amusement plastered in her eyes. Peter had expected her to react this way, but he was in unknown territory now: he had spoken up, he'd stood up to her, he'd told her what he'd come here to say. This was so unprecedented, if she'd reacted by producing a baton and a top hat out of thin air and pulled a white rabbit from it, he would have considered it an equally likely event.

"You must be joking, boy," she said. "I will do no such thing."

His resolve wavered, but he maintained his poker face. "It's your choice," he said. "I didn't expect you to agree immediately, but I'll be in White Harbor for four days. I'll come by tomorrow, and the day after, and one last time, right before I leave. If you forget what I said, I'll remind you."

"Why would I forget my son came into my home to offend me?"

"Never mind." He realized the futility of continuing to argue. "Ignore I said that. I brought this." He reached into his pocket and brought out a laminated card with writing on it. "I will leave this here." He stood up, removed the cover from two small strips of double-sided tape that were already on the back of the card. "I laminated it, just to make sure you couldn't just tear it up with your hands in one of your fits of anger."

"What is that?"

He pressed the card to the nightstand next to the bed, the writing facing the bed's direction, ensuring it stuck to the table hard enough to prevent her from removing it. According to a young man he didn't know, who worked at the hardware store—another stop he'd made on the way to see his mother—this tape could hold up to fifteen pounds, so hopefully, his mother's hands could not rip it out.

"It's a summary of what we just discussed. It will be there at all times."

"How dare you? This is my bedroom, my furniture, my house!"

"It's not, Mother. We already covered that. This is a

hospital. You are a patient. You are sick, Mother. I am offering you a home to spend your last days in, with your son and your grandson."

"Ha! Don't be ridiculous!"

"I will pay for a nurse and a caretaker to ensure you don't hurt yourself and you don't hurt us. I am willing to do that. I want my son to know where he came from."

Even as Peter said the words a second time, he realized how dumb they sounded. He realized she would never agree to this. She would never accept this, and even if she did, she would probably forget the next day and try to hurt William. Why was he even entertaining this stupid idea? No, he had to keep going. He had to convince her. He had to give her the chance.

"I don't want you to die alone, Mother. I want to be there for you, but I also want you to get to know your grandson. He is loving, and smart, and right now he needs his family with him. I know what that's like."

His mother scoffed and suddenly laughed. The hoarse cackle surprised him and made him cringe. It went on for longer than he could bear.

"Oh, you stupid boy. Why would I want to know him? I don't need him. I don't need your help. Your bitch wife is dead, just like God promised. Your boy, that little impure piece of garbage, he will be food, and God will feed. God will feed on him forever. He will beg for the sweet embrace of death, while being endlessly ground by the Lord's teeth. He will be an offering, a gift from me to God, a sacrifice I've already made, and all God needs to do is claim him."

"Shut up," Peter said, goose pimples covering his skin, the freeze of fear running through his veins like air bubbles injected into his bloodstream soon to reach his brain.

"The bitch is dead, your boy will be devoured, and God will bring you back to me." Her voice reached a rapturous crescendo. "God will bring you back to me. His Glory will be upon the world, and I will rejoice with my son by my side."

Peter stood quietly by the nightstand, unnerved. Staring at the blazing insanity in her face.

"It starts tonight, boy."

"The card," he said, with a resolute tone and a stony face, pointing at the laminated nonsense he'd stuck to her nightstand. "Read it. Think about it. Four days. Last chance."

Peter hurried toward the door, past his mother, who sat grinning. He tried not to make eye contact. His back was to her now. He was almost at the door.

"It starts tonight, boy," she cackled, a rough throaty sound, like the staccato coughing of a chain smoker.

Peter stumbled out the door and into the hallway, attempting to escape her voice, but it still followed as the door closed behind him. The elation in it was earth-shaking.

"It starts tonight!"

Chapter Seventeen

The Meeting at Cunningham's

Thursday nights were always slow at Cunningham's. The usual drunks that came every night got there later than 9 p.m. and right now, there was only one customer occupying a table.

It was a tall guy with broad shoulders and a thick body that couldn't decide whether it was made of fat or muscle. He was dressed in a beautiful purple plaid flannel shirt over a light violet t-shirt, dark blue jeans, and brown Timberlands. The long flannel sleeves were rolled up to show thick hairy arms with meaty hands and fingers. The man's hair was done in a short side-part haircut, with a slightly receding hairline and a dense but perfectly trimmed brown beard. He looked like he'd gotten a haircut just that very day.

The man presented "fancy lumberjack", Jess Cunningham thought, as she approached with a pint of beer, fresh from the tap. He would've been just the type she'd asked out if she were still into men—a nasty habit she'd quit completely the night Cassie Robertson had made her moan, "So, that's what an orgasm is!"

In either case, she knew the man had a wife.

She put the pint in front of Barry Giffen with a tired sigh. "Let me see if I get this, Barry," she said. "We all got the text from Nadine."

"Save it, Jess. I don't wanna hear it," he said.

"No, Barry. You *are* gonna hear it. Nadine said Peter asked to move the get-together to nine, because he wasn't feelin' so good. I know you got it, you replied 'Ok' on the group chat, same as everyone. But here you are, just past seven-thirty, all done up like a virgin on a blind date. Normal people usually get to the bar a little past the hour they agree upon, but I guess you're just that fuckin' punctual, aren't ya?"

"Jess—"

"Also, you see that thing over there?" She pointed at the bar and the stools on the other side of her establishment. "That's a bar. That beautiful thing I just wiped shiny as a mirror actually gives the name to the fine business you find yourself in this evening, ain't that fuckin' fascinatin'?" She exaggerated the question, placing her fists on her hips and cocking her head to one side. "Normal people sit at the bar when the place is empty and get their beer there, especially when it's from the tap. You just made me go all 'round the bar and walk all the way from there to deliver a single pint."

"Isn't that your job?" he asked with a raised eyebrow.

"It's 7:30, Barry!" she said with exasperation. "This is my slowdown hour! My sit-down time! If you can't make yourself come in later, you sit at the bar and drink there while you wait for the entire gang to get here, and *then* you all move to a table together. I'm tired, man! You're makin' me walk more'n I have to."

"Have you considered maybe I just wanted some time to myself while I wait?" He snorted through his nose in frustration. "Not like I get a lot of that. Away from work, away from Maryann, away from the kids. Is that too much to ask?"

A heavy compress of guilt wrapped around her chest.

It made her remember a time, back when they were kids, when she rode by on her bike near a small playground. They would've been maybe seven or eight, and Barry was sitting in a swing, completely alone, not doing anything in particular. He had always been bigger than most of the other kids, so he appeared incongruously out of scale in the small swing, just moving an inch back and an inch forward absent-mindedly.

"Hey, Barry," she called out, riding her bike in a circle. "The hell you doing? Shouldn't you be headin' home?"

He flashed a nervous, lost expression her way, and hesitated before shifting toward anger and that intimidating tone he always used on other kids. She had never been impressed by it, though. "Why's it any of your business?"

She shrugged. "Just asking. Had to do a double take 'coz I thought there was a rhino tangled in the swing set."

Barry raised a middle finger. "Fuck off, ginger bitch!"

She rode away laughing, and it was only later, talking to her dad, he told her Barry's mom had been on a four-day bender, and Barry probably hadn't wanted to go home, because that meant she'd take it out on him.

Jess had always had the tendency to mouth off without thinking.

"Connecting your tongue to your brain is like pulling down your pants before you take a shit," her dad always said.

Barry's wife was, to put it in the mildest words she could use, a goddamn fucking psychological abuser. A vicious, bloodthirsty leech, who sucked on his bank account more often and more vigorously than she'd ever sucked on his cock. A soulless monster who dangled their two precious children in front of the man like a bottle of ice water in front of someone dying of thirst in the desert.

"Connecting your tongue to your brain is like pulling down your pants before you take a shit."

Fine, Dad, she thought. *The woman ain't nice, is all I'm saying.*

She noticed how Barry's posture had changed slightly. He was slouching a little. He had already taken a drink of beer and had foam in his beard. Jess humphed, pulled out a small dirty rag from her black apron's pocket and quickly wiped the foam off his face, eliciting a surprised expression from him.

"Wha—"

"You had a bunch of foam on your face." She put the rag back in her pocket. "You looked like someone jizzed all over your beard!"

"Jess, what the hell?"

"Connecting your tongue to your b—"

Oh, shut the fuck up, Dad!

"Goddamn it! You know me, Barry, don't act like you don't." She blew air out with frustration. "I'm sorry. Alright? I'm sorry I mouthed off at you. You know I got no filter on me. It's like a syndrome, or some shit." She signaled with her head toward the pint of beer. "That one's on me. Enjoy your quiet time. The rest of the gang should be here soon. I'll go get you some garlic bread while you wait."

She walked away, shaking her head, and sighed once more, scratching her freckled nose. She could feel Barry staring at her.

"Thanks, Jess," he said.

She smiled. "You're welcome, big guy."

Instead of walking back to the bar, Jess busied herself

wiping tables, moving chairs, mopping floors, and getting the restaurant area back in tip-top shape for the next day. She closed the restaurant for the night since she didn't want to be busy during the get-together with the gang. She would only keep the bar area open, and she'd asked Louis, her bar helper, to arrive at nine o'clock to take over for her.

As Jess put the mop and the bucket away, she exhaled deeply, not from exhaustion, but a strange feeling in her chest, a strange sense of gravity pulling her heart down. She didn't know what had gotten into her this evening. She was in a bit of a wistful mood. It was a sensation she got those days when she allowed herself some time alone at home and she stared out the window to see rain clouds approaching from the sea and heard distant thunder. There was always a feeling of melancholy associated with it. She had always been sensitive to changes in the weather, to changes in the mood inside a room, even to changes in the town's mindset.

In Blight Harbor, you mean, she thought.

She knew Blight Harbor had been in overdrive that day with Peter's visit. Could that be it?

Why, though? Nothing of notice has really happened.

She guessed she was probably feeling this way because the entire gang was coming back together one more time to rally around a comrade who'd lost a loved one. It had been the same when her brother Jonah died and they'd been there for her, or when Royce's twin brother, Leroy, was killed by Freddie Parham, along with five other children.

Before Leroy's death, she had been considering asking Royce out to go watch a movie, but after everything that happened, Royce hadn't needed a girlfriend—he hadn't had the emotional availability. He'd needed a friend, and that's what she'd become.

Would things have been different if she'd ever asked him out when they were kids? Would she have let Cassie Robertson show her what she'd been missing her whole life?

Most likely. If it hadn't been Cassie, it would've been some other beautiful curvy girl with carefully shortened fingernails and lipstick that tasted like strawberries in cream. Sooner or later—she was happy it had been sooner—the Big L realization would've hit, and she would've broken Royce's heart. She might not be a gold-star lesbian, but she was proud that once she dipped her toe in the water, she dove in and never looked back.

It wouldn't have been so weird if they had gotten together, though. The "friends-to-couple-to-friends-shuffle-repeat" dance had happened a few times within their little group. When you grew up in such a small and isolated town, it was difficult not to have a couple of bed partners in common with your friends, she supposed.

There were the early pairings, like Peter and Nadine. *Until that crazy woman came after her with a pair of scissors.*

There were also the regrettable ones, like the time she

and Barry got drunk after their graduation and had probably the worst sex she'd had in her life. It felt like neither of them wanted to be there, but they'd already started going at it, so they might as well finish the damn thing.

Then, there were the late pairings, Callum and Sylvia, or Bobby and Angie—though, technically, Angie wasn't part of the Vigilantes

(*Stupid fucking name, by the way*)

but they seemed to be doing quite well.

Finally, there was Raymond, who had the absolute misfortune of being one of only a handful of out, gay men in a tiny town, so she only knew him to have dated Hank Marsh for a couple years before Hank got out and moved to New York. Ray often joked he'd have to buy mountain gear, since the closest Grindr hookups he found were on the other side of the hills.

Rain and thunder from the sea... The thought appeared in her mind unprompted. *And we're surrounded by the mountains.*

By ten to nine, Sylvia and Callum had already arrived. He, looking like he'd been genetically designed to be a librarian, and she, looking like she'd been genetically designed to be the girl of her dreams.

That lucky, short, bespectacled bastard! she thought. *Happy for them, though.*

Royce came in shortly after, and they had done their usual back and forth. Trading jabs and insults like all besties did, followed by a tight embrace, and their customary exchange of "I love you's", concluding with Royce asking, "Am I your daddy?" and her giggling with a schoolgirl's voice and answering "Yes, Daddy!"

Two more of the bar's regulars, Riley Estrada and Mason Owen, walked in and sat on their usual barstools. Jess did her usual song and dance, bantering and trading jokes, throwing a "fuck" here and a "hun'" there. She popped the cap off two cold beers, the caps hitting the pile of their fallen comrades with a quiet clink. As she put the two bottles in front of Riley and Mason, she heard the front door open.

"A'ight boys," she said. "Enjoy. There's a fridge full of those waiting for you. Just gimme a holler." She spun on her sneakers to face the door and the reaction exploded out of her without filters or red lights on its way out. "Well, skull-fuck me with a red-hot chainsaw. If it isn't Nadine fuckin' Schaefer, out on the fuckin' town!"

Nadine, taken aback by the sudden outburst of profanity, stopped in her tracks, causing Bobby to smash the footrests of Angela's wheelchair into her calves. She let out a loud, "Ow!"

"I'm sorry," Bobby said.

Angela, sitting in the wheelchair, only concealed a giggle with her hand.

Nadine gritted her teeth as she rubbed the pain off her left calf. "That's gonna leave a bruise. Thanks for that, Jess. What the hell do you mean I'm out on the town? I come here at least once a month with the other teachers for Happy Hour."

Jess pointed at the two regulars sitting at the bar.

"See those two? They're here every night because they don't have a life and spend their whole paycheck drinking like the world is gonna end. It's goddamn sad, really."

"Hey!" she heard Riley or Mason—didn't matter which one—protest from behind her.

"I'm also here almost every day, so unless you come visit daily, I don't even realize you left your house. As far as I know, you might be stuck in a month-long hostage situation, and I wouldn't find out until you appear on the news on that TV over there." She pointed at a TV on a nearby wall. "Just like you, I have no life eith…er…"

Her speech petered out as she saw the essential thing she had failed to notice, right in front of her.

"Angie?" she said in a thin, quavering voice.

Nadine moved aside to reveal her younger sister sitting in the chair.

Angela's body had become incredibly thin, but Jess saw that her friend's cheeks were rosy, and she was smiling.

Her complexion had regained so much of its color. She was wearing make-up, she noticed, immediately. The sunken eyes she had gotten used to seeing whenever she took some time off to visit were gone. She was wearing a long, tan skirt with a blue-and-black ink-strike print, knee-high black boots, and a blue blouse under a black leather jacket. She was such a delicate, beautiful thing her heart swelled, and—she thought again, as if needing confirmation—she was smiling, but the most important of all, she was—

"You're outside." Jess's breath was stolen by shock, forcing back tears.

"The nurse couldn't take care of her tonight on such short notice," Nadine said.

"Tomorrow, they're taking me to the park," Angie said.

What made Jess lose the battle against tears was the huge, beaming grin Angie gave her as she said this. She hadn't seen her smile like that in a very long time. She wiped at her eyes, sniffled once, and caught herself from leaping over the bar and hugging her. "Fuck, see what you made me do?" She wiped the tears on her apron, shook her head, turned her gaze toward Bobby, grinned, and said, "God bless your magical dick, Bobby Novak!"

"My what?"

Angie burst out cackling while Bobby just stared at his girlfriend, realizing exactly what she'd told Jess.

"Angie!" His face turned bright red.

Before the moment could become even more awkward, Jess pointed at the table from which Cal, Sylvia, Barry, and Royce were staring at Angie in shock.

"You might wanna hurry and step right over there to say hi, since they also want to see Angie, I guess?"

"Yeah," Nadine said and waved at the table group. "I'll probably have to explain why Angie came when Peter had asked for only the Vigilantes."

"Oh, c'mon," Bobby said, his skin slowly regaining its "whitest guy in America" complexion. "Nobody will mind. Much less Peter. You know him. I'd be shocked if he isn't happy to see her."

"Who gives a fuck if anyone minds?" Jess said. "Anyone bats an eye the wrong way at my Angie, I'll kick 'em out, see if I don't."

"Thanks, Jess." Bobby turned Angie's chair to push her toward the others.

"Wait, listen to me, young lady." Jess was now pointing a finger at Angela. "Once you say your hellos, and everybody's asked all the obvious questions, I will expect Magic Dick here to roll you to that separate table over there, and you and I will catch up, alright?"

Angie grinned again, and it was the most refreshing smile Jess had ever seen.

"Now, go." Her voice was choked up. "You're gonna

make me cry again, and I have a reputation to uphold."

She watched them rolling Angie to the table, where everyone stood to give them a warm welcome.

The night had officially gone from a simple, friendly reunion to a celebration.

A few minutes later, the door swung open so suddenly Jess's heart nearly jumped out of her mouth.

Swiveling her head toward the door, she noticed a young man wearing a black jacket over a security guard uniform. She'd never seen this person before. He was young, roughly twenty-five, tall, Black, head shaved bald, with big, expressive eyes that held an edge to them. He walked to the barstool furthest from the entrance, where people rarely sat, since it was right by the door to the men's room, and settled into the padded seat.

Jess found it odd that he didn't call or motion her over, but he appeared to be one of those quiet types, so maybe he wasn't comfortable engaging first. She walked over, placed a small bowl of salted peanuts in front of him, and said, "What can I get you, hun?"

"Ginger ale would be just fine," he said without looking at her. He took a handful of peanuts, popped them in his mouth and chewed.

While Jess's first impulse was always to strike up a conversation, this young man didn't appear like the chatty type. She grabbed a glass, scooped some ice and poured it in, filled the glass with ginger ale from the tap, then placed it on a coaster right in front of him.

She stood in front of him as he took the first sip without saying thanks. She got curious and decided to poke a little. "You new in town?"

He swiveled those big eyes toward her, studied her face for a few seconds. It wasn't a friendly look. "Yes," he said.

"You a…security guard or something?" It was a stupid question, but it was asked on purpose just to get him talking a little more.

He only glanced at his uniform and took an exhausted sigh, gave a tired nod. "Mm-hmm."

"That's nice!" She gave an awkward smile. "Where?"

"Look," he said, eyes drilling into her now. "I just got off work. I'm tired. I'd like a quiet moment to myself."

"I'm sorry." She raised her hands in a gesture of apology. "I'll leave you to it."

She shot the unfriendly security guard a suspicious look, pondering what his deal was. Was she actually being too nosey? Her attention was pulled elsewhere, though, as she heard the door open yet again. Standing at the entrance, she saw a figure wearing a tan denim jacket, an olive-green shirt, jeans, and fancy black boots.

A strand of thick, black hair fell over Peter's right eye as he peered in her direction. He pushed it aside, giving her an awkward grin.

"Hey, Jess."

"You're late!" she said with a frown. "I thought being raised by an abusive, religious nut meant she'd beaten some discipline into you."

Peter's grin went flat.

Not even noticing his discomfort, Jess said, "Bad boy!" and clapped both her hands together twice as an admonishing gesture. "Come, give me a hug, and I'll consider not telling 'Mother' about it."

Peter sighed, leaned over on the tips of his toes, and threw his arms around her.

"It's good to see you again, Petey-boy. We've missed you." Jess closed her eyes and squeezed extra hard. Something popped in his back. She could tell he was tense.

"The place looks awesome, as always," Peter said, shooting a casual glance around the old bar.

"Aw, you're always so sweet, hun. You can be honest, it's a shithole."

"No, I mean, uh…" Peter cast a more attentive glance around, taking in the red brick walls, the ugly neon signs spelling beer brands, the pool table with the long straight scratch in the middle of the bed cloth. His eyes lingered for a second on the old incandescent light fixtures that hipsters might call "vintage industrial décor", but which he knew were just old. "I…love that wall with framed pictures of your dad with people from town. Is that new?"

"Nice try. Those pictures have always been there, and all of those smiling with my dad are dead already." She pointed at the first picture and went down the line. "Cancer, heart attack, heart attack, bullet, car crash, cancer, cancer, cancer, car crash, drowning, heart attack, and so on, and so on."

"Oh." Peter's mind went blank, his mouth hanging open. "Sorry."

"Well, that guy over there, he was a funny case." She pointed at the last picture in the bottom row. "Paul Vickers. What an asshole! Treated his employees at the docks like shit. One day, he didn't watch where he was going and, right in front of his entire crew—BAM!—walked into an open septic tank. He banged his head on the way down and drowned in shit before they tried to pull him out."

"Tried?"

"Well, I'd say let's leave that in Blight Harbor, but it's pretty easy to guess few people were willing to dive into shit to get Paul Vickers out." Jess stretched an arm toward Peter and clamped a hand on his shoulder. She glanced into his blue eyes, and with a grave frown, studied the dark circles under them. "Now, let's get serious, Petey-boy. Tell me. How bad was it today?"

"How bad *what* was?"

"Stop acting stupid. The whole town knew ten minutes after you walked into the hospital. Blight Harbor has been growing fat with gossip all day about what the conversation was between you and your mom."

Peter shook his head and chuckled. "What's the worst one you've heard so far?"

"I will not dignify rumors with giving you any details, but it involves you, a pillow, and that horrible bag of crazy that gave birth to you not breathing anymore."

"Is it me, or are people in this town the worst at *not* giving details?"

"Hun, when have I ever been subtle?" Jess accompanied this with a crooked smirk. "Can I say something positive, though?"

"Will you be okay? Are you sure it won't hurt?"

She rolled her eyes. "Sarcasm noted. You're learning. Good! I was going to say, you reacted with humor to that remark. That's a change. You know? Compared to the old Peter, who would've probably said some shit like, 'A boy's best friend is his mother.'"

Peter's smile diminished, but he still nodded in understanding.

"So," Jess pushed. "How bad was it?"

He wiped his mouth with his hand, and his eyes rolled to one side, considering. "It was…" He paused. "It was worse than I expected, but still not the worst it's been.

388

You know what I mean?"

She nodded and her throat tightened, but she remained quiet as she noticed his mouth was still slightly ajar, as if he had more to say.

"It's like when there's an earthquake that doesn't knock your house down, but it leaves some cracks in the structure," he sighed. "My talk with her today shook me… it, uh…"

"Left cracks?"

"Yeah."

"Look." She imbued her voice with as much care and love as a sailor-mouthed cynic like she could. She motioned to the gang, who were all facing him and waving. "You see those people over there? Those people are your family, your *actual* family. I consider myself your family. William, your aunt, even that fat maid that lives in your house here. They're your family."

"I know."

"No. Look at me. Eyes right here!"

He met her gaze.

"That old bitch might have pushed you out of her guts, but she ain't your family. Anyone who leaves cracks in your structure, *especially* after you just lost your wife a month ago, they're not family."

"Jess, I appreciate what you're trying to do, I do,"—Peter seemed a bit flustered—"but you don't understand."

"No, Petey-boy." She stared him down. "*You* don't understand. I might talk like a not particularly pricey hooker, but I ain't stupid. You don't understand because you're inside the house. *She's* the earthquake. *We're* the engineers that assess the damage you don't see, because you only see the rooms in the house, not the structure."

Peter didn't answer.

"Also, don't forget who was the one that called the police the day they finally got you away from that monster. Who found you in that crawlspace?"

"You did," Peter admitted, appearing embarrassed.

"I did."

"You know I'll always be thankful for that."

"Oh, fuck thankful!" she blurted, back to her loud self. "You wanna thank me? Really think about what I'm telling you. This is your family, right here. That woman is just an earthquake."

Peter gave her a sincere smile, his eyes filled with gratitude.

"Go," she said, pointing her chin toward her friends' table. "I'll join you guys when Louis gets here to lend me a hand. Unlike your lazy asses, I'm working, you know?"

"Thanks, Jess."

"Oh, and,"—she pointed a stern finger at him—"don't give Nadine shit for breaking your stupid 'Vigilantes Only' rule. Angie's out of the house for the first time in ages."

Peter noticed Angela at the table and gasped.

"If you say anything negative, I swear I will destroy you."

"I would never do that." His face beamed with a big smile. "I can't believe she's here!"

"Great," Jess said, looking satisfied. "Have fun."

Peter grabbed her hand and squeezed it with appreciation.

His friends had put three of the square tables together and were now all sitting as a group, leaving Peter to sit not at the head of the table, but at the center chair, with his back against the wall. From where he was sitting, going around to his left were Nadine, Angie—who was at one end of the table, in her wheelchair—Bobby, Royce, Callum, Sylvia, then an empty chair at the corner of the table, and finally Barry, sitting next to Peter.

"Well, we look like the lamest last supper ever," Royce said. "Bunch of early-forties boys and girls sitting in a shitty bar."

"I heard that! Fuck you, Royce!" Jess shouted, all the way from the bar.

"Can't hear you! I don't talk to the help!" Royce retorted and everyone at the table burst into laughter. "What do you think, *Jesús*?" He gave Peter a nod. "Is this our last supper? You here to tell us you're never coming back to town?"

"We placed bets," Nadine said, and furtively averted her gaze, taking a sip of beer.

Peter gawked at her, blindsided. "Um… I…"

"Woah, woah," Barry said, interjecting before everyone could start piling on top of Peter. "We're not getting into important topics just yet. We haven't officially started this meeting of the Vigilantes. We have an empty chair."

"Oh, c'mon, Barry!" Royce said. "Are we still doing this? Can't we just be a bunch of grownups having a beer together?"

"I'm with Barry," Sylvia said. "We're waiting for Ray."

"Noted," Royce said, then shouted toward the bar. "Can we at least get some wings going already? I'm hungry!"

"Sure, but I'm spitting in yours!" Jess said from the bar.

Royce exhaled in resignation.

"I'm not leaving White Harbor forever," Peter said, sounding done with all the silliness.

"Oh, c'mon, man!" Barry elbowed Peter in the arm. "Protocol!"

"Barr, you're literally the only one that cares about Vigilante protocol anymore." Peter gave him a pleasant smile and a pat on the shoulder. "Thank you for caring, though."

He turned toward the bar. "Jess, seriously, let's get some wings going, please! We're starving!"

"You got it!"

"And don't spit in Royce's!"

"I'll consider it!"

"Thank you!"

Peter surveyed the table and a feeling of warmth and contentment swept over him. Jess was right. This felt like family. It felt like home. For his own peace of mind, he had to have the conversation with his mother, and he planned to have it each day of this weekend, even if it was fruitless. He owed it to his own soul to go through with it. But this, he thought, this was family. This was home. Everyone was treating him as the guest of honor, which felt like a pleasant position to hold.

"We don't really need to follow Vigilante protocol. We should probably get started, because it's nine-forty, so we can't just keep waiting for Ray."

"Oh, is that how it is?" said a laughing voice approaching the table.

Everyone turned to see Ray ambling toward them from the bar with a big smile, having missed Jess, who was in the kitchen checking on the garlic bread, onion rings, and wings.

"I left the hospital late because your mom was so riled up she wouldn't go to bed, and *now* you're too good to wait for me before you officially start the meeting?" Ray said hello to Sylvia with a hug, then Cal, Royce, and Bobby as he continued to talk. "Do you have any clue how many times your mom asked me to mow her lawn today?" He gave a pleasantly surprised embrace to Angie, then Nadine, until he reached Peter. "And all that time, she kept calling me every type of Asian in existence. I think at some point she switched to Asian food names."

Peter stood up, and Ray threw his arms around him, giving him an enthusiastic hug, moving side to side, then held him by the shoulders.

"Why does she even have to call me anything Asian? Why can't she just call me Raymond? I'd settle for 'Hey, you', but nope."

"I'm sorry." Peter blushed with embarrassment.

"Eh." Ray threw a dismissive hand. "It wasn't you. Also, I spend more time with your mom than you, remember? I'm used to it." Ray stood in front of Barry and gave him a rushed pat on the back.

"Hey, Ray," Barry said. "Saved you a seat."

Ray regarded the corner chair next to Barry for a few awkward seconds.

"Thanks, Barr," he said without looking at him, "but I'd been meaning to have a quick chat with Royce about the music for my nephew's birthday party, so I was hoping to sit next to him."

"Oh," Barry said, looking disappointed. "Oh, okay."

"Hey, Cal. Wanna switch?" Ray did a back-and-forth motion with both his index fingers.

Peter and Nadine exchanged a knowing glance, and she mouthed the words "Blight Harbor" back at him.

"Sure," Cal said, with little thought. He stood up, went around the table, and sat next to Barry. "I just wanted to make a quick correction to your last supper comparison," he said to Royce. "Most likely, a majority of the apostles were under the age of forty, so your comparison was incorrect."

Royce's face did not seem amused. "I'll make a note of that important piece of information, because it's going to be useful to me…never."

"Alright," Ray said, and clapped twice. "I officially call this meeting of the Vigilantes in session!"

"Here, here," Barry said, raising his pint and struggling to brush aside the awkwardness of their previous exchange.

"What's the first order of business?" Ray asked, looking at everyone but him.

"Um," Peter stood up. "I'm moving back to White Harbor."

Chapter Eighteen
A History of Violence

Freddie Parham examined, with meticulous, childlike wonder, the painted canvases, the charcoal sketches, the cotton paper that had thirstily drank his watercolors from his brush, and even the doodles and words he'd lazily scribbled on the walls, the floor, and the ceiling.

"Beautiful things," he whispered in wonder.

Beautiful things that were the collection of his life's work. Over twenty-five years' worth of work, of putting dreams and nightmares on any material that would allow him to tattoo them on its surface. Twenty-five years of listening to voices, of decoding dreams, and rendering them into a darkly wondrous sort of still life filtered through the eyes of his soul.

He would never get to publish that storybook with accompanying illustrations, inspired by *Scary Stories to Tell in the Dark.* No monthly horror comics, penned and inked under the *Hyena Publishing* brand he'd always dreamed of creating. Instead, he had to compress all of that work into the many creations he now beheld. He combined, and cut, and curated only the finest his brain could concoct—distilled it, and poured it into his paints, and laced the graphite and charcoal with it.

Only the best for the Lord. Only the best to save my family.

His eyes stopped at an oil painting of a magnificent creature with a long tentacle coming out of a great lipless mouth lined with white human teeth. This one was an evolution of one of his earlier sketches. Back when he'd first envisioned it, he'd thought the tentacle was missing something, but he couldn't figure out what, until much later. It was so obvious, he one day realized. The creature had *no* lips, only an enormous mouth, with exposed *human* teeth. What the great tentacle was missing was a pair of *human* lips around a mouth with *no* teeth. It balanced the creature perfectly. It was, quite simply—

Beautiful!

He was thankful to Bobby for advocating for him when others tried to take his art—his life—away from him, under the pretext it was harmful and only empowered the violence in his mind. If they only knew how stupid that was.

He was extracting these violent, beautiful things

from his being, otherwise they would tear at his flesh and his skin from the inside and cut their way out, destroying anyone who stood near, and then himself. On the canvas, on the paper, on the walls, they were dormant and harmless, until it was time for God to use them for his holy purpose.

There was a charcoal doodle on the wall that made him very curious, mostly because it was just a few lines that formed a stick figure that appeared more insect-like than human. From what he could gather, the "arms" had three segments with two inward elbows per arm, ending in a little hooklike claw. The head was a single squiggly line and the knees bent backward. But what made him curious was a triangle-like shape on top of its body that was placed like the "dress" shape on a women's restroom sign.

He smiled, thinking of a praying mantis in a dress.

Freddie was not a violent man. Quite the contrary. He loathed violence, which was why he put it into his art. His art was his worship. God showed mercy to him, a cursed wretch, by allowing the violence to be expressed in his creations, so it wouldn't remain to fester in his soul.

This didn't mean he had never hurt others. He had. He was locked up for a reason, after all. But any violent incidents after he was locked up had been caused by some thoughtless idiot that made his violence leave the paper and reenter him. He'd warned them. It wasn't his fault if they were irresponsible and didn't pay attention.

He once bit a hole into the cheek of a female security guard.

All her fault. I warned her.

She restrained his hands, then collected his smaller sketches, crumpling them into balls, and throwing them in a garbage bag. What else was he supposed to do? Let her? He couldn't snatch the drawings off her hands, all bound like he was. He couldn't strangle her until she stopped breathing, like he wanted to, more and more, as the violence flew from the crumpled paper back into his brain. So, he lunged at her, teeth first, and the one thing he caught was her right cheek.

He felt bad when he hurt others, especially because Bobby then had to come running to advocate for him—his knight in shining armor. He couldn't imagine how much shit Bobby had had to make up to make that specific mess disappear.

Poor Bobby probably had to blow a judge to get that sorted out. He's a good friend.

Many argued Bobby could not be his psychiatrist because they were childhood best friends. There would still be times when someone would get cute and tried to replace Bobby with someone else. But all Freddie had to do was stop talking, stop bathing, and stop eating, until they realized it was useless to try to make him talk to someone else. With Bobby, at least, they were getting some new info on "The Vanek House Killer" from time to time.

A quick snicker pushed up from his chest and between his teeth.

What a ridiculous name.

Eventually, they reached a compromise. Bobby would be his secondary psychiatrist, while some other shrink would be his primary. This was mostly for show, since Bobby was the only one that ever came to talk to him.

Bobby and his savior complex. That boy is priceless.

He worked so hard to interpret the message behind his art. Freddie found these moments entertaining. It was like watching a dog try to understand why the people on TV weren't the right size and constantly flickered.

Surprise, Bobby! There's no message!

Well, that wasn't entirely accurate, he admitted to himself. There was a certain perspective, a certain abstraction, but just like the horror comics he used to read as a kid, they were what they were. In those comics, a vampire was a vampire, a werewolf was a werewolf, a zombie was a zombie. His renditions were what they were. That thing on the drawing, shambling toward Sam Becker Jr. as he walked home, simply was what it was. All Freddie had done was see it in his mind, filter it through his hand, and draw it.

That single black claw I added looks pretty nasty, though.

His mouth stretched into the widest grin just thinking about it.

He was *not* a violent man.

It was 7:00 p.m.

Two hours until the Mother came to visit.

1991

Monday

The water was so close it was almost touching the tip of his nose. An unyieldingly strong hand held his head inside the toilet while the voice of the owner of said hand echoed against the walls of the school bathroom, strong, authoritative, but above all, full of malevolent amusement.

The voice repeated that impossible and meaningless order: "I already told you, Lange, all you have to do is stick out your tongue and take a drink of water like an obedient dog. Once you do, I'll let you go."

"Please," Peter implored. "Don't make me do this."

"In that case," Barry Giffen said, laughing hard, "we can go with Option Two, which is I push your entire head into the toilet and see how long it takes before you pass out."

He gave Peter's head a slight nudge, and he saw the water get dangerously close to the tip of his nose. He could hear the trio of sidekicks, who always hung around Barry, laughing too, making fun of his predicament.

"If you ask me," Barry continued, "I think the first option is much easier and saves us time, Lange."

Peter knew that even if he had the strength to stick his head out of the toilet, it would only give Barry and his two cronies—the third being Kirsten Holmes, who was standing guard outside the door—the excuse to beat him up. He didn't want to imagine what Mother would do if she found out what they were doing to him. Her reactions were always unpredictable. She could lose it and hurt Barry,

(How dare you touch my son? Only I get to discipline him!)

or she could punish him for letting this happen without defending himself—

(Weak. You're a weak boy! A useless coward!)

after all, Peter was the son of the Circle's Mother. Barry had put him in the predicament of having to decide between drinking a few ounces of toilet water and risking a parasitic infection, or having his head pushed all the way inside the toilet and getting pinkeye.

"I'm gonna start counting," Barry said. "The toilet in the next stall is not as clean as this one, and you're rejecting my kindness. Oscar did us a solid by not flushing when he went a few minutes ago. So, if you don't decide by the time I count to three, we're gonna go to the toilet next door, and I'm gonna dunk your head in that one. Trust me, you don't wanna see what Oscar left behind, but we can all smell it from here."

Oscar Young, one of Barry's henchmen, gave a laugh

that sounded like braying into a pipe as it echoed off the walls.

"What's it gonna be, Lange? A little water from a toilet that has just been flushed, or your entire head in the one we can smell from here?"

"Those weren't the options you gave me!" cried Peter desperately, his voice turning to a grunt with the effort of staying as far away from the water as possible. His hands were planted like gargoyle claws on the edge, where he could feel sticky traces of dried urine and who knew what else.

"I decide what the options are. Which is it gonna be?… One!"

Barry's companions laughed as Peter met the eyes of his terrified reflection on the surface of the water.

"I haven't done anything to you!"

"Two!" Barry said, not even paying attention to Peter's imploration.

"Please, let me go!" He felt Barry push him down again, and for a shaky moment of utter panic, he felt his right hand lose its grip on the rim of the bowl. "I promise not to tell anyone. You can hit me if you want. I'll take it, but please don't make me do this."

Barry sucked in air through his mouth and an immediate blast of terror washed over Peter, who didn't know if he was going to respond to what he had just said or simply shout, "Three!" and drag him to the toilet next door.

Before Barry could say the next word, Peter closed his eyes and stuck out his tongue.

Tuesday

Peter had left his backpack at his desk since the beginning of recess and, just like every day, he strolled quietly, all alone, toward the classroom. His daily routine at school was automatic, mechanical, predictable.

There were already students in the classroom by the time he entered, but this was of little consequence to him. He couldn't talk to others because it was something God didn't like. He didn't want to risk Mother finding out. He kept his conversations to a bare minimum, nothing more than absolutely necessary, otherwise that would result in

(*The Hole*)

severe punishment.

Without a word, he walked toward his desk by the window. As he crossed the classroom, the voices hushed, and he could feel the piercing gazes of every student following him. He kept his head low, but he thought he could hear their voices, full of laughter and whispered mockery.

A pale, cold, and uncomforting light shone through the glass. He cast his gaze outward, where the slope at the edge of the wall dipped down, and he could see the other pavilion nearby, and beyond—despite being at the lower end of the slope—the tops of the trees that made up The Pines.

404

Little by little, other students joined in the classroom, and eventually, Mr. Jenkins, his homeroom teacher, arrived, gave them his usual offhand greeting, and took his place behind his desk to set up his things to begin.

The silence now felt sepulchral and unnatural, as if everyone around was holding their breath. Not giving this much thought, Peter undid the two buckles that held the lid of his brown leather backpack closed and, without thinking, reached inside.

A legion of insects assailed him: cockroaches, spiders, centipedes, crickets, and beetles came out of

(*The Hole!*)

the backpack and washed over Peter like a wave—climbing up his arms into the spaces between his shirt buttons, sneaking down his collar, scuttering under his arms and through his sleeves, and finding their way down his back.

In his utter terror, Peter let out scream after desperate scream.

The Hole. This reminded him of the Hole.

The space under his house where his hands touched cold, damp earth that had not known the sun for years, where earthworms writhed, where cobwebs clung to his hair and clothes, where insects crawled over his body. A dark space where he was powerless to avoid them, powerless to see them, powerless to shake them out of his clothes, as they found new places to crawl into.

The classroom erupted into utter chaos. A pandemonium of students screaming, fleeing from the insects, running, climbing on chairs. Some students ran out of the classroom in terror, while Mr. Jenkins tried to bring the mayhem under control.

Peter fell to the ground, convulsing with fear. Kicking and flailing his arms and legs, trying to get rid of the besieging insects.

From their corner of the classroom, Barry Giffen and his three cronies, Oscar Young, Drew Mills, and Kirsten Holmes, laughed their heads off at a prank they had clearly authored, and which had exceeded all their expectations.

Wednesday

His black shoes appeared and disappeared in his field of vision. First one, then the other, making a soft sound as they shuffled on the linoleum. Left shoe, right shoe, left shoe, right shoe. Clomp, clomp, clomp, clomp. It took a lot of concentration to isolate that sound, given the din of students, faculty, and staff that filled the hallways between periods.

Peter always walked with his eyes pointed to the floor when he traversed the halls. It was the way he could most easily avoid eye contact with others and prevent anyone from walking up to talk to him.

He had to be invisible.

Sometimes, he looked up just to make sure he was

going in the right direction or that he wouldn't end up bumping into another student, or worse, a teacher. But the primary goal was to blend in with the crowd that flowed in both directions.

This time, he raised his gaze for a moment, just to find himself on a collision course with Kirsten. She made a beeline toward him, close to the wall to his right, staring at him with an evil smile. Peter moved to the left to avoid her, but not fast enough, allowing her to push him to the left.

He stumbled to the other side of the hall, where Oscar was already waiting for him. He grabbed him by the straps of his backpack and, following his forward momentum, threw him further down the hall, making him stumble once more toward the right side.

Peter tried to regain his footing, but before he could, he felt Drew's hands on the straps of his pack, followed immediately by another push.

He flailed his arms, sensing he could not stop without falling on his face. That was when he glimpsed Barry, who was hurrying toward him, and before Peter could steady himself, for a microsecond, there was the blur of Barry's fist already coming toward him. The next thing he felt was the most perfectly placed gut punch of his young life.

Barry continued on his way, fist-bumping his friends and laughing, as Peter fell to his knees, gasping for air. He could only hear the echo of Barry's laughter and that of the

other students, as the quartet of thugs walked away, trium-
phant.

Thursday

The school gym locker room was now empty, and that was
his signal. As he always did, Peter timed entering the shower
once the last of his classmates left the vicinity.

Having left his clothes on a bench between the tall
blue lockers, Peter wrapped a towel around his waist and
hurried over to one of the shower stalls. His showers were
never long, but he cherished the moments of relaxation as
the hot water trickled down his skin. For a few brief minutes,
he could escape the overwhelming anxiety of being among
people but being unable to engage with them.

The sound of the running water drowned all the
noises around him and it felt like it was washing his very
mind, taking all the stress and unease of the day with it. A
relieved smile drew itself across his face. All that existed was
the echoes of the water pattering against his skin and the
surrounding tiles. He didn't like the loneliness imposed by
his mother, but he loved this specific moment of solitude.

Sadly, the sound that so relaxed him was exactly what
prevented him from hearing the footsteps of the tall, bulky
figure approaching from behind.

He felt a vice-like grip clamp down on him from behind, so tight that he could not move an inch. For Peter,

there was no doubt about who was dragging him out of the shower. Few other boys were this strong, and of those that were, only one had dedicated his existence to tormenting him.

"Barry!" Peter shouted, realizing how naked and vulnerable he was at that moment. "What are you doing?"

"Thank you, Lange!" Barry exclaimed, carrying him as if he weighed nothing. "I feel so special that you recognized me without seeing me."

Peter shouted, struggled, and tried to break free, but Barry's strength was impossible to match. Peter's grunts echoed through the cavernous space of the showers.

"Barry, stop. Stop!"

Barry didn't answer. He just laughed and carried him out of the shower. As they approached the locker area, Peter heard Oscar's and Drew's hoots and taunts echoing in the air. They were joining the party, witnessing Barry impose his latest torture on him.

"Please don't!" Peter yelled, knowing in his panicked mind that they were headed for the door. "Don't! Don't!"

Beyond the door was the gym. The students of the next P.E. class should start trickling in. Showering last meant Peter had little time to finish and get out before the next group came in, and by the time he got out of the shower, there were usually several of them outside, chatting and waiting for others before going into the locker rooms.

"Let me go!" Peter yelled. "Get off me, Barry! I'm begging you, don't!"

"What are you afraid of, Lange? Thought you enjoyed playing the invisible boy. Nobody will see you. Especially not the group of girls outside, about to start P.E."

Clawing, kicking, contorting. Nothing broke Barry's grip, no matter the primal panic that now took over Peter. Oscar and Drew got their hands on him; together, the three of them reared back, holding him like a battering ram, and—

"No! Barry plea—" Before he could finish the sentence, he felt a powerful push and felt himself flying through the air.

His terror-filled vision was so clear that he could make out every detail of the locker room ceiling, with its crossword pattern of pipes, as it panned before his eyes and was abruptly cut off by the undeniable boundary of the dressing room doorframe, and immediately, brightness: the sudden change from the dim light of the locker room to the bright lights of the gym.

No, was the single word that crossed Peter's mind as his flight seemed to take place in slow motion.

He fell naked to the floor with a wet sound, like a fish fresh out of water hitting the deck of a fishing boat. His dripping skin slid against the gym floor. He hadn't finished raising his head when the next thing he heard was peals of screams and laughter from the students outside. A group of girls sitting on the bleachers with Kirsten Holmes pointed and laughed, egging on the rest of the crowd.

He moved his scrawny limbs to stand up, clumsy like a newborn fawn. He turned around, giving the onlookers an undeniable view of his pale, naked ass, and ran back toward the locker room. The image that greeted him trampled all hope of escape.

Drew had all of his clothes in his hand rolled up into a ball, and was lifting it over his shoulder, preparing to throw it like a pigskin. Still seeing everything in an adrenaline-induced slow motion, Peter clearly saw when Drew made his throw. His mind set the arc the fistful of clothing drew in the air, and he followed it with his head, watching how the clothes untangled from one another—they looked almost graceful, like a fancy kite—and fell, spread out, far away from him.

Before he could decide if he should run toward the clothes or run into the bathroom, the decision was made for him when he heard the door close.

Peter banged and banged on the door, trying to get in. The sound of the other students, laughing and shouting and heckling in derision, turned into a cacophony of horrors. But even through the noise, Peter could faintly hear Barry and his companions exiting the locker room through a window on the other side. He heard their laughter again as they ran away, escaping so as not to be seen by some teacher.

He let his body fall to the ground, drew his knees to his chest, and hid his head between them, trying to hide his humiliation.

Friday

Shop was always one of Peter's favorite classes.

Although his interests were always more in letters, reading, and the arts, crafting and building things with tools served a more practical purpose in his mind. Shop class broke the monotony and allowed him to work with his hands, with tools, with textures, with materials, with instruments with which he did not interact every day.

At home, Mother always hired a handyman to come to do the repairs or did them herself, so there was never a need for Peter to learn how to do certain housework. That made him feel useless sometimes. After all, Mother had told him that since his dad left them, Peter was now "the man of the house". Some man of the house he was turning out to be, he thought, when he hadn't even been taught how to hammer a nail. Workshop allowed him to learn all these things in a way that Mother, miraculously, did not object to. She saw it as an innocuous part of his school curriculum. If the boy learned a skill by just being there, good for him, as long as he didn't do it at home.

Today, however, his little Zen space was sullied by an invader. This was a class Barry didn't take in the same period as him, but he'd had to make up class that week, and the big ape had purposely sat down at the worktable right in front of him.

Although Barry had said nothing since the class started, just seeing his big back in front of him gave him indescribable anxiety. He couldn't stop himself from scanning the area, searching for any potential avenue of escape, for when Barry eventually turned to him and his cohorts suddenly materialized to initiate their next attack.

But Barry didn't turn around.

Peter watched as the steady movement of his shoulders indicated he was focused on his work, completely unmindful of Peter's presence.

As the minutes passed, with Mr. Morales going from table to table evaluating their work and making observations, Peter felt that maybe there was a possibility today was one of those days when Barry was too busy, distracted, or tired, to make his life hell.

"I know something about your dad that you don't, Lange."

The words seemed to come from thin air since Peter didn't see anyone looking in his direction or making any gestures showing they were speaking to him. It was Barry's voice, but he still had his back to him. If he was talking, he did so as if talking to the table.

"My dad once told me something very interesting a

long time ago about why your dad left," Barry's back said.

Peter did not answer. He'd prefer not to be drawn into a confrontation he knew he couldn't win.

"Your dad left White Harbor because of that strange religion of your mom's. Everyone's afraid to talk about it. They dump all that occult shit in Blight Harbor, but my dad told me the truth."

"Shut up," Peter finally said. "You're lying."

Barry let out a low, evil laugh from deep in his chest. That this blow was being dealt so calmly, in such a casual manner, suggested that the boy knew his words would cut deep.

"My dad said your crazy mom was planning to sacrifice one of you two to make herself live longer."

"That's enough!" Peter whispered hard. "Mother would never do that!"

"Oh, Lange, you're so naive."

Again, the laughter from deep within his chest, as if it were his stomach that was laughing instead of him.

"I'm not naive!"

"Your dad chickened out and ran out of town, so 'Mother' would have to sacrifice you instead."

Peter felt dread and anger building inside him. It kept bubbling, boiling, rising like milk forgotten in a pot on the stove.

"Your mom is a crazy psycho, and your dad is a coward who abandoned his son to save his own ass."

Peter could only see the back of Barry's head, but he could just imagine the ear-to-ear grin on the caveman, the bastard, the jerk.

No more, he thought.

Peter's hand slid across the table to a carpenter's T-Square, with a short, heavy wooden head and a long, horizontal portion made of thin wood with a fine plastic edge. These rulers had been designed so that the horizontal portion was the exact length of the worktable—the student could use them anywhere on it.

No more.

Peter stood up, gripping the T-Square firmly in both hands. He walked around his worktable.

No more.

He could still hear Barry's deep laugh taunting him. He positioned himself behind him.

No more.

And raising the T-Square over his shoulder as if he were about to hit a large piñata, he yelled: "NO MOOOOOOOOOOOORE!"

Every head in the classroom turned toward Peter as he struck Barry the first time, with the head of the ruler descending from right to left. He raised it again and hit him back in the other direction. Another blow fell and another and another, drawing X's in the air.

The entire class erupted into excited and panicked yelling. Right before their eyes, one of their classmates had gone completely berserk and was assaulting Barry Giffen.

Peter didn't care.

Barry screamed in panic, taking blow after blow from the edge of the T-Square, which left red cuts on his arms.

Peter didn't care.

Let him scream. Let his classmates scream. Let the world scream.

Peter didn't care.

"He went crazy!" Gabriela Cardenas yelled. "Help! He went crazy!"

Their screams were drowned by the roar of animal fury that came from Peter's throat as he landed blow after blow after blow. Finally, Mr. Morales appeared out of nowhere and caught the T-Square midair with one steady, calloused hand, and with the other, he swiftly pushed Peter against the wall and held him there.

Peter, his eyes brimming with tears, was shocked to see Mr. Morales's horrified countenance as he looked from him to Barry.

"Principal's Office! Both of you!" he said breathlessly, and it seemed to be more from fright than exertion.

Together in the office, waiting for what would likely be a suspension, or in Peter's case, even an expulsion, Peter and Barry sat side by side in silence.

A thick tension permeated the principal's office.

Without turning his head, Peter swiveled his eyes to one side to see Barry, his arms covered in straight red cuts that were already lined with bruises. He also had a couple of cuts on his head and one on the right side of the neck that appeared very painful. The cuts were no longer bleeding after the nurse carefully applied alcohol to each of them with a cotton ball.

Barry was breathing deeply and loudly. From where he was sitting, Peter could feel the fury and anger radiating from his body.

In a timid voice, almost a sigh, Peter said, "I'm sorry."

Barry didn't answer.

Peter hung his head, his hair falling into his face as regret and shame replaced anger. His palms still had the red streak from where he had held the T-Square so tightly.

A sound slipped into Peter's ears. A sound that seemed incongruous with the situation. It was the sound of sobs from his right. This time he couldn't help turning his head completely in surprise, because the person next to him was Barry Giffen. Barry Giffen would never start crying.

Peter gaped, silently watching Barry's large frame, hunched over, pathetic, his back and chest shaking in spasms of inconsolable sobs. And on top of all this, Peter could see how his hands were shaking. For a second, he thought the trembling was from the pain of the bruises and cuts, but he knew almost immediately that wasn't true. If it had been pain, Peter would've seen his hands trembling a moment ago.

What Barry was experiencing was fear.

Barry's back collided with his living room wall, causing several hanging frames to fall and a ceramic ornament that was sitting on a shelf to plummet and shatter into hundreds of pieces on impact.

"ARE YOU RETARDED, OR WHAT?" his momma yelled. Drops of saliva flew from her lips and landed on his terrified face.

"No! I…"

His momma's eyes were aflame with anger and bitterness. Her teeth were bare, her expression was insane, her eyes bulged out of their orbits, her clenched jaw quivered, her complexion turned beet-red. With one hand, she grabbed Barry by the hair and shook his head violently, as if trying to detach it from his shoulders.

"How can you even think of saying that to Peter Lange? Do you have any fucking idea who he is?"

"Momma!" Barry said, pleading, grunting through

clenched teeth, his scalp burning in pain, feeling like it would come off at any moment. "I—"

The slap came out of nowhere. An open palm exploded against his cheek. He gawked at his momma's face and what he saw was a wild beast with deranged eyes and gritting teeth, as if she were about to bite into his neck and rip out his jugular.

"Momma!"

Another slap.

Another.

Another.

Another.

"Haven't you realized how dangerous that woman is? Fool! Retard! Animal!"

"Momma, I don't understand—"

"I thought today was the worst of it, but then I find out that you've been tormenting that boy for years…" His momma put her hand to her forehead and flattened her hair back in frustration. Her jaw tensed and the tendons in her neck stood out. Her complexion was red from boiling blood and anger. "Wasn't it enough for you to see your dad hanging from a beam? Do you want to see me die, too?"

"No, Momma. Never. I swear!"

"You're going to stay away from Peter Lange. If I find out you laid a finger on him again or continued to mess with him, I swear to God, I'll kill you myself to make sure Martha

Lange doesn't come after me. Better you than me."

By now, Barry was sobbing unreservedly. Ugly, convulsive sobs, with ragged breaths and snot running from his lips to his chin.

"And to think you were supposed to be the man of the house after your dad died. You are *worthless*!"

"Momma." Barry implored, tears streaming down his face. His breath caught in his throat. "Please, no more… It really hurts when you say that."

"Do I look like I give a fuck if it hurts? Be a man! Crybaby. Pushover. What good does it do ya to be so damn big, if all you'll grow up to be is a big faggot! All you'll ever be good for is to get fucked in the ass! FAGGOT!"

"Please, Momma, no more. I'm sorry! I'm so sorry!"

"Sometimes, I wish I'd birthed a roll of razor wire instead of a moron like you."

Barry's red, trembling gaze met his mother's, his face full of grief. He saw in her eyes she meant every word from the heart. That day, his momma hadn't gone drinking with Neal Parham because she picked him up at the principal's office, so he knew she was completely sober as she said these detestable things.

As if responding to his imploring face, she slapped him again over the red mark she'd already left on his cheek.

She turned and walked away, leaving him sobbing on the floor.

2022

"Freddie."

A deep voice. A man's voice.

It came with that strange distortion. Like when sounds squeeze through the small circular holes in the thick plexiglass separating his room from the hallway. But it was definitely a male voice.

Freddie turned to see a security guard he'd never seen before. He was a rather tall man. Shaved head, large eyes, an angular jaw. He was young. Very young. Black, wiry, late twenties perhaps, but those eyes, staring at him from a face shaded by the light coming from a lamp above his head, were older than what was immediately apparent.

"Oh, hi there!" Freddie greeted him with his usual toothy grin. "Let me guess. First night at the madhouse, and you're coming to meet the celebrity inmate?"

"Freddie, please." The guard's tone was somber. "There's still time. You don't have to do this."

"Oh!" Freddie feigned shock. "For real? I don't have to? Well, thank you, complete stranger! That's a relief!" He let out his "Hee-hee-hee!" giggle.

"Listen to me! This is important. You have to—"

"Ah-ah-ah! Hold it!" Freddie held a hand up. "You're confusing me now, new guy. First, you say I don't have to, but now I *do* have to. So, which one is it?"

The young guard glowered at him. He was not amused by his deflections. "Pay attention, Freddie."

"Why?" Freddie's response came out like a slap in the face. "Shouldn't I know who I'm talking to first? Seems you know my name, new guy. What should I call *you*?"

"My name is not important."

Freddie rolled his eyes and sarcastically bobbed his head up and down, saying, "Mm-hm, mm-hm, mm-hm." He rested his hands on his hips, pondered for a second, then raised his index finger. "Alright. Let's say it's not important. It's just, you know, there's the fact that you come here, out of nowhere, doing the whole 'Ghost of Christmas Future' routine, all ominous, and cryptic and shit, telling me I don't have to do…whatever '*this*' is…but I can't have your name." He shrugged and raised his palms. "Does that sound like someone I should trust?"

"My name is John Hitch."

"There you go! See? Now we can start talking. Now I feel like I've known you my whole life. 'Sup, John?"

"Freddie, you can still put a stop to this. You know what I'm talking about."

Freddie cocked his head, raised an eyebrow, and stuck out his lower lip, still exaggerating every expression to make himself appear as condescending as possible. "I see. So, we're still going with the cryptic and ominous approach, then. You know what? Not feeling it. That's boring." He turned his back on the man. "Speak clearly, or we're done here, Johnny-boy. I'm expecting a visit in a couple of minutes, and I have to be relaxed."

"I will let you walk out of here," the guard said, then shot a furtive glance over his shoulder toward one end of the hallway, then back at Freddie, who was now staring at him with curiosity.

"You'll what?"

"Right now. I will open this door and let you walk out. There will be a boat on the dock for you. You can go somewhere else, live the life you never—"

"No." Freddie's response was blunt, dry, completely devoid of his previous sarcasm. "If I leave, I won't be able to redeem my family. They'll stay in the void forever. I can't."

"You will never redeem your family, Freddie. Your family is cursed, but not because of what you think. That woman, Martha—"

"The Mother!" Freddie interrupted in a sudden outburst of anger. "Show some respect and call her by her proper name!"

"That witch is manipulating you! She brainwashed you!" It was clear John Hitch did not share the same devotion as Freddie, nor wanted to even try to show respect for

Martha Lange. "You're the last of the Parhams. She's using you. She needs you. If you leave White Harbor, you are out of the game. You will be forgotten with time. It's not a bad thing to be forgotten. Trust me. If you do what the Lange woman is asking you to do, you will make your family's curse complete. You will finish what Dorothy Parham started!"

Freddie took a step toward the man, teeth bare, stabbing an index finger in the air toward him. "She promised! The Mother promised! She promised I would redeem my whole family! I'm the last, so I'm the one that will release them from the void and lead them into the arms of God!" He raised his arms rapturously. "I'm the sword of the Lord! I'm the architect of life! I'm the one that will save my ancestors, my dad, my mom, my—"

"Sister?"

Freddie choked on his next word, his fanatical fervor cut short.

"No, Freddie. That woman is lying. There is no way to save your family. Let this end with you."

As Freddie prepared to shout a retort, a hand—thin, light, translucent, but tangible—touched his shoulder.

"Don't listen to him Freddie," a woman's voice said.

The shape of the Mother was standing there, fading in and out of existence, barely visible, but her hand now squeezed his shoulder reassuringly. She had apparently felt his distress and come sooner to rescue him.

"That's a disguise," the Mother said. "He's hiding behind that young man's face."

String-like figures intertwined in her face and eyes, giving her form and texture and expression as they moved. She regarded the man with what Freddie understood as fascination.

"You say your name is John Hitch. Is that what you're calling yourself now? You've had many names, and you've deceived many people, sacrificed many more. One could say one of those sacrifices is here in this room. Am I lying about that?"

The young security guard's face grew stiff. His muscles tensed. His glare drove itself into the Mother's shape, almost staring holes into her.

Freddie could see her fully now as she took a step before him. Her body was made of black, red, brown, and white mist. Swirling, like earthworms that changed color as they slithered into each other, throbbing and squirming. He did not intervene in the exchange. He owed respect to the Mother. She'd get rid of the meddler.

"You took advantage of him," she said. "Freddie is here because of you."

A strange smile formed in the swirling mass of vapor and shifting colors that was her face. The Mother could sometimes be cryptic and rambling before she gave him God's message—he supposed appearing to him in this form took a lot from her—but this night, she was sharp as a dagger, and cutting as deeply. She was present and focused.

Freddie felt a chill travel up his spine. Had she just said he was locked in here because of the man behind the glass?

(*Don't leave me here! No! Don't leave me here! Please!*)

His eyes seemed to move of their own accord, darting back and forth between the Mother and John Hitch.

"Tell him your name." The Mother said with a taunting inflection.

The security guard said nothing. He stared at her with such contempt, Freddie could picture him breaking through the dense glass, putting his hands around her neck, and strangling her.

"Tell him who has kept White Harbor in its current state." The Mother continued, relentless. "I could even say *you* started it all. The illnesses? The tragedies? The deaths? I am trying to put a stop to that. You want it to continue forever. Go ahead, tell him your real name."

The security guard stood there, quiet. There was no hesitation in his face. He would not give her a loose thread she could pull on. The man's eyes, unblinking, stared at her.

Who was he? He seemed

(*Don't leave me here! No! Don't leave me here! Please!*)

so familiar, like a face he'd seen in a dream.

"John Hitch." She chuckled at the name. "I can still

remember when you called yourself Ben Curling."

Freddie gasped.

The guard's face became suffused with anger and hatred, completely directed at her.

"You ruined Freddie's life," she said. "He'll never live a normal life. All he has is the hope of redeeming his family and himself, and you're trying to rob him of that, too, Ben?"

In an angry snort, hot air left the guard's nostrils and misted the plexiglass.

"You disappeared after the Vanek House burned down," the Mother said. "For a time, I honestly thought you were dead, until God told me otherwise. The Lord said you'd be back to interfere, and here you are, looking…like this…" She gestured with a misshapen foggy hand at him. "I suppose it's an improvement. This isn't the first time you've tried to thwart God, Ben, but this is the end. I thank you for your role in the Lord's grand design. It was not insignificant. I thank you on behalf of all the Faithful, but this is pathetic and fruitless, and it must stop."

Without a word, John Hitch—Ben Curling, according to the Mother—gave one last scowl of revulsion, turned around, and disappeared into the hallway's darkness.

"I can't stay much longer." The Mother turned to Freddie, her empty eye sockets staring into his soul. "Tonight, and the ones to come, will test you, my boy. They will demand a lot from you."

"I know, Mother," Freddie said with a solemn nod. "I'm ready."

"Frederick Parham, you are admirable." She placed a barely tangible hand on his left cheek. He could feel the movements and changes in the hand's texture as a caress. "God will be pleased."

"I'm doing my best, Mother." His eyes showed genuine passion and devotion. "I know I'm not worthy."

"That's true." Her hand did not leave his face. It had no warmth, but it almost felt to him like an actual palm, under which veins carried actual blood. "But after these four nights, you will be the worthiest of all. Your family, dating back many generations, will finally rejoice in the light of the Lord."

"Thank you, Mother." His breathing was heavy as a single tear ran down his face, and before it could reach the Mother's hand, he felt it leave his cheek.

"Your hands. Hurry."

Freddie put both his hands forward, palms up.

The shape of the Mother became more and more dispersed every second.

She put her hand forward, and it solidified. The nail on her index finger turned hard and sharp. Carefully, she cut the Sickle of the Moon symbol on both his palms. Red lines that grew with the warmth of blood now stained them.

"*Tjenaf egoikaat gozun-Uolmin yggshe,*" she said.

He repeated it after her, solemnly.

"*Tjenaf egoikaat gozun-Uolmin yggshe.*"

"Hurry now."

As she dissipated, he put out a bleeding palm toward her and said, "Wait! Mother! Wait, please!"

"What is it?" She sounded aggravated. Her tone went down a little, just enough to sound like a warning.

"Please, Mother. I'm begging you. Only a minute for a question."

The mist and smoke particles making up the Mother's form once again gathered close together, more solid. It was almost like she was standing there, but there were still the shapes, like intermingling strings, that formed her every detail. He could see her face clearly, as if she were standing in front of him, not across a mile of ocean.

"You're right, my boy. Ask me. I am here for you. It's the least I can do."

Her voice now took on a benign tone. She sounded not just like the Mother, but motherly. He hesitated, nevertheless. It was not his place to question, but the urge to know was bursting out of his chest.

"What did you mean it was Ben Curling's fault I'm here?" His gaze examined every minute change in her face. "I was the one that killed those children, Mother. Sure, it was inside the Vanek House, but Ben Curling wasn't there. I don't understand."

She smiled sympathetically. "Yes, you killed those children, but this started long before that, Frederick. You were led there by Ben Curling. He took advantage of your family name, the only name equally or more infamous than his own in White Harbor. This is why it has to be you. This is why you have to keep going. Otherwise, he wins. You were only a tool for him to do the horrors he needed done."

Freddie felt the onset of tears building up again in his eyes, but he blinked them away.

"I saw Gerardo Valencia's mother," she continued. "I witnessed the aftermath of what you did. What she did to herself in her madness."

"That was my fault." His voice sounded regretful. "I heard they moved to another state. They locked her up. If they had stayed in White Harbor—"

"She would've been locked up in here with you. You killed her son. She would have killed you like she tried to kill me."

"She had every right—"

"No."

He saw the figure before him shake her head gravely as it began to disassemble and dissipate once again. "Mother, I failed God when I killed those children inside that house."

"Yes." Her assertiveness left no room for doubt. "But if Roberta Valencia had gotten her hands on you, you wouldn't have been here to do God's work. It was God, in his wisdom, that moved them away from here, because you needed to be here tonight."

Freddie nodded.

"Don't fail me, my boy. Go with God." She disappeared completely now.

Freddie marveled at the many drops of blood that had fallen from his bleeding hands, forming round spots of varying sizes on the floor.

Beautiful things.

The symbols cut into his palms could no longer be seen as the Sickle of the Moon—the mark of God—but he could feel them burn with intent, urging him on.

"*Tjenaf egoikaat gozun-Uolmin yggshe,*" he said.

God will feed.

Chapter Nineteen

The Hole

Everyone at the table stared at Peter after he made his announcement. Awkward glances were exchanged between those present, almost as if they were waiting to see who would speak first. Eventually, all eyes fixed on Nadine as the group wordlessly agreed she should be the one to voice the question.

Nadine, feeling put on the spot, shot a withering look that swept across the table like a scythe, but her face soon changed to one of resignation, knowing that it was, in fact, her question to ask.

"I think you know what I'm going to say, Peter." She tried to keep the disapproval out of her voice, but failed. "Why would you ever consider coming back here having the means to give William a better life, somewhere less…"

"Less what?" Peter asked.

"Less isolated?" Royce chipped in, then continued without stopping. "Less boring, less retrograde, less gloomy, less likely to make him develop a lethal tumor or have an 'unexpected accident' before he's fifty?"

Peter stared at him, frowning in thought, as if trying to come up with a rebuttal, but Ray spoke up before he could.

"Not to mention less racist," he said, and took a swig of his drink. He then shot a laser-sight stare toward Barry before saying, "Less homophobic?"

With a determined motion, Barry raised his finger and pointed it at him. "Hey, that's not—"

Nadine gave the table a light but firm thump with her palm. "Can you all let me finish, please?"

Barry lowered his gaze, while Ray stared him down and took a long, slow sip from his glass, the clinking of the ice cubes audible in the awkward silence.

Nadine cleared her throat. "Well, I think they said it less diplomatically than I would've." She shot the table another sharp glance. "But seriously, Peter, make it make sense. Please?"

"My mom is close to dying." He checked if any of his friends reacted as if this was bad news, already aware they wouldn't. "Jenny is dead. I'm exhausted of doing literary tours, tired of cities, of noise, of everything that comes with being, let's call it, 'known.'" He highlighted this with air quotes. "I need peace. I know that getting out of White Harbor is seen as a medal of honor, as a step up, but I don't see it that way. If Mother"—he cleared his throat—"if my mom hadn't done what she did, I would never have made the choice to leave, as strange as it sounds. I took a liking to the outside world because they *forced* me to leave, but I don't think I would have left by choice."

Bobby raised his hand. "I can understand that, but every time we've talked, you've told me you were afraid if you kept coming here, one day you wouldn't be able to leave."

"That's still true. It's not a permanent move. A few years, at most, for William to grow up in a place that's a little less…stressful…less demanding…simpler."

"Ladies and gentlemen," Sylvia said, raising her glass, "we've just been called bumpkins. Cheers!"

"No!" Peter put his palms forward in a panic. "What I'm saying is William has always been sensitive and losing his mom only intensified that. I want him to grow up in a place where people care a little more about people, not so much about looks, money, status. When he's ready for college, we'll leave again. Also, here are eight uncles and aunts who can teach him a lot about life, and whom I trust unconditionally."

"Aw, how cute," Sylvia said, and then turned to the others. "So, we're both bumpkins *and* babysitters."

Peter laughed, shaking his head.

"Peter?" Barry said. "I think I understand what you mean. I just have the question of how realistic you are in those expectations. White Harbor isn't a place free of pressure or appearances or people who could harm William. I don't think I need to remind you how I earned this scar." He pointed to the scar on the back of his neck from where Peter had attacked him with the T-Square as kids. "I was a goddamn nightmare, I know that. I'm sure now there are kids who are the same, or worse. Right here, you're surrounded by people who didn't have such a good time growing up in this town."

Barry went around the table, pointing at each of his friends, starting with Callum. "Living on welfare."

At himself. "Suicidal father, abusive mother."

At Peter. "Well, you know your mom."

At Nadine. "Taking care of everyone but herself."

Nadine felt an icepick pierce her heart at this remark.

At Angela. "Victim of slut-shaming."

At Bobby. "Best friend of a psycho child killer."

At Royce. "Brother killed by said psycho child killer."

At Raymond. "Um…"

Ray gave him a hostile look, then faced Peter. "You know what, Pete? I believe if you feel it's in your son's best interest, we'll welcome you back. Now, if you'll excuse me, I have to go pee."

Having said his piece, he got up and walked off in the bathroom's direction, but not before giving Barry one last look of contempt.

Barry lowered his head, looking like he was trying to get his train of thought back on track. He tapped his fingers loudly on the table, but instead of speaking, he shook his head, pushed his chair back, stood up, and said, "I'll be right back."

He strode after Ray as the others stared in confusion.

"My life is fantastic, if I'm being honest," Sylvia said out of nowhere, and they all turned to stare at her. "What? Barry didn't make it to me on the list, and I didn't want to be left out."

Royce pointed in the direction the other two had left. "Anyone know what that's all about?"

A plate of barbecue wings clanged on the table, followed by a plate of crispy onion rings, making Royce jump in shock.

"Blight Harbor is what's that's all about, chubby. Stay out of other people's business." As she said this, Jess put a third plate on the table, this one with spicy wings, blue cheese dip, and the mandatory celery and carrot sticks.

Peter and Nadine peered at her inquisitively.

"No," she said, before they could ask. "I honestly don't know what that's about!"

All eyes were suddenly on her. Not a single person at

the table had any doubts that she knew something.

"Well, since you're twisting my arm. I do know something, but I don't have all the details…"

"Usually, in this town, that means you're going to go into details," Peter said with a raised eyebrow.

"Usually, but in this case, I really *don't* have details." She exhaled, and her expression became serious. "All I know is that *cuntata dentata* named Maryann said something incredibly offensive to Ray. Barr—ever the rug on which Maryann wipes her hooves—sided with her, instead of standing up for Ray, and since then, Ray can't stand the sight of him."

"Shit," Royce said.

Nadine turned to Peter. "Seems you made the right call to say only the Vigilantes at this meeting."

"I'm not a Vigilante," Angela said, raising her hand.

"You're an honorary Vigilante, Angie," Jess said. The little bell on top of the door rang, and Jess turned to see Louis walking in. "Oh, thank God. Be right back. Let me go give Louis a quick rundown of what to do, and I'll have my hands free for the rest of the evening. Bobby, could you be a dear and roll Angie to that table over there, in the corner, so I can sit down and chat with her for a while?"

She shot a smile at Angie.

"I'll have Louis bring more drinks and refill those pitchers."

"Thanks Jess," Peter said.

Bobby stood up to roll Angie toward the other table as Jess made her way toward the bar, already assailing Louis Foley with the barrage of profanities and quick jabs she used in place of "Hello".

1991

Barry had a stubborn habit of always going to The Pines after school, even though he knew none of the other kids wanted him there. But as far as he was concerned, they could all go to Hell since The Pines were a safe place for everyone.

From time to time, he took part in the conversations, but he noticed the way the others exchanged glances and rolled their eyes as if wondering: "And who invited this one?", but given the rules of The Pines, no one could tell him to go away.

Now more than ever, Barry had a reason The Pines were his haven. That wimp, Peter Lange, never went there. "Mother", as he called that strange woman, didn't allow him to socialize, so this was a space in which he didn't have to run into the little shit

(who kicked your fucking ass)

whom his mother had forbidden him to approach.

What's so special about that pathetic asshole? he thought.

He's a bitch in sports. I have better grades than him, and the only unusual thing about him is the creepy woman he calls Mother. Why is everyone afraid of him? What's the deal with her? She's just some crazy witch, the same age as my momma. No big deal!

For now, overwhelming himself with questions wouldn't do any good. He only kept leaning on the pine tree he'd claimed as his spot several years earlier. There was nothing to lose by coming here.

Who knows, he thought, *maybe someday, someone in The Pines would want to speak to me without me speaking first.* Although, to date, that hadn't happened. *Not that I care.*

His only friends—and it was a word he'd always used with difficulty to refer to them—were Kirsten, Oscar, and Drew. They never came to The Pines. Unlike him, they didn't expect or want anyone to speak to them. They were a perfect foursome.

Well, he thought, *they're a trio now.*

In the week and a half after the T-Square incident, they had drifted away from him, making fun of his decision—forced as it was—not to torment Lange anymore. In a matter of a day, he'd gone from being the most feared kid in the entire class to the faggot who became afraid of one of the weakest boys in school after he'd given him a scare.

That humiliation was not enough, apparently. Now, from the shadow of his pine tree, he saw his safe space being invaded by Peter Lange, who, after almost eight years since preschool, had appeared in The Pines and jumped into the conversation.

For a moment, the rage he felt overcame him and he walked menacingly toward the tiny insect, to the point of making him trip over a root while trying to run away from him. Lange was still afraid of him, despite everything, he thought with a smile, but Bobby Novak had made him think twice before doing something completely stupid.

Sometimes Novak, with his airs of referee and saving hero, was useful. Going too hard after Lange, here in The Pines, would have resulted in him being cursed, and no one, no matter how brave, dared challenge the curse of The Pines.

That didn't mean he had to put up with the little worm playing smart-ass just because "Mother" claimed to know the secret of the Vanek House. Although, if Barry was honest with himself, he was dying to find out what the big secret was.

There was a deathly silence when Peter Lange—Norman, as Barry had called him—finished the story of Walter Parham and the Parham curse.

The crowd exchanged furtive glances. A feeling of fascination and doubt, but also of common knowledge, passed over everyone, like a fine transparent voile fabric, caressing

440

their faces in an almost intrusive way.

Blight Harbor, Barry thought. He knew everyone here had thought the same thing.

The Pines was a place where you could talk about Blight Harbor without fear because it had no power in this place. What was said here did not feed that dark entity that grew fatter with each piece of gossip, with each secret.

That didn't mean that it ceased to exist in The Pines.

That slight shiver, caused by the tickle of ghostly fingers they had just felt, was Blight Harbor letting them know it was aware they were reaching into its cavernous belly, trying to pull out some of its contents.

"What else did your mom say?" Leroy Howe asked from his side of the circle.

"And where does Ben Curling fit into the story?" Royce Howe asked, from his own side, completing their "stereo effect".

"Nothing else," Peter said with a shrug. "She didn't mention Old Man Curling. After she told me the story of the Parhams and how it relates to the house, she took me to the pantry to…" He clammed up, his eyes shifting away from the group.

Everyone's gaze was fixed on him with anticipation.

Barry recognized that thousand-yard stare and the fearful eyes. He felt something in his chest twist, something familiar. Something like

(*Blight Harbor*)

empathy, which, despite his best efforts, now grew toward the skinny, pale kid.

"It doesn't matter," Peter said. "It's not relevant to the story."

"Come on, Lange!" Jess Cunningham said with her freckled brow furrowed. "You haven't talked to us in eight years, and now you're going to pussy out on us?"

Barry noted the shocked stare Lange gave Jess as if scandalized by the language. He'd heard his former friend Kirsten swear worse, he thought.

"She…" Peter began, but once again stopped. "She punished me."

"What do you mean, she punished you?" Bobby asked. "Wasn't she all thoughtful and happy and telling you she loved you after telling the story?"

"Yes." Peter nodded, his eyes downcast and sad. "But with her, you never know. She found out I was lying to her. She found out where I was hiding my books from her."

A sudden breath of surprise shook the entire group. With what little they knew and what Lange had told them, they could imagine what it meant to have lied to "Mother".

"Where were you hiding the books?" Nadine asked.

Barry already knew. He guessed it right away.

Just seeing the twerp's face a moment ago, he'd recognized someone who'd been punished and abused by his mother, just like he was. That face, on the verge of tears, barely contained, could only be caused by the most severe of punishments, repeated over time. That could only mean Lange had lied to her about this one thing.

I would've never thought you were so brave, Lange, Barry thought. *Or so crazy.*

Lange surveyed the crowd once more as if measuring his audience and, realizing that he had to say something, finally said, "At the Vanek House."

1989

As the electricity hummed back to life, Mother stood up. She had a smile on her face as she placed the leather-bound book on the chair in which she had been sitting. She ran her hands over her skirt, smoothed it out, and said, "Come with me. I want to show you something."

Peter rose to his feet from the banquette in front of the fireplace and followed Mother deeper into the house. She turned on lights as she went, and Peter felt that sense of relief that came over you after a blackout ended and the dark spaces became bright and welcoming. He followed her into the kitchen, which was spacious and well-equipped, so she could prepare the meals she delivered around town.

Mother stopped in front of the pantry, a small space, no bigger than a closet, to the left of the entrance. She opened the door and with a flick of her finger, a bulb that hung from the ceiling bathed the small space in warm light. From where he was standing, Peter could see bags and cans and bottles—everything his mother used to prepare her dishes.

He stared at her, confused. What was she going to do? Was she going to cook dinner? It was possible, but what did she want to show him? Just then, Mother stepped aside.

"Come here, boy." She was still smiling pleasantly as she called to him with a wave of her hand.

Peter walked closer to the pantry and saw how, with the same hand that Mother had called him, she now pointed to a small trapdoor on the floor. It was the trapdoor through which workers accessed a crawlspace under the house when there was something to fix in the pipes or wiring, but it was not something he or Mother ever used. He noticed the old latch that closed the little square door had been replaced with a sturdy metal brace and a padlock, which gleamed under the bulb's light. He turned his head toward her, confused.

"The padlock is open," Mother said. "Remove it and open the door."

Not wanting to question her or disobey, Peter crouched down. He turned the hook of the padlock, removed it from the latch, and lifted the door open.

The small door swung noiselessly on recently oiled

hinges, and as soon as it was fully open, Peter wished by all the holiest things in the universe that electricity hadn't returned. The bulb in the pantry illuminated what was underneath, lying on the damp and smelly earth at the bottom.

"You lied to me, boy," his mother said, her tone venomous.

Before Peter's stunned eyes, in a rectangle of light slightly out of phase with the square shape of the trapdoor, were three books. Three books that shouldn't have been there, because

(*they were in the Vanek House*)

he would never have put them there. Three books with library tags that he had left inside the Vanek House the day before. In the closed room where he sat to read several times a week with a flashlight. His secret space. His impenetrable fortress.

"Mother…" It was a false start. He choked, his voice hoarse and breathy, trailing off after only one word, so he could swallow hard and continue to formulate a sentence. "I can explain."

"You don't have to explain, Peter."

He turned his head toward her, almost afraid that the books—the evidence of his sin—would jump out of The Hole, grow teeth, and bite him while he couldn't see.

Mother's face was stern, fury contained in a stony expression. "You entered the Vanek House. No matter how many times you've done it, one is too many. I found the place where you crawled under the house. There is a hole in the floor that leads to a room. That's where I found your books. Do you think I'm stupid, boy?

"No, Mother! Never! I—"

"Did you think I wouldn't see the marks you left on the grass every time you crawled under the house? You might as well have left a sign pointing to the exact spot."

"Mother, I'm sorry!"

"I might even have forgiven you for going into that house since we talked about it until today." The calm in his mother's voice terrified him to the limits of his endurance.

Mother was infinitely more threatening when she took on this cold, expressionless tone than when she was yelling and ranting with threats about God. These were the moments Peter knew she was truly furious. The moments when she saw no point in berating, only in punishing.

"What's more," she continued, and the sound of her calm voice jolted him from his fearful thoughts so violently it made his heart jump as if he'd heard a gunshot, "I had already forgiven you before we talked, Peter, I just hoped you'd have the decency not to lie to me. To admit you had entered the house. But you lied to me, and not only lied, but I also go there and find this." Without moving her head or her body in the slightest, she just pointed her eyes at the books and back at him, the tell-tale books.

Villains! Dissemble no more! I admit the deed! he imagined himself shouting, like the protagonist of Edgar Allan Poe's *The Tell-Tale Heart,* a few minutes ago, an hour ago, a day ago, a century ago, when his confession would still have been worth something. *Tear up the planks! Here, here! It is the beating of his hideous heart!*

Peter saw Poe's book on the ground behind the door and imagined, all the time he had been talking to Mother by the warmth of the fire, the book had been pulsing under the boards of the cupboard, but he had been too stupid to listen.

"Books," Mother said, and he turned his already sweaty face and terrified eyes to her. "Fiction. Lies."

"Mother, I'm sorry. I'm sorry."

"Lies that required lies to stay hidden." She regarded him with disappointment and grief. "And after I expressed my love for you."

"Mother, I promise—"

"Don't promise, you liar." Her eyes shifted to the books again. "Go down there and take them out."

The sound of a thousand alarms went off in Peter's mind. He knew without a doubt that if he set foot down there, he would never come out again.

"I can reach them if I just lie down on the—"

"Go. Down. There. And. Take them out." His mother's tone made it clear the topic was not open for discussion.

Fearfully, tentatively, Peter sat on the floor. The beads

of sweat on his forehead ran a snail race down his skin. It was a combination of the heater kicking in and the heat from the incandescent light bulb, and the enclosed space of the pantry, but mainly it was cubic tons of fear. His feet hung four inches from the bottom as he lowered his legs through the opening. He jumped that short distance and saw, when standing on the ground below, the edge of the opening just barely reached up to half his thigh. He bent down to pick up the books, being careful not to let his whole body into the gap, so Mother couldn't close the door.

"Kneel," Mother said, almost reading his mind. "As if you were asking God for forgiveness for your sin of reading lies and speaking lies."

Saying nothing, the feelings of trepidation and fear taking over his entire being, Peter obeyed. He could feel the moisture from the earth soaking through his knees and imagined how many rodents had urinated and defecated in that space.

"Put your forehead on the books on the floor," Mother ordered calmly.

Knowing what was coming, tears finally escaped Peter's eyes. He leaned forward, his head pressed against the books, his hands on the stale earth. Seconds later, he heard the slam of the door closing over him, and the padlock going through the latch, leaving him locked in the crawlspace. In an immediate panic, Peter rolled over, his back flat on the ground, since there was no room to sit up.

"Mother, no! I'm sorry! Forgive me! It won't happen again!"

Peter started pounding on the trapdoor, yelling and begging.

"Of course, it's going to happen again, boy," his mother said, and Peter thought he heard a smirk form on her face. "There is much of your father still in you. This is going to happen many more times before you bow in obedience to God."

"Mother, I'm sorry. Please let me out!"

"No, boy. You are going to spend the night there."

Peter was speechless, flabbergasted, trying to comprehend what his mother was saying, because the very meaning of those words was inconceivable.

"Don't worry about the cold. The heating will eventually pass through the spaces between the boards. It's one advantage of living in such an old house."

She was really going to do this. It wasn't just to scare him. She actually meant to do this.

"What you have to ask yourself is: what creatures are huddled in the warmer corners that are going to come out and explore once it warms up down there?"

Peter's first scream exploded out of him.

He saw the light in the pantry go out, and the thin slivers of light that passed between the boards disappeared, then the light in the kitchen, until everything went completely dark. Peter's screams echoed all night, his throat becoming raw from pushing his vocal cords to the limit.

Mother did not take pity on him.

When he emerged the next day, covered in dirt and cobwebs, and still feeling the insects and rats crawling over his body in the dark, Peter knew one thing for sure. This would not be the last time he'd be punished by spending the night in "The Hole", as that horrible place was named.

1991

The Pines' exit was a makeshift opening that had been cut in the school's wire fence many years ago, and the administration had never fixed it. Peter supposed it was because they knew the students would open it again the next day. The Pines were a traditional aspect of the school, it was assumed future students would continue to make use of the area.

This opening was at the bottom of the slope from where they had been sitting. The wire mesh could be raised high enough for two or three children to pass through at a time. Most of the students went out that way, instead of going back up the slope to the school to go out the front door.

A majority of the other kids were gone by the time

Peter climbed under the wire.

Bobby said goodbye and ran off, saying he had to go check on Freddie "the Hyena" but promised they'd talk the next day. They had something important to discuss, according to him. This only made Peter anxious—he hated uncertainty. But Bobby appeared to be a good person, and this eased his worries a little.

Royce and Leroy ran past him, one on either side, and each bumped into one of his shoulders, startling him. They both turned toward him with a big grin.

"You're crazy, Norman," said Leroy or Royce. Peter wasn't sure.

"But you're cool, man," said Royce or Leroy.

Callum Baker walked next to him for a quick moment, his eyes scrutinizing every inch of his face.

"I think there are several inconsistencies with your story," he said, walking beside him, "but it fits into the general historical framework based on what I've read about the early years of the town."

"Uh…" Peter stared at him a little confused, not sure if he should say "thank you", or "sorry". "I like to read," he said, "but I'm not doing very well in history. I'm terrible with dates."

"If you can get away from your mom one day," Callum said, "I can show you some books with interesting notes."

Peter smiled and nodded. Callum said goodbye and went on his way.

Nadine ran up to him and shouted, "Wait a sec!"

Peter stopped immediately, frozen on the spot, as if he'd been caught shoplifting.

She walked past him, turned around, and stood in front of him. "Hold on, Peter."

"Hello, yes, I'm Peter."

"What?"

"Nothing," Peter said immediately, feeling stupid. "How can I help you?"

Nadine laughed, and Peter thought the sound of her laughter was like the voice of an angel turning into raindrops and falling onto a grassy meadow. Although his mother's religion didn't have angels, he'd always heard they were beautiful beings, made of light, full of goodness, but also power, and that was what he saw in the girl in front of him.

"Relax, I don't need your help," she said. "We've talked before. I don't know if you remember."

Yes, I do! he thought. *A year ago! You had your hair tied up in a ponytail with a lime-green hairband!*

"Yeah," he said, doing his best to keep his cool. "In math, last year. Mrs. Norton sat me down with you and with…uh…"

"Rebecca Dobson. Yes."

"That's right." He didn't actually remember Rebecca.

"It was nice."

"No," Nadine laughed again. "It was not. I wanted to apologize to you."

"What for?"

Peter knew exactly why. That day, their math teacher had seated them in trios to solve various operations as a group. Peter had been assigned to work with them. He sat, greeted them, and, seeing that there were three operations, asked, "Maybe we can do one each?"

Nadine had turned to him, regarded him as if he were a slimy toad, and said, "No way, creepy boy. We're not going to work together. I don't know why, but my mom is afraid of your mom. *We're* going to do the work together, and *you* do the operations on your own. You can sit with us, but you're not working with us. Is that clear to you?"

Peter had nodded dejectedly and done his work on his own, sitting next to two classmates who were acting like he didn't exist. Peter knew it was his fault and he couldn't be friends with them anyway, so what did it matter if they talked to him or not?

"Oh," Peter said uncomfortably. "I remember now."

"I acted like a complete asshole. I didn't know why you kept away from everyone, or what your life was like at home. I mean, let's be honest, I had no way of knowing, and you always acted really weird, and we were all like, 'Okay, something's not normal with this one.'"

Peter gave an embarrassed laugh, and Nadine giggled.

"But that doesn't justify how I acted. Could you forgive me?"

He gave her a slow, reassuring nod, followed by a soft smile.

"I think Mrs. Norton knew you hadn't actually worked with us because you did horrible on that exercise. You really suck at math."

Peter's eyes lit up as he burst into laughter. "To be fair, I also suck at history, all the sciences, P.E., and I don't know if you heard, but I can't go to Shop anymore."

Nadine cackled like an old woman now.

Peter found this adorable.

"Oh yeah," she said. "Wrecked Barry's shit with a T-Square. That was awesome. Can't say that helped get rid of your image as 'Most Likely to Become a Serial Killer', though."

They both cackled together, loudly.

Peter couldn't remember the last time he'd laughed like this. In fact, he didn't remember ever laughing like this. He felt a wave of joy inside him, a feeling that had been locked away for years.

"Well," she said, "I have to go now. If you need help with math or any other thing, you can talk to me whenever you want. I'll help you."

"Thanks."

"Bye, creepy boy."

Many of his other classmates passed by and said something to him. It was impressive and even overwhelming, after years of being invisible, to be seen and recognized by others. He had no idea what to expect when the last person to come to him appeared a little over a block away from the school.

"Hey, Norman."

Barry saw, even from behind, the boy was hunched over, pitiful, feeble, and little. Then, he thought, what did it say about him that this pushover had survived the same or worse things than him? He considered himself strong and still barely dealt with his own situation at home.

Lange was startled by the sound of his voice. Of course, he'd been startled. That was part of who he was. It shouldn't surprise him, although he couldn't deny that he was uncomfortable with the weakness he saw in Peter Lange.

The boy turned to him and took two steps back, fear in his eyes.

"I liked your story."

Lange stared at him, his eyes moving to different parts of his body, as if expecting an attack from any direction.

"Thank you," he said with caution.

"I also know it's true," Barry said. "I didn't want to admit it, but I believe you. My dad had told me the story of Walter Parham, but he'd only told me about him being hanged for killing the town priest. But everything else fits the story, though."

Lange didn't answer. He stared at him, still wary.

"I only have one question, but not about the story. About you, Lange."

The shorter kid studied him again, suspiciously, but now there was a hint of curiosity.

"If your mom finds out you're talking to us, will she put you back in that space under the house?"

A shadow fell over the boy's eyes, and he nodded.

"Why did you take the risk of coming to The Pines then? Why did you talk to us?"

Lange's gaze met his, and he frowned, his eyes filling with steely determination. "Because no matter what I do, she'll always find an excuse to put me in that hole. The last time she did it, it was because I didn't fully learn a prayer in that weird language of her stupid religion."

Barry's breath caught in his throat. He didn't know what strange language he was talking about, but Lange's words surprised him, anyway. They presented the boy in a way that was unlike any concept he'd had about him previously.

"I love my mom," Lange asserted, clenching his fists. Fixing his gaze on a random spot on the asphalt, as if meeting someone else's gaze as he said this embarrassed him, he still decided to come out with it. "I respect her, and I would never directly challenge her because she really scares me. But I think something important changed when she started locking me in The Hole. I stopped believing in her god."

He blew air out of his mouth as if he'd gotten something truly heavy out of his chest. "Anything that makes a parent treat their child like this cannot be a god. It's something evil. I have seen her do things. Strange things. Things that scare me."

His gaze returned to Barry, who was speechless to hear these words come out of this kid's mouth. "But I won't let fear stop me from living my life. If I have to lie to have friends, learn more about the world, read books, and live, I'm going to do it. And if she locks me in The Hole, well, who the fuck cares?" He paused, as if realizing he'd used the F word, but quickly regained his resolve and continued. "It's going to be horrible and give me nightmares for days, but when I'm not grounded, I'll be doing the things I love."

Barry was speechless. Never in his eleven years of life did he think he could admire someone as wimpy as Peter Lange, but here he was, admiring and envying him for doing things he could never do for fear of his own mother.

"I…" Barry said, thinking up a thousand sentences in seconds. "I'm really sorry for what I've done to you, Lange. I'm not gonna tell you why I'm apologizing, because it's really none of your fuckin' business, but I really feel bad about everything I've done to you. Ever since my dad…" He stayed silent. Pondering.

He could feel the smaller boy's eyes studying him curiously. "I have to go now." Barry turned around. "I… We'll talk later, Lange." He walked away as fast as he could.

Three days after the talk in The Pines, Peter already felt like others were treating him differently. Already, other people were greeting him, talking to him about movies and TV shows, things he had never seen—who were *The Simpsons,* and what the hell did *"Cowabunga!"* mean?

Bobby invited him to sit with him, Freddie Parham, and the other kids during lunch, and invited him over to his house one day to watch movies.

Peter wasn't ready for movies and TV yet. His mother told him that television became addictive, which conjured up images of drug addicts, like the ones in the school's anti-drug videos. However, if all the other kids at school were addicted to television, they didn't seem as affected. Maybe one day he would accept Bobby's invitation. For the moment, he enjoyed sitting with others for lunch and talking with them, being able to talk about his favorite books, and even doing group work became more enjoyable. Bobby and the others seemed very interested in how Peter had gotten into the Vanek House, but none of them had tried for fear of going into the place alone. Old Man Curling and his dogs were certainly a powerful deterrent.

Today he was in front of his locker, dropping some books, when reality hit him out of nowhere.

He felt a sudden push and his face collided with the slits of the locker door with a loud *Crash!* A firm hand held him from the back of his shirt and pushed him twice more against the locker—*Crash! Crash!*

The next thing he felt was someone turning him around, and the first image that his mind conjured was that of Barry Giffen and his mocking smile, but he was surprised to see Oscar Young staring down at him. The boy was tall, skinny, but strong. He grabbed him by his shirt and lifted him off the ground, making him crash against the locker once more—*Crash!*—to his right was Drew Mills, and to the left, was Kirsten Holmes, all three of them rejoicing in their sadism.

"Check out the school creepazoid," Oscar said, flashing a crooked-tooth smile. "Thinks he's a celebrity because he's got friends now since he bashed in Giffen's chicken ass."

"N-no, that's not true," Peter tried to say with a stutter, "I-I don't think I'm—"

"I'd like to see you try that little trick on me, Lange." Oscar brought his face right in front of him. "They'd have to X-ray you to see how far I shoved that T-Square up your ass."

The three giggled, mocking him.

Peter was shaking, preparing himself for what would certainly be a beating.

"Kirsten," Oscar said. "Don't you think Lange looks a little flustered? Why don't you share your Pepsi with him?"

Kirsten smirked, lifting a large cup of Pepsi with plenty of ice over Peter's head. But just as she was about to dump its contents over him, something yanked her hard from behind. Kirsten screamed and went flying into the middle of the hall, landing on her ass on the floor. The Pepsi cup that was meant for Peter spilled on her face and over her shirt.

"What the—" Oscar exclaimed, but he cut himself off mid-question. Instead of Kirsten, his field of vision filled up with Barry's furious face, who, with a big arm, grabbed him by the shirt.

"Let him go," Barry said with a growl.

Oscar obeyed.

Peter's feet hit the ground, his face completely stunned.

Oscar said, "Barry, what the hell are you—"

Again interrupting his sentence, Barry moved him to one side as if he weighed nothing. His eyes focused on Drew, who was standing right in front of him, his lips quivering stupidly, trying to concoct a sentence. Barry lifted his foot and kicked him so hard in the balls it knocked the air out of him and made him drop to his knees, landing on his face on the floor.

Having taken care of those two, Barry turned to Oscar, his supposed replacement at the top of the food chain, snorting like an angry bear.

"Barry!" Oscar said, raising his palms toward him as if trying to appease him. "Buddy! I'm sorry! Sorry for calling you a chicken! Sorry for making fun of you! We took it too f—"

Once again, Barry interrupted Oscar's sentence, this time with an uppercut so hard, the taller boy simply collapsed like a tower to the ground.

Barry moved his gaze from Drew to Kirsten. "Get this fuckface out of here!" he commanded. "And if you or anyone else get close to Lange again, I swear it's gonna be worse next time."

Kirsten and Drew didn't bother picking Oscar up and just ran off in opposite directions, leaving him crumpled on the ground, uselessly struggling to regain consciousness.

Barry turned to Peter. "You okay, Norman?"

Peter could see the question was sincere. He just nodded.

"If they bother you again, just tell me, okay?"

"Why did you do that? You hate me."

Barry frowned at him, uncertain. "No, Norman. We're friends. I told you last time."

"I don't remember that."

"I told you, 'We'll talk later, Lange.'" He stared at him with a sideways grin and raised eyebrows, as if that made everything clear. "I thought you got it."

Peter was just as confused, but he returned a nervous chuckle and said, "Yeah, you're right." Peter watched as Oscar, who had risen to his feet, staggered away. "Aren't you going to get in trouble for that?"

Barry directed his furious gaze toward Oscar, who, noticing the menace in that look, hurried away.

"Nah," Barry said. "They're not gonna tell the teachers because they would be embarrassed. And if someone else saw, they won't tell because they are afraid of me."

"And that's…" Peter tried to choose his words carefully. "A good thing? That they're afraid of you?"

Barry considered it, and shrugged. "Sometimes."

2022

Ray faced the wall as he stood in front of one of the three urinals. The echo of the stream of urine was heard as a slight tinkle echoing in the bathroom's space.

Barry walked in and took two steps toward the urinals, but stopped when he heard Ray exhale with irritation. "Ray—"

"Wait right there. I'm almost done." Ray's tone had a sarcastic edge, but was laced with a drop of venom. "You don't want to risk me seeing your dick."

"That is not fair."

"Oh, now you care about what's fair?" Ray let out an angry chuckle.

"I'm just asking you to hear me out for a moment," Barry said.

Ray zipped up his pants, turned around, gave him a split-second scornful look, walked over to the sink, and turned on the faucet. He let the water pool in his cupped hands before he started rubbing them under the stream. "I think you've said everything that needs to be said." He took soap from the dispenser and continued to rub his hands together. "It was very clear. Your homophobe of a wife gave you an order, and you obeyed, like a good little servant. What else is there to talk about?"

"You know it's not that simple, Ray. Maryann…"

Ray took three steps toward him and met his gaze, only a few inches from his face. "Maryann just doesn't want a big, bad homosexual coming into her house and being a negative influence on her children."

Barry's mouth worked, unable to form a word.

"Issue is," Ray continued, "the big, bad homosexual already lives in her house." Keeping his distance from him, Ray walked around Barry.

"Ray, please." He reached a hand toward him.

Ray moved aside, avoiding him. "Don't fucking touch me."

He left the bathroom.

1991

"You have to be careful when you cross," Peter said, pointing to Etenia Creek.

"Careful?" Barry asked, shooting a sardonic glance at the stony little gutter. "I can cross it in one long stride."

"That's not why," Peter said. "See the wall?"

He pointed to the wall separating the Vanek property from the Knox family property. On the other side of the wall was the famous house, the second floor looming above it.

"We have to cross in this direction because, between the wall and the house, they block the view, so neither Old Man Curling nor Mother can see us from the other side of the street. We have to cross at an angle, and after that, the house will cover us. Then we duck down, crawl under, and the entry hole is just about three feet in." He pointed to an ugly shed that stood only two or three feet from the wall on the Vanek side, leaving a gap. "You guys can slide your bikes behind that shed. No one will see them."

Before meeting Freddie at Burkle Park a few moments prior, they had gone to each of their houses and given their parents a poor excuse for being late that afternoon. The party now complete, they wheeled their bicycles to the Vanek home.

"Bobby, this is the worst idea you've ever had, bro," Royce said.

"Worse than the competition to pee off Blue Overlook?" Leroy asked.

"Much worse," Royce replied.

"Uh, I think it's important to clarify," Callum said, holding up a finger, "that it wasn't a competition. It was a test of bravery. One that I passed with all honors."

"Really, Droopy? You only peed for like four seconds," Leroy said. "I'd had three *Mountain Dews* before we left. I was standing with my dick out, on the edge of a cliff, looking down for almost a minute and a half."

"Still counts," Callum said.

"Can I pee off Blue Overlook?" Peter asked. His eyes filled with wonder.

"Sure, Norman!" Royce said, then nodded toward Barry. "You and your new boyfriend can consider it an initiation or something."

"I don't need to pee off anywhere," Barry said. "I don't need to prove shit to any of you."

"Oh, sure," Royce said. "Sorry, Mr. 'I can cross it in one long stride'. My bad."

"Guys!" Bobby said. "Peter has been entering that house for months and nothing has happened to him. Are you going to tell me you're not curious about what's inside?"

"Well," Peter objected. "Technically, I've only entered one room."

"Exactly!" Leroy spoke toward Bobby, but aiming a finger at Peter. "What if, by some chance, Norman has been walking into the only room in that house that isn't filled with demon shit?"

"But that's the idea," Freddie said. "Exploring. Finding the demon shit."

"Bobby, the Hyena shouldn't be here today," Royce said. "You know damn well at some point we're going to find him masturbating in one of those rooms, in front of a picture of Baphomet, or something like that."

"Baphomet doesn't get me hard," Freddie said with a wicked smile. "But if I come across a depiction of Azathoth, I assure you it will end up as sticky as the photos I have of your mom."

Leroy wrinkled his nose. "Something is very wrong with that head of yours."

"Wait for us!" said an approaching voice.

466

Peter spun around; his face lit up with a huge smile. "You made it!"

They all turned their heads in that direction to see Nadine running up, accompanied by Jess. They reached the spot where everyone was. Nadine caught her breath and gave them a grin.

"We want to go in too," she said.

"No girls allowed," Callum said, still unimpressed with the tall popular girl.

"Then why are you here?" Jess said.

"Who made that rule, Droopy?" Royce said, giving Callum the side-eye. "We've never had a girl want to hang out with us, so at no time could that rule have been created."

Callum put on a serious face and said, "Well. That's a valid point."

"Besides," Leroy added, "we let Barry come. Why wouldn't we let them?" He turned his head to Barry. "Sorry, big guy, but if it wasn't for Norman telling us you became his bodyguard, you wouldn't be here."

"I get it," Barry said, trying to sound tough.

Leroy gave a doubtful glance at Peter. "Are you sure we can trust him?"

Peter nodded.

Leroy turned back to Barry. "Okay, but you go in last. I don't know how big the entry hole is, but I don't want to risk those shoulders or that ass getting stuck and the rest of us not being able to get in." He paused briefly. "No offense."

"None taken, and fuck you," Barry said.

"Alright, alright," Bobby said, raising his voice. "Are we going to stay here talking, or are we going to go in?"

Chapter Twenty
Beautiful Things
2022

With growing eagerness, Freddie approached one of the many canvases in his room. The painting before him depicted a sloping residential street, the coastline barely visible in the distance. A car was parked on one side, and a streetlight stood on the sidewalk to the right.

Houses lined both sides of the street, and the full moon glowed in the sky.

What made this street different from what you would find in your average town was that the houses were only husks, remains of an abandoned town: cracked walls, broken windows, and caved-in roofs. Dark mold and plant life had overtaken the entire area before turning brown and withering in a world where the sun no longer shined. The streetlight's bulb was broken, and the pole was bent and twisted. The street had deep fissures and holes, breaking it apart into a jigsaw puzzle of asphalt that sloped down until it disappeared into a body of murky water. The flood stretched endlessly toward the horizon, with roofs, streetlights, and dead trees emerging from it, like the remains of a shipwreck. A drowned world just a few yards away.

All that remained of the car was the rusted, windowless carcass of what had once been a vehicle, now sitting on flat tires. There were traces of dead plants that grew inside it, only to die when the sun itself abandoned the world, turning the car's insides into a neglected flowerpot. Here and there, in this desolated stretch of a flooded town, were silhouettes of animate shapes that came out of the broken walls and asphalt. These shapes seemed to be raw and fleshy, like exposed tissue or twisted, otherworldly vegetation.

Above this view of the ruined town, the terrible moon—glowing blue and unnatural—ruled over all. An eye gazing from a starless sky as if reveling in the sight of a world where life no longer existed—or was no longer defined in human terms.

Beautiful, he thought, as if in a trance. *Beautiful, beautiful things!*

He shook his head, remembering he had a job to do. He couldn't dally despite the magnificence of the world in the painting.

Before the blood on his hands dried, Freddie gathered as much as he could in an inkwell, then walked around the room. One by one, he touched a drop of blood to the shapes and landscapes and beings that would not exist outside of nightmares, marking them with the essence of his heart. These were beautiful things he *made* exist by conjuring them into reality.

They were obscene abominations in the eyes of others, but precious and fascinating to him, as if he had given birth to them. Freddie, however, was also overcome by a sense of dread, despite his awe and fascination, because, despite their beauty, they contained all those violent thoughts—all those cursed impulses—that used to live in his mind and his soul. These things had led him to this room, where he'd remained isolated for almost three decades.

He was, in a way, unleashing himself into the entire world, starting with White Harbor.

The ice cubes in John Hitch's ginger ale were already melted, and it tasted like dirty water. He had let his mind wander for a while, pondering whether it was fate or coincidence that his name was John now, at the end, when another John had been there, so long ago, in the beginning. He would've thought it poetic if he still believed in things like justice, or knew for sure the world would still be the world when this was all over.

He craned his neck to his right and felt the slight tug of tense muscles.

There they were. Five on the joined tables, two on the corner table, two in the men's room. All of them ignorant of what was happening—ignorant of their role, ignorant of what he had to do.

Simply ignorant, he thought, *and that makes it that much harder.*

That night, Freddie Parham would trigger a series of events that would have unspeakable consequences, the least of which might be the death—or worse—of every person in White Harbor. He trembled to think what the worst consequences would be beyond the boundaries of the Crescent Mountains.

If he'd known the Parham boy was going to become that witch's puppet, he would've killed him when the Vanek House burned. Of course, back then, as Ben Curling, he'd had little opportunity to do it. It had all happened too quickly. Then, for years, he wasn't in the position to do much about it. Through contacts in his Order, he found out about Freddie Parham's role, but he was out of his reach in Lighthouse Rock. Martha and Peter Lange were untouchable, period. So, he discovered who the chosen ones were, but he couldn't touch them until the first night of the ritual—it was a strike of dumb coincidence that they were all now gathered in one place.

He and his Order felt secure for years, knowing Peter Lange had been taken away from his mother shortly after the fire at the Vanek House. Martha Lange had been too proud, too fanatical, or too consumed by her illness, to select a successor, which meant if she died, it was over. The legacy of Dorothy Parham and Amias Vanek died with her. All John needed to make sure of was that Peter Lange didn't come to White Harbor under the right conditions and wait until the old witch died.

"Maybe then I can rest," he had told himself like a damned fool.

Of course, she killed his wife, and here was Lange, right at the worst possible time.

John had given Freddie Parham the chance to leave, to have a life, but the old witch had already brainwashed him with promises of redemption for his family. Ironic, really, considering this had all started with Freddie's ancestor, Dorothy.

Freddie Parham was already set on his path. He couldn't change that. He was untouchable to him now, the same as Martha and Peter Lange. His only choice going forward was to interrupt the ritual before he could complete it, and for that, many—if not all of these people—would have to die before the third night.

He drank his watered-out ginger ale until his glass was empty.

He was ready.

He only needed to wait for the blue moon.

Except for the plexiglass wall and door, and his only window to the outside, Freddie's entire room was wallpapered in unspeakable creatures, unseen landscapes, and uncanny creations. He wanted to ensure he didn't miss a single one. The Lord gave him dreams of the life that desired to exist in His new world, and Freddie took those desires and shaped their flesh. He wanted to experience every form, every vista, so he couldn't risk forgetting to bless any with his blood.

As he did this, he entertained himself by reciting the Ritual of the Four Nights, as the Mother had explained it to him. While it sounded very simple, he knew a lot of pieces needed to be in place for God's design to become a reality.

"The first night, four will open the gates," he said, with a certain joyous musicality in his intonation. "The second night, one will seal the town. The third night, four will awaken God. The fourth night will be eternal."

Soon, every image had a mark of blood on it, except for one. He had purposely left it for last: the painting of the abandoned town street under the dark blue moon.

Freddie poured the remaining blood from the inkwell on one palm, put the small container aside, then passed the blood between both hands to ensure they were fully covered in it. He placed both hands together at the top-center edge of the canvas, then he carefully slid them apart to either side, lining the entire border with his blood. Once done, he stood in front of the painting—majestic on its easel—staring at it the same way he remembered staring at those Magic Eye pictures as a child, that seen at the right angle developed depth and became 3-D.

A minute after, the area of the room that was visible around the painting shimmered and gradually faded away. The edge of the canvas expanded, but the actual image did not grow with it. It was like the field of vision was spreading around the canvas, and he could see more and more of the scene. The illusion folded at the top and around him until he found himself surrounded by his own creation. He was standing in the middle of the street in the painting.

There was a moment of disorientation, then a flash of dizziness. His vision needed to adjust because, while rendering the image, he'd exaggerated the light just a little to make it more visible, but the reality of it was that moonlight was not enough to illuminate everything around him. The true environment was coated in stark darkness, as if some inexplicable being had gone over reality with a spray-painter until everything was covered in shades of blue and black.

The silence was complete, to the point he realized how loud his ears were ringing with that tinnitus that was always present in our ears, but our brains mute out completely. The still air was thick with the smell of rot, of mold, of age, and the environment was moist and hot, like he imagined the depths of a tropical jungle must feel.

He knew this world was incomplete. It needed his hand to push it into motion. To stir the dark life it held in its distended gravid womb. He would act as a midwife for the pure and immoral existence that would be birthed into this new world.

Freddie remembered when his sister Laurie was born because he'd seen it in person. Mikayla Parham, his mother, would not go to a hospital for fear that some townie spouting hate about the Parham curse would do the newborn harm, and his dad had been out drunk as usual. Freddie had no choice but to help bring his baby sister into the world. Freddie was there, too, when she'd departed.

He remembered how adorable Laurie was, how tender, how precious. He'd been almost eight when she was born and even pulled her from his mother and cut her umbilical cord with surgical precision—the best artists had steady hands, after all. However, he felt clumsy every time his mom handed Laurie to him, afraid his fingers would turn to butter, and she would slip from his grip, fall, and break into a million tiny porcelain pieces.

Laurie had been the embodiment of everything pretty, and delicate, and delightful ever to be born into that normal world—the human world. This world he'd created contained only terrible, unspeakable things, the exact opposite of Laurie. What type of life would he pull out of its womb? Or, more accurately, which of the many he'd already envisioned would be the first.

He supposed he was about to find out.

Freddie closed his eyes, concentrated, and when he opened them, the twisted vision of the neighborhood was gone. He was standing in the middle of that same street, but just as it would have been on any Thursday night. The streetlight cast its glow on the sidewalk, and he could see lights inside the houses, glowing through curtains, behind unbroken windows. The slope of the street continued all the way down, lined with houses, trees, and lights—*And life*, he noted—everything under a waning gibbous silvery moon. He made a mental note of the single empty lot in the street corner to his left.

That's where the Vanek House used to stand, he thought. *It looks so different now that it's gone.*

For the first time since he was under fifteen, Freddie was actually standing in the town of White Harbor, his hometown—not on an island, away from those he might otherwise hurt. The most fascinating thing of all was, in the distance, beyond the beach, he could barely see the lights of the psychiatric hospital he'd been in just seconds ago. He had traveled all the way from there to here in a matter of seconds.

An elderly woman wearing a pink and purple sweatsuit walked a dog up the slope. She passed by him without even noticing him. The dog, a ridiculous-looking Pomeranian with its tongue hanging out, didn't seem to notice him either. The dog was wearing a knitted pink sweater with knitted letters that read "DOTTIE III."

This made him smile.

He finally recognized the old woman, despite the ravages of age. The last time he had seen her had been in a courtroom.

Freddie had killed her three children, and her husband had died in the ensuing fire.

He shook away the memories. They were gone. Old.

Soon they'll be irrelevant, he thought. *Soon, my sins will be washed away.*

Freddie closed his eyes and took a deep breath of the town's air, savoring the sweet smell of the summer night breeze. It differed greatly from the salty air of Lighthouse Rock. It had the scent of the mountains, of the earth, of the town, of use, of people sitting down to dinner, of humanity, of freedom. He enjoyed this smell while he could, because, while he wasn't privy to God's greater plan, he was certain this world would be unmade to make room for something better, but far different.

He was free!

Freddie grinned with elation, and he wished he could

stay in that moment forever, but he could not. He had a job to do, and he needed to do it now. God had not given him this opportunity to waste it getting nostalgic about a world that would soon fade.

When he looked to the right, he noticed a house built on an incline, its first story larger than the second, which protruded from the back half of the house. The house was white with a dark-gray roof. The building was old, but it had changed a lot from what it had looked like thirty years ago. The owners had remodeled it, but the parts that mattered were still there. He felt his breath catch with excitement when he thought of setting foot in that house where the Mother had once lived. To walk where she had walked.

Freddie ambled toward the house and stopped in front of the porch. It was fascinating. He wasn't sure exactly *what* he was supposed to do, but it was like his body knew.

He heard a television inside. The sounds of a family, laughing, conversing, being happy. There was joy in knowing one of the last images of the current world he would see would be a family. It had been so long since he'd last seen a family in person, in their own home. He raised a hand and touched a thin column that held the roof over the porch, and briefly, he felt it throb in his hand. In a bolt of surprise, the thought that flashed through his mind was

(*It's alive!*)

the tactile memory of his mom's belly when she was

pregnant with Laurie, and he felt the baby kick for the first time. A smile stretched his lips. Tears welled up in his eyes.

God is good!

He went up the front steps and before him was the door, which was locked, but he knew would open for him, because in that other place, in "Blight Harbor"—as people called it, and why not call it that himself?—there was no lock. There was barely a door left, in fact.

Freddie was grinning so widely that his cheeks hurt, but he could not stop.

Would the joys of this night ever end?

The small bowl of peanuts was empty.

John Hitch pressed his eyelids shut and let out a long, trembling breath. A shiver crept up his back as a freezing dread grew in his chest like a ball of ice.

"Hey, bud, how about a refill? Maybe more peanuts?" asked the bartender that had come to replace Jess Cunningham for the night.

He shook his head without opening his eyes.

"You okay?" the bartender asked.

He stared, unblinking. "None of your business."

The bartender responded with an uncomfortable half smile and walked away.

He was not okay. He could sense it now. Freddie Parham was free. It had begun. He had to act quickly.

He heard the door to the bathroom open behind him. He reached toward the holster under his jacket and gripped his gun.

It had been so long since Freddie had seen a child, let alone a baby. On television, at Lighthouse Rock, he'd seen many, of course, but it was different in person. The baby smell, the big eyes, those very tiny, nearly invisible hairs that made a baby's skin appear fuzzy like a peach. It almost beckoned his hand to caress it.

He couldn't touch him, though. Even if there was this instinctive need to remember what innocence felt like, regain a bit of that interrupted childhood of his, he couldn't. He was impure and tainted and cursed. He would never ruin the perfection before him, even if the child could not see him or notice him.

The baby would not make it past the night. A childhood interrupted—much like his—but it would be interrupted without being tainted, without being cursed—much unlike his.

He was so envious, but so thankful to have experienced this.

"Baby's crying," Claudia Felton said to her husband as they watched television on their living room couch. She leaned her head back in the chair and turned her head toward him.

"Isn't it your turn?" Steve Felton asked.

His wife shook her head. "No, sir, last time it was my turn. And your baby boy had filled the diaper with half his body weight. I may be his mom, but that wasn't pretty."

Rudy, their five-year-old son, who until two months earlier had been the only one, laughed when he heard his mom talk about full diapers, which, for a five-year-old, was the zenith of comedy.

"Alright," Steve exhaled in defeat, knowing this wasn't an argument he could win. "But it's your turn to rinse the dishes."

"I don't have a problem doing the dishes, sweetheart." Claudia returned a wicked smile. "If you promise to change Cole's diapers every day, I'm more than willing to do the dishes every day."

"No. I think that's a deal I'd lose out on by far. I'm happy having shared custody of the diapers."

Steve rose from the couch, exhaling wearily, but turned and leaned in to kiss his wife on the forehead. He patted his son's head and moved toward the stairs at the back of the living room. His baby's constant crying aroused an immediate urgency in Steve, making him quicken his pace.

"I'm coming, Shorty, give me a moment," Steve said toward the second floor. "Daddy's almost there to figure out what you want now. Or at least try."

Steve entered his baby's nursery, a pastel light-blue room covered in decals of all kinds of animals. A faint light illuminated the corner, casting a soft, warm glow on the walls and ceiling. In a few places, he saw rubber toys and stuffed animals that belonged to Cole, who was too young to understand what they were. The little boy still had a lot of fun watching them with curiosity, touching them, and tossing them around when they put them in the crib.

Steve smiled, imagining a future in which the room wouldn't be so tidy. Little Cole would become big enough to have all kinds of toys that would inevitably lay scattered on the floor, on the bed, in the closets, along with clothes and other artifacts that he did not yet know he would one day want.

Approaching the crib, Steve noted with relief that his son had already stopped crying. "So, young Master Felton, you made me come here for nothing." Steve smiled at his beautiful baby, who gave him a cheerful smile back. "Well, that smile is worth the trip, I'll admit."

It made him wonder if babies really smiled because

they were happy, or it was their little brain throwing random impulses to their faces, resulting in meaningless expressions. He decided Cole was actually glad to see him.

"You know?" he said, leaning over the edge of the crib. "Daddy's not angry he came, because it doesn't smell like you've got a dirty diaper in there, and that makes Daddy absolutely thrilled. But Mommy doesn't have to know that, right?"

The baby smiled with an open mouth and pink gums.

"'Atta boy. It will be our little secret. Meanwhile, Daddy will stay here with you, keeping you company and boring you with little words you don't understand, until you fall asleep."

Steve rested his head on his hand and extended a finger to his son, who immediately grabbed it in his tiny hand. He was extraordinarily proud of his healthy, precious baby boy. He had already been blessed five years ago with a son who couldn't be more perfect and would soon start school, and now he had been blessed with another beautiful son. The fact both looked so much like him meant they were going to grow up to be very handsome little boys. This was another source of pride in his mind (although he would never say that to his in-laws, who insisted that both boys were gorgeous for looking so much like their beloved daughter).

"Can I give you some advice, Shorty? Never get married. Your mom is one of the best women I've ever known.

Daddy got damn lucky! But even the best women come with in-laws, and that's always going to be a lottery. It also happens to be a lottery that Daddy definitely lost when he got your grandparents."

His baby just gave him that enthusiastic smile, accompanied by frantic movements of his legs and arms. Cole seemed to be thoroughly enjoying hearing his dad sully his concept of his grandparents from such a young age. He also didn't seem remotely close to going to sleep.

"Sweetheart," he heard Claudia's voice call him from the first floor. "You gonna be much longer?"

Steve moved his face closer to his baby and whispered with a complicit smile. "Now Daddy's about to lie to Mommy. Lying is bad, except in certain situations, so remember, this is our little secret."

He turned his head to the hallway and said: "Almost done. This little piggy made such a mess. It's taking me longer than I thought." He moved his face closer to little Cole and winked at him, receiving another smile in return. "You're my champion, so don't think Daddy's serious. You're not a piggy." He turned back to the hallway. "I'm done. I'm going to wash my hands and head downstairs."

Steve leaned over the crib rail, placed a gentle kiss on his baby's forehead, and caressed his cheek. "I love you, Shorty."

Throughout this entire conversation, Steve hadn't

noticed the person standing right next to him watching the exchange between him and his son. A person whom he couldn't see or feel or hear, but who was relishing every second of their conversation.

Steve turned around and headed for the hallway, but as soon as he walked through the door, all the lights in the house went out, plunging him into utter darkness.

"What the hell?"

Even if it had been a power outage, Steve was sure some light would have come in either through his baby's nursery window or through the master bedroom window at the other end of the hall. Instead, everything was pitch black, almost as if his head had been completely covered with a thick rubber mask.

"Sweetheart?" he said aloud. His voice echoed through the house.

There was no answer. The silence felt oppressive, impenetrable.

"Sweetheart? I think the power went out in the entire neighborhood, 'coz I don't see any lights around. Are you okay down there?"

Again, no response.

He always kept an old rechargeable flashlight in the drawer under his nightstand. He just had to feel his way in the dark to his bedroom until he reached the nightstand and pull it out. What he didn't remember was the last time he had charged it, since he hadn't used it for quite some time. Also, there was something strange and disturbing about not getting a response from the living room.

"Claudia?" He raised the volume of his voice a little more, and now there was an infusion of fear in his tone. "Something wrong?"

A viscid fear crept over him, his mind spinning with all the scenarios where his wife wouldn't be able to hear him. Not one seemed possible, though, and even if he took leaps of logic to make them possible, none led to anything good.

Searching for some kind of guide, he slowly reached out a hand toward the wall to his left. It was the one that continued uninterrupted to the master bedroom, but the moment he touched it, he instinctively retracted his hand as if he had touched something dangerous or disgusting in the dark.

His breath was coming in quick gasps. His eyes went wide, trying to catch any light, but the surroundings were pitch black.

"What the fuck was that?"

He was stunned. His head faced the wall, which he couldn't see. He didn't know how to react. For a moment, he completely forgot about the fact that his wife wasn't answering his calls. What he had felt on that wall was beyond explanation. The wall was damp and warm, as if what he had touched was living tissue. It felt like moist, living flesh.

As his mind frantically tried to decide whether to fight or flee—or faint—he remembered he didn't need to get to his room to get the flashlight. His cell phone was in his pocket. His right hand quickly went to the side of his pants and dug the black rectangle out.

Urgently, desperately, he ran his finger across the cell screen until he found the flashlight icon. A beam of light dazzled him while his eyes adjusted. He pointed the light toward the spot where he had felt that impossible texture, and his jaw dropped. His puzzled and incredulous eyes were focused on a patch about eight inches in diameter in which the wallpaper was torn. Underneath, there was something that appeared to be organic tissue, a mixture of red, pink, and white. with the surface sheen of moisture and blood, and most impressive of all, it seemed to pulsate.

I fell asleep on the couch watching TV and I'm dreaming. I never heard Cole cry. I never went up the stairs. I was never in his nursery. I'm asleep on the couch having a nightmare.

Defying his rationalization, the patch of meat on the wall stirred, as if it had shuddered. Startled, Steve took a step back.

Convinced this was a dream, but overcome by hysterical curiosity, he slowly approached the organism on the wall. Tentatively, he brought his gaze closer and noted that the wallpaper was, in fact, just barely covering this surface, almost like Kraft paper covering slabs of beef.

He timidly brought an index finger to the torn edge of the paper, where a portion of it was dog-eared. He gripped it between his thumb and index finger and yanked at the tip, tearing off a piece of the wallpaper and revealing more of what was underneath.

A nervous, intrigued giggle escaped from his chest.

He repeated the action with his fingers, ripping out another piece of wallpaper, again revealing a texture similar to muscle tissue behind it. Now he saw tendons from which pulsing muscle fibers issued forth and were lost again under the wallpaper.

None of this made sense, and it only made him more and more convinced he was dreaming.

Yet again, he reached his hand to the wall, this time wanting to touch the bloody tissue. Maybe if he touched it, he would know if it was real or not. Maybe the sensation of disgust would wake him up, or even the sensation of touch itself. He couldn't remember a time when he had perceived touch in a dream.

When his hand was only an inch from the wet surface, the exposed flesh jerked violently. Two of the muscle fibers relaxed and separated, revealing a hole between them. From this hole came a strange black tentacle that caught Steve by the wrist and continued to stretch and climb, coiling up to his armpit.

"What the fuck?" Steve hollered and tried to pull his

hand away, but the strange black cord tightened and held him in place. Another strand came out of the hole and tied his other arm, then came another and another. Countless of these threads shot to various parts of Steve's body and wrapped around them, immobilizing him.

Steve cried out in terror and felt the black tentacles pull him toward the wall.

His distraught eyes watched as more and more of the wallpaper peeled off. The flesh beneath it heaved, forming ruptures, and soon the black tentacles had him completely pinned against the warm surface. He could feel the sickening heat of a foreign organism against his skin. He could feel the pulse of many pumping veins swelling and relaxing just beneath the flesh. There was blood on his face and arms, and it was soaking into his shirt and pants.

More and more of the black tentacles came out of new holes in the wall and enveloped him until he was finally surrounded by darkness. This was not the intangible darkness caused by the mere absence of light—it was the claustrophobic darkness of being trapped inside a hermetically sealed cocoon that did not give him the ability to move.

With no time to digest the confusion and panic that was shaking his brain, he felt the threads or tentacles or worms—or whatever these things were—opening and penetrating his skin. Steve Felton experienced a new definition of pain. Before he could let out a scream, hundreds of slippery, nauseating fibers filled his mouth and slid down his throat, tearing through his flesh and muscle fibers, ripping his insides apart. He felt them pull at his tendons, break his bones, distend his veins, fill every space, reshape his being, and violate every inch of his humanity.

Freddie allowed himself some light, letting the small lamp in the baby's nursery come back on. He wanted to see what was coming. He stood still, watching in fascination as the first arrival of one of the servants—an Exile—unfolded.

He had taken it upon himself to place the entrance to Blight Harbor in the baby's nursery's door. People had judged him all his life for being curious about the darker side of things, about terror, about monsters, about images that scared others. Because of this, Freddie had expected Steve Felton to freeze up in panic the moment he crossed over to the other side, and for a moment, that was exactly what he did. But what he found most impressive, what he could not have expected, was that once the terror abated, curiosity would take hold of Felton.

He had touched the surface of what, until recently, had been a wall in his house and had even removed the layers that covered the living entity that was Blight Harbor in one of its infinite forms.

Even Freddie was startled when the tendrils belonging to one of the Exiles came out of the wall and caught Steve Felton. Now, he was wrapped in a smooth-surfaced black cocoon that pulsated like the belly of a pregnant mother, carrying the first of his creations.

He was filled with a peculiar sense of pride as he realized he was about to be a father.

No, he thought. The only Father of this new world was God. He only had the honor of helping shape this world and the beings that God wanted to bring into it.

The first night, four will open the gates.
The second night, one will seal the town.
The third night, four will awaken God.
The fourth night will be eternal.

In moments, Felton would emerge. Renewed by the Lord.

The first of many beautiful things.

END OF BOOK 1

THE STORY CONTINUES IN
BLACKOUT: WHITE HARBOR BOOK 2

Continue for a bonus novella

I Am The Door

A White Harbor Story

2022

Sliding his fingers under his glasses, Callum Baker rubbed his eyeballs with his fingertips. Squinting with exhaustion, he turned his head and peered left, using this motion to crack his stiff neck. From where he sat, through the library's glass doors, he could see the school hallways were empty and dark. The janitor, Jenson Harvey, had already made his last round, fooling no one with his lazy mopping technique—he was rushing his cleanup, as usual, so he could hurry out for his nightly drink at Cunningham's, the only drinking hole in the small town of White Harbor.

Callum had ultimately resorted to buying his own mop and bucket, and would mop the library floor himself, since he was apparently the only person in Ann Summers

High School to show any kind of respect for the library. He couldn't expect a nearly illiterate drunk like Harvey to appreciate the reverence humans owed the written word.

He was alone with his books and his files, which he always had a hard time putting down. He knew he should probably be on his way home, but he wanted to finish his notes on the Albright family tragedy of 1968—one of many strange occurrences in a town where tragedy and premature death had become something expected. Callum often felt he was the only person who paused long enough to question why.

"Did you know Victoria Parham was torn apart by coyotes in her backyard?" he once blurted out at the school staff Christmas dinner, earning him a table surrounded by staring eyes, hanging jaws, and dumbfounded silence.

Sylvia Nguyen, the principal—and, unbeknown to his coworkers, his girlfriend—had been in the process of carving a delicious, glazed ham, and had stopped mid-cut, leaving half a slice hanging in a downward concave curve, like a tongue.

Undeterred, Callum continued. "She was! She was torn apart by coyotes as her three children watched from the bedroom window, crying and screaming."

Sylvia shot him an uncomfortable glance and said, "Um, Cal? What are you getting at with this?"

"I don't know," he said. "Just making conversation.

When was the last time you heard of a coyote attack in White Harbor? Now, *four* coyotes, coming out of nowhere to rip apart a middle-aged woman in front of her kids for no reason?" He cast a glance around the table. "Bizarre. That's all I'm saying."

Sylvia had smiled politely and changed the subject.

Why do that? he'd thought with indignation, letting the stress out through his hands as he shuffled papers and files from one pile to the other on his desk. *Aren't they the least bit curious?*

He released a frustrated sigh.

That lack of curiosity he perceived in everyone else was the reason he was compiling and sorting through countless documents, testimonies, books, and recordings. He meant to write a comprehensive study on White Harbor's history. If the townspeople didn't want to look deeper into why their isolated little corner of the world was so different from all others, he would take it upon himself to put together as much research as he could and shove the whole thing down their throats to make them pay attention.

The Albrights—his current subject—were one of those stories that kept coming up during conversations, a story forever intertwined in the town's ever-growing compendium of nightmares.

What Callum's scientific mind instinctively gravitated toward when studying events like these were the facts—

the truth, the undeniable, concrete, recorded evidence. However, even for someone as fact-driven as he was, it was hard to ignore all the "other stuff". The unexplained. The inexplicable. The gossip and assumptions and rumors. Even baseless conclusions held some importance when talking about White Harbor, and that's what made his work more difficult than a simple compilation of cold facts.

His mom—may she rest in peace—used to say stories in any town were living entities that fed and grew. A story could start off as: "Teenager shot when trying to break up an argument", but that story would feed off the trough of public opinion. Each person who told it would add something to it, a supposition, a question, an angle, a suggestion, an unrelated fact that seemed relevant when viewed through a specific lens.

"Oh, yes, the story will feed," his mom used to say, her lips pressed tightly between her pudgy cheeks. They used to make her lower face look like a line between two backward parentheses. How he missed her chubby, kind face.

"*I heard* this."

"*Did you know* that?"

"*I seem to remember* when."

"*You know* who."

"*Oh, it makes sense* why."

On and on, the story would feed. Growing and growing and growing. Until one day the tragic story about a teenager getting shot when trying to break up an argument would become something out of a tabloid blurb: "A young girl, known by townsfolk for her drug use and promiscuity, was shot dead at a local bar, when trying to stop an argument between her two jealous lovers, one of whom was armed. Onlookers commented on her profane language, and the fact she appeared inebriated."

As time passed, there would be no other truth, only "the local truth", even when it was completely fabricated.

So, how complete would his story be if he only included the proven facts and ignored the local truth? How would his study be complete if he turned his gaze from what the townspeople saw as facts and didn't even address it? Sure, he would have a very scientific and historically accurate account of events, but it would be a *boring* scientific and historically accurate account of events…that only he would read.

In the end, Callum Baker resolved, he would divide his book into two sections; first, telling the stories as they were told in White Harbor, then deconstructing them with facts, evidence, and logic. To do this, he'd first have to navigate through all the information before him, and put together the story of the Albrights, as told within the boundless perspective of the ever-changing local truth.

Chapter 1

1968

On the porch of his one-story home, two black dogs lay on either side of Ben Curling's rocking chair. They were known as cane corsos—or Italian Mastiffs—a breed of dog more intimidating than dangerous, a fact entirely dependent on their upbringing.

One of the dogs snorted, leaving a small wet patch of moisture on the wood of Curling's porch. It slowly dissipated into nothingness.

Curling was an elderly man of an age no one seemed to agree on. He was Black, of a very dark complexion, which contrasted with keen brown eyes that appeared to see behind the curtain of a world he had no interest in being part of. His hair was short, curly—more black than gray—and his face was sculpted into a permanent scowl. He sat on his old rocking chair, barely rocking, observing the world pass by. At his age, it felt like faces and names almost blurred together—but only almost—since he never forgot a face, never forgot a name. What *did* blur together was just how much importance he put on each, which wasn't a lot.

His dogs, identical to each other, had no names. Curling referred to them as "this one" or "that one", more based on context cues than any actual recognition of each animal's identity.

The dogs' ears perked up. Silvery blue eyes turned at the same time to peer through the balustrades surrounding the porch, down the slope, toward an approaching figure.

Curling lazily swiveled his head to see the new next-door neighbor walking toward his house. Jonathan Albright. Another name and face he wouldn't soon forget. The man seemed handsome but unremarkable to the point of being generic: tall, medium-build, smooth-shaved, short brown hair. Albright came striding up the hill from the house next door, a house Ben Curling owned—but disliked acknowledging as his—the house everyone in town called "the Vanek House" after its original owner, Amias Vanek.

Curling's eyes tracked Albright's movement, but he made no attempt to stand or acknowledge him. He found Albright's face too stupid to warrant a greeting. The olive-striped, too-tight shirt, checkered shorts, and sneakers all made him look a damned fool. His stupid grin didn't help.

Albright stopped right before reaching the porch's front step and shot a wary glance at the dogs, who stared back attentively.

"Um…" Albright said, pointing at the dogs. "Is it okay if I… Uh… They won't… Will they?"

Internally, Curling cursed the moment he agreed to let these people in the house. If it were up to him, he would've set fire to the damn thing a long time ago, but the house had to stay right where it was, and so did he. Now, these people were in the house, which technically made him their landlord, and this came with the annoyance of having to speak to them.

Albright's face made no sense to him, that stupid grin on the bottom half of it, and the nervous eyes and upturned eyebrows on the upper half. How he disliked that face.

"They won't attack me, right?" Albright asked.

With a tired, growl-like voice coming from right behind his collarbone, Curling said, "Not unless I tell them to." He shot a glance at both dogs. "Used to be three. The other one attacked someone before I told it to… Now there are two."

"At-tacked?"

"You're here for the key to that room on the second floor," Curling sneered, getting to the point as quickly as he could, so the man would just leave.

"Yes!" Albright walked up the three steps to stand on

the porch and cast another wary glance at the dogs, whose eyes hadn't moved away from him. "I mean, yes. My wife, Penny, she—"

"Your wife doesn't know what she's doing," Curling interrupted, against his better instincts. "You don't wanna go in that room. Leave it be."

Albright gave him that squint he'd seen so many times before, that look of confusion. Not so much because he hadn't understood the words that came out of his mouth, but because he was trying to determine if he was only partially or completely insane.

"We're opening a bed-and-breakfast, you know? Would be kind of wasteful not to use one of the biggest rooms in the house."

He gave that stupid smile. Curling narrowed his eyes and wondered if it was a kind of default expression that took over the man's face every time he stopped speaking.

"Bed-and-breakfast." Curling munched on the concept for a few seconds. "That's what you think you'll be doing with *that* house." He motioned with his head toward the Vanek House.

The old, wooden, weather-worn building sat two stories high. Its features were crooked, its windows broken, mold, gaps and cracks scarred its walls, telling the world what Curling knew: It was barely inhabitable. As soon as he was told he had to let the Albrights rent the house, he'd hired a contractor from out of town to come and put some glass on the windows and fix some leaks in the roof, check that the piping and appliances were at least in acceptable condition to sustain a family, at least for as long as this farce lasted. He wouldn't lay a finger on the house himself—not to fix it, at least—and he wouldn't hire someone from town and allow them to have more gossip to throw onto *Blight Harbor*'s plate, to keep it good and fat. If they wanted to go on with this stupid charade, he would comply, but let someone else do the work. The only thing he told the contractor was, "Do not touch the big room on the second floor." Now here was this grinning fool asking for the key because his wife thought herself too clever for him to know what she was really trying to do.

"It's old, and storied, and certainly famous around town," Albright said, leaning against a balustrade, giving the illusion—and it was an illusion—of relaxing into the conversation. His rigid shoulders and arms tightly hugging himself gave him away. "You should've seen the faces people made the first time we stopped at Cobb's Diner for lunch and mentioned we were moving into this house. The whole place went quiet."

"I bet."

"Yeah!"

There was that stupid grin again. Wider now.

Curling felt it was none of his business, and he

shouldn't even care, but he still asked, in spite of himself. "It didn't strike you as odd that people would react that way?"

Albright seemed only slightly taken aback by this. "Well, from a business perspective, I thought it was a good sign. Encouraging even."

The grin. Wider even. Such a stupid man.

Curling gave an extended, tired sigh, and reached into his jacket pocket. He brought out a single brass key. The old key had a perfectly round loop for a head and a piece of blue string attached to it, which was tied to a small metal sigil. It looked like the upper half of a circle, with two horizontal lines under it, and a vertical line that pierced all three elements. It appeared as if the half-circle were resting on a cross with two horizontal lines. Finally, what looked like a "V" crossed the lines and enclosed the half-circle. It looked a little like an anarchy symbol turned upside down.

"That's a nice key chain," Albright said. "Looks familiar."

Curling rolled his big eyes up at him. "Sure, it does."

He handed Albright the key. Curling thought for a second to stay quiet and let things be what they were going to be. But just then, in the corner of his eye, the shape of a little girl. She couldn't have been more than seven years old, and here she came, bounding out of the Vanek House and running toward them.

"Dad!" she called toward Albright as she reached

Curling's front lawn, with a cheery, infectious voice. "Mom says lunch is ready!"

"Okay, munchkin!" Albright answered. "Be right there!"

The girl turned toward Curling, smiled wide, looking very much like her father, but prettier—and definitely smarter—displaying a gap between her teeth where a baby tooth had recently fallen off. She waved her hand and said, "Hi!"

Curling answered the greeting with a single, serious nod.

The girl said, "Bye!", still smiling, then hurried back to the old house.

Albright turned his gaze back to Curling, giving him a comical eye-roll. "I know what you're wondering," he said with enthusiasm. "How the hell are these people cooking, if they've barely gotten set up and they haven't installed their stove yet?"

Curling wasn't wondering that, but held his tongue.

"Got ourselves a Radarange!"

Curling stared with an expression that combined puzzlement with annoyance.

"It's an electronic oven! Microwaves! Can you believe it? We haven't even crossed into the seventies, and the future is here already! Expensive, like you wouldn't believe, but worth every penny!"

"Listen," Curling said, dismissing every stupid word that had come out of the man's mouth. "I'm not the right person to tell someone how to manage a wife." This earned him a frown from Albright, but he pushed on. "But she isn't telling you everything about why you're here, about why she wants to open that room."

"I'm sorry, Mr. Curling," Albright swallowed and glanced at the dogs again, anticipating they might react to his agitation, "but that's really inappropriate of you to say."

"Listen," he repeated in a firm voice, leaving no room for objection. "I don't often *do* conversation. I do warnings even less. If I bring someone into that house of my own accord, I take full responsibility for what might happen. You're *not* in that house because I want you there. You're in that house because someone twisted my arm. So I feel I should say my piece and let you make of it what you will."

He studied Albright's eyes. The man looked like his face could not decide which was the correct expression for what he was hearing.

"Your wife thinks she's clever. She thinks she knows what she's doing. Overconfidence and excessive praise will do that to a person, no matter how clever they are. I don't believe in 'a man does this, a woman does that'. That's nonsense, but I think, sometimes, if a person's spouse does something abhorrently irrational—even dangerous—slapping some sense into them might be justified—"

"Whoa, whoa, whoa!" Albright said, taking a step forward, with his palm held toward Curling.

The dogs reacted immediately by sitting up.

This made him stop in his tracks. He gazed at the dogs, swiveled his gaze toward Curling. He spoke in a careful tone. "Listen, *sir*. I do not believe a man should slap his woman. That's barbaric. I know you're from a different generation, but I will have you show some respect for my wife."

Curling sat back in his chair. His big eyes did not leave Albright's, that permanent scowl firmly plastered on his face. He took a deep breath and nodded reluctantly, conceding.

"Thank you for the key," Albright said, and nodded a polite goodbye.

He watched the man turn and walk down the steps. Albright crossed from Curling's front lawn to the front lawn of the house that would see him leave in a body bag.

Chapter 2

Jonathan Albright sauntered through the Vanek House's front door, pausing at the main hall, which acted as the house's living room. A wide set of stairs, as wooden as the rest of the house, rose to the second floor. He followed the stairs with his eyes up to a landing halfway up, where they angled ninety degrees and climbed the rest of the way.

He stared at the area upstairs where the second-floor landing reached a hallway. It traveled to the lonelier, unused areas of the house, beyond where the bedrooms were. It continued, he knew, deeper into the empty regions of the house...

That locked room.

He tried to shake off the strange sense of dread that

crept up on him, but it lingered like unwanted, velvety fingertips on his heart as he walked slowly through the living room. Against the further wall, he saw the only part of the house not made of wood. There was a great stone-and-concrete fireplace, rising through the house like the backbone of its rickety body. He might consider himself a very optimistic man, but he didn't think himself optimistic enough ever to light that fireplace. The house was old enough that he supposed a spark could burn it down in a single puff of smoke—the way they did in *Looney Tunes* cartoons when Bugs Bunny held a single match to Yosemite Sam's mustache.

Boxes were piled against the wall next to the fireplace, with the words "Living Room", "Kitchen", "Bedrooms", and "Bathroom" written in messy permanent marker.

He walked past the dividing wall, into the dining room, where there was another opening to the stone fireplace. Whoever this Vanek guy was, he definitely wanted more bang for his buck with the huge, double-sided fireplace.

The dining table sat in the middle of this spacious room, seating a fidgeting Sadie, who waited with anticipation for lunch to be served. His baby boy, Nelson, sat in a highchair, playing with a tiny rubber elephant his mom had bought him.

Jonathan approached the head of the table and pulled the chair out. He said, "So, how do you like the house, munchkin?"

Sadie looked around, as if carefully considering her response. "It's like staying at Grandpa's cabin, but ugly." She gave him a big smile, and she giggled, a whistle escaping through her missing tooth.

Jonathan chuckled with his daughter. "We'll make it pretty soon enough. You'll see."

"Did Curling give you the key, hon?"

He turned to see his wife walking in from the kitchen, holding a bowl of salad and some reheated spaghetti from the night before. She placed them on the table.

"Yes, ma'am," he said, pulling the key from his pocket and holding it up to his wife, who examined the odd keychain for a second or two before taking it. "That's a strange individual."

"Who? Curling?" Penny Albright said, serving their daughter some spaghetti and salad.

"I don't want salad!" Sadie said. "I don't like green stuff."

"You know why you have to eat the green stuff?"

"I don't care. I don't wanna."

"I see." She shrugged. "Well, suit yourself. That's just going to come back to bite you in the butt later on."

"Why?"

"Have you ever looked at the mountains? Like, carefully looked at them. How their shapes are curved, and a lot of them are covered in green stuff?"

"Yeah."

"Those used to be giants, but one day, they fell asleep, and the plants ate them because they spent so much time sleeping they didn't eat the plants fast enough. So, if plants can eat a giant, imagine what they can do to us!"

Sadie's eyes opened wide as saucers.

"That's right," Penny said, nodding gravely. "Plants eat people. Even giant people. So, we have to eat them before they eat us."

"You're lying."

"Oh, I'm lying, am I?" Penny turned toward Jonathan. "Ask your dad. Am I lying?"

Jonathan shook his head. "No, your mom isn't lying. In fact, do you know why the top of Grandpa's head is completely bald? He fell asleep without eating his greens once. He woke up in the middle of the night and there was a head of lettuce eating his hair. It never grew back."

Sadie mouthed the words, "Oh my gosh!"

Penny turned to face their daughter, having surreptitiously left the salad on her plate already, and was now putting a tiny amount of pasta into Nelson's little bowl.

"Why doesn't Nelson have to eat green stuff?" Sadie asked.

Penny swiveled her eyes toward her baby, then back to her daughter. "Well, um…"

She shot a panicked glance toward Jonathan, who

inconspicuously showed his upper teeth and pointed at one of his incisors.

"Well," Penny repeated, having caught the hint, "you know how you've been losing your milk teeth, and your new teeth are coming in? That's when you're the most effective at eating vegetables. Nelson just barely got his milk teeth, and they're too delicate to eat vegetables. That's why."

Sadie squinted at her, her eyes narrowing skeptically. "Can I knock all my teeth out, then, so I don't have to eat green stuff?"

Penny narrowed her eyes back at her. "Stop being a smart ass and eat your vegetables. Nice try."

Sadie grinned widely, with the gap in her teeth looking even more prominent in such a big smile. She looked quite satisfied to have outsmarted her mom.

"So," Jonathan said, "as I was saying… That guy Curling is kinda weird. How do you even know him?"

"Church," she said, immediately, serving herself a plate of pasta.

"You know Ben Curling, who lives in White Harbor, from church, way back in Burley?"

She gave him an annoyed eye-roll, passing him the bowl so he could serve his own plate. "No, babe. Obviously not."

Jonathan took the bowl and spooned a generous serving of last night's pasta onto his plate.

"You remember Alberto Ruiz? From Bible group? He came over to dinner with the rest of the group the time it was our turn to host? Had a little boy, also named Alberto?"

Jonathan took a bite of pasta and briefly paused to think back.

"Short-ish? Glasses? Deep voice?"

"Oh!" Jonathan remembered. "The Latin guy! I mean, not the Latino guy—I know he's Latino—I meant the guy who's teaching himself Latin? Oh, I loved that guy. He was so nice!"

"Yes, that Alberto. Well, you also met his wife, Doris. She works here in White Harbor, and they knew we were looking for a place to start our business, and she told Alberto this man from the White Harbor chapter of our Bible group was renting a big fixer-upper with an option to buy. So, that's how I got in touch with Ben Curling."

"I see," Jonathan nodded. "He doesn't strike me as a Bible reader, though."

"He's, uh…" Penny paused, trying to find the right word, "he's a *reluctant* member."

"He was very insistent about you not going to that room on the second floor. Made it sound like it was full of demons or something."

Penny scoffed as she chewed on a forkful of salad. "You know people in these towns. They're all about their little superstitions."

Jonathan nodded, and for a moment the table was quiet. Penny busied herself smooshing some of the pasta and carefully feeding it to her baby with a cute, round-tined, blue Spork.

"You know," he said. "I've been wondering. How come you've never invited me to your Bible group?"

Penny turned a puzzled, flat-eyebrowed glance at him and said, "Jonathan, you're Jewish. Also, you'd probably be bored to death. That's why I only invite you over when they're like social dinners and things like that—that way we won't be going on and on about Bible verses and stuff."

"Okay. Yeah, I was just wondering."

"Uh, hon?"

Jonathan looked up at her, and she was signaling with her head toward the salad bowl.

"You didn't serve yourself any salad," she said. "How about you set an example for your seven-year-old and get some vegetables in you?"

"Ha!" said Sadie, triumphantly raising her fork over her head. "Gotcha!"

Jonathan chuckled and put some salad on his plate.

For the last time, the entire family ate a relaxed, simple dinner together in their new home.

Chapter 3

Penny Albright got up from her bed slowly. Her husband, who was now softly snoring next to her, slept like a rock every night. They'd had to spend most of the day unpacking boxes, carrying things up those stairs she'd have to childproof, and moving things all around the house to make it at least habitable.

The house wasn't habitable, however.

The house hadn't been habitable for most of the twentieth century, and it all had to do with what was in that bedroom at the end of the hallway.

She had been sent here—unbeknown to her blissfully ignorant husband—to *make it* habitable.

Curling had raged, and complained, and threatened, but his opinion was irrelevant. Yes, he had a say, but that say had been unanimously overridden. He was only a glorified caretaker, for all she cared; an old-fashioned asocial grouch in a long line of old-fashioned asocial grouches surnamed Curling. No one at the church took him seriously anymore.

Penny Albright, however, was one of the most recognized members of her church. Everyone in her Order knew if only one person could deal with what was locked in that room, it was her, and she had enthusiastically accepted the honor.

With a cat burglar's careful hands, she opened her nightstand drawer and produced a flashlight, turned it on, and with a smooth motion, stood up from the edge of the bed. She paced with deliberate, silken steps toward a dresser she'd helped her husband carry up to the bedroom, on top of which sat a small jewelry box. The jewelry box had a tiny four-digit combination lock—this was a way to keep the children out of her most prized jewelry, but also to keep Jonathan away from the key. Her husband was a wonderful, sweet man, but he was as curious as a child, and he would not think twice about swiping that key and going into that room to see what the fuss was all about.

She spun each dial into place until the number read "0110". She opened the jewelry box, lifted a small division, and found the key sitting at the very bottom.

Key in hand, she closed the box, set the dials to a random number, and slowly headed out the door. In the pervading soundlessness of the night, each step produced a creak that sounded to her like lightning crashing and splitting a tree in two.

Once she carefully closed the door and found herself in the hallway, she was freer to walk, the socks she wore at night letting out nothing but a soft, padded sound, though the usual cringe-inducing creak would surprise her every once in a while.

As she stopped in front of the door where both her children slept, she cocked her head slightly, listening for the slightest sound that might indicate they were awake.

Only silence.

Satisfied, she continued walking to the end of the hallway, turned right, and saw the door. The only door in this portion of the hallway—and unlike the others in the house—this one had a riveted metal frame. It was old and rusted, but still strong, making the door appear sturdy.

Several seconds passed before she realized she wasn't moving. Her breath was raspy and quivering in her throat, and she could see her breath leave her mouth and nose in a cold cloud, despite it being a warm summer night.

She had to walk there and open the door.

She had to walk there, open the door, go in, evaluate, cleanse.

It was all she needed to do in order to put an end to the many tragedies associated with this house throughout the history of White Harbor. So many unnecessary deaths, so much sorrow, sadness, destroyed families—innocent souls that had met an end in this accursed house. She could end it all. She could banish what lived in that room.

All she needed to do was walk there.

She simply needed to take one step.

One step.

She couldn't take that one step.

Something in that room was warning her to stay away. Something didn't want her there, but she'd prepared for this before she moved her family here in the name of duty. So, if she was that prepared, why was she so paralyzed?

It was only a door.

(A lonely door in a hallway. Cold as winter in the middle of summer. A door. Wood older than my grandparents. Still sturdy. Rusted metal. Absorbs the cold of the hallway. Freezing. My hand will stick to it if I touch it. My skin will rip if I pull it away. Will rip my skin, my flesh, my soul! I want to leave! I want to get out! I want to run! I don't care if I leave my family behind! I want to run away! I want to r—)

"No," she hissed in an angry breath. She was so completely terrified, her lizard brain had triggered an alarm that disgusted her. How could she have thought of something as appalling as leaving her family behind and saving herself?

You brought them here, didn't you? How is that any less irresponsible?

Penny bit her lip. She clenched her fists and took one step.

Another.

Another.

The closer she got to the door, the heavier the weight of a presence bigger than her. Bigger than the house. Bigger than the entire town. It pressed down on her, putting images in her head from years past.

The little infant boy that fell down the stairs and broke his neck.

The man, drunk and unconscious, pulled into the room by a hand that looked female, but so thin and long it could not be human.

A teenage couple. Her knife driven under his jaw, coming out of one of his eyes. She kissed him deeply before pulling the knife out and stabbing herself.

The man lying dead in the flames of the fireplace, his flesh carbonized and consumed.

The twin boys, locked in that room, wallowing in their filth, dehydrated and starving under the gaze of a tall, unyielding, iron-framed door that wouldn't open.

The young, homeless mother in ragged clothes, holding a dead baby in her arms as if breastfeeding it, her gaze lost. A knife on the floor next to her. Her arms slashed and bleeding out. Her breasts slashed as well. The blood from one pouring into the dead baby's slack mouth.

Penny stood before the door. Her entire body shaking from the horrors the house was putting in her mind. Images of others who had dared enter this profane place; threats of what could happen to her and her family. With a resolute but spasming hand, she pulled the key from a pocket in her robe, tried to stick it in the keyhole, missing once, twice, then finally pushing the key in and turning it. With a deep breath, she put her weight onto the door, and it opened inward.

She stepped inside.

She shone the light into the room.

Nothing.

Just an empty, windowless room.

Thirty-one, thirty-two, thirty-three, thirty-four…

"Honey?"

Thirty-five, thirty-six, thirty-seven, thirty-eight, thirty-nine…

"Hey, honey?"

Penny's voice sounded distant, reverberant, as if she were speaking to him through the opposite end of a pipe from the other end of a hill.

Forty, forty-one, forty-two, forty-three…

"Jonathan, hey!"

Forty-four…

Jonathan looked up at Penny, who was standing just a few feet away, staring at him with concern. Bumbling sounds that were meant to be words fell off his lips like drool. He shook his head, and finally said, "There are forty-four Froot Loops in my bowl."

Penny squinted at him. Her gaze flitted down to his bowl, then back to his eyes.

"That's fascinating, honey," she said with a hint of sarcasm. "They're getting soggy too, you know?"

He peered down at this bowl and realized his mouth had been hanging open.

"Are you okay?"

"Uh…" Jonathan hesitated for a moment, then shook his head. "I'm sorry. I'm just… I didn't get a very good sleep last night. I kept having these weird dreams."

Penny nodded expectantly. This was usually the part in which his loving wife waited patiently as he recounted the events of his dreams. Jonathan knew she only pretended to be interested. After all, what could be more boring than hearing someone talk about dreaming he was driving a car fueled by melted gummy bears? Yet, he appreciated her always paying attention to those things.

The issue this morning was he honestly didn't remember the dream.

"Two dots," he said, as if that was supposed to mean

something. It was the closest thing to a memory he had of his dream. "Two blue dots."

Penny looked more confused.

"That's all I remember," he said. "I think, in the dream, I'm looking out our bedroom door, and it's dark, and all I see there are two blue dots, like eyes, on…something." He shook his head in frustration. "I'm sorry, don't mind me. I'm being weird. I just need to rest."

"Okay," Penny said, clearly not fascinated by the subject of "what I dreamed last night," but showing genuine concern for her husband, nonetheless. She came close, gave him a loving hug and a kiss on the cheek. "Tell you what, you finish your breakfast and rest up for a while. I can take care of unpacking for a couple of hours. You try to sleep, alright?"

"Sounds good," he said, his voice groggy and fatigued.

Penny disappeared through the threshold, leaving him behind, and in his mind, it felt like she had been swallowed by the house.

Chapter 4

Jonathan tried eating his Froot Loops but couldn't get through the first spoonful. He chewed and chewed, swishing the sugary circles around his mouth until he finally spit them back into the bowl.

He headed up the stairs to go lie down. As he crossed the hall, he saw Sadie playing on the front lawn with her dolls. Nelson was probably in the kids' bedroom, lying on a comforter on the floor next to his mother as she unpacked things from boxes and sorted through them.

Reaching the bedroom, Jonathan sagged onto the blankets. His head hadn't even settled on the pillow when he fell into a drunken, uneasy, suffocating sleep. He felt he couldn't breathe. He could feel pain in his hands, as if they were curling inward with arthritic tension. Somehow he understood that this was not something from inside the dream, but his physical body reacting to something in the dream, something he saw that his mind refused to show him.

He lay face up, eyes shut. Arms pressed close to his body. His hands—in an epileptic paralysis—were claw-like, trembling and tense. His toes were curled and rigid. He could feel his buttocks pressed tight with stress. His heart thumped fast, hard, loud. He could imagine his ribcage breaking open and his heart leaping out of his chest and onto the bed, where the sheets got soaked in arterial blood. His teeth were pressed tightly, grinding against each other, jaw locked in place. A moan escaped his throat; a pleading, fearful moan.

I need to see it, he thought, commanding his brain. *I don't want to see it, but I need to see it. Not seeing it is worse. Not seeing is worse. Not seeing is—*

His eyes opened.

Seeing was worse.

Chapter 5

Penny sat on the floor of her kids' room, unpacking some of Nelson's clothes and putting them in a small chest of drawers next to his crib. Nelson, inside the crib, was content, watching a small mobile with little plush animals hanging in front of his face.

Once she was finished with the box, before moving to the next one, she disassembled it and folded it flat for later disposal. As she was about to start on the next box—more clothes—a keening wail caught her attention, freezing her soul. It came from the master bedroom.

It was her husband's voice, but it sounded distorted, like slowing down a spinning record where all that's being played was the sound of a man screaming.

Instead of immediately reacting, she froze. The sound wasn't normal, it didn't sound fully human. It was a perverse abdominal howl. The image in her mind was of some pre-historic mammal—not quite evolved to be considered an ape—attempting to scream for help. No words, just a rising and falling noise of alarm, coming from vocal cords she recognized as her husband's.

"Jonathan!" she cried, as she sprung to her feet and ran out of the room.

When he opened his eyes and his gaze adjusted, Jonathan found himself staring into something inexplicable. Just above the headboard, on all fours, on the wall behind the bed, was his son Nelson, but not really. Yes, it was a baby, and he could recognize his son's face anywhere, but Nelson's entire body was charcoal black. There were no shades to this color, no sheen of perspiration like one would see on human skin. It was matte black, as if it absorbed all light.

It stared straight at him with silvery-blue eyeballs. He couldn't look away from those eyes—cold, empty, soulless, like empty spaces in the creature's face, emitting a lifeless glow. Will-o'-the-wisps in a shadowy swamp.

He saw a long black tongue, almost half the size of the entire baby, emerge repulsively from a drooling mouth filled with crooked teeth, and saw it lick its own face, as if savoring what was to come. That face was filled with such malice it made him feel weak and vulnerable. He was at the mercy of a predator who had absolute control.

Jonathan couldn't move. His body felt shriveled and compressed, all his joints ached at once and his eyes were fixed on the abomination on the wall, right above his head. It moved one of its tiny baby hands—velvety, non-reflective black like the rest of its body—and put the fingers on the bed's headboard, as if it was ready to crawl toward him.

These didn't look like real infant fingers. They looked lumpy, joints bending at slightly off angles; tiny broken fingernails, gnarled, malformed, missing entirely from some fingers. Everything in that tire rubber, artificial shade of black. The memory of his baby boy grasping his index finger with his perfect little hands, contrasting with these horrid facsimiles, prompted Jonathan to scream, but his mouth wouldn't open. He was paralyzed, as if by some venom. Tears streamed down the sides of his face and only the corners of his mouth opened—just barely—to let out a terrified moan. His body had become a pressure cooker. Boiling fear, bubbling terror he couldn't let out. It continued to build and build inside him, trying to find an outlet, but he couldn't even fully open his mouth to produce the cry of terror he so desperately needed to exorcise from his body.

And there were those eyes.

Those undeniable eyes.

An inexorable, hopeless blue that negated any other source of light.

The long tongue retreated into its mouth, and an ungodly grin took shape on the baby's face. A very adult, vicious grin that sent chills down his spine. A grin filled with teeth angled every which way and piled onto each other; teeth he knew his infant baby didn't have. He could see each individual tooth, but they were as dark and unreflective as the rest of its body.

The creature moved its other little hand, then one leg, then the other. It now had both hands on the headboard.

Another low and helpless moan escaped the corner of his lips, not loud enough to be heard by anyone.

The baby creature crawled closer. Its blasphemous grin was now mere inches from his face. He could now see the monster wasn't crawling on the wall, but was *growing* out of it. Jonathan could see the point where its tiny knees touched the surface, and there was the slightest hint of it fusing into the wood, into a black patch of a strange mold that spread over the wall and the ceiling, like a revolting snail's trail.

As adrenaline fueled his terror, he saw more detail in the black mold, and he noticed hints of tiny, closed baby eyes on certain parts of the walls and the ceiling, the eyeballs rolling frantically under the eyelids. Tiny infant hands and individual fingers and toes wiggled and curled at random places on the matte-black surface. He saw hair, mouths, and tiny black teeth. It was as if the charcoal stain had been learning to form the shapes that would make up a baby as it spread over the room, but had failed repeatedly until it managed the unnatural abomination now crawling toward him with its repulsive, sinister grin.

Jonathan moaned and wept in desperation and fear, but the scream wouldn't leave his chest, no matter how hard he tried.

He saw the small baby hand reach toward him. Seeing it so close, he could make out just how it had made the effort to recreate a human baby but had failed completely. The artificial material that made up its body was a liquid, trying to be a solid. It emulated the texture and flexibility of flesh, but if it were to stand still, it wouldn't be any different from a statue. A bad carbon copy of his baby boy, offensive and evil.

The second he felt the cold, dusty touch of those fingers, the pressure in his chest finally pushed through his clenched teeth, and something louder than the lamentable moan burst through his mouth. It was still a garbled, anesthetized sort of scream, a wail attempting to form words that seemed too big for a barely opened mouth and an unresponsive tongue.

Jonathan sobbed as the baby's hand caressed his hair

gently, lovingly. Like it knew him. Loved him. The softness of its touch was more frightening than if it had leaped toward him to bite his throat off.

It loved him.

It *owned* him.

He sobbed, he wailed, he shook, his arms stayed twisted against his chest, inward and claw-like and useless. And those blue eyes, looking into his own, pulling him in, pulling him into depths he would fall into forever.

Lost in the blue. Lost in the cold. Lost in its love.

Finally, he felt the rise of a single, high-pitched shriek, gurgling from his throat—

"Jonathan!"

He gasped, and his eyes flew open at the sound of his wife's voice. She was standing at the door, looking at him with alarm.

The baby was gone.

The charcoal mold—with its nauseating body parts—was gone.

Jonathan wiped tears from his face, his hands no longer useless claws. He could feel his pillow was wet, and the bed was soaked with sweat and—

He saw Penny's eyes move toward his shorts.

He had pissed himself.

Chapter 6

Her husband had seemed a little out of it since the strange dream. Even a day later, he was caught in the remnant grip of whatever his brain had conjured. Jonathan hadn't really gone into details. He often did when discussing unusual dreams—good or bad—so she found this to be out of character.

He was often eager to tell her of his dreams, trying to figure out what they meant, even if she rarely had a clue. It was this cute thing her husband did, and it meant something to him, so she often showed interest. However, in the wake of what had clearly been a terrifying dream, he now avoided talking about it.

He had also not eaten a bite since he'd woken.

Penny now stood in the kitchen, looking out toward the back porch. Jonathan sat there, quietly, staring at nothing in particular, writing in his "dream diary", as he called it. Since waking up that morning, he'd had dark circles under his eyes and looked pale. He hadn't showered and had been distracted as he continued unpacking the last of the bigger boxes. The way he placed items around the house without thought was unnerving, like he was operating on auto-pilot. His eyes were vacant, too. Unseeing. Contradictorily, though, there was a keen awareness in them, like there was such a whirlwind of thoughts behind those eyes he couldn't really see what was in front of them.

"Honey?" she called out to him, and he turned a sleepy gaze toward her, slack-jawed. He answered with a weak nod. "I'm going to see if Mr. Curling can let me use his phone. I don't feel like going all the way downtown for a payphone, and I need to call Mom and check in with her, alright?"

He gave a forced smile and nodded in agreement.

"Will you be okay?" she asked.

He nodded again. This time he spoke, but still looked lost—still, there was that oppressive sense of thoughts behind those eyes he wasn't sharing—"I'll be fine, honey. I think I just have a stomach bug or something. Can't really hold anything down for now. I'll be alright."

She gave him a loving smile, which disappeared the moment she turned around and headed toward the front door. On the way out, she spared a glance toward her daughter, who was sitting on the floor, drawing with crayons, next to Nelson's playpen.

"Sadie?"

Her daughter turned her gaze toward her.

"Could you watch Nelson for a couple of minutes? I'll be right next door, alright?"

Sadie nodded.

"You need anything, just holler, and I'll come running, okay? I'll hear you from over there."

Sadie nodded again. That gap-toothed grin she gave her told her whatever was upsetting her husband hadn't touched her children. That was an immediate relief.

Quickening her step, she strode out the door.

She took a deep breath, as if the touch of the bright summer sunlight had given her a boost of energy she didn't know she needed. It was like she'd been subconsciously holding her breath while inside the Vanek House, and the sunlight and outside air reminded her to breathe.

She hurried past the front yard, went up the slope a short way, and into Ben Curling's front yard. From the moment she set foot in it, both of the man's terrifying dogs sat up on full alert—perhaps in reaction to her not showing any signs of slowing down. She glimpsed Curling's fingers doing a certain motion toward the dogs, to which they immediately responded by lying back down. Their gaze would not leave her, though.

She walked up the steps to Curling's porch and regarded the old man with disdain. She thought that rocking chair was surgically sewn to his ass, since he never seemed to stand from it.

Curling regarded her with curiosity, but remained quiet.

"What the hell is going on?" she asked in a firm, assertive tone.

Chapter 7

There was a shed in the backyard, near the very edge of the Vanek property. It was wooden, old, and sat awkwardly on small pilings, leaving a crawlspace of about eighteen inches from the ground. Next to this shed was a dead tree—tall, gnarled, and its bark was peeling like dying skin. Branches like skeletal claws reached out from the top. The tree on its own was ugly and scary, but Jonathan's attention was, at this moment, engaged elsewhere. He was jotting down what he saw in a small diary that rested on his thighs, where he wrote about his dreams, and other things that caught his attention.

Right now, he was staring at the thing in the crawlspace.

Even through the white noise of the pouring rain, he could still hear his daughter, who was playing in the living room with Nelson. She spent her time chatting with her baby brother, her voice loud and brimming with enthusiasm, even when she was lying on the floor drawing, and Nelson was in his playpen. She loved showing him everything she drew, as if the little boy could understand what she was showing him—sometimes even *he* couldn't understand his daughter's drawings.

Jonathan had kept his ears focused intently on his daughter, even when his wife came to ask him if he was okay. He didn't want to worry her about what he was seeing, so he smiled and told her what seemed like the most likely explanation for his current state—he'd caught a stomach bug and would feel better soon. Penny had left him there and gone away to talk to that unpleasant man, Curling.

He needed her gone. He needed to focus and listen. He'd been afraid if he looked away, or got distracted, what he was seeing would disappear because it was so hard to spot in this downpour.

But it didn't.

Yes. His little girl was in the living room. There was no doubt about that.

He wondered, in an oneiric reverie, why then was his little girl staring at him from the crawlspace under the shed with those blue, glowing eyeballs? Why was her skin evenly the color of soot? Why was she grinning at him with charcoal-black teeth and a black tongue that stuck out twenty inches from her mouth? Most importantly, why were her legs elongated and wrapped around each other like two thick lengths of rope? He saw them come out from under the shed toward the dead tree and stretch an impossible length. They wrapped upward around the tree, all the way to the top, where two tiny, blackened feet came out of the end of the long tangle, facing opposite sides, looking almost like a fishtail.

The rain came down hard, sheets and drops of water ran down the trunk of the tree, and formed fat drops that fell down from the serpentine coils of his daughter's legs. Yet, even the water didn't create a reflection or a slickness on that charcoal skin. Through it all, he could see Sadie grinning at him from under the crawlspace, shining blue eyes on a complexion like asphalt under a starless night.

This is a dream, he thought. *This is a dream like the one with Nelson. It has to be.*

He looked into his daughter's revolting grin and realized she wasn't missing her tooth.

Chapter 8

"What the hell's going on?" Penny asked Curling again.

The old man squinted at her, studying her face, but did not answer.

She was overcome with frustration and rolled her eyes, then glared at him. "The room is empty!"

He held her gaze, still squinting.

"I don't know for sure what you did," she said with a huff. "I don't know what you've been doing in that house all this time, and honestly, it's none of my business."

Curling tilted his head and raised an eyebrow. Something like a smile flickered at the corners of his eyes.

"But I didn't move my whole family into that house to find an empty room," she continued.

Curling let out a mirthless chuckle. "You shouldn't have moved your family into that house for *any* reason."

"Don't smart-mouth me, old man. I don't know what I expected to see when I opened that door, but it sure as shit wasn't an empty room."

"I'm not smart-mouthing you," he said slowly, patiently, his cadence and tone going down, as hers went up. "But I have been watching over that place since before you were born. 'Expecting' is not a word you should apply to that house, because you never know what it's going to do. You're like one of those rich people who think just because you tamed a tiger, it will not decide one day to just bite your face off."

Penny felt a small sting of indignation at the comparison and shot back. "You've been here since before I was born, and you haven't done anything to seal that place."

"Hmm," Curling said with a dismissive nod. "You're the expert."

"Did you move it?"

Curling frowned. "Moved what?"

"Whatever was in that room."

Curling finally couldn't stop himself from smiling. He gave a derisive chuckle. "If there was ever proof you have no idea what you're doing—"

"Shut up." She didn't raise her voice or show any emotion. She wanted this conversation to be over, to reach the part where Curling told her what she needed. Then she'd go back to the house to deal with it. "What do I need to do?"

Curling regarded her for a few more seconds, finally sighed, and stood from the chair—*It isn't surgically attached to his ass, after all*, she thought. He headed inside the house, leaving her with the two dogs, who didn't take their pale blue eyes off her. She could hear him rummaging around inside, then there was the sound of his boots on the wooden floor, approaching the porch again.

Curling handed her a brown book, bound in leather and rope. The edges of the pages within were worn and browned, with dog-eared corners and small, improvised separators in between.

She opened the book. On the first page, in perfect penmanship, were the words, "Diary of Amias Vanek".

"Is this real?" she asked.

"My ancestor," he said emphatically, "Rickward Curling, inherited it from Vanek himself. Look in the dog-eared pages. They might have what you need."

She stared at him with mistrust.

"I will want that back before the end of the week," he added.

She let out a chuckle. "Your ancestor." Her voice was full of contempt. "Right."

Without another word, she turned and hurried back to the Vanek House. She could almost feel the man's gaze stuck to the back of her neck, following her all the way back until she disappeared through the front door.

The moment she walked in, she was met by her husband, whose appearance was only a bald head and pointy ears away from Max Schreck's Nosferatu, standing stiffly at the threshold between the living and dining rooms. She was taken aback, as it took her a second to even recognize him.

"How didn't you get wet?" he asked.

She didn't understand what he was asking her.

"You forgot your umbrella," he said, and just then she noticed he had an umbrella in his hand.

Penny looked back through one of the front windows at the sunny day outside, then turned to him, puzzled.

"Jonathan, sweetheart, I think you should go lie down for a while." She saw him glance up the stairs, and a shudder ran through his body.

His lips were quivering. "I, uh…" He averted his gaze from the second floor. "I don't want to sleep right now. I'll, uh…" His eyes darted around with a desperate expression in them, as if trying to find something that would satisfy her questioning. "I'll lie down on the couch and read a bit. While the kids are here, too. That way I…uh… They won't be alone. Is that okay?"

Penny had to stop her face from contorting with worry. "Yes," she said. "Need me to get you anything for the stomach bug? Maybe some chamomile tea to at least help you feel better?"

He shook his head. A look of disgust passed over his

face. "No. No, that's okay," he said. "I don't want to drink anything. I'll just lie down."

She nodded. Held the book in her hand, close to her body, and headed toward the stairs.

"What's with the weird book?" Jonathan asked.

"Oh," she said, waving the book casually in the air, as if it were of no importance. "It's just some Bible group notes from Alberto's wife. She left them with Curling, and he just gave them to me now that I was there."

"Huh," he said, with an unconvinced frown. "Weird."

She grinned nervously. "Yeah, I… I forgot it was my turn to come up with the next meeting's agenda, since we're now moving to White Harbor's chapter of the Bible group, so I need her notes to make sure I don't miss anything for next week's meeting."

"You don't need to explain so much," he said plainly. "Worried I won't believe you?"

She squinted at him. "No, I'm—"

"I'm messing with you." Jonathan waved a dismissive hand, grinning as he sat on the couch and set a couple pillows against the armrest, so he could lie down.

"Look dad," Sadie said, out of nowhere.

Penny and Jonathan turned to face their daughter, who was holding up a childish drawing on a piece of paper.

"I drew a mermaid!"

The crayon drawing showed what Penny knew was

Sadie, but drawn as a mermaid. Brown crayon curls made up the hair, and she wore a green dress, under which came an unusually long tail that looped twice, ending in a funny-looking fishtail.

Penny smiled. "That's beautiful! My talented girl!"

Sadie smiled back at her.

"Isn't it, Joh…" Her phrase petered out as she looked at her husband's horrified face.

He stared at the drawing, as if he were looking at some portent of doom held by the innocent hands of their seven-year-old daughter.

Jonathan noticed his wife was staring at him. He composed himself. He said nothing and laid his head on the pillows he'd set up on the couch. Noticing she was still staring, though, he waved his hand in the air dismissively. "I'm sorry, I'm being weird. I'll just lie down for a while." He looked at his daughter and patted her on the head. "Nice drawing, munchkin."

Without another word, but filled with a renewed sense of dread, Penny headed upstairs.

Chapter 9

That night, sitting in bed—the bedside lamp providing the only illumination—Penny read, over and over, every single one of the diary entries Curling had separated using dog-ears or adhesive tape stuck to a numbered piece of paper jutting from the book itself.

No matter how many times she read Amias Vanek's notes about the house and the profane rituals they had performed in it, nothing stood out as useful. She started feeling like Curling had only given this to her in a twisted attempt to mess with her head, and there was no actual use to the damned thing.

She swiveled her head toward her husband, her eyes full of worry. He was lying on his side of the bed, his back to her. She could see him breathing. Despite his position, she could tell he was awake. Through his pajama shirt, she could see the outline of his ribs.

How could he have lost that much weight in two days? Some stomach bug...

Jonathan's overall attitude and disposition had been as pleasant and optimistic as always, but he wasn't eating or drinking anything—and he looked pale as death—which certainly worried her. Her mind spun yarns about all the potential causes for his current state, trying to make herself believe it was really just a bad stomach bug. They had been eating food they had brought in with them, most of which had actually been cooked before the move. It wasn't that ridiculous to think some of it had gone bad. Except they'd all eaten the same things, and only he was sick.

What if it's the house? The thought popped into her mind like a lightbulb that had turned on and then immediately off, leaving the ghostly afterglow of it in the darkness.

Maybe she had been too proud, too stubborn. The idea she could expunge what had lived in the house all this time and become the new caretaker after Ben Curling—turn it into a good place, something the old man had always failed to do—had been too appealing. The notoriety in her Order was enough to seduce her into agreeing to upend her entire life, not to mention her family's, and move to White Harbor. She had been so sure, so damned sure, she could handle it.

My goddamn hubris.

After Jonathan quit his job, the prospect of starting a family business in a new town had been an easy sale. He'd been excited about the idea and had started drafting plans and coming up with pitches for the local municipality on how their little bed-and-breakfast, built on a historical site like the Vanek House, could attract tourism to the town of White Harbor. Jonathan saw this becoming the business to let them age into that nice old couple who welcome guests and give them that warm feeling of a home away from home.

She also bought into it. She'd felt so confident that everything would go their way. That was up to the second she shone her flashlight into that room to find it completely empty. The moment that heavy door opened, and all she was greeted by were four wooden walls and a ceiling, she had felt completely lost.

She didn't even know what she'd expected to find there.

(*"Expecting" is not a word you should apply to that house, because you never know what it's going to do*)

She didn't trust Curling. Too many people had died in that house under his watch. It was the reason she'd been asked to take over. Rumors had been circulating among the members of her Order that Curling no longer watched over the house and the evil that lived in it, but that he'd succumbed to it, that he did the house's bidding.

She turned her attention to the book on her lap.

And here I am, bringing an old book he gave me into the house, and I'm reading from it. It's like I have a fucking death wish.

She felt her husband stir, and she watched him as he turned around and looked at her. God, he looked pale!

"You know what?" he said. "I think I am going to go make myself some chamomile tea, like you said. Tomorrow, we should get some medicine or something. I feel terrible."

She returned a tender smile. "I think that's the best idea you've had all day. Do you want me to go make you the tea?"

As he sat up, he waved a hand toward her and shook his head. "No, no, no. You're tired too. You just sit there and read your weird Bible group book. I'll make it myself, alright?"

She watched the weak and uncoordinated motion of his legs as he put on his slippers. His pajamas hung from him like curtains—he really had lost a lot of weight—as he stood up and walked out the door, giving her a feeble smile as he closed it. The sound of his slippers receded as he moved through the hallway outside.

Chapter 10

Jonathan sat in the kitchen, on a folding chair, in front of a small folding table. They had bought these in a hurry, and they were incredibly uncomfortable to sit on for a long time, but he supposed they'd do, at least while they got settled in and got a nice kitchen table.

He was leaning back, arms folded over his chest, eyes closed, rolling them under his eyelids from side to side, to massage the pain at the upper part of his eye-sockets. He sat with one leg bent close to the chair, the other stretched forward, the toes pointing up and a slipper hanging off them. His head hurt like a motherfucker, and he just wanted whatever was wrong with him to pass, so he could begin enjoying the remodeling job and his new life with his family.

Those nightmares, though. He'd heard of nightmares caused by an upset stomach, but these new ones—and even the waking dreams he'd had these past few days—had been beyond ridiculous, like nothing he'd ever experienced.

His mother had taught him that dreams don't really have meaning in and of themselves, but he had always thought otherwise. That there was some underlying interpretation to the dreams we had, which went beyond the superficial "uneasy brain/bad dreams" way of looking at it. If he honestly believed this though, what in the world could dreams that terrifying possibly mean?

The water in the electronic oven finally boiled—well, sort of boiled. It just got really hot and steamy, but he never saw it bubble. The loud beeping from the oven made him jump. Some people said electronic ovens gave you cancer or made you sterile or impotent. He prayed it was the middle option, since he was happy with just his two kids. For obvious reasons, he hoped not to get cancer, and he quite enjoyed making love with Penny, which made him hopeful the oven wasn't actually killing his future erections.

The moment the oven was done with the water, he brought it out, grabbed his mug, dropped in two bags of chamomile tea, and poured in the boiling water in. Adding some honey, he stirred the concoction, the swirls of honey and water and stray tea leaves creating a deep brown liquid, and a thick, sweet scent—pleasant under different circumstances, but currently, cloying and nauseating. He supported his upper body with his arms on the kitchen counter while he waited for the tea to brew a little before drinking it. For a moment, the tea's yellow color looked like urine to him, urine inside a toilet bowl. Jonathan blinked the vision away and wiped at his eyes.

Looking around at the old kitchen, with few actual appliances and a sink that looked like the cheapest thing Curling could've bought to make the house livable, he wondered for the first time if he was being too naive about their chances of making the bed-and-breakfast idea work.

Work.

That was the key word. Fixing this place was certainly going to take an insane amount of work.

Am I really up to this?

He blew on the cup. Took a sip.

He was hit by a taste like melted plastic, like someone had stirred gasoline into the tea. With a grimace, he did his best to convince himself it was an aftertaste caused by not having eaten or drunk anything in two days. He forced himself to go for another sip, a longer one this time. Then put all his willpower into swallowing hard.

He breathed in and out, discomfort settling into the pit of his stomach, the organ itself beginning to protest and churn.

"Nonononono," he mumbled.

The nausea struck him like a gut punch. He hated throwing up. That horrible moment of vomit was always preceded by the dread and anxiety of the unavoidable, like being dragged out of his bed by an angry crowd to be pushed onto his knees before a guillotine with no trial or say in the matter. The inevitability settling as the nausea pushed his stomach contents up his esophagus.

He had nothing in his stomach. He hadn't eaten in two days. Why was his stomach trying to push out something that wasn't there?

Jonathan shook his head, as if refusing to vomit would prevent it. What use was there in delaying it when it was coming, anyway? The force pushing up from within him stretched his body upward, and he whirled around toward that cheap sink and, in a powerful heave, he vomited

(*Tea?*)

a thick black thread—a wriggling, liquid worm, or tentacle the thickness of two fingers.

It pooled briefly before going down the drain, and it kept going. It had no slickness, no gloss, it reflected no light. A black pool, like puking out a black hole, endlessly streaming from him. It felt like miles of this substance were unspooling within him and flowing out of his mouth, then went down the drain.

A strange banging sound, like that of settling water pipes, invaded his ears, louder than the sound of his own vomiting. The noise flowed through the pipes—first down-ward, then under his feet, on and on and on—until, simultaneously, the horrible flow of black vomit ended and what felt like an explosion shook the kitchen floorboards, making him lose balance. He fell to his knees in front of the sink, gagging and heaving, no more inexplicable ooze coming out of his mouth.

For a long minute, he remained on hands and knees. He needed an hour, a day, a lifetime to recover from having vomited what felt like his entire soul. He wanted to lie on the floor, hug his knees, and never stand again, but a vibration, a presence from behind, demanded his attention. He heard a strange thumping and scratching under the kitchen floorboards.

Dread felt like a solid mass in his chest as he turned to see the boards were shaking, as if a train were passing right at the other side of the kitchen wall. The boards jumped, their nails shot upward, their sound like the hooves of galloping horses, then—*THUNK!*—one board flew off the floor. He shielded his face with his arms, and didn't see what was beneath, but he heard another *THUNK!* and another, and another, and another—*THUNK! THUNK! THUNK!*—followed by the clatter of each individual board falling somewhere far from where he sat, as he cowered on the floor, arms over his face, clawing at his hair in frantic terror.

Unlike the nightmare in the bedroom, he found he

could actually scream this time, and he did, but the noise of the floorboards shaking, exploding into the air, crashing against walls and appliances, mixed with the banging of pipes, and another noise he couldn't yet identify—a wet noise—drowned his screams out. How could this ruckus not wake his entire family? How could it not wake the neighbors? Was the entire neighborhood deaf?

These questions became irrelevant, as he now found himself unable to scream. *Something* snuck between his elbows, quick as a striking snake. It covered his entire mouth, like a hand, but before he could determine what it was, he felt another appendage come from the *palm* of this hand and crawl down his throat. A strange, viscous fluid bled from the appendage, filling his lungs, and every open space in his ribcage and abdomen. Tears formed rivulets down his cheeks, and his arms fell to his sides, convulsing, as he now sensed his entire body being lifted into the air.

Against every impulse to preserve his sanity, he opened his eyes as wide as he could to see what had a hold of him. He was right—a hand. A matte-black hand attached to an inhumanly long arm, stretching out of a six-foot hole in the floor.

Inside that hole: madness.

He recognized his wife's face—even if it was as sootblack as the insides of an overused furnace, even if her eyeballs glowed blue, even if her face had been stretched to six times its real size and its edges dissolved in a dark, gelatinous mass that flooded the hole in the floor.

Jonathan could see her other arm somewhere illogical in the blob of dark substance, bending this way and that, ending in a hand with three fingers. He saw her toes here, a single breast there, a gaping unshaved vagina opening and closing, obscenely, near the edge of the hole in the floor. All over the inscrutable dark mass were eyes of different sizes that opened and closed before his bulging, paralyzed stare.

Body parts emerged, then sank into the nauseating black pool. It looked as if his wife had submerged herself in tar, and she had dissolved into it, but her face—her enlarged, deformed face—continued to float at the top, her enormous eyes, staring directly at him, and that mouth with black teeth grinned, and he could hear her laugh. The purest laugh of joy his wife could produce, but undercut with a gurgled, deep, mannish sound, which made it sound choked and wrong.

The terror was so intense, he barely felt the tube violating his throat or the substance it was pumping into his insides. His mind could only keep check of so many horrors at once. That was until he felt the black goo worming out his nose and ears and tear ducts. It crawled out of his urethra and his anus, as if he were both pissing and shitting liquefied rubber. The emerging substance branched and crawled down his legs and up his back and abdomen. He was being enrobed, coated both inside and out.

Now, in this mental overload, in the purest of panics, he felt the creature's arm move him closer. The other smaller eyes, all over the monster's mass, now glowed blue—the big ones protruding from his wife's face had stopped glowing. They now looked like Penny's brown eyes, but gigantic. The sound of his wife's joyful, gurgling laugh greeted him as her mouth opened wide, wider than his entire body. He saw the decadent expression of gluttony drawn in her pleasured eyes, which looked horrendously human in their ecstasy as she lowered him slowly into her quivering, open maw.

The almost erotic joy he saw in those eyes, each the size of his head, as he was fed into the enormous mouth, disgusted him almost as much as the sensation of that wet, black tongue, now crawling up his legs and sliding up his back.

She's tasting me, he thought irrationally, hysterically calm. Suddenly, an alarm rang in his head as he saw the lips peel off the creature's teeth. It chomped down, right into his midsection, right into his bowels. He couldn't scream. All he could do was witness his lower body emptying through the ragged hole. Intestines, tissue, and bone—all laced with a matte-black substance, which had made him tastier to the Penny-creature. It chewed with enthusiasm, and he heard the smacking, cracking sound of his flesh and bones being ground by those teeth. The Penny-creature was savoring him. Its enormous eyes rolled up in pleasure.

He even thought he could see a tear of undiluted delight at the corner of its eye, and he couldn't scream.

He couldn't scream.

It was chewing his legs as he watched.

He couldn't scream.

It delighted in his taste. It moaned with pleasure. The taste of his ruined legs and pelvis made it cum.

He couldn't scr—

He bolted upright in his bed, choking on a scream. It still wouldn't come.

"Jonathan, what the—"

He turned his head and saw his wife sitting there next to him. That old book in her hands, the bedside lamp on, her eyes wide open in

(*Pleasure*)

shock, staring at him.

"You just scared me half to death! Are you okay?" she asked.

He felt an overpowering sense of apprehension course through every inch of his body at the sight of his wife.

"I…" he started. Stopped. Considered. "I just had another awful nightmare, that's all. It's the stomach thing. It's like it's messing up my brain."

"Tomorrow morning, first thing, I'm going to the drugstore to get you something, alright?" she said, her brow scrunched up with worry.

He nodded, then wiped sweat off his forehead.

"You want to tell me about it?" she asked.

While he would find this tone of voice comforting at other times, tonight it felt infantilizing and condescending. The sound of her voice repulsed him. He shook his head, turned his back to her. "I'll just try to sleep. Goodnight."

"Goodnight," she said.

Chapter 11

Merrill Yates, the local pharmacist, slipped a blister pack containing eight pills into a small plastic bag, then also put in about nine small, laminated paper packets—they made a soft hissing sound, from a powder or granulate they contained—then, finally, put a big bag of a power next to the bag.

"Alright," said Merrill. "The pills are for the morning. Have him take one before breakfast. It's important he does this on an empty stomach. The little packets—have him dissolve one in water and drink it thirty minutes before each meal. As for the rehydration salts, just take a big pitcher of water and dissolve this whole thing in it. Have him drink as much as he needs, as many times a day as he needs. This is probably the most important part of it. All the other stuff is to control the stomach irritation and nausea while the bug runs its course, but he has to stay hydrated, alright?"

Penny gave Merrill a relieved smile, but couldn't hide the dark circles forming under her eyes. "Thank you so much, Mrs. Yates."

"Oh, no, no, no," Merrill said, wagging a finger in her face. "Call me Merrill, please. *Mrs.* Yates was my mom—God rest her soul. She'd die again if someone ever confused her with this short-haired, pants-wearing, tattooed tomboy of a child she brought into the world."

Penny stared, speechless. That had seemed to come out of nowhere, and certainly caught her by surprise.

Merrill burst out laughing. They let out boisterous cackles, their face turning red.

Penny looked even more confused.

"Oh my God," Merrill said between chuckles, wiping away a few tears of amusement from their eyes. "You should've seen your face, darling. I'm messing with you. Mrs. Audra Yates is still alive and well, and she loves her 'neither-here-nor-there' androgynous kid." Merrill leaned in and cupped a hand on the side of their mouth. "Between you and me, being the local pharmacist means I actually finished college, so she gets bragging rights with the townsfolk."

Penny gave a weak giggle, unsure of how much she was allowed to laugh at this.

"I'm just trying to see if you liven up a bit, darling. Are you okay?" Merrill asked. "When you came here about a month ago to buy some cream for that baby of yours, you looked so happy. Couple weeks ago, when you came to town again with your family—your little girl needed those vitamins—you all looked super excited to be so close to moving in. It's been less than a week since the move, and you look tired as hell." Merrill studied Penny's face. It made her feel like she was under a microscope. "The house is getting to you, isn't it?"

"Huh?" she said with a gasp. "The... The house? What are you talking about?"

"Girl," Merrill said. "What in the world possessed you to move into that place?"

"I don't understand what you—"

"Yes, you do." Merrill's expression was grave. "From the moment you set foot on that property a month ago— even if you were just scouting locations—you started feeding Blight Harbor. Every curious neighbor that approached you with smiles and greetings and chitchat and questions—even if you didn't know—you were feeding Blight Harbor."

Penny took a moment to gauge whether she'd heard correctly. "Did you say, '*Blight* Harbor?'"

"Alright, seems you need a bit of Town Lore 101," Merrill said with a conspiratorial smile. "Blight Harbor... think of it as the dark side of town, but it's not a physical place, it's more of a spiritual, or metaphysical, dark side. Let's see, try to think of the town as a person, right?"

"O…kay?" Penny wondered if Merrill was just giving her the new neighbor's spook story.

"I mentioned my mom, right? I love my mom. My mom and I are A-OK. Nicest old lady you've ever met. We get along like best buddies. Wasn't always like that, though." They raised their index finger and smiled wickedly. "It took her some time to wrap her head around who I was, but she would never let me see that. She would always be all nice and loving in front of me, but I heard her on the phone, a few times, talking to her friends, telling them things like,"—Merrill softened their voice, presumably to imitate their mother's—"'Just my luck. I only have the one daughter, and she goes around wearing man's clothes, like some common dyke!'" They let out a loud cackle. "Sorry mom, I like dick! Surprise!" Merrill put their hands out, fingers flared, as they said this. "Then, as if that weren't bad enough, one day I hear her crying while on the phone,"—they once again softened their voice—"'I feel like my little girl's lost to me. She doesn't want me to call her my *daughter* anymore. She wants me to call her *my child* or *my kid*. One of these days, I'm gonna find out she chopped up her tits and goes around with a sock shoved down the front of her pants!'"

Penny stood there, gawking at Merrill, not following the logic at all, but being shocked at the level of over-sharing in this interaction. While Penny considered herself a progressive, 1960s open-minded woman—heck, she'd even participated in the SDS March Against the Vietnam War in '65—Merrill's unapologetic way of discussing her "situation" was a little more than she was accustomed to. She was okay with it, but it had certainly caught her off-guard.

Merrill's expectant silence didn't help.

"You're confused," Merrill said, staring at Penny's bemused expression. "Getting to it. Hang on. I told you my mom and I get along just great. She's proud of me. She loves me. I love her…but those two things I heard her say—and a lot of other things you really don't wanna hear—completely contradict that. You see, that's not the mother I know *now*. She wasn't even the mother I knew *then*. She and I have always gotten along, but she used to *hide* that nasty, mean, judgmental side of her from me. That ugly person who said those things *is* Blight Harbor." Merrill stopped again to make sure Penny was still following. "If White Harbor were my mom, Blight Harbor would be my mom saying those things in secret. You, my dear…are living inside the phone."

Penny grasped the concept now. She, in her studies, knew it under a different name. It was the thing she was expecting to find inside that empty room on the second floor.

"The gossip you've been stirring up from the moment you moved into that house—every answer you give a neighbor, any visible thing you do around the house, even the times you've talked to Old Man Curling—and, seriously, why are you doing *that?*—that's feeding Blight Harbor. That's why I'm asking you if the house is getting to you. With Blight Harbor as fat and well-fed as it currently is, it mustn't be easy to live in the Vanek House. It's like the grease trap for every nasty thing living in the hearts of everyone in this town."

Penny thought of it briefly. Gave a polite nod. Smiled through those exhausted eyes, and said, "I'm just really exhausted. The move has been very tiring, and with Jonathan getting sick, I haven't been getting a lot of sleep this week." She forced her smile to stretch wider. "Thank you so much for caring, though. You've been so welcoming to my family since we first got here, and you barely know us. I really gotta go now, though. Hope to have you over for dinner once we're fully settled in, okay?"

Merrill gave Penny a knowing gaze from head to toe, then made a corner of their mouth twitch, containing what was obviously disapproval. "You bet."

What Penny didn't know was that Merrill hadn't pointed out two other things she'd just done which were feeding Blight Harbor: that odd sense of discomfort she had been radiating when hearing about what was behind Merrill's particular way of presenting themselves, and the denial she had expressed about what the Vanek House was doing to her family.

Chapter 12

After making a few calls, like she'd done every day since she'd arrived—calls to her parents and her group in Burley—Penny returned to the Vanek House.

Why do I keep thinking about it as the Vanek House? she wondered, feeling annoyed. *It's my house now.*

Something in her head kept nagging at her. Something about Merrill's words had sounded familiar. Something had stuck in her brain like a thin tiny needle from one of those cacti covered in what look like hairs but were, in reality, thousands of sharp little spines.

The diary. It has to do with the diary. She stood in the wide first-floor hall, when the words appeared in her mind again. *Blight Harbor.*

The house was unusually quiet.

"Jonathan?" she called.

There was no answer.

"Sadie?"

Silence.

It was morning. Her daughter should be playing somewhere in the house, and her husband should be… Well, anywhere, really, since he wasn't sleeping well.

As if a hairy spider's leg had brushed against her heart, she felt a wave of fear.

With urgency, Penny went up the stairs. *Maybe he managed to fall asleep, and they're all napping?*

As she reached the master bedroom, she saw her husband sleeping soundly. He showed no signs of being in the throes of a nightmare. He looked peaceful, resting for the first time in days, or at least, he seemed to be.

Penny quietly approached her nightstand, opened the drawer with utmost care, and took out the old diary. She needed to browse the document for a moment to see what it was about Merrill's remarks that had reminded her of it. Once more, she paced toward her jewelry box, where she entered her code, "0110", removed the top layer, and—no surprise to her—there was the key to the lonely room in the back.

She stepped out of the room and softly closed the door, then turned her head toward the kids' room and approached the door, which was slightly ajar. Just because her husband was asleep, it didn't explain why her kids were so quiet. The moment she pushed the door in softly, with the tips of her fingers, she stood there with her jaw hanging open, pleasantly surprised.

Nelson was sleeping soundly, drooling down one corner of his lips, tiny little bubbles of saliva forming as he breathed. Sadie was lying spread-eagled in bed, looking like the enormous plushie dog she slept with had fallen on top of her and flattened her. Penny watched as she adjusted her position to hug her enormous dog.

Surprised, Penny closed the door, and now her gaze moved toward the bend in the hallway that would lead her to *that* room. She stealthily walked toward it and turned the corner. This time, the room did not seem to repel her as she approached. She stood in front of the door, reached into a small pocket she'd sewn into her skirt, and brought out the key.

She unlocked and opened the door.

Empty room.

Again.

What was I expecting?

(*"Expecting" is not a word you should apply to that house, because you never know what it's going to do*)

"Alright." She sighed and looked around. "I guess the floor will have to do."

Penny sat down, cross-legged, on the floor. She was surprised at how little dust there was on the floorboards. She opened the leather diary and set it on her legs and began paging through it with no proper plan in mind.

Merely a few seconds later, she saw it. Written in beautiful handwritten penmanship in the middle of a paragraph:

Blight Harbor

"Blight Harbor," she whispered. She stared at the words, dumbfounded for a moment, as if they hadn't been there before. "They call it Blight Harbor," she whispered, reading off the yellowed, worn page. "A simplistic, scary moniker for something much larger and unfathomable. An eldritch truth that exists in this land, which God has blessed. As we store food and crops for the winter, so does 'Blight Harbor' endlessly store God's source of sustenance and the materials to craft His wonders. God needs only the darkness that lives in our hearts and in our minds. We give to God our fears, our nightmares, our anger, our secrets, our violence, our envy, our greed, our lies. God takes these dark things away from us, and in return, gives us the promise of a better world."

Penny swallowed hard. This was definitely the thing

she was tasked with eliminating from this house, but knowing what the locals called it didn't help her figure out what she was supposed to do.

"The Sanctum is our door," she continued reading, "the place where we perform our communion with God, where we can behold His wonders."

Is this the Sanctum? She looked at her unremarkable surroundings. *It's supposed to be where that evil thing lives. Doesn't look like much, though.*

"The real door, however," she continued reading, "is the house itself and anything in it." She licked her lips. She did not like how that sounded. *The house and anything in it. What the fuck does that mean?* She read the whole paragraph again until she reached the spot where she had been and continued on. "The door moves. All it takes is for the Sanctum to be opened. A willing servant will ask, and God, in his infinite mercy, will move the door."

In a burst of frustration, she slammed the diary on the floor with a grunt. "This is just rambling bullshit from an insane heathen! Fuck! This makes no sense! The Sanctum was closed until I used the key. The door should be here, because *I* opened the Sanctum, and I didn't move the door, so it should be here!"

Did Curling move it? she thought, and without hesitation, her mind removed the question. *Curling moved it. He moved it before we came here.* She gritted her teeth with anger.

*That old piece of shit sabotaged me! He didn't want me to take the house from him, so he sabotaged me! Then, he—*She looked down at the diary—*he gave me the diary to taunt me. He's mocking me! He knew the room was empty! He's mocking me!*

She stood up in one sudden motion and tossed the book to the floor. Her enraged eyes regarded the closed door with the iron reinforcements, and she immediately pulled it open and walked out.

The second she set foot outside, she knew something was wrong.

There was a window at the end of the hallway, to her left.

It was night outside.

The night was almost entirely dark, save for a full moon in the distance. A dark blue moon that shone eerily through the window. There were no street or house lights she could see in the town outside, just that black night and the blueish moon.

No stars.

Only a few minutes earlier, it had been a bright morning outside.

"Jonathan!" She sprung into a sudden dash. "The kids! Jonathan! Get the kids!"

She turned the corner, desperation bubbling in her eyes. She reached the children's bedroom. Upon reaching the open door—which she was certain she had closed—what she saw pulled a scream from her, as if a clawed, spiked arm had been shoved down her throat to pull out her still-vibrating vocal cords and her deflating lungs.

Before her eyes was a spectacle of horrors her worst nightmares couldn't have concocted, because she would be forced awake before her brain even allowed her to glimpse such an image.

Her daughter was lying on her stomach in a pool of her own blood. The little girl's entire body was covered in so many stab wounds they were impossible to count. Her left arm was stretched forward, as if she were trying to crawl away as she was stabbed again and again and again in the back.

She could see Sadie's face—even if she was lying on her stomach—it appeared she had been stabbed in the neck enough times that her head was attached only by a few ragged threads of muscle and skin, and it was fully turned around over her shoulder, one blue eye in a grisly, bloody face, staring directly at the door.

Staring right at her.

By the foot of Nelson's cradle, there was a shapeless lump of bloody flesh—torn, gory—with patches that looked almost like chucked pork. Hints of pink and white, either gristle or tendon or bone, could be seen here and there in this mass. It was only when she saw a small piece of light blue fabric—what should've been the leg of a onesie—that her brain made the needed synaptic connections, from one concept to the next, to realize these were the remains of her one-year-old baby.

The sight of one of only seven teeth in her baby's mouth, sticking out of what she could tell was his gum, nearly drove her insane.

Penny screamed until all that came from her mouth was air and drool. She wanted to run toward her babies and hold them in her arms and breathe life into them again, but touching them was an impossible task—touching them would make this real. She could not allow this to be real. She would not.

Her hands flew to cover her face, and she turned around, sobbing, bellowing, caterwauling incoherently in soul-searing pain.

That was when she felt the knife go in.

It didn't hurt.

It was like getting a shot at the clinic. Once the tip of the needle went in, the rest wasn't really felt.

Cold, she thought, detached.

She uncovered her eyes and stared stupidly down at the half-an-inch of a blade sticking out of her stomach. The handle being gripped by a man's closed fist. She felt a sting of pain as the blade was pulled out of her.

She looked up.

There was her husband's pale face, grinning at her.

Chapter 13

Jonathan Albright assessed his work.

The two creatures who had been pretending to be his children were now dead.

A part of him, somewhere in the back of his mind, insisted that these were not creatures, that these were *actually* his children, but he could see them now, plain as day: asphalt-black, with black teeth and tongues, lying in pools of their black, tar-like blood.

Forty-four times he'd stabbed each. That was how many times the voice had told him to stab them. He didn't know why. Apparently, that was the exact amount that would kill them and send them back to Hell, or wherever they'd come from.

Jonathan felt strangely calm for someone who had

just learned a few days ago that his entire family had been replaced by demons. He even felt proud. He was helping the world by removing these demons from the Earth. That's what the voice had told him, and he had no reason to doubt it.

Three days ago, after getting the key from Ben Curling, Jonathan had gone back home to sit down to lunch with his family, but just as he'd walked in, he'd been overcome by a strange sense of curiosity. Something about Curling's words had stuck in his head, something about his wife not telling him the whole reason they were really there. It had something to do with that room upstairs. He knew that much.

That day, before heading toward the dining room, Jonathan took a detour and hurried upstairs. He walked all the way to the end of the hallway, and around the corner, until he reached that room his wife seemed so anxious about opening. Without thinking twice about it, he opened that old, reinforced door, and what he saw before his eyes changed his perception of life. The door inexplicably opened into the same hallway he was standing in, but in that other hallway, it was night.

In awe, he stepped through the threshold.

Having an approximate idea of the blueprint of the

house, he was certain there couldn't be a hallway like that in this area, and not just that—the walls looked different. The material appeared to be wood, but not really, like some kind of imitation. He ran his hand over the wall right in front of the door, and in parts, it felt like stone, carved to have a wooden texture.

But how?

Then, a few inches to the right, he was touching skin—human skin, with tiny hairs and all—but it was the color and texture of wood, but like a tattoo. It was warm, warm, as if he were touching another person, but the texture of the skin and the stone somehow blended perfectly into each other, as if they were the same material.

Mesmerized, he walked to one side, now placing both hands on the imitation-wood wall, feeling how the texture and temperature changed. The very sensation changed. Here, in another spot, it felt like paper, and looking closely, even in the moonlight, he could see the wooden texture on the paper was made of tiny, printed letters—hundreds of tiny, printed letters, forming the wavy shape of the grain.

This is impossible. This is insane. Am I insane?

BOOM!

The heavy door slammed shut. He hurried back to it and tried to open it. It wouldn't budge. He tried the key, but it didn't work from this side. Fear gripped his heart, and he began looking around for another way back

(*to the light*)

to the hallway he'd come from.

He saw the window, and his heart skipped a beat. The only window on this portion of the hallway was still to his right—when facing the door—which meant, whatever this "other house" was, it wasn't a mirror version of the other house. It was as if someone had simply put two identical houses together back-to-back, and the point they both coincided was the reinforced door.

Outside the window, there was only night. No streetlights, no lights coming from other houses, just the moon, dark, silver-blue, shining over everything.

He'd never seen the moon glow that color before—that preternatural blue. A cold shade of blue. A dead glow devoid of all warmth.

In stunned silence, Jonathan walked toward the window, aware of the way his footsteps sounded different from each other—the floor was also made of this strange patchwork of materials only superficially resembling wood. He stood in front of the window, looking out toward that moon. He could have sworn it stared back.

He tentatively reached a hand to the glass, but stopped short of touching it. A voice in the back of his mind warned him against it, as if touching it would be unpleasant or dangerous. Against this instinct, he put an index finger forward and carefully moved it toward the glass.

He pulled his finger back as soon as he touched the window and stared at it in astonishment. He rubbed his finger against his thumb. It was wet. The window wasn't glass—it was water.

I'm dreaming. I have to be dreaming.

This time, he resolved to put his open palm against the window. When it made contact, his breath caught. It was actual water. He could see ripples over the vertical surface of what should've been glass. Taking quick, shallow breaths through his mouth, he risked pushing his hand further in, and he let out a stupefied giggle when it continued deeper, as if he were submerging it in a small pond—a pond in the wall.

He looked at the moon through the ripples in the water-window. In an impulsive moment of stupidity, he grabbed at it.

"I'll grab the moon and pull it down for you," he remembered saying to his wife many years ago, when he was courting her—younger, stupider, cornier—and he'd gotten a blush out of her.

His fingers moved in a quick motion as if the moon were a sphere lying at the bottom of a pond. He imagined himself snatching it and pulling it out, wet and dripping crystalline drops all over the floor. But all he felt was water moving between his closing fingers as they passed through the image.

He was about to pull his hand out when he felt something wrap itself around his wrist. He couldn't see what it was, but it felt like small tentacles squeezing around his forearm. They wouldn't let go, no matter how hard he pulled.

Then, in a single hard yank, his entire upper body was submerged in the window, as his legs hung out of the surface.

At first, his eyes were closed.

"*Open your eyes,*" a voice said directly into his mind. It didn't feel like someone else was talking to him. It was his own voice. Ordering him to open his eyes and gaze into whatever lived outside that window.

He shook his head like a child. He was terrified. Whatever was on the other side of that window, he didn't want to see. The strange certainty that—if he opened his eyes—his heart would stop from terror pulsed in his veins.

"*Open,*" the voice said.

No. I'm scared. I don't want to.

"*Open,*" it repeated.

He opened his eyes.

He was awake.

He was standing at the doorway of the Vanek House—*his* house—just coming in from Ben Curling's porch, as if he'd lost track of time. The key to the upstairs room was in his hand. Aside from a strange moment of déjà vu, he remembered nothing of what had just transpired.

Chapter 14

For the rest of that day, Jonathan hadn't remembered what he'd seen through that window. He hadn't even remembered going upstairs, having crossed to that moonlit world on the other side of the door. But that had been *that* day.

Today, four days later, after nightmares and visions that had shown him the truth—all of which he'd recorded in his "dream diary"—he'd awakened in bed with total recall of the event.

He remembered what he saw through that window.

He saw the other side.

He saw the Moonlit World.

He saw the truth of *our* world.

He saw the roiling chaos, the mass of *everything*, the all-consuming darkness coming for us all. It was a pitch-dark wasteland where unending rot met unending restoration. Where nothing ever died, but everything prayed for death. Where all variations and all possibilities in which everything could go wrong with each individual existence had already happened and was replayed endlessly, simultaneously. Where one entity's pain and sorrow was felt by every other entity, and everyone experienced the suffering of all the others, at once, forever. An unending cacophony of tortured human, animal, and sentient being yet to be discovered, breached only by three words that came to him in that voice that sounded like his own, but belonged to someone else.

"*Be the door,*" the voice said.

He remembered, through the panic that assailed his mind, a single word broke through in response: "Yes."

The other voice didn't need to say it, but he knew "being the door"—whatever that meant—would help prevent the inexorable horror he saw on the other side of the window from crossing to his side. He knew he would happily die, and he would kill, if it helped prevent—or even briefly delay—what he saw in the Moonlit World from coming to this side.

The voice had shown him the truth of what had already crossed over.

Penny.

Sadie.

Nelson.

They had never existed. They had never been real. His family were *things* that had spilled over and wanted to multiply.

I am the door, he thought with both regret and pride.

Even the things that made him want to feel the ache of loss, like the sight of his little girl—no, the *thing* pretending to be his little girl—staring vacantly at the bedroom door, with a gap between teeth exposed by a dead slack jaw, seemed little compared to the pain and horror on that other side.

She was starting to lose her teeth.

A pang of grief cut through his heart.

Her teeth are black. Her tongue is black. Her blood is black. If she was my baby girl for real, her blood wouldn't be black.

As he'd been straddling his demon daughter, stabbing her repeatedly, he'd had to halt. His demon wife had come over and stood at the door, peering in.

He'd frozen in place, thinking the shadowy creature at the door, with the glowing blue eyes, could see him, crouched, covered head to toe with his daughter's—*the demon's*—blood. He was convinced the creature at the door would charge at him, coming to stop him, summoned by the loud shrieks of the baby demon in the crib.

Jonathan had turned his gaze toward the crib, his face covered in black blood, the piercing cries of the infant abomination drilling into his ears. He'd turned his face again toward the door to see the woman creature take the doorknob and slowly, almost tenderly, close the door.

Whatever supernatural force—*God?*—had set him on this mission, had stopped the demon from seeing and interrupting his work.

Jonathan had stabbed the Sadie-creature the last two times to be done with it, then stood and went to work on the shrieking creature in the crib. It had stopped squealing after the first stab, which had almost nailed it to the floor, and he'd had to struggle to pull the knife out and continue stabbing, forty-three more times.

His job almost done, he had to remind himself these were demons. *These aren't my children. These aren't my children.* He was doing his part to keep the invasion from the other side at bay. *These aren't my children. These aren't my children.* He was doing God's work.

He smiled again.

I am the door.

He had to take care of the demon posing as his wife now.

Chapter 15

Penny saw the knife slide out of her abdomen. She saw her husband grinning insanely at her, as if he'd pulled some funny prank only he understood. She saw their children's blood all over his face. The first instinct that kicked in was to slap him, then push him away as hard as she could. It was a strange slap and an even stranger push—completely non-dramatic and utilitarian—like she was pushing away some creep who'd gotten handsy in line to a Pink Floyd concert.

Jonathan stumbled backward, and she took off running, holding her stomach. Adrenaline had kicked in so quickly there was still no pain. There was a lot of blood, however.

Penny ran past him as he struggled to regain his balance. She made a sharp left from the bedroom door, then another quick left, where the hallway became the second-floor landing and—

"What the fuck?"

—she was met by a hallway that simply did not exist in the house—or, more accurately, that did not exist in this area of the house. The wall to her right had a single door at the very center. A door reinforced with rusty iron, and at the end of the hallway, a window looked out toward the dark town, over which only a dark blue moon glowed.

"What the *fuck?*" She gawked. The house appeared to have suddenly flipped into a mirror image of itself.

Footsteps.

Her husband was coming.

She ran toward the door that wasn't supposed to exist and tried to pull it open. It wouldn't budge. The effort made the stab in her stomach burn and sting, but it was a dull sort of pain. Her body was here, but the pain, for now, was nowhere near her. The pain was in another room.

She looked to the right, saw Jonathan turning the corner, knife in hand. Her babies' blood all over his face and clothes, a deranged grin on his face. She spun her head left, saw the window—the window that was supposed to be entirely on the other side of the house. It was her only option.

Penny had always known Jonathan to be gentle but

even sick and skinny as he'd suddenly gotten, he was still taller and larger than her—not to mention he had a knife.

She ran to the window and raised her hands to push it open, but stopped when she noticed something impossible—as if the hallway even existing on the opposite side of the house wasn't impossible enough—the window was painted on the wall. It was not an actual window, just an image on the wall. It was completely flat, but even then, she could see outside, she could see depth. Her view angle changed as she moved from one side to the other, but the window was a flat image on the wall.

That was when she felt the entire length of Jonathan's knife being plunged between her shoulder blades. A guttural "Oof!" escaped her, and her back arched in reaction. The knife was violently pulled out, then went back in without hesitation. By the third stab, an expression attempting to be words came out of her mouth, something that sounded like, "Nahagharg-johna-nah! Naaaagh!" followed by a desolate, sobbing, pleading noise.

The knife came out again. She spun, reaching her arms out to try to push her husband away, but her hands missed him completely and the knife came down on her shoulder. Immediately, Jonathan's strong arm pushed her down to the floor and continued stabbing her without saying a single word. He did this mechanically, as if it were make-work, as if he were hammering down on a nail.

Before he could straddle her, which would've made her end quicker, she landed a well-placed kick in the balls. He recoiled and fell sideways against the wall. She followed this with a second kick, right in his bad ankle—it had kept him from the draft, now it would keep her away from her. He howled in pain.

Finding strength from wherever she could, her body blazing with pain from every wound she'd sustained, Penny stood. Just as she was about to flee, she heard Jonathan roar with anger, and felt the knife pierce the back of her leg, right above her knee. She fell down screaming and banged her head on the floor.

Dizzy, but still trying her hardest to run, Penny pulled herself to a standing position with an angry holler. The knife was still stuck in her leg. She limped away as quickly as her protesting body would allow.

She turned right at the corner and stopped cold.

She was bleeding from every stab wound, but what she saw still made her cry in rage.

Penny had turned the corner and expected to see the doors to her bedroom and the children's bedroom. Instead, there was the hallway leading to the window at the end, with the dark night and the blue moon. More baffling still, there was Jonathan just a few steps from the reinforced door, now to her left, groaning as he stood, a hand over his aching crotch, flinching from his injured ankle.

Terrified, Penny spun and doubled back the way she'd come, and to her bafflement, there was the hallway with the reinforced door, now on the wall to her right, and Jonathan, now walking toward her.

She shook her head, sobbing, screaming.

As her husband's fingers wrapped around her throat and he lifted her in the air, one thought crossed her mind in plain words.

The house is going to kill me.

As her husband pulled the knife out of her leg and slammed her on the floor, the fight had almost left her body. The house was trying to kill her. It was not playing by rules she could figure out and defeat. Regardless of what she did, it would lead her back to the tip of her possessed husband's knife as many times as it needed to until she was dead.

My possessed husband, she thought, seeing him grin down at her with a deranged sort of love in his eyes. He raised the knife, ready to bring it down, when the thought flashed again in her mind. *My possessed husband.*

She pulled Ben Curling's keys from her jacket pocket and pressed the symbol on the keyring against his chest. This made him recoil more violently than when she had kicked him in the balls. He winced, retreated, and fell on his ass, shrieking. That revolting grin suddenly gone from his face. The impact as she fell to the floor made every stab wound roar with pain.

Blindly, groaning, desperate, she turned on her stomach, pushed herself to her feet and she limped down the hallway that was supposed to lead to the master bedroom. She made a quick estimate of the portion of wall where her bedroom door would normally be located—a couple of feet to the left from where the reinforced door now stood—and she held the keyring flat against the wall. The wall shifted before her eyes. The symbol on the keyring melted into the wall until it disappeared. The bedroom door now stood before her.

Footsteps again.

Jonathan was coming.

She grabbed the knob, pushed it in, and hurried inside without even thinking.

Time slowed in her mind, and the next fraction of a second let her brain know that there was no floor beyond the door. The sight before her was the first-floor hall coming up to meet her. She had walked through the wooden balustrade of the second-floor landing and was now falling.

She tried to put her arms up to shield her head. Tried to turn in midair. But when she hit, she hit hard. The left side of her body hit the back of a chair and she heard her ribs breaking before the jolt of pain coursed through her body. The chair fell, and her mass followed, dropping to the floor with no grace.

The air knocked out of her, indescribable pain racked her entire body. Her world was pain. She gasped, croaked, and moaned. She was convinced she wouldn't move an inch from her current spot.

It was over.

Penny caught a glimpse of Jonathan ambling calmly down the stairs. That gaunt complexion that had taken over his face and body, their children's blood—now mixed with hers, soaking his clothes—and that grin, that proud grin that made him look like he'd found a true purpose in life, or that life had lost all serious meaning. He strolled toward her, gripping the knife in his hand. Every alarm in her brain told her to stand and run away, but her body was no longer capable of such movement. She was trapped in a car with no battery and broken locks on a railroad crossing, and the train was coming.

It was so clear now. She saw her husband's eyeballs had turned completely black, like a void. Why hadn't she realized it? All the effort spent on keeping the key hidden in her little combination box, and it was all for nothing, because her dear Jonathan had gotten curious and gone into the room before giving her the key.

That was why the room was empty.

(*The door moves. All it takes is for the Sanctum to be opened. A willing servant will ask, and God, in his infinite mercy, will move the door.*)

The house had tricked Jonathan.

He went down on one knee next to her, reminding

her of the wonderful man who had kneeled in front of her over a decade ago and asked for her hand in marriage. The way she'd cried as she said yes, and he'd cried when he heard her say it.

Still smiling, without a word, he raised the knife and drove it between her ribs, then her kidney, then her arm, and so on, and so on. His pleasant smile never broke as he continued to stab her as if it were sequential factory work, counting steps in a process. He simply kept stabbing without stopping or acknowledging her pain, the reactions of her body to the knife piercing her flesh, or the horror of what he was doing.

The last thing she thought before she died was, *The house killed me.*

Chapter 16

He watched black blood swirl down the drain as he washed his hands. His entire face and clothes were soaked with the disgusting liquid, but it didn't matter. He was almost done, but he only needed clean hands to do this one thing before continuing.

While he knew time was of the essence, Jonathan took a moment to sit at the edge of his bed and jot down a few words in his diary, which he now resolved did not contain dreams, but glimpses into that Moonlit World. He was quick, succinct, but he believed he'd communicated the most important part of it.

He put his diary in his bedside drawer, stood from his bed, and walked out of the room, his bloodied socks squelching inside his shoes. His shirt clung to his body as if his fake family's blood was still trying to build a bond with him, even after death.

The demons were dead, but they were still on *this* side, and he was the door.

Jonathan moved the bodies to the dining room, put them against the wall, one next to the other. There was a brief flash during which the demonic illusion came back over his eyes. For the briefest moment, he saw his wife, his little girl, and his baby boy, their bodies almost unrecognizable with wounds and blood

(*The gap in Sadie's teeth*)

but so human, so dead, so lost to him.

His chest nearly collapsed, and his body bent as he let out a pained, keening, "Aaaaahh!", as if he was letting his soul leave his body, but his body could not die until his mission was done.

The illusion was suddenly gone, and Jonathan once again saw the twisted monsters on the ground, and his grief turned to rage and spite. He felt betrayed. He felt robbed. He felt violated. These creatures had made him think he'd had a family. He'd made love to whom he thought was his wife. It had given him whom he thought were his children. He had played with them, taught them, *loved* them. They had made him think he was happy, and it had all been a lie.

Jonathan ran the edge of his knife, one side then the

other, over a honing rod. Stabbing the creatures so many times had blunted the blade. As he slid it back and forth, his rage kept building in his heart. Every memory, every hug, every laugh only increased the level of betrayal he felt.

Once ready, he crouched next to each of them and started cutting. It was interesting to him that, despite his rage, his cuts were gentle, careful, as he took each piece of their bodies, each no more than an inch all around. He took fourteen pieces out of each of the children, and sixteen from his wife, who was the first demon to cross over. Forty-four pieces in total, which he put on a plate.

Jonathan closed his eyes and lowered his head, and he forced the image of his family—not the monsters—into his mind, and whispered, "Thank you for any part of it that was real."

He stood and moved to the table, plate in hand.

Jonathan didn't sit at the head of the table as he normally would—he didn't feel he should. He wasn't the head of the family anymore. He never was. Instead, he pulled out one of the side chairs and sat down. He briefly considered a rolled-up napkin on the table. He took it, unrolled it, and placed it over his lap. When he tried smoothing it, some of the black blood that soaked his pants was absorbed by the napkin, leaving a black stain on it.

The plate barely made a sound as it touched the table's surface.

He looked at the chunks of black-blooded flesh on the plate in front of him. The plate was cheerful and colorful, contrasting with the grimness it held. A pang of nausea ran up his throat.

I am the door.

He smiled again, reminding himself he was serving a greater purpose. He was setting right a great wrong.

Jonathan took the first chunk, placed it in his mouth. He expected the taste to be sour or bitter or rotten, or even artificial, like nothing he'd ever tasted before. Instead, there was something gamey about it. The taste reminded him of veal, the undeniable taste and scent of blood hanging over it like an unpleasant spice, floating to the back of his throat and into his nostrils. Without chewing, he swallowed the first piece—the first of forty-four neat little pieces he had cut—which would force the souls of these creatures to cross to the other side.

He was beyond full by the time he let the last piece slide down his throat.

It was almost over. Two more things needed to be done for the ritual to be finished. The first one he dreaded, the second one he anticipated with eagerness.

Jonathan glanced at the knife he'd placed next to the plate. He took it in his hand. Closed his fingers tight-ly around it, as if imbuing the knife with every iota of his strength and willpower.

He put his left hand on the table, his fingers flared as far apart from each other as he could get them. He touched the tip of the knife to the table, about two inches from his middle finger, then curled his other fingers. His hands trembled, as if warning him not to do what he was about to do, but he had to.

I am the door.

Then, in a single chopping motion, he brought the knife down, cutting off the tip of his middle finger. Right at the very joint of the last phalange. He felt the pain burn from his finger up his arm, but he didn't scream, just gritted his teeth. Jonathan had already felt the most unbearable pain a man could feel as he came to terms with the notion that his family did not really exist.

This was necessary. The voice's instructions had been very specific. He was the door. He needed to send a part of him to the other side to act as a key he could use to lock the door.

Jonathan took the severed piece of his finger and placed it on his tongue. The taste of blood and severed flesh hit his tastebuds right away. He was surprised to realize it didn't taste dissimilar to the pieces he'd cut from his false family. Once more, without chewing, he swallowed. He felt the fingernail touch his palate as he forced the piece to slide down.

The penultimate step of the ritual was done.

It was time for the last step. The one he wanted to reach as expediently as possible.

Once more, Jonathan took the knife.

He turned the blade toward himself with both hands—the remains of his finger sticking out, dripping blood on the table and his clothes, which were blood-soaked already.

Upper quarter of the torso. Then divide that quarter into four. Find the upper left quarter of those.

His heart.

I am the door. The door has to be closed.

Jonathan pulled in a deep breath. He plunged the knife in with all his strength, with no hesitation. As his chest collapsed, an emotionless exhalation escaped his open mouth.

Slowly, he leaned against the back of the chair and let his arms fall to his sides.

It was finished.

He turned his head to look at the dead creatures near the wall to his right, but then he looked away. They didn't matter. They weren't his family.

He had never had a family, but he had freed himself from their spell.

Jonathan Albright smiled with satisfaction as his sight darkened.

One of the front doors creaked open, letting in just enough moonlight to illuminate the main hall.

Padded feet crept silently into the house, with the very slight click of nails on wood. These were followed by a man's boots, which were not as quiet.

Even in the darkness, Ben Curling could see the signs of what had happened. The turned-over living room chair, the bloodstains all over the floor, even coming down the stairs.

His two dogs were looking up at him, expectation in their blue eyes.

"Upstairs," Curling said with a low grumble.

Both dogs padded up the stairs, leaving him alone.

He turned his flashlight on and, careful not to step on any blood—yet knowing he was in no danger in the house—sauntered to the dining room, where he knew he'd find them, if the streaks on the floorboards were any indication.

Curling passed the threshold and shone the light in. He saw Jonathan Albright dead at the table, a bloody plate in front of him, a knife in his heart, and his stomach distended.

Curling sighed. "So, this is what you did."

He wasn't talking to Albright's corpse.

He shone the light toward the three bodies resting against the wall. He saw the copious amounts of blood, the stab wounds, nothing he hadn't seen before. There were also the *other* wounds, which confirmed what he thought when he saw Albright's swollen belly.

He heard the soft sound of the dogs' feet coming toward him. He put a hand out toward the floor, and one dog touched the keyring to his fingers. He took it, then put his other hand out. The other dog placed the diary in his hand. Curling put the key in his pocket, gripped the book. He took one last glance at the family, shook his head exhaustedly. Then, he turned around and headed back toward the front door, followed by the dogs, this time not caring if he stepped on the blood at all. Now that he knew what had happened, he had no concerns about someone questioning the fact that he was in the house after the family died.

Curling stopped, holding the door open. As the dogs slinked out, he turned and cast a glance at the house, a glance with a derisive frown. He was glancing at a house, objectively speaking, but he was also frowning at it as he would at an old, strained acquaintance—a being he despised, but with whom he had no choice but to maintain a relationship.

Curling turned and left.

He would call the police when he got to his house, then provide the most basic of answers to the most complex of questions.

"Too much speculation," Callum thought, removing his glasses this time as he rubbed his eyeballs.

He considered the way he had separated the sources and versions of the tale. The official record was dwarfed by the size of the town rumors and the statements of people who hadn't been there, but had, of course, added a tiny piece to the whole.

Even people who had been inside the Vanek House at some point in history—Callum himself had been in it and had taken notes of his own observations—had only uncovered tiny pieces of the full story, and he had to take some pieces of those observations to fill in the blanks.

Interviews of people who belonged to the same Order as Penny Albright were very superficial hearsay, state-ments resulting from letters that Mrs. Albright had sent and phone calls she'd made during the few days she'd lived in the house. The one thing they had in common had been how damning of Ben Curling these remarks had always been.

Curling appeared to have wronged this group, be-yond merely what had happened to the Albrights. Knowing what he knew of Curling, he had a hard time disagreeing with those accounts, but he had to force himself to find the objective truth in them, and not let confirmation bias get the better of him.

He had the handwritten "dream diary" of Jona-than Albright, and even that was sparse. The relevant sec-tions seemed like the ramblings of a madman, dream logic, stream-of-consciousness, digressions. He would have a hard time distilling what really happened from Albright's notes about demons and what he called the "Moonlit World". There were also mentions to the importance of stabbing each "demon" forty-four times, but no reason was given anywhere. However, he saw the number forty-four in other notes, such as the number of Froot Loops in his bowl—an odd thing to make a note about. He remembered this number also ap-pearing in notes unrelated to the Albright case, but he hadn't been able to make heads or tails of it.

His cell phone rang.

It was Sylvia.

Callum picked up, and immediately said, "I know, I'm late for dinner. It took a while." He listened for a moment. "Okay, fine, I got distracted working on the book and lost track of time. I'll be there soon, okay? Need me to get anything?" He nodded. "Sure! Oh, believe me, you'll love this one once it's compiled. I could use some help, though?" He smiled with pleasant surprise. "You would? That's amazing! You're the best."

He put the papers and books in order, based on category, holding the phone between his ear and his shoulder. He closed his laptop, turned the lamp off, grabbed his jacket. "On my way." He hung up the phone and headed toward the door.

Before leaving, he stopped. He turned and looked toward the darkness of the library. Everything was quiet, nothing moved. Nothing *appeared* to move. The empty spaces between the books on the shelves, the darkness under the desks, the dirty water in the bucket where his mop lay submerged. There could be something there.

The mental image of the Albrights dead in their dining room was still vivid in his mind, and he couldn't shake it off.

Blight Harbor was watching him from every dark crack and in-between space. It was watching him dare to shuffle its contents around.

That phrase his mother always said crossed his mind.

"That's in Blight Harbor. Leave it there."

Only he couldn't. He couldn't leave it there. Callum wanted to know. He promised himself, ever since he was a child, that he would write the stories, that he would find the truth. He couldn't just let it lie in Albright's "Moonlit World" when the point of his whole life was uncovering it and exposing it for the world to see. Each story had a piece of the puzzle, and he had to investigate them all.

"That's in Blight Harbor. Leave it there."

"I can't, mom."

He took one last nervous glance around and hurried out the door.

Acknowledgments

White Harbor is based on a short story I wrote twenty years ago. Why does this matter? Because I sat on this story for half my life because I didn't believe in myself. Anxiety is a bastard. It takes on the voice of everyone who's said you're not good enough, magnifies it and repeats it forever, so the voices that say the contrary have a hard time breaking through. It's thanks to those other voices that White Harbor exists.

The voice of my husband Jimmy, who has always believed me capable of anything, who listened to me rambling during road trips and dinners about the background and story arc of every character in these pages, and has listened intently and asked questions, and given his thoughts, and above all things, has loved me at my most unlovable.

The voice of Jose Villalobos (Maroto), who was my first vocal supporter and who gifted me the keyboard these words are written in, after mine broke… and I was too broke to buy one.

The voice of Fabio Melendez, whom I can say was my first fan, reading each chapter and being excited about where the story would go next.

The voice of Carlos Alberto Ruiz, who showed me my small actions can inspire others.

The voices of my Patreon supporters: Xavier Poe Kane, Kento, Brians Vargas, Alonso Arrieta, Fabian Pupo, Michael Garro, Myles Rich, Luis Castro, Avatar-of-Chaos, Carlos Andrés Soto, A.M. Blackwell, Edie Tuck, Jean-Louis Ghazi.

The voices of people who contributed to or read this story early on and gave me their honest feedback: Josh Hagaren, Eric Woods, Eryn McConnell, Aquino Loayza, Jacy Morris, Wynward H. Oliver, Josephine Curwen, and I'm sure I'm leaving many out.

Finally, the people who now give me a voice: David-Jack Fletcher and Leeroy Cross James at Slashic Horror Press.

Thank you. This story took form thanks to you.

About the Author

Carlos is a Costa Rican gay writer and former English teacher. As an anxious, introverted kid growing up in Costa Rica during the 80s and 90s, he always felt like an outsider. His refuge was escaping into and devouring sci-fi, fantasy, drama, crime thrillers, and, above all things, horror. For years, these books, movies, comics, and even video games became his life.

He dove into the horror-next-door of Stephen King, the ineffable cosmic abominations of H. P. Lovecraft, the disturbing atmosphere of *Silent Hill*, the dreamlike imagery of David Lynch, the sheer unnerving strangeness of Junji Ito, and many more; they got mixed in with his country's folk stories and his own life experiences, resulting in a peculiar blend readers might feel is familiar but askew.

And isn't that the foundation of horror?

Doesn't horror begin with something mundane that, seen from a certain angle, feels a bit off?

For updates on Carlos's work, follow him on Facebook, Instagram, X, and TikTok: @carlosriveraauthor

Author's note

Independent authors are admirable. Faced with impossible numerical odds, having to perform like seventeen different roles *other* than "author", and opening ourselves up to a world that still isn't quite convinced we're good enough, we still think *But I have this really cool story I want to tell!*

What nobody tells you is going to be your biggest struggle—at least it was mine—is impatience. Right before I self-published the first book of my "White Harbor" trilogy, I already had several chapters drafted that were supposed to go at the end of Book One and bring that arc full circle, but I kept looking at the calendar and impatience won out, and I said, "Screw it, they'll be the first chapters of Book Two". Don't get me wrong! I was happy with how Book One originally ended, but I kept thinking it could be so much better.

Well, now it is better! In this second edition, you get Book One the way it was supposed to be: polished, extra chapters, and with a glimpse into the darkness to come. As if that weren't enough, you're gifted the prequel novella, *I Am The Door*, a horrifying story from the town's past.

I want to thank Slashic Horror Press, for giving me this unique opportunity, and I want to thank YOU for visiting White Harbor, when you could've spent your time anywhere else.

I hope you enjoy your stay. I hope you visit White Harbor again.